THE AWAKENING OF JOE BOWEN

B. L. SHERK

ISBN: 978-1-968397-03-6
First Edition
Published by Viral Book Nation
Artesia, California, USA

CHAPTER I

Three days before Midsummer's Eve
The Zion Crossroads Plantation Hotel
1980

*"Nobody knows how the Crossroads came to
be, or why or when; for it has always been.
Though it has borne many names, the ancients
simply called it 'The Gate'."*

Chief Louah

"What are you doing at this hour that you feel the need to lock the door?" The knocking, that had torn him from a dream, grew more insistent.

"Nothing special, Fleming!" Murphy fumbled blindly for his glasses and the room came into focus. The clock read ten past ten and, to his horror, he realized one of his father's notebooks still lay open on his bedside table.

"It may interest you to know that Mrs. von Hassel has been in the shower now for eleven minutes and counting," announced the voice behind the door. "I thought you'd spoken to her on this matter!" The doorknob turned impatiently. "Did you hear me, Brother?

Murphy lurched out of bed. Thank god he'd set the bolt. "Sorry, Fleming! I'll remind her." Meanwhile, he was hastily stowing the notebook along with the others, into the bottom drawer, beneath the wool sweaters. It was a place Fleming would surely never see it, the place where they'd been hidden since that fateful day last August, the day of his father's final 'disappearance'.

Murphy strictly avoided the word suicide. It was just too upsetting. Still it was comforting to think that his father's last earthly act was to leave these notebooks by his bedside. Yes, perhaps his father had loved him after all. That's what Murphy wanted to think anyway, so he'd kept them, incomprehensible as they were, filled with grotesque drawings and even stranger poetry.

His father must have come secretly in the middle of that final night, because when Murphy had awakened the next morning, there they were, stacked on his bedside table with the Ancestor's ring sitting right on top. What had his father been thinking as he'd gazed upon his sleeping son? Murphy could only wonder. They'd never really talked, at least not about anything that mattered. Now reading these notebooks was the last chance to finally understand this stranger he'd called father; and so he'd kept them hidden where Fleming would never find them. Otherwise, they would surely have been pitched into the fire. Fleming would have called them the demented writings of a madman or worse, the work of the Devil, and perhaps he'd have been right. But there was something in these pages that Murphy understood all too well, a theme tying it all together. The 'Dark Thorn' was what his father called it, something Murphy had always simply thought of as 'The Curse'.

The irony, that he should now find himself longing to talk with his father just once more, did not escape him for how many times had he secretly wished that Joe Bowen would simply die or disappear and never come back? Of course when it did happen, it was not the relief that Murphy had always imagined it would be. Instead, it had trapped him in a netherworld of 'what if's'. What if their mother had never left? What if Joe had never fallen off the roof? Maybe the story would have turned out differently. Maybe they could all have lived a different life, grown into different sorts of people; better, smarter, stronger—happier. But Life is a blink and then it's gone and now it was too late. Murphy quickly shoved his legs into his pants, pulled a shirt over his head, then hurried up the back stairs to the second floor bathroom and knocked on the door. "Mrs. von Hassel?"

In her own good time, a woman in a red silk kimono emerged through the steam, wearing sunglasses and a towel wrapped like a turban around her head. She attempted to sweep past him, like an empress wishing to avoid a distasteful peasant, but he timidly detained her.

"Mrs. von Hassel---!"

"What?" she snapped.

His resolve spluttered. "I just wanted to say, good morning!" Perhaps, he would remind her about the drought and the three-minute-shower policy another time.

The sound of an approaching car drew them both to the second story french doors leading out onto the balcony. In the distance, a vehicle could be seen doggedly bumping up the potholed drive, a great billowing cloud of dust trailing behind like a long dragon's tail, as it made its way through the grand arch of ancient live oaks leading to the Zion Crossroads Plantation Hotel.

This was the moment Murphy had been dreading---when Fleming would find out about the new guests he'd scheduled without permission. Unfortunately they were all northerners, too. But after nearly two years of complete stagnation in their hotel business, when three reservations called in on the very same day, how could he have said no? The hotel was desperate for money and had been for years. So in direct violation of Fleming's 'No New Guests' policy Murphy had gone ahead and booked them.

He and Mrs. von Hassel continued to watch covertly from the upstairs window as a pair of brothers in a dusty white Chevrolet rattled to a stop in front of the house.

With a long metallic screech, the driver's door opened and Jack, a dark haired man in his mid thirties emerged, wearing long khaki pants, cowboy boots, and a red tank top that revealed a tanned muscular physique. He took one look at the surroundings and shook his head in disgust. "I knew we shoulda gonna the beach." He lit a cigarette, and squinted up into the white humid sky where vultures circled, silently watching, along with a solitary black man listlessly chopping at a weedy rose garden.

Meanwhile, Tommy, a dreamy eyed Huckleberry Finn, standing head and shoulders above his older brother, busted out in a wide grin. "Oh, my god, Jack! This is exactly what I saw in my dream!"

Jack rolled his eyes and clomped up onto the splintery porch in order to take a closer look. "I must have been crazy drunk out of my mind to let you talk me into this!"

People were often disappointed with their first glimpse of this plantation turned hotel, the elegant fossil of a grander age in all its white pillared glory. From a distance, it still retained its charm, framed by gentle blue mountains, and fields of wildflowers rolling down to a small green river; but upon closer scrutiny it was clearly falling apart.

"So what's with this anyways? Don't these people know the war is over?" Jack flipped up the corner of a limp confederate flag hanging in front of one window revealing an old pizza box taped over a broken pane.

Tommy fished a crumpled pamphlet out of his pocket and waved it in the air. "Follow your dreams, Jack!" Suddenly, it hit him---the flag had been in his dream, too.

"Yeah? Well, I never had a dream worth remembering!" Jack sucked one last drag off his cigarette and crushed it under his heel as he headed through the door. "All I can say is--- if a place could be haunted this would be it!"

Back at the upstairs window, Mrs. Amanda von Hassel turned to Murphy with a predatory smile. "You'd better get your ass down there before Fleming does."

Cringing, for such crude references to body parts always made Murphy cringe, he scurried downstairs but, too late! Fleming was already there at the registration desk, glowering sullenly at the newcomers. Meanwhile, the black man in the blue fishing hat had slipped into the back hall to listen in.

Entering the disintegrating grandeur of the front hall of the Zion Crossroads Plantation Hotel, the alert visitor was immediately struck by the subtle atmosphere of defeat. Indeed, it clung to the very walls like the odor of an ancient resentment eternally recorded in the grim ancestral portraits hung in stately procession up the wide sweeping staircase. Yet, despite the cobwebbed and threadbare conditions, clearly this building had been conceived by a rich artistic imagination, from the elegant brass chandelier, the white paneled walls, elaborate molding, and rich carpets, to the gorgeous mahogany registration desk carved by Italian craftsmen and the stained glass window on the stair landing, casting ruby and gold colored shards of light across the floor. It takes money, however, to keep up old buildings and the business had been skidding through hard times since after the second World War. Now the only source of life in the room was the profusion of spider plants crowding the desk and hanging overhead, giving it a sort of jungle effect.

"You must be the two brothers, Tom and Jack Spratt!" cried Murphy, arranging the mournful geography of his face into a forced cheeriness.

"Sprack! Sprack with a 'k'," corrected Jack, rather testily for 'Jack Spratt could eat no fat' had followed him relentlessly through school.

"Sprack! My apologies! Sprack! Um---." The poor man glanced like an injured pup at his brother. "Fleming? These are the two gentlemen from Baltimore that I told you about?"

"Then again---perhaps you did not," was Fleming's terse reply and with a withering glance, he sat in the corner to read his Bible in murky silence. A small effigy of Jesus hung in agony on the wall above him.

Often it took seeing the two Bowen brothers side by side to realize that they were twins, with the same dark wiry hair, the same gaunt, elongated face, the same pinched nose, and bulging forehead. This wasn't obvious at first glance partly because Murphy was clean-shaven and Fleming wore a long, flat, shovel-shaped beard of almost biblical proportions but it was also something about the eyes.

Murphy alone wore glasses, thick heavy black framed spectacles, and the magnified eyes blinking through them were as harmless and vulnerable as a guppy. Fleming's eyes, on the other hand, were narrow slits, suspicious, and hard, and regardless of how hot the day, he always wore a long sleeved white shirt buttoned to the hard knob of his Adam's apple.

Murphy was just handing over the registration form to be filled out when an unkempt, bearish figure suddenly appeared, sniffing his way to a box of donuts arranged on an antique sideboard against the far wall. "You got glazed *again*? You know I only like cream filled!"

Murphy quietly scurried over to snatch the donut away. "Mr. Puffenberger, please! These are for the *new* guests!"

Mr. Puffenberger's small black eyes now fastened intently on the strangers. "But I'm hungry."

"Breakfast was at seven," was the icy pronouncement from the Bible study corner.

"And whoever heard of eating breakfast at that ungodly hour!" grumbled Mr. Puffenberger. He was extraordinarily obese and now winded from the simple exertion of fighting over a donut.

"It's not our fault that you can't seem to get yourself out of bed on time," snapped Fleming with open distaste for the greasy locks hanging over Puffenberger's collar and stained shirt stretched tight across his prodigious belly.

"Don't think I don't know what you're trying to pull, Bowen," growled the interloper. "If you think you're going to starve me out, you've got another thing coming! I know my rights!" He glared thoroughly at Jack and Tommy then shuffled out the front door, his full rosy lips poked out into a determined pout.

Murphy took a deep breath and handed the information form to Jack. "So sorry about the interruption. You will have the Jefferson Davis room in the historic section which will be upstairs, second door to your right. Here are the keys and you will find the lavatory right across the hall."

"You mean we don't have a private bathroom?" exclaimed

Jack.

Fleming sniffed and turned the page.

"Jack!" the tall brother lowered his voice, "It's historic." He flashed an apologetic grin at Murphy.

But Jack persisted. "So how come the pamphlet don't say nothin' about this?"

Murphy blinked like a big slow-witted bird. "I beg your pardon--did you say---'pamphlet'?"

Suddenly Fleming was on his feet, elbowing his more timid brother out of the way. "What *pamphlet*?" He stressed the word with an aggression that seemed out of all proportion.

Jack snapped his fingers impatiently, "Give it-a me, Tommy!" Tommy reluctantly handed the pamphlet to his brother, who waved it like a war flag under Fleming's pinched nostrils then commenced to read in a loud, mocking northern working man's accent.

TREASURE! TREASURE! TREASURE!

BURIED CIVIL WAR TREASURE

JUST WAITING TO BE DISCOVERED

MAYBE YOU WILL BE THE LUCKY ONE!

COME JOIN THE HUNT

AT LUXURIOUS ZION CROSSROADS

A PREMIER CIVIL WAR PLANTATION

GOLD STAR HOTEL

GOOD FOOD!

REASONABLE RATES!

HORSEBACK RIDING!

SWIMMING!

COUNTRY LIVING!

REST & RELAXATION!

His sneering rendition was greeted by a deadly silence from the twins; Murphy's expression, waxen with fear and Fleming's clearly murderous.

"You---didn't happen to save my father's life---did you?" squeaked Murphy timorously.

"Did I save *whose* life?" Jack's brown eyes narrowed sharply.

"Never mind! Where did you get this?" Fleming's tone was unmistakably ominous.

"None of your damned business," bristled Jack, for he was a man who went into the world expecting a fight and usually succeeded in getting one.

"I found it on my windshield," interceded Tommy, quick to be diplomatic.

Fleming turned away as if suddenly indifferent. "Well, I'm sorry to say that it's expired."

Jack's eyebrows lowered. "What do you mean 'expired'?"

Murphy opened his mouth to speak then thought better of it.

"I mean, it's out of date. There is no treasure hunt," replied Fleming as if nothing more needed to be said.

Murphy nodded weakly.

"Well, at least you've still got horseback riding, right?" Tommy only asked because this had been the bargaining chip he'd used to convince Jack to come here at all. Ever since he was a kid, his brother Jack had wanted to ride a horse.

Murphy looked mournful. "Oh, that—well, not anymore. So very, very sorry—very sorry---." His voice trailed off into a whisper.

"Well, then I would call this false advertising, wouldn't you Tommy?" his older brother declared triumphantly.

"And you are certainly free to leave, as you please." Fleming's smile was not a friendly one.

"You're damned right I am but not without my two hundred and fifty dollar deposit!" Jack shrugged off Tom's restraining hand.

"Not without 48 hours notice, *sir*," came Fleming's steely reply.

"Well then how does Better Business Bureau sound to you, *sir*?" This was Tommy's cue to drag his brother back out onto the porch.

"Look, Jackie boy, remember this is supposed to be a *vacation* not a war. We came here to *relax*."

"Yeah, well not before I sue the sons-a-bitches for false advertising!" Jack often ended conversations in this manner. "They can't say they have a treasure hunt and horseback riding and not have a damn treasure hunt and horseback riding!"

Puffenberger was sitting on the swing at the end of the porch watching as if this were a sporting event, a small bag of candy clutched to his round belly, his great jowls moving in a staccato grinding action. "Go ahead and do it. Those bloodsuckers deserve to be sued." His eyes lit with interest on the pamphlet in Jack's hand. "So, did Joe give you that?"

Instinctively, Jack drew it behind his back. "Who's Joe?"

The man acted like this was something that could hardly be believed. "You don't know Joe Bowen?"

"Never heard of him."

Puffenberger's eyes hardened. "Then what the hell are you doing here?"

Jack pointedly turned his back on the inquisitor and said to Tommy in a low voice. "Let's hit the road."

"So, you think I could take a look at the pamphlet?" interrupted the man from the swing.

"Why? You ain't seen one before?" retorted Jack with growing suspicion.

"It's been awhile that's all." Back and forth went the porch swing, with alarming creaks and groans under Puffenberger's great weight.

The two men stared each other down. "Don't think so, pal," said Jack

"Jack! Let the guy look at it!" Tommy reached for the pamphlet.

"No!" Jack drew it out of reach.

"What the hell? Why are you being like this?"

"I just want to know why he wants to see it, is all."

"You really think you're going to find it, huh!" interjected Puffenberger with poisonous mockery. "Don't lie. You wouldn't be here if you didn't! But don't kid yourselves. Nothing comes free here and you will pay---one way or another." With a wheeze and a grunt, he hoisted himself onto his feet. "Gents, it's been a pleasure."

Jack stared bullets as Puffenberger sallied forth like a great ship at sail, disappearing from view around the side of the house. "There goes a Class A jerk if I ever saw one!".

"Shh! Listen!" Tommy put a finger to his lips.

The sound of heated voices arose from within the house. The Bowen twins were having an argument.

"What kind of weird shit you got me into this time," muttered Jack darkly.

Tommy sighed. "So you still wanna hit the road?"

Jack paused for consideration. "Nah. I'm thinking they're lying their faces off, Tommy! Clearly there's a treasure and they don't want us to know about it!"

"And?" Tommy was trying to push down the big grin that wanted to bust out all over his face.

Jack paused to light another cigarette then blew out a long stream of smoke. "Yeah-- I never been the type to get lucky but if anybody's gonna find that treasure, it's gonna be you, baby brother! I mean, face it, 'Luck' is your middle name!"

"So we're staying?"

Jack scowled. "I must be crazy for following your bony ass!"

"We're staying!" Tommy fell on his brother with a great bear hug.

And though he tried to hide it, Jack was grinning, too. He leaned back against the railing then jumped back. "Christ! Look at this!" He vigorously started brushing the thick pollen dust off the back of his pants. "Jesus!"

While Tommy went in to take care of the details, Jack went out to unload the trunk, cursing Tommy's sloppy way of packing all the tools on top of the luggage.

Nearby the young black man was back to hacking without conviction at the weedy flower bed, but lit up with sudden interest when Jack took out two shovels and a pick. "So where you from?" he called, crossing the shaggy, sunburnt grass.

"Baltimore," replied Jack, finally wrestling the last suitcase out of the tangle.

"Oh, really." The gardener removed his hat to mop his brow. Without it, he looked younger than he'd first appeared and good look-ing in a striking kind of way. It was the eyes. They weren't a normal color---almost yellow. "So whatcha gonna do with the shovels?" he asked, nonchalant but friendly.

Jack gave him a sidelong look. "Dig."

Gardner nodded in a thoughtful sort of way. "So, how did you know Joe?"

"Joe?" Jack narrowed his eyes. "Everybody keeps talking about this guy Joe. I don't know nothin' about no, Joe."

To this the gardener made no reply but only watched with even more curiosity as Jack continued unloading the trunk. "So you're from Baltimore, huh? I've been there. Had lobster on the pier in some amazing little shack of a place."

Jack stopped. The man suddenly sounded educated and northern. Something did not fit. The name tag on his shirt read, 'Gard-ner'. "So is that your name or just your job?"

"That's my job and my name." Gardner's expression turned stony as if he did not find this amusing. "Well, back to the chain gang," he muttered, seemingly more tired than offended, and started hacking at the weeds.

Just as Jack was nudging their bags through the front door, Amanda von Hassel made a dramatic appearance on the landing of the grand staircase leading into the front hall. She was dressed now in a wide straw hat, and a long airy white dress that clung to her voluptuous body in translucent layers. Pausing, as if waiting for an entrance cue, she announced in a deep sultry voice that 'the rat' was back. Large sunglasses concealed most of her face, except for a mouth glistening with metallic pink lipstick and a strong Roman nose dusted unevenly with powder.

"Mrs. von Hassel, please---!" Murphy scurried towards her solicitously, speaking in a lowered tone, in hopes she would do the same. "I told you yesterday that we'd take care of that little problem just as soon as---."

"But they're in the walls!" When disclosing potentially embarrassing pieces of information, Mrs. von Hassel seemed compelled to project strictly from the diaphragm.

"Please---Mrs. von Hassel, can we discuss this some other time?" Pleading now, Murphy glanced furtively at the new guests.

"And another thing," she continued full voice, "Must you keep pounding on the door while I take my showers? It's indecent! I don't know where you get this idea that I stay in the shower for an hour! I do not shower for an hour!'

"You are always welcome to leave, Mrs. von Hassel," observed Fleming without bothering to look up from his Bible.

Mrs. von Hassel ignored this comment as her attention had wandered to the two newcomers passing her on the stairs, luggage in hand. She regarded them like a cat intent on small prey and when they had disappeared from sight, loudly demanded to know if they were 'homos'.

Murphy looked as if he might die from embarrassment. "No, ma'am. They are brothers."

"Then are they single? And for heaven's sake, do not call me, ma'am."

Murphy looked heavenward as she unconsciously shifted her bodice, like a cowboy adjusting his holster, and turning, headed back up to her room. Mrs. Wilhelm von Hassel, previously Mrs. Chauncy Wilkerson, previously Mrs. Jakob Schneck, previously, Mrs. Reynaldo Marquez Hernandez, previously Mrs. Chick Moran, previously Mrs. Harry 'Spud' Brown, had in her glory days been what she chose to call an actress, although for the most part she'd dedicated her life to the art of love and beauty.

Memories of the time Mrs. von Hassel had turned her attention to him, flooded Murphy's mind unbidden. He would be mortified if anybody ever found out about it and even thinking of it now made him blush to the tips of his large protruding ears. His only consolation was in the fact that no one knew about their little evening of indiscretion---possibly not even Mrs. von Hassel who was at the time extremely intoxicated which was her customary condition every evening along about eight o'clock pm.

Meanwhile, Fleming was holding the Sprack brothers' registration gingerly between thumb and forefinger like a dead rodent. "Brother, I thought we had agreed not to open Zion to the general public any longer."

Murphy's ears grew red with shame. "What was I supposed to do? They called and we need the money!" He handed Fleming the dark yellow envelope from the Muldoon & Crock Mortgage & Loan Company. During the height of their father's period of recurrent mental breakdowns, a second mortgage on Zion Crossroads had been taken out and a balloon payment would be due within the next three months.

But Fleming tossed it aside, with contempt. "Oh ye of little faith! We don't need their money." By that he meant northern money. No, Fleming had determined that God would deliver the family treasure into his hand. The fact that they didn't seem any closer to finding it now than they had been a year ago did not cause Fleming to flinch from his conviction that God was on their side. "Fear is just another way of slapping the Lord in the face, Brother," continued Fleming sternly.

Murphy dutifully tried to pay attention. After all, Fleming was smarter and he did read his Bible every day. Besides, he was a man of the world. He'd gone to college and even lived in Richmond for eight years. In contrast, Murphy had never gone anywhere or done much of anything and somehow this had always made him feel less worthy of an opinion on the really important things.

But as Fleming stroked his esteemed beard and started in on the inevitable subject of the New Confederacy and the 'Higher Purpose', Murphy's mind wandered. That advertisement in the last issue of 'Hospitality Monthly' came to mind; the one with the disturbing byline, "If not now---when? and the picture showing a gray person in a gray room gazing forlornly at a colorful world outside his window, full of birds and flowers, full of life, but sadly out of reach. Murphy knew he was that person.

In October Murphy had turned forty. Forty years old and he'd never really accomplished anything, not like a real man should; never pushed himself beyond but now he had a dream. It had arisen rather unobtrusively while poring over the 'Hospitality Monthly'. It was a daydream about going to big conventions in exotic places like Atlanta or Miami and taking workshops, making contacts, becoming a true professional! Maybe, just maybe he could turn this slipshod operation into what it deserved to be, a five star hotel again, like it had been in the 1920s when his grandparents created it! He didn't know if this was really possible but all he knew was that he was ready to do something real, so ready it hurt. The only problem was Fleming.

Fleming had always felt disdain for the 'hospitality' business. The thought of complete strangers tramping through the sacred ancestral halls, gawking at the portraits of his ancestors, sleeping in their beds, feeding at their table like pigs at the trough, repelled him to his very core. It was a desecration of the memory of those who had struggled so valiantly for The Cause, and a bitter reminder of their humiliation and defeat.

Now that their Father was thankfully and finally dead and buried, Fleming was determined that things were going to change. Zion Crossroads would be restored to her 'rightful identity'; a term floated around in meetings of a group of Civil War 're-enacters' that met at Zion Crossroads once a month and called themselves the *Society of the Gray Knights.*

Fleming was the Historian of the group and wrote articles for the newsletter. Lately, he'd been spending more and more time in his attic room, writing newsletters and manifestos about the rise of the New Confederacy, with headlines like: *The Only Reason You Are White Today Is Because Your Parents Practiced Segregation* and *Justice For Our People Now!*

Ever since Murphy could remember, there had been loose talk in the community about the South rising again, but secretly Murphy felt that this group, the Gray Knights, took it to unnecessary extremes. After their father's death, that's when Fleming had started holding the meetings at Zion Crossroads. Murphy knew that if he'd still been alive, Daddy would never have stood for it.

"The Gray Knights won't be having their monthly meeting this Thursday will they, Fleming?" asked Murphy, suddenly realizing what an awkward combination it would make---the Gray Knights and these new guests.

Fleming halted his sermon in exasperation. Of all Murphy's bad habits, this one vexed him the most, for Fleming absolutely hated to be interrupted. "No, Brother---they will not!" He lowered his voice to an angry hiss. "Do I look like a fool? They could all be spies, which is why I don't want any more strangers coming to this house!"

"Oh," replied Murphy, fervently wishing he had never brought up the subject. Murphy used to sit in on the meetings of the Gray Knights but after getting a whiff of what this cast of wild eyed, bristle bearded characters were up to, he began to find excuses to be else-where. They were all just like Fleming, so negative and violent in their opinions that it made him want to hide inside a 'Hospitality Monthly' magazine for the rest of the afternoon.

Like a company of ghosts, reeking of mothballs in their an-cestral uniforms, they might have stepped right out of a history book, solemnly addressing each other as 'Colonel' this and 'Major' that. The 'General' was the most notable figure, with his meticulous white beard, and scent of lavender; the perfect gentleman, slow and gracious in speech and deportment. Everyone deferred to him as if to Robert E Lee himself. In fact, his surname was Lee.

Their opening creed, repeated in unison at the beginning of each meeting, declared that they were not "Americans but citizens of the Confederate States of America which has been under military occupation for over one hundred years." In fact, they saw themselves as the architects of a second secession from the Union. And though the law had been passed years before, they were still obsessing about the 'forced' integration of the schools, something that in their view flew in the face of their fundamental freedoms. The federal govern-ment should not be permitted to march in and tell the states what to do. This was the true reason, they told themselves, that the first 'war against northern aggression' had happened in the first place. But the bottom line was that they feared that mixing the races would lead to the ultimate destruction of the White Race and the Nation as a whole.

Fleming's view, which he elucidated in his articles with fiery or-atory, was that this also went squarely against Biblical Law. The Black Races had obviously been cursed by God. Fleming was a proponent of returning government to Biblical Law, which would naturally include stoning culprits, cutting off limbs and so forth. Fleming was consid-ered the Biblical expert and was often referred to as 'Reverend' or al-ternately 'Colonel' which was his great-great-great-granddaddy's rank during the War of Northern Aggression.

Recently, many had vowed to become tax objectors. A petition was passed around the room and everyone signed, pledging not to pay federal taxes ever again. "It's time we put our money where our mouth is!" cried General Lee, prompting many boasts and passionate vows. Fleming was the first to sign and unlike some, truly meant to follow through.

After that they'd taken to holding closed-door sessions to which Murphy was not invited. Fleming said he was too much of a 'wiener' to be trusted. But from random scribblings on crumpled sheets of paper left over from meetings, Murphy had pieced together the plan they were concocting; namely that of turning Zion Crossroads into the *Center In Support of the Round Table of the Gray Knights,* the purpose of which was to *Unite in Truth and Brotherhood for the Rise of the New South'.* And in fact, they had already begun developing their arsenal of ammunition in the old summer kitchen.

Murphy was used to Fleming getting his way and maybe it was just for peace of mind that Murphy had taught himself not to care. After all, he'd had little reason to expect much from life up to now; and wasn't Fleming a part of himself? Did they not have the same face, the same body, and blood? Indeed, in some deep and mysterious way, Murphy understood that they were truly 'one' and for the most part he'd contented himself with feeling proud of Fleming's achievements as though they could stand in for his own. Besides it was useless to argue with Fleming anyway, being that he was hardheaded as a piece of stone.

As a child, Fleming had been largely indifferent to Murphy, usually preferring his own company, except when it came to fighting his secret underground war against the housekeeper, Leonora, whom he called the 'Nigger Hitler-ina'. For this, he often needed an ally and for lack of anyone else, Murphy was recruited. Though he was little more than a gopher in Fleming's elaborate pranks, Murphy had lived for these moments of camaraderie.

But the year they'd turned twelve, things had changed drastically. Their father fell off the roof and their mother had packed up and left, never to return. That same year, Fleming declared his independence by moving into his own room up on the third floor, leaving Murphy to battle the dark ghost ridden nights of Zion Crossroads alone.

On the full moons, it wasn't uncommon for the ghost of their great-great-great-granddaddy Colonel Carter Meriwether Bowen to roam the halls the whole night through, banging and thumping and bumping around. Fleming bragged that the ghost didn't bother him a bit, knowing full well that Murphy had spent entire nights sweating under the sheets. As a consequence, Murphy was nicknamed 'Weiner' early on.

Still, no matter how Fleming bullied and manipulated, Murphy had always steadfastly revered him, admiring his defiant strength, his knifelike intelligence, his total lack of caring for what others thought. (And wasn't that Murphy's downfall? He cared too much and it made him weak.) After college, and after working in that New Republic Book store, Fleming had returned, pious and distant, spouting high sounding words and `principles' that created an invisible wall between the brothers.  Murphy did not `get it' and that made him `irrelevant'. Now more than ever, Murphy did not exist in Fleming's world and it was devastating. The loss of an arm or leg could not have pained him more. But since last summer he'd begun seeing Fleming through different eyes.

For Murphy, the first turning point came when Fleming decided not to pay the taxes. Down to his core, Murphy was a rule-follower and frankly he was shocked by Fleming's cavalier disregard of federal authority; not to mention that he would even go so far as to hold a bloody standoff in the halls of Zion! At least that's the way he talked in those manifestos he wrote. Well, it was beyond imagination!

For the first time in his life Murphy had disobeyed his brother and filed the taxes in secret. Any day now the refund check would be arriving in the mail and in a show of real daring, Murphy had decided that his brother would never know a thing about it. No, it would all go towards buying a new refrigerator.

"Look...the Professor is coming. Now is the time!" Fleming stepped inside the broom closet under the stairs. Murphy knew what his brother was up to. He wanted to spy on poor Professor Valentino through the two-way mirror he'd had installed in the door.
Murphy glanced furtively at his reflection in the gilt framed mirror hanging behind the registration counter. Fleming had installed the two-way mirror back when he thought the housekeeper was stealing from them. Murphy had always disliked it. It made him edgy, knowing there was the possibility that he was being watched.

But this was quickly swept away by the wave of good cheer that always accompanied the dapper Professor, as he opened the screen door, newspaper tucked under his arm. Valentino was the one person Murphy looked forward to seeing every day.

"Good afternoon, Professor. Are you sure you should be out in the heat like this with your heart condition?" Murphy always talked extra loud because Valentino was hard of hearing.

"Oh, my yes," Valentino said, in his soft faded voice, "The heat is marvelous. Makes one feel so alive!" Every afternoon it was his custom to go out for a stroll to the mailbox with Willie, a dog that no one else could see.

"Well, it's time to take your pills," announced Murphy, removing a tray of medicine bottles from the drawer.
The old fellow smiled like a mischievous child. "Oh---my magic pills!"

For a man with half his mind gone and a long list of medical conditions, he did seem amazingly healthy. Clearly, at one time Valentino had been unusually handsome and fastidiously groomed. His thick wavy hair, already silver by age thirty, was combed straight back, revealing an elegant widow's peak and accentuating a high noble forehead. Everyday he still dressed in a suit and tie and though a bit shabby, still bore himself with regal authority. Overshadowed by great bushy eyebrows, his china blue eyes, once icy and incisive, now bore a soft inward expression, as if all the world were inside himself.

After Valentino had tottered up to his room on the second floor, Fleming came out of the closet and stood in front of Murphy, arms folded. "You didn't even ask?"

"It wasn't the right moment, Fleming. He was in such a happy mood!"

"So you're waiting for him to be sad?"

How many times had they gone round and round on this issue?

"For someone hell bent on following the rules, I would think you'd be just a little worried," said Fleming. "What will happen if the fire inspector shows up and we still haven't cleared out that room?"

He was referring to the stacks upon stacks of newspapers clogging up Valentino's room, not to mention `scientific samples' ranging from rocks, sticks, dead insects, and the occasional decaying animal. (Mrs. von Hassel's olfactory senses had sounded the alert on that issue more than once). Of course, Murphy knew full well this wasn't about fire hazards. Fleming was after Valentino's copy of the treasure map.

Just a few days after their father's hasty burial nine months before, Puffenberger, Mrs. von Hassel and Professor Valentino (the 'intruders' as Fleming chose to call them) had arrived at Zion Crossroads without the slightest notion that Joe had just passed away. They claimed to be his friends and each bore a notarized letter written by Joe himself, authorizing them to live at Zion Crossroads "in perpetuity" and at no cost "in return for having saved his life."

Needless to say, the news had dropped like a bombshell on

the twins who had never even heard of these people. Fleming was all set to kick them out when Joe's Last Will and Testament mysteriously surfaced, only to reveal another shocking revelation. Not only did it bestow upon the three intruders free room and board but a co-equal partnership in a so-called 'Zion Crossroads Community Inn & Plantation Treasure Hunt'.

The 'treasure' in question was the Colonel's long lost treasure---the treasure he'd buried before rushing off to fight for the Confederacy---the treasure he was never able to find when he returned because the map had gone missing. The story was that the old veteran had slowly gone mad, leaving the forests of Zion Crossroads riddled with holes like so many empty graves, as he dug for the lost treasure. Even after his death, it was said, the Colonel's ghost could be seen, roaming the haunted forest, searching for it.

Over the years, the idea of a treasure map had been passed down through the family like a fairy tale that only grew increasingly more difficult to believe. After all, it was well known that the old Colonel had gone crazy. However, the arrival of these 'Intruders' caused Fleming's already suspicious mind to go into overdrive. If the treasure really did exist then perhaps what his mother had always suspected was true. Joe was purposely hiding the map from them.

Fleming made a holy vow right then and there that no stranger would ever take from him what was rightfully his, no matter the cost and he made Murphy put his hand on the Bible and swear to it, too. Later, Murphy would look back on this moment with shame. He should have known. If he hadn't been such a coward he would have made himself see that Fleming's long-held resentment had finally gone to madness.

Murphy was jolted out of this revery when his twin turned to leave and banged his head on the mother spider plant hanging above the registration desk in full spidery splendor. Never one to admit physical pain, Fleming stood in ominous silence, his hand pressed to his head.

Murphy held his breath. "Oh, Fleming---!" He stopped short of apologizing. Nothing aroused Fleming's contempt more thoroughly than pity.

"What did I say about all these plants, Murphy?"

"I know, I know! I just haven't had time to move them but I will! Don't worry. I will!"

"Your promises mean very little, Brother!"

"Yes, I know. I'm sorry." Murphy had to admit they'd been going through something of a population explosion for spider plants were everywhere, occupying every possible surface and hanging on hooks from above. Fleming had ordered him to get rid of them weeks ago but for Murphy, they were more like the children he'd never had, and he couldn't find it in his heart to destroy them, so he'd procrastinated.

He could feel Fleming glowering at him as he climbed the ladder beneath the mother plant, watering can in hand.

"Be careful, Brother," warned Fleming just as Murphy was stretching precariously from the top step. "You wouldn't want to fall now would you!" Fleming knew very well that since the day their father had fallen off the roof, Murphy had had a fear of heights. It was only love for the spiders that could make him set that aside.

With that poisonous comment, Fleming left. A moment later, Murphy was startled by the sound of the front door opening. Down he went, bringing the ladder and the mother spider crashing to the floor along with him. From where he lay sprawled beneath the overturned ladder, Murphy squinted up into the blurry face of a stranger.

"Are you all right?" asked the man.

"I need my glasses---." It was an awkward moment as Murphy pawed around like a blind mole in search of his spectacles.

The man's name was Stephen Andriot. He was perhaps thirty-five years of age, light brown hair pulled neatly back into a ponytail, handsome, with an athletic build. His eyes were unusually wide set and this, combined with a mouth ever on the verge of a smile, gave him a look of permanent bemusement. An escapee from the country club lifestyle he'd been raised in, he'd turned to freelance journalism, roaming the continents on expeditions of one sort or another. An inquisitive dare-devil, he thrived on dirt, sweat, and deprivation. The glory of danger, the magnificent sunrise from a mountain top, or the mystery of midnight in the jungle was his drug of choice. And now for the strangest of purposes, he found himself here.

Andriot quickly retrieved Murphy's eyeglasses and offered him a hand up. "Are you sure you're all right?"

Murphy bravely shrugged off the assistance. "Oh, don't worry about me! This happens all the time!" He struggled to his bony knees then hoisted himself to his feet, grimacing mightily. "I guess you could say I'm just an accident waiting to happen! Ha, ha!" He bent forlornly over the plant lying amidst the debris. "This was my very first plant." His chin trembled.

Andriot's response was resoundingly cheery. "Just stick it back in the dirt. It'll be fine!"

Murphy flashed a martyred smile but he'd stood up too quickly and everything turned black. He started to wobble. "I think I need to sit down." Leaning on Andriot's arm, he limped over to a threadbare chair in the hospitality corner.

"You've hurt your ankle. You'll need some ice."

"It's nothing, really. I've had much worse. I'll be perfectly fine," the victim chirped but it was a false note. Plainly, he was not perfectly fine and his face immediately fell into despair. He asked Andriot to guess how many mirrors he had broken in his life.

"Well, I suppose everyone has broken one or two."

"Seven! Seven mirrors! Do you know how many years of bad luck that is? Forty-five!"

"Well, forty-nine, actually."

"That's right! Forty-nine!" Murphy's eyes slowly filled with pain, his thin shoulders sagged. "I could be dead before that bad luck runs out."

After a moment's consideration, Andriot said that he didn't believe in bad luck but Murphy only smiled tragically. "Trust me! When you've got it, you believe in it all right."

"But don't we make our own luck---good or bad? Isn't it all in how we look at things?"

Murphy immediately withdrew like an injured turtle into his shell. He'd been a fool to reveal his inner pain to a stranger. Limping and hiccoughing furiously (his usual response to a stressful situation), he began lugging Andriot's luggage from the porch to the registration desk. This was his way of punishing Andriot for implying that suffering wasn't inescapable. "Fill this out, please," he said, coldly indicating the registration form.

Thinking that they took their curses very seriously around here, Andriot cleared a spot among the spider plants and began to fill out the form. There was an uncomfortable silence, as Murphy continued hiccoughing in the most impersonal and businesslike manner he could muster.

"Hey, listen," Andriot said, casually scanning the ancestral portraits gazing down in cold superiority from the walls. "I'm looking for the owner. Mr. Joe Bowen?"

Murphy's magnified eyes widened with alarm. Loose papers fluttered from his hand. "You didn't by chance--- `hic`--- save his life---`hic`--- did you...`hic`...?"

At this precise moment, Fleming entered the room. Andriot

looked from one to the other, quickly calculating the resemblance. "Actually, it's interesting that you should ask because, as a matter of fact, he saved mine. A psychotic moose on the rampage was headed straight for my back. Joe stopped him dead in his tracks with a single shot straight through the eye socket. That's why I'm here. I've got the head stuffed and mounted in the back of my truck. Thought I'd give it to Joe as a little memento."

The twins exchanged furtive glances. "Joe was our father," replied Fleming stiffly. "Unfortunately, he passed away last August."

Andriot looked dumbstruck then his mouth slowly spread into a wide grin. "But you're kidding! Right?"

Fleming stroked his dark beard with pale womanish fingers. "Why would we 'kid' about something like that?"

Andriot looked from one to the other, an incredulous smile still hovering on his lips. "Because I saw him not six months ago on New Year's Eve."

Their jaws dropped and suddenly Fleming and Murphy looked the way identical twins should look---identical. "Are you sure?" they croaked with one voice.

"We're talking about the same Joe Bowen, correct? Owner of the Zion Crossroads Hotel? This is the Zion Crossroads Hotel?"

"I'm sure it's a very common name, 'Zion Crossroads'! Very common!" blathered Murphy but Fleming silenced him with a murderous look.

Fleming coldly inquired as to what he looked like---this person Andriot claimed to know as Joe Bowen.

"Tall, thin, dark hair---I don't know, fairly regular looking."

"Lots of people fit that description!" blurted Murphy cheerily.

"Did he wear glasses?" Fleming's tone was nothing short of sly, as if he knew he held the trump card.

"No." Andriot's shit detectors were now on full alert. These guys seemed inordinately rattled. But why?

"Well that settles it then," Fleming sneered. "Our father was legally blind---almost completely helpless without his glasses!"

"Oh, yes! Completely helpless!" echoed Murphy, blinking like a guppy.

Andriot tilted his head, quizzically. "Hmmm. Well, maybe you're right then. This guy could shoot a damn quarter at thirty paces. My mistake! Still what an amazing coincidence, eh?" Owing to years as a reporter and excellent peripheral vision, he did not fail to notice their obvious relief.

"So what the hell do I do with this stuffed moose head? You want it?"

Murphy paused thoughtfully. "I suppose we could hang it on the wall someplace." He brightened. "Perhaps in the library! It could go with our fox hunt theme."

"That's somewhat of a stretch but whatever suits," murmured Andriot. His attention had strayed. He had the habit of seeing people as backdrop to his own movie, so to speak. When he was interested, he gave his full attention but when his attention shifted, it was like they no longer existed. Next scene.

Now he saw something curious through an arched door. With Murphy at his elbow, he drifted into the dining room, a very grand paneled room, painted in a dull powdery green with an ornate tin ceiling. An opulent chandelier hung from a faded mural inset featuring a naked Venus, thinly draped, and floating on yellowed clouds against a cracked greenish blue sky. As if drawn by a magnet, he headed straight for the other end of the enormously long banquet table, where an oil portrait of a nineteenth century man hung over an imposing mantlepiece. "Who's this?"

"That's our great-great-great granddaddy, Colonel Carter Meriweather Bowen," announced Murphy with a note of pride. "The original owner of this house."

Andriot stared. The resemblance between Joe and the man in the portrait was uncanny; the same hawk like expression around the eyes, that double-dare-you kind of look born by a man who thrives on risk and competition. They had to be related. He was puzzled now more than ever. Why were these men, his sons, lying to him?

Meanwhile, Murphy was reciting the history of Zion Crossroads and how in 1699 their brave Ancestor was orphaned at the age of twelve and worked his way from Ireland to America as an indentured servant; eventually buying his freedom and this piece of frontier property. He seemed especially proud that his great great great granddaddy Colonel Carter Meriwether Bowen had been a war hero, fighting alongside the likes of Stonewall Jackson in the War between the States.

"So I understand this hotel was sort of big deal back in the 1920's."

"Yes, Grandfather Fairchild Meriwether Bowen turned it into a hotel in 1913 and it was very popular until the Great Depression hit and then---."

Suddenly there was a tremendous jolt, as if a bus had rammed

into the side of the house. The whole place shook for a seemingly endless moment, then subsided, the sound rolling off into the far distance.

"What the hell was that?" demanded Andriot, his heart pounding. Murphy was clinging to him as if he were a life raft.

"Earthquake." The word floated in from the front hall on a note
of satisfaction, as Fleming apparently enjoyed being the bearer of this
piece of information.

"I didn't know there were earthquakes in Virginia," said Andriot,
returning to the counter, amazed and shaken.

"These are the last days, my friend. There will be earthquakes
wherever the Lord deems there to be earthquakes," answered Fleming
and with that returned calmly to his Bible.

CHAPTER II
Dinner Time
The Zion Crossroads Plantation Hotel
1980

"From the day we're born, the most important thing is to be understood - for how else can one find any comfort? How else to still that hunger which is pain? To be understood is always of prime importance and it remains so until the end."

from the notebooks of Joseph Meriwether Bowen
Spring 1978

Mrs. von Hassel also lived on the second floor of the main house. Her room was in the northwest corner at the back of the house. It suited her. She didn't care for morning sun anyway. She was usually sleeping off her vodka lemonade from the night before, for though she was an actress and astrologer by trade, she was an alcoholic by vocation.

As dim as the light already was, she kept the blinds shut to make it even dimmer mainly because she looked better in lamplight. As a rule, she strictly avoided direct light of any kind and absolutely never went out into the sun. She was by nature, a nocturnal creature, a stargazer, rising at noon stiff, head-achy, and strictly incommunicado except for a few shrill commands if anyone should be so foolish as to get in her way.

It was her habit to spend summer afternoons languishing on the front porch, a diminished, veiled presence in a straw hat and sunglasses, sipping lemonade spiked with liquor. Today she withdrew to her room to begin the evening ritual of making up her face with the anticipation of having new guests to charm at dinner.

Sitting before her three-way mirror was the only time she ever permitted her real face to be revealed in unflattering light. She had inherited her father's strong Roman nose and bad skin, which in her mother's judgment would always prevent her from being a true beauty.

It was the challenge that God had given her, yet it had become her ally as well for it had imbued her with strength of determination. Thankfully, as her body ripened, it had proven to be as lavish as her face was plain and the homely girl would come to reinvent herself as an `exotic' beauty. For if she knew anything it was that without beauty a woman was a nonentity in the world of men.

Her beauty was a spell she cast, having little to do with the details of her face but more a product of her daring glamour and by the way her spirit animated her face. However in unguarded moments, naked behind her mask, a very different face emerged, the face of someone who worked the soil with her hands, a practical face, an unremarkable, and ancient face.

Today when she looked into the mirror, that ancient face looked back at her, hardened by sorrow, the eyes hollow and empty, the mouth bitter. It was nothing she dared show to the world so she turned to her pallet of colors and creams, her wigs and hairpieces and busied herself with the work of transformation until the face she knew and loved returned to her. Tonight at least there would be three new men at the dinner table, and that alone gave her a lift.

It had been such a long dreary winter with the dreariest of companions. Even the spring had not been much comfort, remaining cold and rainy long after its due.   But she would not allow herself to think about that right now. When she thought such things, the creases in her face deepened in an ugly way. Her newest motto was: A smile is an instant face-lift! That's right! There's a girl! Keep it bright and charming!

Dinner was served at 6 pm sharp so at 5:55, dressed and `presentable', she would make her earthly descent, to the dining room, fittingly elegant. She'd quickly learned that to be fashionably late was to go without, as Fleming was very strict about latecomers not being served.

The dining room was large and square, with a long mahogany banquet table that could easily have seated twenty people, casting a lonely effect with the mere handful scattered among the empty chairs. Fleming sat morosely at the far end, mirroring the grim-faced portrait of the ancestor suspended above the mantlepiece behind him. Mealtimes were his only concession to being sociable, and these he spent in an unapproachable silence, meticulously subdividing his food into mounds of eatable and uneatable and in general, amplifying the portrait's gloomy effect on the room.

A few seats away to his right, Mr. Puffenburger waited, fork in hand, a cloth napkin spread across his great belly, waiting for what would hopefully be the highlight of his day but which, more often than not, was a disappointment. At the opposite end of the table on the same side was Mrs. von Hassel strategically positioned so she would neither have to look at or speak to Mr. Puffenberger whose eating habits she despised.

Opposite her sat Professor Valentino. She didn't mind sitting with him so much because most of the time he had the wit (or the lack thereof) not to have anything to say and served as a fitting audience for her nightly monologue. True he was prone to unusual behaviors that in any other setting would have been embarrassing, but she had learned to draw upon her acting skills, and go on as if nothing were out of the ordinary. For example, on this particular evening, and just as the new guests were filing in, he had taken it into his head to measure all the plates and silverware with his little retractable tape measure and was diligently recording them in his little black book.

The two brothers, Jack and Tommy Sprack sat somewhere in the middle of the table, side by side, Tommy smiling all around, and Jack keeping a wary eye on Valentino. Andriot showed up at 6:10 and sat between Mrs. von Hassel and Puffenberger just as Murphy emerged from the kitchen with steamy spectacles and announced that dinner would be a little late due to `complications'. He vanished again behind the swinging door.

Fleming fixed Andriot, the latecomer, with a cold stare. "Lucky for you our evening meal has been detained."

Andriot looked up, merely curious, that unnerving hint of amusement playing about his lips. "I beg pardon?"

"Read the policy," the management sniffed and with a superior air continued his meditation on the far wall above the other diners' heads.

The new guests laughed nervously, thinking this was some sort of awkward attempt at dry humor but the other residents did not look up or share in the mirth. As if on cue, Mrs. von Hassel coughed politely, resting a bejeweled hand lightly on her throat. "I don't believe we've met. My name is Amanda." Her voice was dusky and reeked of experience. Tonight, she was wearing her hair swept up in a mass of platinum blonde curls, a low-cut lavender silk dress and rhinestone-studded sandals.

Jack straightened up like a kid in a bad school play. "Jack Sprack, that's S-p-r-a-c-k. And this is my brother, Tommy."

Tommy would have liked to have introduced himself, but instead just closed his mouth and grinned his sheepish grin. He tried not to stare at Amanda's glossy pink lips and the mesmerizing way she shaped her mouth around each word. He also noticed that the cords in her neck stood out when she asked Andriot to `please.' pour her a glass of ice tea.

"So where are you two boys from, Jack?" her eyes, still a trifle bloodshot, widened into that well-practiced vacuity women instinctively use to draw in their prey.

"Baltimore, m'am."

"Really?" Her smile acidified. He had spoken that poisonous word, `m'am'. "And what exactly do you do in Baltimore?" She said the word as if it were the lowest place on earth.

"I work road construction and Tommy is a---he works in a nursing home."

"Massage therapist," added Tommy.

Jack winced noticeably. "Yeah. One of those."

"Oh," she said, stifling a dainty yawn then turned to Andriot, purring that she knew he had to be a Scorpio.

"Aquarius, actually," said Andriot, exuding an off handed charm and self-confidence.

Amanda smiled knowingly. "Oh, but I'll bet you have Scorpio rising. I'm rarely wrong about Scorpios. I married seven of them." She laughed, exhaling the sour smell of a serious drinker. "So where are you from?'

"Well, that's a long story." Andriot discreetly held his breath. "You mean recently or originally?"

"A traveling man, I see!"

"But not for long if you get your way, right Amanda?" glowered Puffenberger from the opposite end of the table.

Mrs. von Hassel glided past the interruption without missing a beat. "So where were you from recently *and* originally. I want to know it *all*." She positively glittered now, as if Andriot were the most fascinating man in the world.

Rebuffed, Puffenberger rolled his eyes for the benefit of the Sprack brothers, as if they were his private audience.

"Originally, I'm from Connecticut." replied Andriot, seemingly unaware of the crossfire.

"I adore Connecticut! All those charming country roads, the stone walls, white board fences, the horses---." She beamed a defiant look of gorgeous well-being towards Puffenberger, who merely burped without apology.

"But I've lived all over the world, really. The last six weeks I've spent climbing Machu Pichu, actually."

"A mountain climber? That must be what all those muscles are about." She dropped her creamy lavender lids seductively.

"Watch yourself, buddy," muttered Puffenberger. "She's got her eye on you. Guard your wallet."

Mrs. von Hassel's face froze in a terrible smile. "O bitter man."

"Careful, Mandy! Your claws are showing!"

At that moment, the swinging door opened and Murphy popped his head out, along with an odor of scorched food. "We're ready!"

"At last!" murmured Valentino, putting his hands together and looking skyward like a choirboy.

Gardner, the young black man with the golden eyes came out first, sweaty and beleaguered, bearing a large tray of sliced, slightly shriveled roast beef. Murphy followed with bowls of scorched potatoes and lumpy gravy.

"Bon appetit!" Gardner sat down with a flourish opposite Mr. Puffenberger. "And there'll be cake for dessert. So how was the sneak preview, Puffy?"

Puffenberger pretended not to hear.

"Oh, the collard greens---Gardner?" But Gardner stoically refused to take the hint. Relenting, Murphy himself darted back into the kitchen and returned with a large bowl of collards.

"In my day the help ate in the kitchen," sniffed Mrs. von Hassel.

"Yeah, well by my watch, your days are pretty much over, Mrs. von Hassel." The cook smiled boldly and reached for the roast beef. "Folks, the beef's a little dry so you might want to put some extra gravy on it."

"The beef is always a little dry," complained Puffenberger, but he still forked a large mound onto his plate.

There was an impatient clinking of a knife upon a drinking glass. It was Fleming, glaring like a wrathful prophet until a dutiful hush fell upon the diners. "Let us pray." Knitting together his soft white fingers, and tilting his head back on his long bony neck, he shut his eyes into their shadowy holes. "Heavenly Father," he began in a quiet voice, as if this were a private matter between him and God and did not concern the others. "Seize these sinners gathered here. Purge them of their iniquities, their lying blasphemous ways. Cast their false gods asunder. Annihilate all that doth offend thee, O God. Amen." There was a weak sprinkling of 'amens'. The newcomers exchanged guarded looks.

"And on that cheery note," added Gardner, holding his fork aloft, "lez eat." A brooding silence descended on the group as everyone sawed away at the roast beef. "So how's about that little earthquake we had today, huh folks?" he continued amiably. "I bet you thought the whole damn place was gonna come piling down on our heads, didn't ya!"

"For a minute I thought a semi truck had just rammed right into the side of the house!" replied Tommy, looking to the others for agreement, but they only slid wary sidelong glances at Fleming, as if waiting for him to speak first. He said nothing.

"Has this ever happened before?" asked Andriot.

"Since last September, oh I'd say at least once a month," said Gardner, chewing briskly. "Right Murph?"

Murphy nodded, his face giving an odd twitch.

Everyone stayed in their own thoughts until Mrs. von Hassel began a rambling monologue about her third husband Reynaldo, a ballroom dancer from Queens, tragically run over by a cab on 49th Street.

After dinner, Jack and Tommy had immediately gone back up the creaking staircase, past the glowering ancestral portraits to the carved wooden door bearing a small plaque reading, The Jefferson Davis Room. It was a spacious room that still bore the high born elegance of a bygone era with its tall ceilings, long windows hung with rich brocade, and twin four poster canopy beds. Still there was an overall atmosphere of brooding decay, like a photograph yellowed with age and something else slightly less tangible. No, it wasn't just the heat but Tommy couldn't quite identify it. It was too ephemeral--like the subtle smell of anxiety lurking in the sweat on one's skin.

"It's hot as hell in here!" muttered Jack fumbling impatiently with the switch to the ceiling fan. "Just our luck! The damned thing doesn't work---!".

"Here, let me!" Tommy gave it a try and in a few moments, it started to whirr. "See it works!"

"It better work! For this amount of money? Shit. Open them doors, will ya--- so we can get some air in this place."

Tommy opened the french doors and stepped out onto a white columned porch that ran the length of the front of the house. It wasn't much cooler outside for the sun was still burning brightly in the humid haze of the sky; still there was a great view of the surroundings, the magnificent oaks lining the front drive, the fields of wildflowers rolling down to a placid green river, the blue mountains beyond. To the east, he felt the wild presence of the ancient forest beckoning---all of it just like the dream he'd been having almost every night.

It was one of those traveling dreams. That's what he called them now; the ones that felt completely real and normal, except you could fly and do amazing things because you knew you were dreaming which was why this place felt so familiar. Suddenly other memories tucked in the hidden folds of his brain started riffling through his mind like a deck of cards---memories that he didn't quite understand.

"Cheers!" It was Jack standing there with two glasses of whiskey. He drank his in one long draught. The first swallow was always the best. After that he forgot to notice.

Tommy waved his glass away. "Nah, it's too hot." Tommy never liked the burning sting of it going down his throat.

"Come on! It's your vacation!" Jack's mood was already improving. Soon he would feel the lid coming up off his head, setting his thoughts free. Then he could relax a little and really be himself. It used to be he'd laugh and do crazy things when he was drunk but he was a kid then. Now he just thought about things. It was probably the only time he ever really did just think.

Tommy sighed. As usual he would give in but he'd be doing it more for his brother than for himself. After a few sips, he'd leave the rest sitting in his glass then Jack would yell at him for wasting and finish it off himself. That's the way it usually went. He just hoped Jack wouldn't start obsessing about lawsuits and all the people who'd ever screwed him over which was usually what happened when he drank.

"This place sure makes you feel like you're back in the olden days, doesn't it?" said Tommy finally, hoping to keep the conversation positive.

"Yeah, but if we had to go back to the 'olden' days, why couldn't we have gone to a place where we had our own bathroom---and horseback riding?" said Jack, who always found it more interesting to complain. He headed back into the room to get a refill and stretch out on the bed. "Man, I'm wiped out."

"Still, it's a small price to pay," said Tommy following him in. "Think big picture, Jack. We could be rich this time tomorrow!" He pulled out the rumpled pamphlet and sat on the opposite bed. "According to this, the first thing we gotta find is a riding trail called Gwyneth's Way, then let's see---the Tree of the Hollow Man from there we go due north to the Wall of Survival along Slave's Run. What is it with these names---Wall of Adversity, Fortune's Ladder, the Mirror of Reflection, the Stone of Destiny?"

Jack grimaced but Tommy knew it was because he was afraid

to hope. He was just wired that way. But Tommy wasn't worried because he'd had that dream. In fact, the moment the wind had smacked that pamphlet onto his windshield, he just knew that something was up---something big. It was like---a summons.

Of course, he had to be careful talking like that with Jack who'd say it was just airy fairy bullshit. It would make him angry. *Don't get your hopes up*, he'd say. *Don't count your chickens!* Even so, Tommy had been having a hard time containing his enthusiasm. *The Universe will show us the way!* he'd told Jack. But that had definitely been a mistake for it had only aroused Jack's contempt.

"I'm sick of all this hippy dippy philosophy shit! Universe! Why the hell can't you just say God like everybody else?"

"Because to me that word isn't mysterious enough. People say God and think they know what they're talking about! 'The Great Mysterious' would be much better."

"Or how about the Wizard of Oz?" Of course this had made Tommy laugh and Jack liked to make him laugh so he'd laid off and lit his last cigarette.

"Hey, Jack. You're not supposed to smoke in the room."

Jack blew out a stream of smoke. "Forget about it! For this price I'm smokin' wherever the hell I want." He was small for a man, but powerfully built, with a deep indelible streak of rebellion. In his younger days, he worried he was a little too pretty with the long thick eyelashes so in high school he'd taken up cigarettes to make him look tougher. Now he was hooked on two packs a day and already dried out looking with a deep smoker's hack.

"When are you gonna cut down, Jack?"

"Next week---maybe." This was his usual answer. He thought it was funny but Tommy refused to laugh.

"You need to get something positive in your life, Jack. You gotta have dreams to live for or what's the point?"

"Dreams, huh?" Jack regarded his long legged brother, with that sheepish grin of his, the long blonde hair tumbling into his eyes. What an interminable kid he was, getting all excited about this treasure hunt thing! But just the sight of his simple happiness only made the dark cloud settle a little more firmly around Jack's head because of course he was right.

No matter what, you're never gonna be happy, Tommy would always tell him. *You're too negative*, he'd say and then launched into all that hippy dippy garbage about how you create your own reality through your thoughts. Which made absolutely no sense to Jack since why in the hell would he have ever created the mess his life had turned into---and on purpose? No way!

He knew from experience that no matter how hard he dreamed, none of them ever came true. No, it was the fickle finger of fate that set your course in life---a fluke of the genes that had made him short and Tommy tall. And yeah, he was negative---but negative was good. It was reality. Not like this fuzzy headed "it's-meant-to-be' shit. No, Jack was never going to be like Tommy who was almost idiotically 'positive'. Sometimes Jack wondered if his brother didn't do it just to be irritating.

It was a mystery how the two of them could have ended up so different. After all, they'd had the same parents but somehow Tommy was golden from the beginning, with that big smile busting out like he was embarrassed to be so happy. For him life had always been a walk in the park. 'Don't get your hopes up' was the message Jack got growing up: You're short. Somehow Tommy had missed all that. Or maybe he was just tall.

"Come on," said Tommy suddenly. "Let's go out and take a look around."

"I told you, I'm tired, man."

"You need some fresh air, Jack. It's cooling off outside and it'll be good to get some exercise." Tommy started dragging Jack off the bed.

"Hey, now! What the---!" Jack instinctively grabbed onto the bedpost and it gave an alarming creak. "Damn, Tommy! Break the bed why don't you!"

"Come on! Get your butt up and let's go!"

"All right! All right! Just let go of my arm, ya big ape!" Though he acted grumpy, a smile was creeping in because he always secretly liked the attention. "I gotta get some more cigs outa the car anyways."

"I thought you were cutting down."

"That's next week, remember?"

They passed Mrs. von Hassel holding court on the front porch with Professor Valentino and Stephen Andriot. Gentle laughter surrounded her like she was belle of the ball. Following the stone path that led around towards the back of the house, they saw that the house had a large two story addition extending off the back with long columned porches above and below.

Beside a cracked cement pool in the center of a stunted rose garden, Puffenberger was seated on a stone bench, listening to Dixieland jazz on a cheap portable radio. On his lap, he clutched a rumpled grocery bag and appeared to be chewing but surreptitiously as if he did not to want anyone to know what he was doing.

"Wow, this place must have been really something back in the day," commented Tommy, nodding towards the building.

"That's what they tell me." Puffenberger seemed remote in his great body as if disinterested or slightly miffed---yet watchful.

"Those rooms got private bathrooms?" asked Jack, nodding to the addition.

"Yeah."

Jack's face lit up with new hope. "Tommy, let's get them to switch us."

"If you like taking cold showers and toilets that don't flush," added Puffenberger calmly with a certain malicious satisfaction.

Jack scowled. "What kind of hotel is this anyways?"

"A disintegrating one."

"Damn!"

Meanwhile, Tommy was looking at the pamphlet. "Listen, how do you get to---*Gwyneth's Way?*"

Puffenberger paused long enough to swallow. "You mean the Loop! Past the stables, you'll see the sign that points the way---only it's kinda late to be going out there."

"I figure we got a couple more hours of light."

"Still, sometimes a mist rolls in. If you see that happening, I'd get the hell out."

"A mist, huh?" said Jack, rolling his eyes dramatically. "Ooh, I sure hope a ghost ain't gonna try to snatch us or something!"

Puffenberger grinned malevolently. "Suit yourself."

"Thanks, man. We'll be careful," Tommy nudged Jack to get moving before he had a chance to make another tactless comment. You never knew what he was liable to say when he'd been drinking.

"Dude, got anything in that sack for me?" called out Jack.

Puffenberger stopped chewing abruptly with a stony gaze and clutched the bag tighter as if afraid that Jack might grab it from him.

Tommy gave his brother's arm a rough yank. "Come on, Jack!" Jack waited until they were almost to the stables before letting out a howl of laughter.

"Did you see that guy's face?"

"Would you tone it down? He can still hear you!"

"So?"

"You are such a jerk sometimes, Jack!"

"Lighten up, man! I was just joking with him."

"You don't joke with people like that. He's probably very sensitive about that stuff."

"Sensitive? You mean about his blimp-ness? I bet he weighs 400 pounds!" Tommy moved ahead with long strides, leaving Jack to catch up from the rear. "What is your problem, man? It was funny! So did you see that old Professor guy measuring the spoons at dinner? Hey, wait up 'til I catch my breath." Jack was already winded.

"Then stop smoking those fucking cigarettes," called Tommy and purposely increased his pace.

Despite the comment, Jack's snarky good humor remained undimmed. "Half the people at this place belong in some kind of institution if you ask me---especially that creep, Fleming Bowen. What do you make of him---hotel manager by day, psychotic killer by night?"

Tom picked up a large branch and threw it as hard as he could by way of saying he was still mad and didn't want to talk to him. Jack's cheerful mood suddenly evaporated. Insults generally didn't bother him, but he didn't like to be ignored. He fell back now to sulk as Tom continued at a determined pace.

At the beginning of the trail, a wooden signpost identified it as Gwyneth's Way. A diagram on the map showed that the picturesque trail made a giant loop like a figure eight. It was a walking and riding trail for the genteel guests who in former days came on trains from distant cities.   A cooling breeze made the trees dance high above them---huge and ancient trees; watchful and silent.
Tommy came to a stop, gazing up into the canopy of leaves above them.

"So what are we doin'? I thought we were lookin' for the Stone of What-cha-ma-callit, the Loopty loop or whatever!"

Tommy raised his hand for silence. "This is what they call an old growth forest, Jack," he said, softly. It had been awhile since he'd been in a forest like this---not since his Earth People's Park days--his hippy dippy adventure days, as Jack called them. Tommy closed his eyes, breathing it all in. Stepping into a forest was like entering another world; the energy field was so different, so full of life. It felt somehow irreverent to even speak. Sanctuary. A voice in his mind spoke the word. Sanctuary.

Jack rolled his eyes. All this meditating and yogi-guru-stuff that his brother was into did not ring true for him. In fact, he'd always been a little embarrassed about his younger brother's choice of a life path. Massage therapist? That was just not a man's type of thing to do. "What? You gonna go hug a tree now?"

Trees had not played much of a role in these two brother's lives growing up as they did, in a working class neighborhood of row houses with front yards the size of postage stamps and narrow weedy backyards bordering trash-strewn alleys. Old junk cars and a vacant lot up the block had been their playground.

"I'm tryin' to feel peaceful, but someone keeps runnin' his mouth!" Usually Tommy felt okay about letting Jack rule the roost but today his patience was worn thin.

"You want peace, bro---? Let's go get the Jack Daniels."

"Jack, why you gotta always be that way?"

"What way?" Jack gave a wolfish grin. He would relish seeing his laid-back, peace-nik, unconditional-love-brother lose his cool.

"Annoying as hell!"

"I can't help it! I'm bored!"

"How can you be bored in a place like this?"

In disgust, Tom picked up his pace again and soon was far enough ahead of Jack to prevent further conversation. In the silence, as they continued on, their feet tramping in rhythm on the uneven trail, the presence of the trees grew thick around them, the air moist and close. Soon the green tinted light, the clean earthy smells, the sounds of the birds lulled Tommy's mind into a dreamy stillness and he felt himself grow large, as if the forest itself were part of his own body. It was a feeling he'd had many times throughout his life, like being small and yet very large at the same time.

Now he had this same mysterious feeling only stronger than ever before. His body carried him effortlessly down the path, his feet meeting the earth as if they knew each curve, as if an inevitable momentum were taking him somewhere but when he suddenly veered off the trail into the undergrowth, Jack balked, breaking the spell.

"Now where you goin'?"

"Down this path."

"What path?"

"This path."

"That ain't no path." Jack stared dubiously down what was at best barely an indentation in the foliage. "I ain't goin' down there. There's bugs and shit down there. Why can't we stay on this nice open trail, instead?"

Tommy hesitated. Normally, he would have bowed to Jack's wishes but something beckoned him that he could not ignore. The light had turned a rich gold. The sun was starting its slow descent into the west. It was not quite eight o'clock just a few days from Midsummer's Eve. They still had plenty of daylight left. "Suit yourself," he said and plunged ahead into the undergrowth.

Not about to be left behind, Jack quickly caved but not without complaint. He'd never liked the woods. He didn't like the branches touching his skin. They made him itchy---not to mention the bugs everywhere. As for Tommy that was precisely what he wanted---to be touched, to completely immerse himself in the essence of the forest. Soon they were both drenched in sweat and the further they walked, the more deeply relaxed the younger brother became, as if bathed in a cocoon of peace. Even the sound of Jack thrashing noisily through the vegetation behind him had no power to disturb him.

After a time, the terrain became rocky and steep. Prickly vines snatched at their arms and legs until they were forced to a complete stop, faced now by an impassable wall of briars. All around them stood the white trunks of ghost trees, long ago choked in the prison of that deadly tangle. A stealthy low-lying mist, thick as soup, had begun to creep in among the trees.

"Shit, Tommy! Ain't this what the blimp guy was telling us about? We need to---." Jack turned and with a genuine stab of fear realized that Tommy was nowhere to be seen. "Damn it, Tommy! Where the---?"

Presently, a gray form emerged from the earthbound clouds. Relief immediately turned to anger then back to fear for the shadowy figure passing within a few feet of him wasn't Tommy. It was Gardner, the cocky black gardener with a shovel on his shoulder but he walked right by, as if totally unaware of Jack, muttering a steady stream of curses.

The moment the gardener had disappeared from sight, Tommy was there at his elbow, as if nothing had happened.

"Christ, Tommy! You scared the b'jesus out of me. Where have you been?"

But Tommy was ecstatic. "I think I found something!"

In the mist, Tommy had suddenly found himself in a clearing, encircled by enormous stones of carved crystal standing some twelve to fourteen feet tall, great hulking forms. For a moment, within the sound of the rustling leaves, he'd thought he'd heard an eerie chorus of voices whispering to him but like a dream, it was gone and next thing he realized it was only Jack's voice calling out to him.

"You gotta see this, Jack! Come on! I'll show you!"

"No way!" muttered Jack. "Let's get our asses out of here before it gets dark! Now which way do we----?" As if in answer, the mist rolled back revealing the path. "Now that's what I'm talkin' about! Let's go!"

"Weird. That was weird."

"Yeah, it's weird. That's why I'm getting the hell out of here!"

"Wait a sec." Tommy ripped off the lower edge of his yellow T-shirt and tied it to a branch.

"What's that for?"

"A marker so we can find it again!"

By now the light had thinned into a watery murk distorting the true shape of everything. Trees and bushes appeared monstrous and sinister. They quickened their pace, oblivious now of the thorns, the darkness and the mysterious mist pressing them forward as if they were being encouraged to leave.

The sound of Puffenberger's Dixieland jazz music greeting them on the soft summer breeze was the first sign that they were going to make it out in one piece. Soon, the main house came into view, lights shining from the windows, spilling out onto the lawn. The devilish heat had turned playful and benign, the air a fragrance of sweet honeysuckle. The world gave a collective sigh. The torturous day was finally done.

They found Puffenberger still sitting on the bench beside the cracked cement pool, cradling his paper sack in his lap, the little radio beside him, mashing handfuls of popcorn into his mouth, grinding his jaws in a quick staccato rhythm.

Tom approached, saying, "Man, you were right about that mist. That stuff is wicked."

"It wasn't that bad," countered Jack quickly. He found it irritating the way Tommy always turned belly up for people, showing his weakness like a badge that said, `I'm safe. Please like me'.

Puffenberger smiled, the whiteness of his teeth showing up in the shadows. "I told you." He was clearly pleased.

"So you ever been lost out there?" continued Tommy, hoping to start a conversation.

Puffenberger's smile promptly disappeared. "Everyone gets lost. Everyone." An ominous silence followed.

Someone was coming up the path from the direction of the stables. As he came closer, they recognized that it was the gardener, but he was no longer carrying his shovel. Nodding, he walked briskly past them, and disappeared into a room in the North Wing.

"So what's he doing in the woods so late?" asked Jack.

"Says he's searching for Indian artifacts." Puffenberger arched an eyebrow.

"Indian artifacts, huh?" Jack looked skeptical.

"My feeling exactly. However, I've yet to determine just exactly what he is doing here if he's not looking for the treasure."

"Is that why you're here, Mr. Puffenberger?" Tommy was just about the only person who could ask personal questions like that and get away with it. Maybe it was that bashful 'aw shucks', apple pie kind of goodness that he had about him that made people let down their barriers.

"Another thing I've yet to determine," answered Puffenberger. He seemed genuinely sad. "Well, time for me to hit the sack." With a grunt, he moved his bearish bulk up off the bench and with his radio and paper sack tucked under his arm, shambled off to his room at the far end.

Jack clapped Tommy on the back. "Come on, Tommy---time to get some sleep and see if you can dream up the directions to that treasure!" He headed off towards the house, chuckling to himself.

"You mean---?"

"You said it yourself, right? It's kismet!"

CHAPTER III
Gardner the Gardener
The Zion Crossroads Plantation Hotel
1980

"Since the beginning of memory the Gate has been here and thought always active, once it was much more so - back when They came and walked freely among us - but those days have long gone."

Chief Louah

Though he hadn't shown it, he was no fool. Gardner could read the suspicious looks as he'd passed by. For a moment, he considered whether or not to worry. He didn't like to be seen coming out of the woods at that hour. He really didn't like to be seen period. Normally, he didn't worry about Puffenberger---that is, not as long he kept sliding him extra desserts at night. Ol' Puffy might not like it, but he wasn't going to start trouble now. He knew he was caught in his own trap.

But this short suspicious guy from Baltimore---he was territorial, like a small dog, the kind that bites. He didn't like the way he looked past him in the house, either, as if he were just an un-important black servant. Of course, that's exactly what he was---a servant---which was why this whole situation was driving him nuts. With new people suddenly showing up, he had to define himself all over again. It was humiliating but in the end it was just vanity and he couldn't let that get in his way. Not now, not when he was finally getting somewhere. He couldn't be positive, but he was pretty sure he'd found Indian Rock or at least he'd had it in his sights. For the first time in months, he felt something akin to hope.

Gardner lived in the `new wing' built in the 1920's when Fairchild Meriwether Bowen, the only successful businessman in the family line, turned his family home into a hotel. The two story addition off the back had been quite ambitious; each room with its own bath and entrance opening onto a long graceful veranda. Of course, the fact that his room was located just behind the kitchen only added to his shame and embarrassment. What would his friends at the university think of him staying in the servants' quarters that his own mother had used those many long nights she had tended Mr. Joe after his fall off the roof?

Gardner had not been raised to cook or tend gardens. He'd been raised to read books. He'd been raised to use his mind to better himself, to rise above; and though he recognized the irrationality of it, he despised physical labor and couldn't help but feel contempt for any black man doing it.

His family had been living and working here at Zion Crossroads in some capacity since slavery days, something he hated to admit because it made his parents look like weak, illiterate black people; the kind his new colleagues at the university held in such contempt. But though his father Philip had been a menial laborer all his life, he had also been a man with a lifelong passion for reading. Gardner had learned to read sitting on his lap.

And as for his mother, Leonora ---she had literally run the Bowen household for years. It had been out of necessity. `Mr. Joe' had been breaking down and falling apart over a period of years, like an avalanche in slow motion. For all intents and purposes, after his wife left, Leonora had pretty much raised Joe's twin sons, Fleming and Murphy. For years, she had been the rock and the anchor of that entire household. Without her, Zion Crossroads would not have survived intact.

Pride swelled painfully inside his chest until he felt his heart would break. So what if she wasn't `educated'. So what if she didn't know Shakespeare from Aristotle? The truth was---and he knew it now---she was the strongest and smartest woman he had ever met and that included all those intellectual airheads he'd known in Chicago.

His throat tightened. It was so unfair---no--he had been so unfair to judge them. His parents had continued to live here for the same reason most people stayed in familiar surroundings, because family was here, because it was home. And `Mr. Joe`, had always been a good and kind employer.

But Gardner couldn't get away fast enough. He'd left home when he was seventeen, gone off on a full scholarship to study art at the University of Chicago and never looked back. He'd made a new life in a community of progressive artists and intellectuals determined to free themselves from the chains of the past. Almost the first thing he'd changed was his accursed name…a name that to him had always reeked of servitude and thus 'Gardner' had become Garner. It was that or Garnet but he opted for the more conservative name. He was not into flash. He was a prep all the way.

Of course, since returning to Zion Crossroads, the 'management' had never been able to get the hang of his new title, and so 'Gardner' he had remained. He wore it every day, like a badge of shame; an image he would have to fight forever to overcome. That he, of all people, could wind up back here was the bitterest of ironies---he who had always prided himself on being ambitious and intelligent, someone destined for success. Yes, brooding about what people thought of him was something he struggled with everyday yet he found solace in knowing something they did not know.

It was hard to believe that he'd been here at Zion this long. That had never been in the plan. Nine months ago he'd come back for his father's funeral and had remained here ever since.   Just two years before that it had been his mother's funeral that had brought him home---the first time in seven years that he'd stepped foot into the crumbling cottage of his youth---a place that to him represented nothing but wasted gifts and missed opportunities.

After his father passed, he'd come girded against any sentimental feelings about the past. No, he'd learned to block all that a long time ago; otherwise, he would never have had the fortitude to leave home the first time. So he'd told himself that he was only there to pick up his father's belongings---the tired old work clothes still hanging on a hook behind the door, the old blue work hat, and his father's books. It was the books Gardner wanted more than anything. They had been a treasured part of who his father was; something Gardner could hold in his hand, and make a part of himself as well.

But he wasn't going to get off that easy. It was his mother's clothes. His father had never managed to clear out his mother's clothes. In fact, all of her possessions, her face powder, her hairbrush and pins, everything was still sitting in the order she had left them before her death. Her passing two years before had come completely out of the blue. She'd only been in her mid fifties---much too young to die. Her husband, Philip, who was 13 years older than she, had been on a downhill slide ever since. He'd lost interest in living and so his death had come as no surprise and in fact was something of a release. But for Gardner, her death had been a tragic blow only made worse because of the bad blood between them ever since he'd gone off to

Chicago.

It wasn't that Leonora was against him going to college. It was just that she had always had dreams of him becoming a doctor, or maybe a lawyer---even a minister but an artist? The rift had never properly healed and for years he'd stayed away. Now he was learning one of the hardest lessons of his life---that people can die. He'd never considered that possibility before.

The rest of their belongings were so beat up and old, just junk really. Not worth keeping. The little four-room cottage was in such sad shape it needed to be torn down as well. The night after the funeral, Gardner had sat in his father's broken down recliner and let the anger fill up inside him like molten lava. Through the window he could see the lights of the main house, the Big House as they'd always called it. He could be damn certain none of them would be sitting in such a ripped up old recliner like this but how could his father have done any better with the miserable wages they'd paid him?

His father had given the Bowen family the best years of his life, working diligently, always at their beck and call, day or night. Philip Bell had been proud of his work as an 'upkeep' man, as he'd called it. Though he had a humble station, he'd had an inner spiritual compass that gave him stability and peace. He'd lived a good life. Gardner tried to think about that. He didn't want to poison this moment with the hatred he felt—the hatred he thought he'd finally escaped by living in Chicago. There he had insulated himself in an academic world where people were sophisticated, civilized--- where he could stand a chance of being just a guy doing his thing---not always the black man---just a man.

His eye led him to a photo album and raw emotions he didn't know he had caught him unexpectedly in the chest as he opened the front page and saw the family as it had once been---a little child held in the strong arms of a smiling father, a beautiful woman in her Sunday clothes, standing in the shelter of his other arm. The smiles were brilliant because they were real. His parents had been rich. They'd known genuine love. He had sense enough to know that now. He'd judged them harshly when he was younger, but now he had to admit, that with all his degrees and fancy talking women, an honest love relationship had eluded him.

In his pursuit of experiences, of education, of money he hadn't felt the need for love up until now---but he was almost thirty and a chill had settled in around him. As much as he hated to admit it, the silence in his apartment at night was stifling. Socializing had been getting more and more hollow, the books drier. Words like `abstruse' were creeping into his day to day conversations. He watched himself erecting sentence structures like high rise towers. His head was so stuffed with information that when he lay down at night, it leaked out and ran into his dreams like a suffocating sludge, a stifling din, an incomprehensible roar. His head hurt. His eyesight had gone weak. Maybe it was living in the city with everything right on top of you, so close you couldn't stop to breathe, never able to see a real horizon. A man couldn't step back far enough to even focus his eyes. The world was a blur and he was living inside his head.

For years he'd blamed his parents for allowing him to be so idealistic, so gullible. They'd protected him too much. In college, he'd soon learned the real world was not interested in pure love for art or knowledge, or anything else for that matter. It was sarcasm that won respect and which would become his sword and shield. His art became abstract, reflecting the alienated, deformed angst that was so in vogue among the cultural elite. He'd developed a taste for marijuana and atonal jazz, the crashing, colliding discords sent him into altered states---his favorite place from which to create art.

Never known for her tact, his mother had demanded to know why he didn't paint something that showed his `real' talent. Why, a child could do better than this! He'd never quite forgiven her for that comment. From then on, he would love his parents but from a distance. They were, he decided, of two worlds and would never understand him.

That night sitting in the deteriorating cottage, the stink of slavery in the slow humid air, his anger had started to burn, desecrating the sanctity of his grief. He should have been thinking only of his father, not obsessing about the whites and how much they had taken from him. The bookshelves in his father's house were crammed with books. He'd suddenly realized he would need boxes to put them in. He hadn't thought of that. Where was he going to find boxes around here?

Irritated with himself, he headed outside to look around. As he passed the old summer kitchen across the yard from the Big House, he remembered it had always been used for storage. He tried the door but it was locked. Inside, he could see, through the dirt encrusted windowpanes, that it was stacked to the ceiling with wooden crates. Despite the warm evening, a chill went up his spine as the beam of his flashlight caught the word `ammunition' stenciled on the sides.

About a month before his father's heart attack, Gardner's father had written, complaining of some `crazy nonsense' as he'd put it, going on at Zion Crossroads.  Joe had been staying out in the woods, refusing to come back to the house.  There was some kind of `stand-off `between him and Fleming and `things were really bad'. His father was sick of being at Zion---something Gardner had never in his life heard him say. He just had to get out, he wrote, and so for the time being he was going to stay with his niece Lorraine, who lived nearby. Gardner still felt guilty for not having gone down to check up on him right away but he'd been so busy. How could he have known that it would be their last conversation? Still determined to find boxes for his father's books, Gardner had noticed the root cellar entrance, two heavy wooden doors low to the earth, fastened with a simple latch. Stuff had always been stored down there, as well.

Touching the latch triggered a memory of the day that Fleming had bribed him into going down into the root cellar alone. Gardner had not been more than five or six at the time, putting Fleming at about age twelve. He could still see him straining to lift the heavy wooden doors with those skinny white arms---white as a frog's belly, his mother used to say. Fleming's menace had never been physical brutality but that of cunning and psychological treachery. He had lured Gardner with the promise of a candy bar.

"I'm scared," Gardner had protested, clinging to the older boy's hand.

"You don't want to be a chicken, do you?"

For some reason, at that time in his life, there had been nothing worse than being called a chicken and so in spite of his fear he'd gone down into the darkness alone.

The stone steps still looked as they had so many years before, worn out and weary, vaguely ominous, the clammy darkness still infused with the same sour earthy smell of an old grave. As an adult he had the advantage of a small key chain flashlight, something he'd not had when he was five years old shut up in that tomb of darkness.

He could still see it in his mind, Fleming's form against the light, a shadow, inscrutable, as he had lowered the heavy wooden doors and thrown over the latch. Gardner could not remember screaming. He could not remember any sound at all, as if the whole scene had taken place under water, muted and surreal. But he must have screamed because that was what finally drew his mother's attention, and resulted in his rescue.

His mother, Leonora had `whupped' Fleming until he howled like a dog.  Gardner vividly remembered how the tall skinny white boy had finally twisted out of her hands, and called her a `nigger bitch' before running off into the woods. Leonora had run right after him, and when she couldn't catch him, had thrown a bucket after him. That was the first time he'd ever seen his mother lose herself to rage and it was the first time he'd ever seen her cry.

His mother carried him, sobbing, to Mr. Joe who was propped up on a cot on the front porch, in the shade of the honeysuckle vines. He'd fallen off the roof not long before and there were white casts on his arms and legs and with his head all wrapped up in white bandages, he looked like the Mummy in Murphy's comic book. Gardner had been a little afraid of him, but Mr. Joe had lured him to his bedside with a sucker, the kind with the twist of white cotton twill for a handle. He said the doctor had given it to him but he didn't want it. Gardner remembered that it was orange.

He wondered if Fleming would still recall the incident and what he would say if Gardner were to bring it up. Remember the time you locked me in the old root cellar? Ha, ha, ha! But he couldn't imagine Fleming ever laughing about anything.

All of this had flashed through Gardner's mind in the time it took to descend the stairs and now his attention was directed back to the business of finding boxes. There were stacks of cardboard boxes in various stages of disintegration. He picked one with a lid. It contained some worn out clothes, flannel shirts, a pair of torn jeans, some tennis shoes. When he dumped it out several books fell to the floor, along with a typewritten manuscript entitled, "Albatross IV" and several panic-stricken cockroaches scrambling for cover. Grinning, he picked up a volume entitled, `Steal This Book'. Who at Zion Crossroads would have been reading this? Mildly interested, he tossed it into the now empty box and headed back to his father's cottage.

After several hours of cleaning and packing (there was more to do than he'd thought) he'd taken a break in his father's chair, deciding to browse "Steal This Book." But what he found concealed inside the jacket cover was not the icon of the sixties rebellion that he'd expected but a leather bound, handwritten journal inscribed with the name of none other than Haden Meriwether Bowen, dated 1859.

"Well, I'll be damned," he said aloud. This was Haden, the old Colonel's twin brother. He'd seen the names on gravestones in the Labyrinth Garden where he'd played as a child. Twins ran in the Bowen family and that name---Meriwether---had been tacked onto every male Bowen since the beginning of time, apparently.

The journal was part sketchbook and part diary. The opening sections mostly concerned plantation matters--the lack of rain, problems with the horses, and other mundane details almost as if he had originally intended this to be a farm journal, with some attempt at recording expenses. But soon little sketches began to pop up, almost as if he hadn't been able to fully concentrate. These were of interest to Gardner, as they were everyday scenes; a man kneeling in a garden, a woman filling a bowl with flowers.

Then there were more personal references. A social gathering at a `Mrs. Fitzhugh's' house was commented on at length. It seemed that she was intent on matching him up with one of her daughters both of whom he found to be "entirely boring and tediously vain."

Gardner rifled through the pages, and towards the middle of the book was caught by the stark contrast of a mysterious name written in a childish halting hand, an entirely unfamiliar name: `Abanetha'. The next several pages were covered with individual letters crudely formed, then page after page devoted to one name painstakingly repeated. `Abanetha'. After that followed simple sentences like: `The dog ran over the hill.' `The cow ran over the hill`, and so on---almost like a school primer.

He was just about to close the book when a lone phrase caught his eye: `Abanetha, the lovely'.  Again repeated over and over and on the opposite page another name: `Haden Meriwether Bowen' was likewise repeated in the same childish hand.
Intrigued, he'd continued on until he came to a very different sort of message. The spelling was incorrect, the lettering as crudely formed as before:

Otobr 21 1860
To My Jul my Chil,
I onle hop Sum da yo wil be techt to red my chil
and yul wil no to red this mesij wich I lev
wit Perl for saf kippin. I don trus nobode
I tol Perl to tel yo mi Jul Yo papa lav yo for he eva ses
yo an yo mama lav you for I eva ses yo. Yo papa he
lav you so he lef a trasha jus fo yo. I pot it in th ey of th Inan rok.
Wen you git gron an yo ned it
go an git it. I hop you haf it beta dan yo mama wen dat day cum.
Yo mama Abanetha

Gardner had to go over this message several times because it was like reading a foreign language but she was only writing the words the way they sounded to her. It wasn't until he pronounced the words out loud that he recognized who this letter was being written to---

someone named Jewel.

"Jewel!" he muttered. "That name sure rings a---!" Then it struck him like a chorus of trumpets that his own great, great grandmother had been named 'Jewel'. "Oh, my God...Jewel Bell!" He immediately went and got the family Bible, a huge ornate thing, with beautiful colored pictures depicting Moses parting the Red Sea, Jesus feeding the multitudes, Jesus ascending into heaven on a cloud of glory. There was the family genealogy recorded in the front, encircled with lilies, first in his grandmother's formal hand, and then added on to by his own mother's graceful and precise hand.

Sure enough, Jewel was right there at the top----the very first name alongside her husband, Marcus Bell. Jewel Bell had been her name. Jewel Bell. As a child, he'd always imagined her looking something like the picture of Bathsheba with eyes that glistened like jewels and a voice that sounded like angel bells.

To my Jul mi chil.

Could this Abanetha have been Jewel's mother? Gardner's heart beat faster.

I onle hop Sum da yo wil be techt to red (read) my chil
and yul wil no (know) to red this mesij (message)

Tears jumped to his eyes with the thought of his ancestors being deprived of something he took for granted---the ability to read.

wich I lev (leave)
wit Perl for saf kippin (keeping).
I don trus nobode (nobody)

Why? He wondered.

I tol Perl to tel yo mi Jul
Yo papa lav (love) yo (before) for he eva ses (sees) yo
an yo mama lav you for I eva ses yo.
Yo papa he lav you so he lef a trasha jus fo yo.

This word brought Gardner to a screeching halt. Trasha? Then it came crashing in on him. The word was 'treasure'! Of course, it had to be but the next line---.

I pot it in th ey of th Inan rok.

Put it in the what? Put it in the eye? Of what? The eye of the what? The last word had to be rock but what did she mean by Inan?

I hop(e) yo haf(ve) it beta (better) than yo mama wen (when) that day cam. I love you, Abanetha

He had sat there stunned for a few moments. If this were Jewel's mother, what had happened to her? Why had she written this tragic letter to her child, as if she would never see her again? As if her father would never see her again? And who was her father?
He had turned back to the page before—'Abanetha the lovely. And Haden Meriwether Bowen.' Why had Haden been teaching her to write? And how long had this notebook been down there in the root cellar? Had his parents ever seen it? He'd turned back to the beginning of the diary of Haden Meriwether Bowen with renewed interest and read until dawn.

CHAPTER IV
Haden's Diary
The Zion Crossroads Plantation Hotel
1855-1860

It was well known that twins ran in the Bowen family. The original twins, Haden and Carter were sons of a wealthy plantation owner, Josiah Meriwether Bowen who was so extremely wealthy, that when his sons reached adulthood, he gave each of them identical mansions. Erected according to the fashion of the day in the Greek style with columns, they were extravagant in every way. Carter's holdings East of the River were named 'Clarendon' and Haden's plantation was situated to the West and would be called 'Zion Crossroads'. Gardner remembered having heard stories about the twin mansions, and how one had burned down long ago. As a kid, he'd used to explore east of the river, and had found the old foundations in the earth, covered over with vegetation.

From Haden's diary, Gardner learned that the brothers apparently had been nearly identical in every way but as they grew into manhood, Carter spent his time gambling and carousing with unseemly women, while his brother Haden preferred to spend his time practicing the violin and painting landscapes. When Carter was at the point of financial ruin, his brother's good fortune west of the river began to nettle him.

"September 13, 1859
Today, Father arrived unexpectedly in great distress. He and Carter have had another falling out.. As usual my brother blames Father and myself for his own miserable failures. He accuses Father of giving me the better land. He declares that his portion, Clarendon, is nothing but a rock pile, and was doomed to failure from the beginning.

I dare say my brother's failures have more to do with the fact that he spends the better part of his time drinking and gambling. I did not want to press my father any further with these details, though he would surely have to be deaf, dumb and blind not to see it!

According to Haden's diary, Carter had always accused his father of showing favoritism to his twin so to avoid more conflict and for the sake of his father's failing health, Haden decided to make peace by sending Carter his head man, Maximillian.

"I will sorely miss him, as he is exceedingly industrious and clever but this is the only way to satisfy my brother's need to better me. If anything, Maximillian will improve the relations among the slaves, for I know he will treat them well. A condition they are ill used to, as I know how brutal my brother is with his slaves."

Haden seemed to have little interest in business, and gladly left his farm affairs up to his head man, a black slave by the name of Maximillian. Maximillian and his wife, Abanetha had originally been owned by an eccentric Frenchman who'd dabbled in a sugar plantation down in Barbados. When he'd died, the slaves were inherited by the Frenchman's niece living in New Orleans who had apparently not appreciated Maximillian's prideful ways, which she felt had been encouraged by the fact that her uncle had even taught him a bit of reading and his numbers, widely considered a very dangerous practice surely bound to encourage rebellion. So when she sold them to Haden's father, it was with a warning that Maximillian was headstrong and that Abanetha had 'witchy' powers and would prove difficult to handle.

Even so they were bought as a gift from his father and despite the dire predictions of the previous owner, Maximillian proved to be capable and intelligent. It wasn't long before Haden was leaving the details of running a plantation up to his head man and this suited him as he had little interest in business but preferred artistic pursuits. Consequently, much of the journal was a record of the meetings, morning and evening, with Maximillian to discuss the day's affairs.

September 14, 1859
Today, I made preparations for releasing Maximillian into Carter's service. Once again, this makes for yet another instance of sacrifice due to Carter's selfish ways.

The first week of Maximillian's absence, Haden soon realized that he was going to have to spend more of his time managing the business of Zion Crossroads as there wasn't anyone with Maximillian's capabilities to replace him. This was extremely distasteful to Haden, and he wrote longingly of his paintbrush and his music and the bitterness he felt towards Carter who was the cause of all this disruption. Perhaps he had been a little hasty, he thought. Why should he be expected to make this sacrifice to someone who made so little effort to better himself?

And after a month had passed, and on the very day he had decided to visit his brother, and see about getting Maximillian back, news came that Maximillian was dead. During an argument, Carter had taken an ax and split Maximillian's head right open. The slave that reported the incident, said that there was so much blood that "nobody could ever wash those steps clean again" In a cold fury Haden saddled his horse and traveled immediately to his brother's home. He arrived to find that an unearthly silence had descended upon Clarendon.

"Not a leaf stirred, not a bird chirped, not a soul breathed. The slaves were grimly silent and stared as I rode past. The house slave that came to the door bore an angry bruise on her cheek and her eyes were swollen from crying. Her terror was plain and I didn't need to ask who had dealt her the blow. I found my brother in a drunken stupor in the library.

"What has happened here? Where is my head man?" I cried.

"In the ground," he said, and spat whereupon I struck him sharply across the mouth. Carter knows, that though I am usually peaceful, when my temper is finally riled, I can be a savage fighter. Hence, my admirable brother took up his station, cowering behind a chair, from which he tried to defend his heinous action by once again placing the blame on me. If I had whipped my slave as I should have, he said, Maximillian would have learned to show proper respect. According to my brother, Maximillian had been lording himself around the place as though he were somehow superior to Carter. He feared the slaves would lose all respect for him and so he had had to 'stand his ground' or else 'all hell would have broken loose.' I should be thanking him instead of blaming him for surely we would have had another slave rebellion on our hands.

"Fool!" I cried. "Maximillian would have made you rich! As it stands now, please understand that you owe me double the value of my property!"

He started in to whine about not having any money but when I showed that I was in no way moved to pity, he turned on me with venomous hatred, calling me 'the perfect little prince', and that Father had always favored me. Still, he was sober enough to know that the law stood firmly on my side so he withdrew a sack from his safe and in it were the gold coins that father had divided between us. "Take them, like you have taken everything else," he said and ordered me to get out of his house.

"Our disaffection is now complete, Carter!" I told him. "As far as I am concerned you are no longer my brother!" With that, I left for I am convinced that if I had stayed a minute more, I would have killed him myself."

When Haden returned to Zion Crossroads, he went directly to the living quarters above the summer kitchen where he knew he would find Maximillian's wife, Abanetha. Hearing no response when he called out her name, he impulsively mounted the steep and narrow staircase.

Gardner had been there many times as a child---the tiny room beneath low rafters, lit only by a small window on one end. Now he could see her in his mind, Abanetha lying *"motionless as death"* on the rough sack that she and Maximillian had called a bed. Haden reported that the eyes she turned towards him, *"though they were open, saw nothing of me."* And that the *"fire of life that usually shone there had gone out."*

Haden confessed to having been, *"suddenly possessed by a deep shame upon the intrusion into her private grief."* He had apologized for the evil thing his brother had done but she had gone beyond hearing. He laid the money on the floor and left.

In the morning, he awoke to find the sack of coins lying on the threshold of his bedroom door. The intent of this act was like a slap. He'd been refused by a slave? In anger, he went immediately to her quarters and demanded that she take the coins but she merely pushed them away. She'd been crying and there was a bruised sullen look in her eyes.

He'd pressed the sack upon her again, and then a third time at which point she had thrown it back at him, striking him full in the face. "Kill me, too," she'd cried. "Kill me, too!"

"Ignorant woman! I am trying to help you!"

"Ignorant man! Take your money!" and she turned away and went back up the stairs. In most households she would have been severely punished for this behavior but Haden was no ordinary master and seemed to truly feel compassion for her and so let it pass.

A few days later, Haden took his easel out into the forest to do some painting and came upon Abanetha unawares, collecting wild plants. He knew she was rumored to have the ability to work earth

magic for when the babies were born among the slaves, they were always taken to her for healing and protection against demons---so he'd
remained out of sight to observe.

This was the first entry in which he made any comment upon
Abanetha's beauty, for she had apparently bared her arms and legs to
the sun. Haden was unmarried, though well into his thirties, and by
his own description lived a monkish existence, an artist devoted to the
goddesses of art, literature, and music. But after seeing this "wild figment of beauty so utterly at one with Nature" he was consumed with
forbidden thoughts of Abanetha. She disturbed his dreams, her long
beautiful legs, her smooth belly, her full breasts. By night, he dreamed
of being swept into dark swirling waters in search of her. By day, he
found himself looking for her, secretly following her just to gaze upon
her unnoticed.

He agonized, for though white men had taken their slave wom-
en to bed for generations, he knew this was no common lust. It was
not only her outward beauty but an intangible inner power, something
willful and wild. She was entirely her own and would never be possessed by another. In the end, this was what had rendered him so
helpless; yet though he thought about her incessantly, she only ignored him.

"Clearly, she blames me for Maximillian's death," he wrote in
exasperation. He endured the sight of her back turned towards him,
his pride *"reduced to rubble"*. He ordered that she be assigned as a
house slave. He determined that he would have her near him. *"This
longing unleashed in my imagination has now taken on a recklessness
that I no longer question,"* he wrote.

Six months passed, during which time, she served him in stony
silence, never looking at him. He spoke to her anyway, more and more
freely---often keeping her there in the room as he went on and on
about whatever it was he was reading or thinking about. He shared
his inner world with this shadow that stubbornly resisted his every
kindness. He left gifts, a sweet, a peach, a flower---all remained untouched, left in precisely the spot in which he had set them. And then
things changed.

*"Today, I caught Abanetha smiling. Perhaps it is the breath
of spring which has warmed her heart for despite her best efforts I
do believe the prison walls of grief and vengeance are slowly coming down."* And, *"Today for the first time since Maximillian's death,
Abanetha spoke, though it was without thinking that she answered, for*

During this time Haden changed profoundly as well. *"I now realize that for the first time in my life, I am aware of someone outside of myself. By her presence, merely, I am calmed."* He described her long graceful hands daily winding the clock, the meticulous care with which she dusted the finery, swept and mopped, methodically clearing out the old dust, creating a new freshness and order to the muddle of his belongings. Never before had he trusted any slave to go into his study, where he kept his painting, his music, his books. She, and she alone, had been allowed into his private sanctuary. And the only reaction she had thus far permitted herself was a look of skepticism when faced with the monumental chaos.

As she cleaned, he secretly drew sketches of her, kneeling on the floor, reaching to a shelf. Feeling his eyes upon her, she turned and he'd look away, as if nothing at all were happening but she could have no idea the profound effect this was having on him.

By watching her simple daily work, Haden began to understand the world in a different way. *"For the first time, I feel empty of all desire to do anything but be in her presence."* It was madness, he wrote, but her presence felt more necessary than food or drink.
Because she never spoke to him aside from very basic pieces of information such as, 'shall I dust the cabinet, suh?', he attributed to her words, a wisdom that he finally realized she did not possess. She was as much a figment of his imagination as any goddess. *"Yet, though I idealize her, in truth, I know that it is her very essence, her presence of strength and intelligence that speaks to me, even in her silence".*

Later on, when he knew her well, after they had been living as lovers for some time, he would look back to his first vision of her and marveled at the comparison. For he would come to know her as sweetly ignorant of all the things he prized most highly. She knew nothing of the greater world, of art, of music---yet, this came to matter nothing to him. For in truth it was her very being that he loved, not what she knew, not what she could do. That, for him, was miracle enough. *"I have never loved another living soul beyond a friendly toleration, never felt anything this passionate, this consuming. I have never felt this alive."*

The day they became lovers was the day he asked to paint her portrait. She forgot herself and laughed. "To have made her laugh gave me more joy than I had ever known at one time before, for in that moment, she laid down her hatred and let me in."

Gardner could see it all as if it had happened to him: Haden, carefully sitting her down on his fine brocade settee, gently taking the dust rag from her hand; she, stiffening when he reached out to remove her headscarf, and then relaxing. He then bending close, his shaking hands laboring to untie the knot, breathing in the calming scent of wood smoke and soap; posing her like a doll, turning her slightly towards the light, her face, so serene, so sweetly rounded, a face better designed for laughter and smiles than for anger, so composed now, the natural light inside her, shining in her eyes, on her lips, her skin.

Tilting her chin just slightly, theirs eyes meeting as friends who knew and trusted one another and then, wrote Haden, *"her eyes blurred with tears. Impulsively, I leant forward and kissed her eyes, first one and then the other. I pulled back, and we looked at one another for a moment before I leant forward again and this time kissed her mouth, and she answered my kiss with one of her own."* He later wrote, *"It was some time before the painting was ever made."*

The brothers had not seen or spoken to one another for one year; not since Maximillian's death, not since the day Haden had humiliated him in the study.Then without warning, one day Carter arrived at his door. By then Abanetha was six months pregnant and she made the mistake of coming into the room where the two men were sitting drinking brandy. Carter must have quickly sniffed the air of ease and openness that existed between the two and Haden probably didn't have the sense enough to conceal his happiness until it was too late.

However, according to Haden's account, Carter said nothing directly about Abanetha's relationship to Haden but clearly went out of his way to demean her during his visit. Haden was keenly aware of the bad blood between them and uneasy about the visit. *"Knowing him as I do, I can safely say that he is up to no good, though he makes gestures of reconciliation."* For Haden, this marked a grim turning point

"Until this moment, I have been in the happy embrace of a dream." But now reality was closing in, and he was waking up to realities he would have otherwise preferred to ignore. A few days later, Carter returned, only this time he was drunk and his message was blunt. What the hell did Haden think he was doing? Then Haden did something he would later regret. He told Carter the truth. He attempted to explain to his brother how this was a pure love, something different from what the world saw as love, something higher ---only to be met by the full force of Carter's contempt.

"I have ever had the complete and utter confidence," wrote Haden, *"that everything that I am, everything that I say, think, or do is completely acceptable. All of my needs and wants have always been easily fulfilled and I have grown up to expect nothing short of perfect satisfaction. In knowing Abanetha as I do, I have come to see that if I have any shortcoming, it is the naïve belief that this is the way things are supposed to be."*

"Old Carter was correct," thought Gardner. The abundance had flowed quite naturally to Haden, making him supremely ignorant of the privilege of his birth, an unconscious arrogance that whites rarely perceived in themselves. The golden light that had always shone on Haden would have, in the comparison, cast his brother deeper into the shadows.

Along about the time when Abenetha's child was to be born, Josiah Meriweather Bowen died. Haden wrote:

April 10, 1859

"Last night Father confided that he was preparing to die and no matter how I tried to convince him that he was going to get well again, he insisted on telling me how he wanted to divide his property. Everything, his house, land, slaves, all are to be sold and the profits divided between myself and Carter. Everything is to be equal except for one small matter, a certain chest, and a diary--- things I did not know even existed until a day ago. Father says it was brought over from Ireland by our Ancestor, Meriwether Bowen and has always been kept hidden due to its heretical nature. Father made me promise that it never see the light of day and warned me that even to read it could jeopardize my soul. He himself has never looked inside its covers. It has been passed down from father to son for generations and no one has dared to read it.

But though the very title, Boke of Shadows, made me uneasy, I determined that his fears were nothing but superstition and that I would read it for myself. This being the only record of our ancestor's life seemed reason enough and surely a loving God would not condemn a man for simply reading a diary!

However, after reading it---I found myself in agreement. It must be hidden. For though I myself do not find it offensive (on the contrary, it is extraordinarily stimulating, opening the imagination to new levels of wonder) there is no doubt that others would. As a result, I determined that this kind of knowledge must be protected in secrecy. Even so, it has given me the inspiration I have craved for a new direction---a sort of Greater Life; something I have long recognized as the Muse.

So I will honor Father's wishes. I know a hiding place where no one will find it---a small cave in a great stone outcropping that we call Indian Rock. I go there often for renewal. I find have the amazing dreams up there.

April 16, 1859
"Last night, Father passed away. Unfortunately his final moments were tainted when Carter burst into the room. Upon seeing Father and myself in earnest conversation and thinking the worst, he accused us of conspiring against him. I begged him to be silent and to show respect for Father's condition but he started his usual rant that Father had always set me above Carter. If it were not for Father, I would have laughed out loud but the horror of it was beyond comprehension and poor Father was in such grave distress that his heart gave out utterly and in that moment he died.

If I ever felt any desire to placate Carter's selfishness for the sake of keeping the peace, it is now forever gone. I am determined not to give him an inch more than his share and I will fight him at every turn if he should try to take his advantage---which I am confident he shall."

April 19, 1859
"Today, Father was buried. It was a fine ceremony conducted by Rev. Ailsworth and many fond remembrances were shared by old friends and relations. Carter appeared sober and pious and gave a flowery speech on behalf of our father and anyone would think him the most devoted son that ever lived. Even I indulged in the thought that perhaps Carter had been miraculously altered by the event of Father's death. Such things have been known to happen.

"However, the moment we were alone, Carter's true feelings were again made clear. He claimed that stories were being circulated around the county that Haden Meriwether Bowen was living openly with his slave mistress. Was I completely insane, and what on earth was my intention? To live with this woman as my wife? I answered calmly at first, but I admit, impetuously. "Yes, she is my wife."

"By what law?"

"By God's law---the law of love."

"This isn't God's law," he said. "This is an abomination and I shall not allow you to make a mockery of our good name!"

"I'm sure you yourself do that quite well enough, brother," said I.

Carter had no answer to this but turned and walked out. However there was no mistaking the murderous look in his eye as he left the room. He aims to make trouble, of that I have no doubt."

This was where his journal entries stopped, leaving Gardner sitting completely stunned. Secret laughter rang out among the ghosts of his ancestors. What could this mean but that he, Gardner David Bell, was a direct descendant of Haden Bowen? But the real kicker was that Zion Crossroads rightfully belonged not to Carter's descendants but to him!

Oh, this joke was too rich. The cosmos had outdone itself. Laughter boiled up inside him, and he hopped around the room like a crazy man on hot coals. It was too much to comprehend, too much to contain. This was solid evidence here and surely there were other documents, letters, contracts, something. He'd get a lawyer!

He hooted and hollered and then came that familiar bitter pain pressing against his lungs---that old thorn of injustice. He could just imagine the whites closing ranks. He would never be able to challenge their right to Zion. Who was he kidding? There was no proof that they would ever accept and he wouldn't subject himself to the kind of treatment he would surely get for trying.

Flattened by this insight, he sank back down into his father's old chair. He could feel it coming, that wistful acceptance, that resignation to loss, the knife twisting in the heart of desire, the bitter taste he'd been bred on. The urge to weep rolled up from deep within and suddenly he leaped up as if the place where his father had sat in resignation for so many years had the power to swallow his soul. He wanted to strike at it, to smack it down No, he would not give in. There had to be a way, otherwise, why had he been given this knowledge? Some Power beyond wanted him to know this, of that he was certain. He'd never felt anything more strongly.

Deep in the night, he'd slipped finally beneath a thin veil of sleep, hovering between dreams and reality; so he wasn't the least bit startled to hear noises suddenly coming from the next room. In the dream he'd called out, "Is that you, Mama?" But the woman who came through the door wasn't anyone he'd ever seen before. She stood, hand on hip, a tall coffee colored woman, so natural, so dignified. There was no apology in her, no hiding. She looked him straight in the eye. "It's yo turn now," she said, like it was a matter of fact.

He awoke with a start, the diary on his lap opened to the pages where she had written her name so long ago. Abanetha. The room smelled of ashes and soap. He closed his eyes in order to see her again. What did she mean by that—-it was his turn now.

He flipped idly through the book and suddenly there it was, a sketch of Abanetha herself; strong, elegant even in her simple dress, her head wrapped in a scarf, large doe eyes, full mouth, wide cheek bones. There were numerous drawings of her on her knees scrubbing, dusting; daily activities, just as he had described in the book.

And then there were sketches where she was the focal point of outdoor scenes: Abanetha by a great tree, in the flower garden, by a stream, and finally sitting in the shadow of a giant rock. The woman's figure here appeared so small that the only way he knew that it was her was because it was titled, "Abanetha at Indian Rock." On second glance, the rock did appear very much like a man's profile, with a great sloping brow, a shadowy indentation for eyes, a hook for a nose and a terse gash representing a mouth. This was the moment that the missing piece of the puzzle suddenly slipped into place...In the letter to her daughter, Jewel, Abanetha had written: *"Your papa loved you so he lef a trasha jus for you. I hid it in the Inan rok."*

Haden had left a treasure for his child and Abanetha had hidden it in the cave at the top of Indian Rock--in the Indian's eye. And it was still there! It had to be! All he had to do was go and get it. Out of the shadowy world of childhood a memory surfaced—his Dad taking him out into the woods and pointing down into the ravine, "See? See the Indian Man's face, son?"

Gardner's head swam with dizzying comprehension, and suddenly he knew what it was he would have to do...what he was meant to do. That was the day he strode directly to 'the Big House'. The heavy front doors had been pulled shut and the place seemed strangely abandoned, so he sat down to wait on the old rocking chair, the one Mr. Joe had always sat in. The place had really gone to the dogs since he'd been here the last time---and it'd never been all that great to start with. The grass hadn't been cut and was starting to look like a regular hay field, the windows were dirty, some of them broken, shutters hanging in disarray. The paint was peeling.

He smiled sadly to himself when he realized he was looking at the place the way his father would have looked at it---as an 'upkeep man'. His father had always been proud of a job well done but in the last several years of his life, especially since the death of his wife, he'd been in pretty bad shape, suffering from arthritis and dizzy spells and obviously there'd been nobody else willing to take up the slack.

And then Gardner noticed something else, something that he'd been looking at all his life and never really seen. It was a symbol carved into the lintel over the front door but it wasn't a symbol at all. It was an elaborate monogram---HMB---Haden Meriwether Bowen, *his* great great, great grandfather.

Triumph trumpeted through his body like the Hallelujah Chorus! Maybe Mama had been right after all. Maybe he really did have guardian angels watching over him! Yeah! That 'trasha' belonged to *him*. And damn it, blood was blood. If anybody was going to find it, it was going to be him!

CHAPTER V
Three Women Arrive
The Zion Crossroads Plantation Hotel
1980

The next morning, Tommy was still dreaming when Jack jostled him awake. He'd been up since dawn and there was news to report. "Guess who I saw sneaking into the woods before dawn with a shovel and some hedge clippers?"

"I don't know, who?" Tommy closed his eyes and tried to slip back into that beautiful dream he'd just been having.

"The gardener dude, that's who!"

"So?" Tommy put the pillow over his head. He'd been in a primeval forest, suffused in a misty green light, running naked, just running, his blood singing in his veins.

"So? So! What do you want to bet he's onto something? Now get your ass out of bed!"

It was unheard of for Jack to be up this early without someone holding a gun to his head. He was usually thick and cranky but suddenly Jack had a case of gold fever.

"Jack, he's a gardener. Of course he's going to be walking around with a shovel." With a jolt, Tommy remembered one more thing from his dream—there's been a woman there.

"At 5:30 in the morning? Get real!" Jack was chuckling. "Come on! We got work to do!"

The amazing thing about Jack was that once he made up his mind to do something, come hell or high water, he was going to do it no matter how stupid it was. However, as they were getting the metal detector and their shovels out of the trunk of their car, a woman drove up in a gray BMW. She was long legged and beautiful, elegantly dressed in a red silk blouse and short, short white shorts, her coffee colored hair twisted into a knot on top of her head. She passed them by like a brisk wind, all business-and-behind-schedule, her ruthless red high-heeled shoes clicking in staccato purposeful strides across the porch.

Quite suddenly Jack wanted to go back inside for a donut.

"What about all this 'work' we got to do, Jack?"

"It'll wait, Tommy. It'll wait!"

Tommy shook his head. Jack was too easily distracted by women especially those who were out of his league. It was all part of his need for rejection.

Inside, the woman was already looking impatient as if she'd been standing at the registration counter all day, tapping her long red fingernails on the counter and giving every possible signal that she was not in the mood for conversation. This however did not seem to penetrate to Jack. Exuding supreme self- confidence, he swaggered up to the counter and picked up a pamphlet which he pretended to be reading, meanwhile, straightening himself up as much as possible as she turned out to be a tad taller, (though, in fairness, she was wearing heels).

"Do you know where the manager is?" she asked, removing her sunglasses, and pushing dark strands of hair from her rich brown eyes. She could have passed for a fashion model and sexy too, but after two seconds it was plain she was all business and cold as a fish.

'He should be around here somewhere." Jack's eyes were shamelessly running up and down her shapely form when he thought she wasn't looking.

Tom cringed to see his brother popping a stick of gum into his mouth. Chewing gum only magnified his cockiness as he chewed with a quick rotating motion of the lower jaw, exposing his front teeth in a kind of sneer. "Things were getting a little slow around here but now maybe we're coming up to speed, eh Tommy?" said Jack with a sly wink.

"Oh, there's the bell!" she cried, pouncing on the bell lurking among the spider plants and punching it several times. Jack hung there in limbo for a few seconds, grinning for no apparent reason.

Meanwhile, she pretended to be reading a stray 'Hospitality Monthly' magazine.

"Had a long trip?" he asked, bobbing right back up for the second slap.

"Not too bad," she replied, turning her back as if totally immersed in the magazine.

Tom grabbed his brother's arm. "Come on, Jack. Let's go."

Jack waved his brother off. He was just warming up. "You gotta be from someplace up north. Let's see if I can guess. Philly, maybe?"

"No." She gave a flat dismissive smile and turned the page.

"Okay." Jack rubbed his hands together like this was a game of twenty questions and she was just teasing him along. "I had a feeling you weren't from Philly. And definitely not Jersey."

God, was he utterly unaware that he was getting blown off? Tom turned away. He just couldn't watch.

"All right, I got it! I got it! A classy girl like you (he'd never gotten it how politically incorrect it was in 1979 to call a woman a girl) has got to be from one place and one place only---New York City---am I right? Or am I right!"

"Mmmm." She was refusing to look at him at all now and her voice was sounding further and further away.

"What'd I tell ya, Tommy? I got instincts!" He stabbed the air with his index finger. "Even though you don't have that 'New Yawk' accent!" Jack was chuckling as if they would both somehow find this amusing. "I been to the Big Apple lots of times. Got an uncle in the Bronx." He was leaning back with both elbows propped up on the counter like he was a man of the world.

At this point Murphy appeared. The woman sprang to life.

"Hello, my name is Katherine Pierce.   I believe my husband arrived here yesterday---Stephen Andriot?"

"Oh, yes m'am. We have you in the Jeb Stuart room, upstairs, room 4."

Jack's smile stiffened and faded. "Yeah, so---Tommy, I suppose we ought to get going here. Nice to meet you and, uh---." But they were busily discussing details and he found himself in the background foolishly muttering something about enjoying her stay. Tom now easily pulled Jack away, like a weed suddenly loosened from its roots.

They headed back out to the car in a gloomy silence.

It wasn't until they were in the woods that Jack exploded. "Where the hell was her wedding ring? She wasn't wearing a wedding ring!"

"Sometimes people use other kinds of rings now, Jack."

"But who ever heard of having a black stone for a wedding ring! She ain't even got his name."

"So she's a modern woman, Jack! Forget it! It's no big deal."

"I am such an idiot!" He slapped himself on the forehead.

"Come on, you know women love it when guys come on to them no matter how stupid you are---I mean how stupid `they' are."

But Jack wasn't listening. He was brooding. If he had a fatal flaw this would be it. "So she's married to *that* guy, huh!"

"Look, Jack! Leave it alone! You don't need this! I mean, give yourself some time to recover! You've just been through a pretty hard break up!"

"Yeah, well I dumped her not the other way around, in case you didn't know!"

"Still, that kind of thing is a major jolt to system!" Tommy knew for a fact that she had dumped Jack but he wasn't about to say anything.

"All we ever did was fight anyway! I'm glad to be rid of her, frankly!"

"Exactly! So you came out a winner, if you ask me."

"Yeah, we had no compliment-arity. A huge attraction but always like two firecrackers, you know? I'm definitely better off without her."

Tommy pretended not to notice the contradiction between the truth and what his brother was telling himself but he had that wounded look in his eyes. Yeah, this woman had really hurt him. Poor Jack, he'd been battling all his life. Sure, he'd called 99% of the fights down on himself but being short was not easy for a guy like him. He had a chip the size of New Jersey on his shoulder but underneath he was a loving kind of guy who didn't know how to show it.

As for Tommy, he was the 'little' brother and God forbid Jack should ever bear him a grudge but everything had always gone down way too easy for him. Plus, he was tall---not to mention the nice personality and good looks. Of course, no matter how hard Tommy tried to get it through to Jack that he too was good looking and had personality, Jack would hear none of it. "Not like you, bro," he'd say, with a sad smile. "Not like you. Naw. I'm just irritating. I make people want to punch me. You? You're so laid back and you got that grin! Who could resist you! Besides, I'm short."

"So what does that have to do with anything?" Tom would say.

"When you're short people always gotta mess with you. Every macho pig out there is gotta mess with you, just to make himself feel like a big man." Jack was stubborn like that. When he was convinced something was true, nothing in hell could shake him loose from it.

His main problem with women was not in the initial attraction phase. That wounded slightly feverish quality to his brown eyes was often a real selling point--- at least until he opened his big mouth and started to complain; then they couldn't get away fast enough. But rather than taking this as a hint to change his ways, it merely confirmed Jack's steadfast belief that the world was out to get him. Tommy tried to tell him different but it always fell on deaf ears.

Once they were out in the woods, they had a problem relocating the path they'd been on the day before. Somehow, every one of them ended up in a dead end but they did discover one of the Colonel's holes when Jack fell into one roughly the size of a grave---six feet down. This did nothing to improve his mood, which had turned dark. After Tom helped him out, Jack insisted on trying out the metal detector, which, of course (because God and the universe were against him) wouldn't work so he spent the better part of an hour cursing and tinkering and cursing and shaking and finally hurling the damn thing against a tree. Meanwhile, Tommy sat on the ground and got comfortable. He decided Jack's temper tantrum was probably a good way for him to blow off some extra steam.

Later just before dinner, they had an opportunity to witness the married couple in action. All afternoon, they'd not seen a trace of her as she was taking a nap. Then about 3 pm, she'd gone down to the front desk and asked if there was a phone she could use for some business contacts. Murphy said okay, just so long as she paid for any long distance calls. She proceeded to spend an hour and a half in animated discussion, pacing back and forth like a tigress on a short leash. Meanwhile, the husband sat upstairs on the balcony, hair uncombed, in a torn t-shirt, feet propped up on the railing, acting like he was asleep.

When it came time for dinner, she was still immersed in a conversation and apparently deeply annoyed. Andriot tried to get her attention but she was completely oblivious. Finally, he got directly in her field of vision, shouting as if to a deaf person, "Katherine! It's time to eat. You can't be late here or they won't let you eat."

In the dining room, she took her place beside her husband across from Tommy and Jack. Puffenberger had already parked his bearish hulk at the far end beside Fleming who reigned over all in grim meditation. Amanda, in layers of gauzy mauves and pinks, made her well practiced entrance precisely at 5:55 and sat in her customary place across from Professor Valentino, who was absorbed in some note taking in his small black book. Meanwhile, Murphy anxiously popped in and out through the swinging door, burbling about minor glitches and small delays in the kitchen.

There were two additional women sitting at the table, as well. Surprise guests, actually, since no one had seen them arrive. On Tommy's right sat a slender young woman, her blond hair, caught up in a ragged wisp at the back of her head. Her large doe eyes and small rather pointed ears jutted out ever so slightly from her head giving her an elfin appearance. She wore no makeup. Her beauty was simple and unadorned, someone who would, at first glance, not attract much attention. She radiated the quiet patience of a good listener, a careful speaker, while giving the subtle impression that she knew something that she wasn't saying. There was no doubt in his mind that Tommy had seen her somewhere. He smiled at her with recognition but she acted like she didn't know him, so he backed off. He didn't mind. He'd ask her later when no one else was around. Maybe she was just shy.

Beside her, and sitting at Fleming's left hand, was a slightly older woman, heavy, with pasty white skin, and short bleached blonde hair that had been mercilessly permed. Her wide mouth was firmly set in a flat, no nonsense line, slightly soured at the edges. She seemed entirely focused on rearranging her silverware, then smoothing the napkin in her lap and looking blankly at the flower arrangement in the middle whereupon she would start the process all over again. First impression: she didn't want to be here.

Tommy told the elfin woman his name, whereupon Jack quickly jumped in and spelled it for her to prevent the inevitable, 'Spratt' mispronunciation. "That's my brother," added Tommy. Jack nodded.

The younger one introduced herself as Nealy Brown, and the other as Portia Reed. They were sisters.

"Oh, how nice! I always wanted a sister. I never had anyone to swap clothes with," gushed Amanda von Hassel, despite the obvious fact that neither of these women would fit into the other one's clothes.

Nealy nodded politely. Portia lifted her upper lip in a smile that could just as easily have passed for a snarl.

"And what brings you out to these particular boondocks?" inquired Puffenberger loudly overriding Amanda's thoughtless comment.

"We came for the healing springs." Nealy's voice was feathery soft, causing everyone to lean slightly forward in order to hear.

Murphy dropped his fork with a loud clatter. "The---- what was that you say?" he asked, looking like he'd swallowed something that hadn't gone all the way down.

"You know, the one in the pamphlet where it tells about the

Indians and how they used it for healing ceremonies---and things." If Nealy noticed Murphy's obvious consternation, she did not show it.

Fleming raised one eyebrow. "And where did you get this 'pamphlet'?"

She hesitated, "Well---"

"You're not going to tell them that story now are you?" muttered her sister, Portia.

"Oh, tell us a story!" Professor Valentino's face lit up with childish delight.

"Well, it *is* rather strange." Nealy paused.

"Who cares about that?" Puffenberger beamed at her in a slightly lewd manner from across the table. "The stranger the better, I always say! We specialize in strange around here!"

"Of course, it is true---" continued Nealy, mysteriously hesitant.

Portia scowled and turned her head away.

"Go ahead and tell it," prodded Tommy quietly from beside her. Yes, he'd definitely met this woman before and now he knew where.

"Well, I was working in my garden one evening," she said. "A storm was coming, and a hard wind was blowing, slamming doors shut, knocking stuff around, when all of a sudden I looked up and there was this tiny whirlwind filled with dried leaves coming right up the alley, into my gate---and it moved right through me---." She hesitated again.

"Right through you?" prompted Puffenberger. "And---then what?"

"Yes, it actually came right through me and this--this pamphlet wrapped itself around my leg!"

"Like the wind delivered it to you," murmured Tommy, trying to conceal his excitement. "Interesting."

"Yes, and strange," repeated Puffenberger. The penetrating gleam in the big man's eyes made Nealy slightly uneasy.

Meanwhile, Tommy wondered if she remembered him, too---and if that's why she was avoiding him.

No one else ventured to comment except for Murphy Bowen who muttered, "Indeed," while loudly stirring his iced tea and looking anxious.

Tommy then started asking questions about the Indians that had once lived here. Murphy, looking painfully distracted, answered in a vague sort of way that yes there had been Indians, he supposed.

"Actually the ghost of an old Indian Shaman still lives here in the forest. That's what they say anyway. Lots of ghosts around here----," commented Puffenberger gruffly. All eyes slid unconsciously up to the portrait of the old Colonel, glowering from over the mantel.

Suddenly, as if he could bear it no longer, Murphy jumped up, exclaiming that everyone must be absolutely starving and what could possibly be the hold up, before hastily excusing himself. The sound of heated voices from the kitchen rose to a quick crescendo before Gardner burst through the swinging door with a platter of meat announcing that dinner was served.

Nealy quietly refused the meat, saying she was a vegetarian which evoked a disapproving scowl from her sister, Portia. Meanwhile, Mrs. Amanda von Hassel was antsy to begin her monologue. She did not care for the fact that there were suddenly additional women in what had previously been her exclusive domain. She'd taken an immediate dislike to Katherine whose beauty and cool self-possession were reason enough to ignore her completely. Portia, the dumpy sullen one with the cheap perm was all right. She was certainly no competition and perhaps she would speak to her at the appropriate moment. Nealy, on the other hand was just too earnest for her taste. Earnest people bored her.

Tonight, she would focus on her fifth husband---the one who'd been `filthy' rich and a special buddy of Frank Sinatra, just to let them know that she had used to be somebody.

CHAPTER VI
The Labyrinth Garden
The Zion Crossroads Plantation Hotel
1980

By nine a.m. the next morning, the heat was already oppressive. An overbearing sun glared through low gray clouds, imprisoning the wilted world in a humid haze. Ah yes, thought Gardner---his very favorite kind of weather for hacking away at the weed patch still referred to as the 'Rose Garden on the South Lawn'. This was all part of Murphy's Grand Plan for the restoration of Zion Crossroads and Gardner had become his drudge.

Gardner had made a good show of it long enough to determine that Murphy was not spying on him from the rear study window, before drifting off towards his usual hideout in the Labyrinth Garden--- the safest place for a nap. He'd been up since 3:30 a.m and had already spent a couple hours in the forest bush-whacking through briars so he could be back at the house by six to have breakfast on the table by 7 a.m. Which was why he was already pretty much wiped out when after washing dishes for twelve people (by hand because these people had never heard of something called a dishwasher). Then there was the the hanging of the stuffed moose head over the mantelpiece in the library. That had put him behind on his nap-schedule. Of course, on the plus side it was a definite break from the monotony.

After said moose was hung (albeit a bit crookedly) he, Murphy, and Stephen Andriot, the journalist, had engaged in an interesting bit of conversation.

"I never realized that a moose could be so---big," began Murphy, gawking with a sort of stunned admiration.

"Sorta takes up the whole room, don't it?" added Gardner.

"Though I'm sure we are so *grateful* for this wonderful addition to our---art collection," added Murphy with his usual Southern gentility.

A little more than a hundred years ago this had once been

Haden Bowen's sunlit library where he'd devoted himself to his art and music. The walls were still lined with his books and paintings, but now an enormous Confederate Flag had been draped over one window, cloaking the room in a gloomy reddish glow. Stone busts of Confederate War Generals crowded the mantelpiece.

Gardner happened to glance over the journalist's shoulder just as the latter quickly jotted the words, "The stale atmosphere of defeat..." into his ever present notebook.

When Andriot looked up, Gardner pretended to be examining the moose. "Huh! Is it mooses or meese?" he asked, casually flicking at its enormous snout with his dust cloth.

"Just moose," answered Andriot.

"But a very *noble* beast," chimed in Murphy on a generous note.

"Looks sort of like a pirate though, don't he?" Gardner pointed to the silver dollar set in one eye socket. "So you say old Joe really shot this sucker right through the eye, huh?" He and Murphy exchanged a look that made it plain that they thought this was not to be believed.

"That's right," said Andriot with his characteristic cool. "I've never seen a marksman like Joe. He could shoot a silver dollar out of the air. That's why I asked that it be put there in the eyehole."

"Well, stranger things have happened, I guess," said Gardener, but he looked doubtful.

Murphy cleared his throat. "Of course, this was *not* my father. My father *died* last September. And *this* man shot the moose in *January*. So it wasn't my Father. But it was an amazing shot."

Gardner could see that ol 'Murph was intimidated by this Andriot fellow. Though admittedly, there was something vaguely unnerving about the guy; the way he watched you out of the corner of his eye with that crooked little Cheshire cat smile---like he wasn't saying what he really thought.

To everyone's relief, Andriot changed the subject with a question about the battles the Colonel had fought in during the civil war. Murphy puffed up a little with pride; the light striking his glasses making them perfect reflections of the red flag hanging in the window. Then he started recounting the long boring tale of the Colonel's wartime exploits.

When Gardner felt he couldn't take it one more minute, he pointed at a spot near Murphy's feet. "Well, excu-u-u-use me? But would you look at this?" Murphy froze mid-sentence. "Somebody must have tracked in some dog shit? Or is it deer shit?" Everyone peered down at the smudge in question. "Check your feet, Mr. Bowen. I do believe you've stepped in something!"

Murphy obediently checked the bottoms of his shoes. "No, Gardner. My shoes are quite clean."

"Well, maybe it was nothin'!" announced Gardner. "False alarm! Course you never know when shit's gonna get tracked in." Gardner rolled his eyes. "And dust---let me tell you it collects. In my 'bid-ness', if I learned one thing is that these ol' southern plantations do get so dusty!"

With his dust rag, he vigorously attacked a painting of a dead rebel soldier lying in the arms of a winged angel, holding forth a laurel crown with the words Deo Vindice emblazoned on it.

"You know what *that* means, don't you! Deo Vindice? With *God* as our Protector? That's right!" Gardner reached out with his finger to flick an invisible piece of dust from the soldiers' crotch area. "Yes, sir they're very religious around here. Very religious. Of course seems to me the whole idea of God getting involved in helping one race own another race seems to go against the whole main idea of Christianity---but what do I know!" Gardner continued to dust the marble statues on the mantel.

Murphy muttered that he had some work to do but Gardner rolled right over him. "Of course, now here on the altar we got Jefferson Davis, a real dust magnet. Then there's Stonewall, and Jeb Stuart, and we can't forget good ol' Robert E. Gotta take real good care of Robert."

The phone rang in the foyer and Murphy made a hasty departure. Gardner and Andriot eyed each other with a level gaze until Andriot finally broke the silence.

"Can I ask you something sort of personal?"

"Sure." Gardner was breathing hard like he'd just run a race.

"What's it like working here?"

Gardner reflected for a moment. "You mean how does it feel working for people trying to keep the past alive? Or maybe how does it feel to be working for people whose ancestors fought a war to keep my great-great-great granddaddy in slavery?" Gardner looked rhapsodic. "Well, I can't say it makes me all warm and fuzzy inside."

"So what does it make you feel?"

"Truthfully? I've got one word for those people---Appomattox. End of story. You were on the wrong side of history and you lost so get over it."

A nervous cough at the door, announced that Murphy had

returned from his call whereupon Andriot made his excuses and left.

After this brief moment of elation, however Gardner's energy had all but fizzled so when Murphy had tasked him with weeding the rose garden, he instantly began plotting his escape. But just as he'd gotten to the intimidating pair of stone lions guarding the grand entrance to Labyrinth Garden, Fleming had appeared, seemingly out of nowhere.

"What are you doing?"

Gardner sighed deeply. This man had a nasty habit of materializing exactly at nap time. "I'm gonna go weed the ornamental gardens."

In lieu of a response, Fleming stared like an x-ray machine scanning for the lie.

"Like Murphy told me to do," added the gardener with a yawn. "So if you will pardon me."

"He did?" Fleming's dark eyes narrowed.

Gardner felt the weight of Fleming's suspicion bearing invisibly down upon him. No doubt it had something to do with the fact that Gardner had a Master's Degree while Fleming had dropped out after his second year of undergrad. Even so, Gardner had become very good at playing his part. The main thing was to keep his eyes down and act humble.

"Well," Fleming fixed him with a stern look, an unspoken warning that he would tolerate no shenanigans, then turned on his heel and departed towards the house.

Muttering a few choice words, Gardner headed into the shady refuge of the boxwood maze. The sharp, musky scent brought back childhood memories of tagging along with his father who had always kept the labyrinth well clipped and in good order. But in his later years, the Labyrinth along with everything else had been neglected, the towering hedges grown misshapen and wild, the once manicured paths, turning into dark eerie tunnels.

As a young child, the Labyrinth had always felt mysterious and scary and his mother had warned him that a child could get lost there and never be found again. Indeed at times even adults had difficulty making their way out, for the maze could be a trickster---leading its victims endlessly down false paths.

Later, when Gardner was older and braver, he'd explored the Labyrinth and discovered unexpected things, like graves guarded by blind stone angels. The Colonel was buried here---Carter Meriwether

Bowen. From the dates on his magnificent tombstone, he had lived to the ripe old age of 93. His twin brother, Haden, was also buried here but in another even more secluded spot. Gardner had been about twelve when he'd stumbled upon that second grave but though he'd searched for it many times after, had never been able to find it again. That was the way it was in the Labyrinth---for though from the outside, the Labyrinth was a fixed size, and one could walk completely around it; from the inside it seemed infinite with possibilities and wrong turns.

Now he knew to follow the little stone markers that someone, most likely his own father, must have used to mark the way into the center where it opened into a wide grassy circle. Here, lay the remnants of a spacious garden, subdivided by stone walkways radiating like spokes on a wheel, where perennial herbs and flowers grew up with the weeds. The centerpiece was a round stone temple supported by Grecian style pillars, overgrown with wisteria and honeysuckle---his favorite spot for a nap.

Today, however, he hadn't yet come round the last bend in the path when the sound of a loud curse floated over the tall boxwood hedge. Damn! Someone had beat him to it. It was a woman's voice---the dark haired one married to the journalist---the one with the queen complex. Yeah, he'd seen how she treated her husband, heard her talking on the phone with that loud voice, as if no one else existed. He knew the type---ambitious, condescending, an agenda for a brain. He'd just gotten out of a relationship with one exactly like her.

For the moment, her back was to him, providing him the chance to observe her unnoticed. She was doing T'ai Chi but not very well or at least not to her satisfaction because she kept stopping with a loud expletive and starting over.

"I thought T'ai Chi was supposed to be calming to the spirit," he called out cheerily.

She turned and instantly erupted with an ear splitting scream.

"Sorry, sorry!" He raised his hands in a show of peace.

"You startled me!" Her tone was accusatory.

"That's why I said I was sorry," he muttered, trying to cover the dislike he felt for her. "Well, as much as I'd like to stay and chat, I have an appointment with some weeds over there, so if you will excuse me." With a tight lipped smile, he tipped his father's blue work hat and headed over to the furthest patch of weeds. Just to show how little her pretentious T'ai Chi routine interested him (or her beauty for that matter because he sure as hell wasn't about to trip over himself like all the other dumb asses around here) he turned his back and started scraping the weeds out of the hard baked dirt with a vindictive fury.

Yeah, he hated this damn job and the fact that she was here, was forcing him to work when what he desperately wanted to do was to take a nap! Then to make matters worse, when she was finally through with her set, instead of leaving, she went and sat on the stone bench under the shade of the Temple where she began to watch him like someone at a sporting event.

"You're going to kill your back, doing it that way," she called out.

He turned in her direction with a dull expression that plainly communicated that he did not want or need her advice.

But she only persisted. "Gravity will do most of the work for you, if you let it. And you should alternate from one side to the other."

With pained dignity he offered her the hoe, "Be my guest."

Instead of showing offense at his brazenness, she laughed, then with supreme self confidence, sauntered over, took up the hoe and started expertly chopping the weeds. Within minutes she had cleared a wide swathe. By the time she'd finished, she was breathing hard and glowing with sweat. "Wow," she said. "I'd forgotten how good that feels."

He gave her a grudging look of admiration, "You got some mean hoe'in action goin' on there---m'am."

She gave him a calculating look. "Thanks," she said and handed him the hoe.

"Now I *know* you didn't learn that on the mean streets of New York City."

"Illinois, actually."

"Ever been to Chicago?" He had the distinct feeling that he'd seen her somewhere before but no way was he going to say that old pick up line.

"No." Her hard professional beauty softened. "Actually I grew up in central Illinois." This sounded almost like a confession for indeed it was not something she often shared with people. Middle Western farm people weren't taken seriously in the circles she aspired to. "Soybeans, corn fields, for miles and miles as far as the eye can see. But for the past 12 years I---we've been in New York." She touched the back of her neck self consciously, as if this were too personal. "Um, have you---have you seen Andriot?"

"You mean your husband?" he said, making motions of getting back to work. *She calls him by his last name*. Interesting.

She hesitated. "Yes."

This was the signal, the cut off where the conversation was to end. It was all manners now. But that weird familiarity kept tugging at his memory. Yep, without a doubt that they had met before but so what? All he really cared about right now was that she get the hell out so he could finally take his nap.

Something about that gardener made her feel uncomfortable, she thought.   Maybe it was his eyes, that golden color---so strikingly beautiful, she almost felt shy to look at them. But he was no country boy---and no gardener, either. Gardner, that was his name. He didn't fit here.

As she headed back through the boxwood maze, a dream from the night before nudged her like a dark cloud. Suddenly the heavy air, the flat colorless sky, the silence pressing against her ears felt ominous. Images of murder crowded her mind. She tried to brush them aside but they persisted and now the details flooded in. She was running through the maze but the light was weak, the colors drained away. Shadows pressed upon her at every turn. Something terrible was waiting for her, a hand gripping her throat…

It was with relief that she burst out of the Labyrinth as if coming back into the full light of day after being somewhere very dark. She stopped just to breathe and quiet her racing heart. Something weird had just happened and she had no idea what it was but suddenly she understood how her novel was going to end. The woman would have to die. It couldn't be any other way. A wave of sadness swept over her. She knew it was not uncommon to feel so strongly about a character but this was strangely intense.

She wasn't quite sure what to do with this feeling. The very fact that she'd ever gotten involved with this character still mystified her. For one thing, whatever made her think she could write through the eyes of a black slave and be convincing? She couldn't be more out of her depth. So how could this be anything but pretentious? Yet, from the beginning, this character had possessed her and almost against her will (and certainly her better judgment), she had submitted to this story that just wouldn't leave her alone.

Her main character, an illiterate slave woman, couldn't be more different from her yet the story flowed so easily as if it were writing itself. Sometimes she wondered, could she be unconsciously copying something she'd read long ago? Still, she couldn't seem to get away from it. She'd been working on it for several years now but the direction the ending should take had always eluded her until this moment. Now she realized that deep down she'd known it all along but just hadn't wanted to know.

For the past two months she'd been in the throes of a killer writer's block, her mind jammed into a dark corner. Everything she'd already written was dead to her. Maybe the entire project was a waste of time---just like this trip.

This morning, Katherine had awakened later than she liked. The sun had already risen and it was heating up outside. She felt instantly out of step with the day. Stephen Andriot had already dressed and left the room taking with him any hopes she'd had that this was going to be a romantic get-away.

The last time they'd even spent an evening together face to face with no television or phone calls, they'd had a terrible fight—or rather she had had a terrible fight. He had just walked out. He didn't do emotional scenes. And that had been the extent of their communication for the past two weeks, aside from superficial conversations mostly on the phone. He was in and out, busy completing projects, avoiding her whenever possible. She'd been consumed with work. If they had a strategy this was it: stay so busy that you don't have time to figure out your relationship is on the rocks. Last night they'd barely spoken and she was so exhausted she'd passed out the moment her head hit the pillow.

The week before, when he'd told her about his plans to visit an old plantation house called Zion Crossroads, she'd invited herself along, even though something told her he didn't really want her there. It had sounded quaint and charming---the Zion Crossroads Plantation Hotel---but the moment she'd gotten here it was clear that this wasn't going to be a place where they could mend their fences, not while sharing the bathroom and eating every meal with strangers. She felt like they were under a magnifying glass every moment. She didn't need this!

She tried to console herself with the notion that it wasn't a complete loss. From another angle, this could be research for her novel, which oddly enough did take place on a pre-civil war southern plantation but just thinking about her book made her feel even worse. For the past six months, she'd been bothered by a vague undercurrent of doom. Was she supposed to persevere or give up all together? But giving up was too frightening, as if it meant---well, what did it mean? That she had no purpose? Cold fear---that's what it meant. Death.

She reminded herself to call the office so her assistant, Leo, could update her on the subversive new manager's latest maneuvers to sabotage her promotion. After struggling to get to the top of the magazine publishing business, who would have thought it would be another woman who would be trying to block her way? Of course, Katherine never had gotten along with other women. They didn't trust her. She was too beautiful, too smart. No woman wanted a friend like that. Thank God for Leo because she couldn't talk about this with Stephen. He had zero interest in power struggles and gossip.

As a result, she was usually on the phone every night with Leo, analyzing and reanalyzing the situation, while Stephen hibernated in semi-darkness in front of the TV. She had been so obsessed with her problems, she'd been almost relieved when he was called away on an assignment. He would be gone until early May, right about the time Katherine's nephew was to be born, an event which would unexpectedly plunge her into an even darker crisis of the soul.

Not used to sleeping this late, her head felt like it was stuffed with wool and she was cranky. When she finally did make it downstairs, she was informed that breakfast had been served at 7 a.m---over two hours ago. The only things left to eat were donuts and coffee from the hospitality table. Against her better judgment, she gobbled down two chocolate donuts and a cup of coffee that left her stomach churning then headed out into the steamy morning. The sun was already bearing down relentlessly out of a white humid sky and not a breath of wind stirred. Vindictive little scenes rolled through her mind's eye, previewing just exactly what she was going to say to Stephen when she did find him.

Katherine had met Stephen Andriot on a wilderness survival training course and the attraction had been strong and physical. He was the rock climbing instructor, a free thinker, the kind of man who never questioned that he deserved the best of life, the perfect antidote to soothe her carefully hidden insecurities.

After growing up with mid-western farm people who scorned her dreams of being a writer even as her mother withered and grew old washing and rewashing the same dish, she'd rebelled and went east to study journalism and did quite well. Yet, no matter how high she rose in the magazine industry, beneath her New York veneer, she was still plagued by an inexplicable lack, a fear that she never truly belonged and if she wasn't vigilant, she could miss her chance and be overlooked. So maybe she guarded her boundaries a little too ferociously. Maybe that's why she called her lover by his last name—Andriot—as a way of keeping a certain distance, a hard line, like a stick to keep him at arm's length; her way to remind him that they were equals.

Even when they walked, it was competitive, aerobic not romantic; as if she were always out to prove herself, to test her limits, be the best---win. She'd just finished graduate school at the time she'd met him. After the wilderness training, she'd gone back east and landed a position in the editorial department with a magazine in New York. Two weeks later he'd appeared at her door. He'd fallen into a photo journalism job by sheer magic and family connections. Meeting her had inspired him, he said, and so on a whim he'd interviewed for a travel journalism position and got it.

That's the way it was with Stephen Andriot--- so careless, yet everything just fell into place for him. He only had to think--- yeah, okay, I'll try it--- and it was there. He'd never worked for anything in his life which had fascinated Katherine who'd had to work and sacrifice. But that was in the beginning when love was new. Now his luck just irritated her.

They'd been living together for almost two years now. Neither one was sure if they 'believed' in marriage; though when necessary, she called him her husband. At the beginning both she and Andriot had been satisfied with their arrangement because of the space and independence it had given them. Constant travel exactly suited Stephen's nature. He was like a beam of light shining here, shining there but nothing you could hold onto. He had a voracious curiosity, loved people but felt no real need to attach. In the beginning what he'd seen in Katherine was a strong, sexy, and independent woman, someone with dreams of her own; someone who could allow him to live his life as he wanted.

But then reality had set in. While, she was tied down in New York, he was off on a never-ending series of adventures in obscure places all over the world---Nepal, Antarctica, Afghanistan, Africa. Last month it had been Peru. She would fly out once or twice to visit him on location but soon learned that traveling threw her off center. With too much uncharted time, her emotions started coming out of their boxes, and her mind got messy. It was safer just to be ruled by a jam-packed agenda, a clear and orderly progression that left no room for questions.

And then lately she'd been having weird thoughts---about babies, actually--- imagining what that would be like. This made for a peculiar mixture of excitement and doom. Nothing could have been more out of the blue for her. Never would she have ever imagined herself even considering such a thing before. She was on track to becoming a success---not sit around changing diapers and burping babies! Still, maddeningly, when she did have the time to write, she'd found herself staring off into space daydreaming---about babies! Horrors!

Even though she would never admit it, it had all started when she visited her younger sister who'd recently come forth with nine pounds of bouncing baby boy. This event had been unexpectedly traumatic for Katherine. Before the birth, she'd bustled around the city shops, playing the good auntie, buying all kinds of tiny clothing. (Were babies really that small?) And all the equipment! It was something she had never thought about before. Suddenly, a whole world of mothers and infants opened up in her perception. (Where had they all been?) Apparently she hadn't been paying attention because they were everywhere.

The full impact did not hit until she went to visit the newborn nephew and his deliriously happy mom. Her younger sister, Trisha, had always been a close competitor with Katherine. When Katherine had joined the track team, Trisha joined the track team, when Katherine decided to learn how to shoot guns, or ride horses, Trisha would do the same. Katherine had always taken it for granted that Trisha wanted to be her. Katherine was the winner, Trisha, the second runner up. That was the way it was supposed to be. And now Trisha had disturbed the natural order of things---she'd gone ahead and had a baby. Of course, it wasn't like it was really premature or anything. Trisha was after all twenty-eight and Katherine was just about to have her thirtieth birthday.

While staying at Trisha's (she'd only stayed overnight because she had a meeting the next day) Katherine had had the opportunity to hold this child creature. For the first time since she could remember, she felt awkward and unsure of herself. Give her a mountain to climb, or white water to navigate, or a board of directors to intimidate, but this wobbly, spitting, puking, fussy little being absolutely terrified her. Of course, the moment she handed him back to Trisha he was transformed into a placid little bundle of love.

She also felt a little put off by the way her mother and father seemed utterly transfixed by this little person. And there was absolutely no conversation she could relate to. They talked of nothing but how the baby slept, when he last ate, when he last pooped. Her mind strayed. The smell of warm wet diapers was suffocating. And she worried about her sister. She noticed Trisha had put on weight, her face was full, her stomach pooched out. Katherine feared it would be all downhill from here. And that husband she'd managed to procure---already showing signs of the suburban couch potato sitting in front of the TV, drinking beers at three in the afternoon.

The longer she stayed, the more alienated she felt as if an invisible black line had been drawn, separating her from them. She watched herself with disgust, fidgeting, and sulking like a ten year old. Some obscure pressure was building up inside her and she felt like she was going to burst. At the soonest possible moment she found an excuse to leave.

She had pantomimed her way through all the niceties, the sweeties, the hugs, and plunged towards the door. Trisha appeared at her elbow at the last moment, trapping her on the front porch. Katherine felt obligated to say something open hearted, something generous, possibly profound but her good will was hopelessly stuck. All she felt was terribly envious and horribly alone.

Trisha suddenly embraced her tightly, her shoulder unerringly digging into Katherine's windpipe. "Isn't he beautiful?" she said, tears welling up in her eyes. "I'm so glad you came, Kath. It means so much to me. I just want you to know that I hope that you'll be able to spend lots and lots of time with him so he can grow up knowing his auntie!" She was laughing even as the tears trickled down her nose.

"You look so---happy, Trish." Katherine's words felt wooden and false. Trish couldn't know that the word `auntie' made her feel---so---what was it? Irrelevant? False?

But thankfully, Trish was oblivious. "Oh, I am! I am so happy! I just---." Tears choked her voice off for a moment. "You just have no idea until it happens, how you're going to love that baby! I mean, God, Kath! It's like falling in love only so much more powerful! I can't explain it. You just have to experience it, I guess."

Katherine reminded herself that she was the one who had never wanted kids. She had other goals. She had a novel to write, a career! All this melodrama was insane. She hugged her sister and managed to make her exit with a smile but inside, she was falling into a dark crevice of doubt. On the way home, she conjured visions of Trish in ten years, divorced, overweight, overworked, bitchy---a slew of brats tearing up her house---and jealous of Katherine's freedom. But this gave only temporary respite from the onslaught of fears slowly invading her mind like an enemy army.

Suddenly, everything she had been seeking seemed utterly meaningless and all her knowledge just empty clatter. Everywhere she went, a conspiracy of mothers and infants followed, glowing with peace and happiness. She felt downsized, decreased, demoted. But the panic didn't set in until her best friend from college called. Unbelievable! Now it seemed that even Page was pregnant! Page, the biggest partier that had ever hit the planet---Miss Independent, the one who'd worked as a welder, for God's sake! Page? Pregnant? No amount of reasoning could save her now. Katherine was being left behind and where was Stephen? He obviously didn't care. He'd scoffed when she once made the mistake of mentioning a baby.

"Come on, Kat get real! Writing means more to you than anything or anyone. You'd make a lousy mother." This comment had remained like a thorn festering in her mind. Maybe it was true. She'd always felt so driven. The thought of surrendering her independence to anyone was suffocating, to the point of panic.

Lately, he'd been accusing her of getting 'weird' on him; that she was always cold and distant but when he asked what was wrong, she'd only say, "Nothing," and pull away. But all in all, it wasn't his style to be confrontational and issues of conflict only made him drift further away from her, his edges dissolving when she reached for him.

Stephen's take on all of this was simply that Katherine was hitting the hump, the big 3-0, and true to her fashion, making it harder than it had to be. Her thirtieth birthday was coming up. And that was it---a simple, elegant explanation. His plan was to keep his head down and keep it light until it blew over. He did not do well with dark emotional scenes. However, this only confirmed her belief that he did not care.

So why had she come here, she asked herself as she stepped onto the front porch of the hotel---to patch up a doomed relationship? To get pregnant? She felt a chill just thinking about it. Or maybe she had gone completely insane. Yeah, maybe that was it.

Gardner's nap in the temple was short and restless and he awoke with the beginnings of a dull headache. The interactions he had had this morning had left him feeling frustrated. How had he allowed himself to get into this trap? It had been nearly nine months since he'd decided to stay on here as the 'upkeep man' and he still hadn't found the treasure. He should be back in Chicago, grading papers, and going to the movies with beautiful women instead of hacking away at the damn weeds! He despised gardening. Gardening was a futile battle, a waste of human energy. Just thinking about the sweat and aching toil of his ancestors cultivating tobacco (the most useless thing in the world) so some white-ass son of a bitch could live like a sultan made him want to blow the whole damn thing up---the garden and that big house right along with it. In fact, the mere thought of gardening made him exhausted! It made him sick!   To hell with the garden! The weeds would be there tomorrow and tomorrow and tomorrow. Enough already! He was going back to the kitchen for a drink.

On the way back he obsessed about the white woman and his father's old blue fishing hat. No doubt, she looked down on him because of that hat---and of course, yeah---the hoe didn't help. And he was black, of course---that too. Back in Chicago there were places he could go where that had ceased to matter---where he could forget all that bull shit and just be. It hurt him to have to be back in this world, the old world where it did matter, where people couldn't just be themselves. They had to be the 'black man' or the 'white woman' dragging their entire goddamn history of identity along with them.

It filled him to the brim with spite just to think about it. It was suffocating. Originally he'd kept his father's old hat, the soft misshapen fisherman's cloth hat, for sentimental reasons---not because he thought he'd ever actually wear it. It wasn't his style. But he soon learned while working out in the blistering sun, that you damn well better keep your head covered. (He could hear his father chuckling over this, his `preppie' son, always too good for manual labor, wearing an old work hat. Oh, yes, a father lives for such moments.) So he wore the hated hat as a penance for his own arrogance and to honor his ancestor who had toiled so humbly in its shade. But he still hated to be seen in it. Maybe it was his competitive streak acting up, but it galled him not to be recognized for who he really was.

"Listen, could I talk to you for a second?" It was the Andriot dude, standing by the old cement pool, in his open neck linen shirt, khaki shorts, and hiking boots; a worn brown leather hat mashed down over his wild curly brown hair. He looked the type, all right. They were all over the university---a free thinker, his own man, everything Gardner wanted to be---correction---everything he knew he was.

It was too late for Gardner to pretend he hadn't heard so he couldn't really escape although if he could have, he would have turned around and gone the other way. Something about Andriot's wide set eyes and crooked half smile gave Gardner the feeling he was being secretly laughed at and his dad's old fishing hat was just about burning the top of his head off. He could almost hear what this guy was thinking---house nigger two steps up from slavery. And though he told himself he wasn't here to impress *nobody*, Gardner slipped it off and looked Andriot straight in the eye because sometimes eye contact is all the dignity a person's got.

"You just missed your wife. She was doing T'ai Chi in the Labyrinth Garden but she left."

Andriot gave him a look because it was 1979 and most people didn't know what Tai chi was; certainly not a black gardener out in the middle of nowhere. But that wasn't what he wanted to talk about. He wanted to know about Joe. They had been friends, he said, and he wanted to know where he was buried.

Gardner frowned. "Well, it's kind of complicated and as you can see I've got real important business going on here, you know---these weeds to pull and all that fetchin' and totin'." Ordinarily, white people almost never showed any reaction to his jokes. He called them 'black humor bombs' because they shook things up and also because they bombed in the sense that nobody ever seemed to 'get' that they were even jokes. People were either too polite, too racist, or too stupid (and sometimes all three), so they just continued on, bleeping it out of the conversation entirely.

But Andriot was not your usual white people. "Can I ask you something kind of personal again--Gardner? That's your name, right?"

Gardner nodded then shrugged. He'd given up on 'Garner' for the time being. It was too complicated.

"Who are you, I mean really--who are you?" Andriot took out a cigarette and lit it while it dangled from his lips just like actors do in the movies. The guy was just naturally cool without even trying.

Gardner smiled sagely. "Believe it or not, I teach Art History at Northwestern University." Talk about a bomb. He tried to act nonchalant but his insides were churning and his face grew hot as if he were lying or something. He wanted to kick himself. Why the hell did he have to add the 'believe it or not'? Okay, so he had an assistantship, but it was still true. He did teach at a university.

Andriot looked like he had just added 2 plus 2 and gotten 5. "So what the hell are you doing here?"

Gardner paused for a moment, trying to capture exactly the right word. "Let's just say I'm on sabbatical---doing research."

Andriot looked at him intently. "Research in what?"

"History. Family history---diggin' up the past, you might

say."

Andriot took a long slow drag on his cigarette, evaluating. "Cool."

Gardner smiled inwardly, thinking how this was true in more ways than one.

"Listen, I was wondering if you knew where Joe Bowen was buried."

"Oh, yeah! His grave is in the Labyrinth."

"You think you could take me there?"

Gardner took a quick gander of the windows. Nobody was looking. "Sure thing. Come on." With that he led Andriot into the maze. After a series of turns leading to one dead end after another, Gardner stopped at a fork in the path and scratched his head. "Nothing in here ever seems to want to stay in the same place but---oh wait, here! This way!"

"You sure you know where it is?"

"I should, seeing as I was at the funeral." His eyes brightened. "Yeah, it's this way."

"You *saw* him buried?" demanded Andriot as if this were suddenly of great importance.

"Yeah, I was there...although not by invitation."

"And this was last September?"

"No, August...August 19th."

The day after stumbling upon Haden Meriwether Bowen's diary and the summer kitchen crammed with crates of ammunition, Gardner had gone up to the Big House to see Joe. Although he had vowed never to return to Zion Crossroads again, suddenly he had every intention of staying. The decision had come like a thunderbolt in the night. He would sign on as his father's replacement. He'd be an 'up keep' man by day, and undercover treasure hunter when no one was looking. It was an insane plan and it thrilled him to the marrow of his bones.

It had been many years since he'd last seen Joe, but he remembered him as being gentle, distracted, preoccupied so he would be easy to convince. Gardner had been surprised that Joe hadn't shown up at his father's funeral just a few days before. Maybe he had a broken leg or something. With Joe that was always a high probability.

Gardner had been just five years old when Joe fell off the roof. His mother used to set him beside the bed with a checkerboard to help keep Joe entertained and run to get things when he needed them. Joe used to pat him on the head and call him, "Little Tiger." This nickname had pleased him. His favorite picture book was about tigers. Joe had always tried to amuse him in some way but even a child could see that he was sad, stuck in all those casts and bandages. That's how he remembered him most---for it seemed that Joseph Meriwether Bowen was forever getting hurt.

As far back as he could remember, Joe had always had problems of one sort or another. It was something Gardner's parents used to discuss at the supper table. Gardner's mother, Leonora, had been a little obsessed with the situation but that was understandable since she was the one who'd inherited the burden of the house, the twins, and of course, Joe after he fell off the roof.

For her, it had never been just a job. She seemed to have truly cared about Joe and she worried about him and wanted to help him out of his depression. For a time, it was feared that Joe might even take his own life. Her solution had been to put a Bible on the table beside his rocking chair on the porch. She'd set a little sunflower seed on the cover just so she could tell if he'd opened it at all. That had been his mother's answer to every problem: a little Bible, a little prayer. Doubtless, she'd waited in vain for that seed to move off that cover.

Thinking about all this, as he'd waited on the porch that day, Gardner had realized Joe Bowen was the one white man from his past that he would actually like to see again. It was then, by an odd stroke of fate, that Gardner became witness to a peculiar procession---a line of men dressed in Confederate uniforms marching with an attempt at military precision behind the flag of ol' Dixie while bearing a plain wooden coffin into the boxwood labyrinth. Gardner had recognized Murphy immediately, the same gawky near sighted creature, only older now. However, Fleming, who had grown a great bristling black beard, was harder to pinpoint being that almost every other man in the group sported similarly outlandish facial hair.

After the disappearance of the little group into the hedge, Gardner had stood around for close to three quarters of an hour, not knowing whether to leave or stay. Common sense argued to get the hell out even as a stubborn attachment to his crazy new plan made him linger just long enough for the plot to thicken in a most unexpected manner. It so happened that a white Chevy Impala bearing a Mr. R.J. Shifflett, the county coroner himself, arrived in a cloud of urgency and red dust. R.J. was a small egg shaped man, with a waist somewhere near his armpits, with a green and yellow John Deere cap set high atop his moist bald head. He was sucking on a lemon drop and before saying a word, gestured for Gardner to take one from a white paper sack but Gardner politely declined.

Mr. Shifflett had heard rumors that apparently there was a funeral for Joe today and he had come to pay his respects. Gardner said this was the first he'd heard that Joe had died and Mr. Shifflett responded, "Well, that goes for you, me, and everybody else around here. So, do you know where the grave site is, son?"

Gardner pointed to the Labyrinth. The old man tipped his hat politely, walked a few yards and then turned. "Comin'?"

And that's how Gardner came to be at Joe's burial. Finding the spot in the maze would ordinarily be no easy enterprise, as the maze was extraordinarily tricky and complex, but just as they entered, voices arose in a loud rendition of Dixie.

They'd arrived at the gravesite situated in a roomy cul de sac just as a man, dressed all in white, with a curly white beard and looking all the world like Robert E Lee, was engaging in a flowery prayer, praising Almighty God, thanking him for the safe delivery of this poor misguided soul who was mentally ill and surely not responsible for his actions. There was a slight disturbance as those assembled suddenly realized two uninvited guests had joined their ranks. With grave solemnity Lee completed his prayer and then raised his eyes questioningly to the intruders.

Mr. Shifflet cleared his throat politely, as he ambled up beside Fleming. "Hey, y'all," he said. "Hey, there Murphy, hey Flemin'. Sorry about yo' Daddy passin'. Just come to pay my respects is all." Meanwhile, Gardner had casually positioned himself near the exit, carefully looking down in response to some of the hard looks he was getting.

The twins stared. After a short silence, it was Fleming who spoke. "Thank you, RJ." Murphy seemed tense and very pale, even for a man who was already white as a frog's belly. Fleming on the contrary was steady as a brick.

"What a turrible shock. Turrible, just turrible. " observed RJ Shifflett, in the reverent tones of an undertaker.

"Yes, it was. Such a shock." Fleming's tone was, however, not in any way sympathetic.

"I didn't even know he was sick, truthfully," continued RJ, conversationally. "He was in the care of a doctor before he passed, was he?"

"No, sir. He didn't believe in doctors."

"I see. Well, I suppose that's not uncommon---not uncommon

a' tall." He hooked his thumbs through his belt loops and rocked back on his heels.

"He'd been very confused for a long, long time, RJ."

"Well, that's too bad. So there was no doctor in attendance, you say?" He asked again, as if he wanted to be absolutely sure.

"No, sir. There was no doctor," repeated Fleming politely.

Shifflett lowered his voice, eyeing the fresh grave. "You realize, Flemin', by law and under these circumstances I'm supposed to have his body exhumed for examination."

"Why?" Fleming's response was more a demand than a question.

Sensing opposition and fully aware of the ticklish situation this presented, Shifflett became appropriately conciliatory. "Now, Flemin' I don't know as you are aware but this is against *procedure*. You can't just go on and bury people like this on your own."

"He was my *father*. This is his *home*. I don't see why this is wrong."

"Well, because it's against the law, that's why."

Fleming straightened his back and proudly lifted his chin. "Sir, my father suffered greatly in his life so surely in death, you will afford him the respect of privacy. I cannot believe that you would impose on him the indignity of digging up his remains like a---like a dog. In the name of God, leave him lie in peace!"

"That's right! Yeah!" rumbled those assembled, all listening intently.

"Oh, yes I know as well as anyone about your Daddy, son. Joe had some hard knocks. Yes, indeed," answered the old man, mildly. "Now I'm not trying to cause trouble but I am the county coroner and I could get in some real hot water if they find out I've been derelict in my duty. Now by law---."

"Law? Don't you think it's time we stood up for ourselves, RJ? How long are we going to continue to let the government into every nook and cranny of our lives, snooping around, digging up our dead?"

The group got enthusiastic about this and threw in a few choice words.

Eyeing the crowd, Shifflett knew better than to go against the odds. "Well---I just need to know for the record then---how *did* he die? Heart attack, you think? Or stroke? Murphy?"

Taken off his guard, Murphy nervously, pushed his spectacles up his short pinched nose. "He was perfectly fine in his body." His eyes darted sideways to Fleming. "It was his mind that was gone. He was---confused." He broke off abruptly, looking ashamed.

"Oh, yes---I know. Poor Joe." Shifflett paused delicately. "So, Murphy, are you saying he *wasn't* ailing?"

"He took his own life." Murphy's face crumpled and for an alarming moment, it seemed as if he weren't breathing at all, but then he exhaled a long womanish sob. Those present looked away in embarrassment.

RJ placed his hat over his sunken chest, and nodded sympathetically. "Poor Joe. He was a good man but he shore did have some hard knocks.'

Fleming seemed to be staring right through him at something far away.

Murphy had removed his glasses, overcome with weeping. Soon strings of mucus were hanging out of his nose and dripping off his lips. "He was just so---confused!"

Shifflett gave Murphy some good hard pats on the back, like one would give a hunting dog. "There now, there now! That's tough, ain't it?" One last time, he turned to Fleming. "And so you did not have a doctor present at death? I'm only asking because you see, that would make it so much simpler in terms of the paperwork and such."

"Of course not." Fleming's tone softened unexpectedly. "My father was an intensely private man, RJ. It's very important that you understand that he just could not bear public scrutiny of any kind---not at the end. Privacy was his dying wish but I have the letter right here, if you wish to see it."

"He left a letter? Huh! Yes, I'd very much like to see it, if you would."

"I will have a copy sent you, RJ."

"A copy---of course. I'd say take your time but---" He shook his head sadly. "Poor old Joe. Had some real hard knocks."

Fleming looked grave. "He would never have done something like this---not in his right mind."

"I know it. I know it. He was a good Christian man, Joe was. He didn't go in much for church, but I firmly believe the Lord don't know the difference. It's what's in your heart that matters."

Fleming nodded.

For a moment, it looked as if RJ were preparing to leave, but he hesitated and in the gentlest possible way asked how it was that Joe took his life. "By what means, I mean."

Fleming raised his eyebrows and hesitated. "Poison," he said. "I think."

Carefully now, Shifflett asked with utmost delicacy. "Might you have the, uh, *sample* of what, uh, was consumed?"

A wave of restlessness rippled through the group. "Now RJ... is that really what you need to be askin' at this particular time and place?" demanded Robert E. Lee in a fiery tone.

Fleming calmly raised his hand to silence the questioner. "We have the empty vial, if that's what you mean."

"That would be greatly helpful. I realize this is a delicate subject, and I truly don't intend to cause you distress. It's just my job, you understand and if we can take care of this little matter, then I'm sure we won't have to pursue it further."

Fleming bowed graciously. "No offense taken."

Whereupon, R.J. Shifflett raised his speckled hand and bid the group farewell. "Gentlemen! Y'all keep up the good fight, heah?"

After listening to Gardner's story, Andriot asked if the Bowens were especially into hunting.

"Hunting? No, not really."

"So how come they've got a building full of ammunition boxes?"

"Be careful, man. Fleming wouldn't like to know you're snooping around. But I'll tell you one thing, they got shit going on around here you wouldn't believe."

"Try me."

"Ever hear of the Gray Knights?"

"A neo-confederacy group?"

"Neo-fascist, New Confederacy, white supremacist--call it what you like, but they're all nuts! He's the historian for the group. They meet here once a month."

"And they let you hang around?"

"Hell, no! They always send me off to town on errands. But Murphy tells me stuff."

"Murphy? The one with the glasses?"

"Yeah, he's a good guy. No guts but a good heart. "

"What about his brother?"

"Fleming? If there were ever such a thing as reincarnation, I'd swear he was some kind of a Hitler or Mussolini in his past life. Deep down---he's evil, man."

"He knows you had a university job?"

"Oh, yeah, but I told him I got fired and that seemed to make him feel better seeing as he never made it through college. Murphy says it's because he got sick of all the liberal propaganda so he quit and went to work in one of those right-winger bookshops."

Andriot looked at him again, with that cool little smile, measuring. He's wondering what the hell a guy with a Master's Degree is really doing here playing upkeep man, thought Gardner. Well, let him wonder.

But of course the real reason Fleming Bowen had never liked him had more to do with his golden eyes--- like sunlight reflecting off a sandy river bottom--- something Gardner wasn't about to share with this Andriot guy. Gardner still remembered the day a lady in town had looked down at him and exclaimed, 'Why this child has got Joe Bowen's eyes in his head, plain as day! What kind of hanky panky's been goin' on over there?' And the other lady had said, 'What did I tell you? This is Joe Bowen's child sure as shootin'.

He was about six at the time and had innocently gone home and asked his mother what was 'hanky panky' and was Mr. Joe his daddy? Leonora had promptly given him a hard slap. "Don't you ever say that again! Hear me?" But then she started to cry. "Don't you listen to their garbage mouth nonsense. That's all it is. People spreading lies are just paving their way to hell is all and we don't need to follow along after them, now do we? We just do our best to stay in our own business and leave the Lord to take care of them. They'll get what's coming to them, they surely will."

True, it was common knowledge in the Bell family that these golden eyes showed up now and then---just an inherited trait. That was his mother's explanation but no doubt it put her in a tricky spot when her baby was born, light skinned and with eyes the color of her employer's.

Looking back, Gardner had to wonder what had prompted his parents' loyalty to Joe. He didn't pay them well, but when his wife left and he fell off the roof, Leonora and Philip had stepped in to run the household. Yes, there were plenty of malicious theories whispered in the community though never within earshot of Leonora. Nobody wanted to risk her ire, for though she could be a powerful ally you would never want her for an enemy.

As both men stood staring at the wooden cross, Andriot's mind snagged on the one glaring inconsistency that made this whole thing so impossible to understand. The lopsided cross plainly stated that Joe had died August 17, 1978---but how was that possible? How was it possible that on New Year's Eve, four months after Joe's alleged burial, Andriot had gone hunting with him in the wilds of Alaska?

Andriot remembered it like it had happened only yesterday. They were tramping through a field of snow at twilight, the northern lights dancing above in a tremendous display. He had just confessed something to Joe that he had never told another living soul. Andriot did not admit many people into the inner sanctum of his emotions. He liked to play it nice and easy on the surface, never getting bogged down in the details, always free to move on. But something had happened that caught him, like a briar that he couldn't quite free himself from, and somehow out there in the wilderness, hidden wounds started welling up like old blood.

They were building a fire and he'd start to talk. It was a weird and potentially awkward moment and in a sense, the moose had saved him from further embarrassment by crashing out of the woods at the moment that it did. So there he was, in the path of certain destruction, looking death in the face and thinking, what the hell kind of crazy timing was this…when CRACK, a deafening shot resounded, echoing off the hills. Amazingly, the Moose had lurched to it's knees then crumpled in a splatter of blood on the fresh December snow but he said nothing to Gardner about any of that.

Meanwhile, cursing under his breath, Gardner reached down and tried to straighten the cross but it just sagged again to the side. "Joe was a good guy. I'm actually sorry he's gone," he said softly.

"You sound surprised—."

"Yeah---well, I thought there was absolutely nothing for me to miss about Zion Crossroads, but---maybe I was wrong." He plucked a dandelion and placed it on Joe's grave.

Suddenly Gardner wondered if he'd been wise to confide so much to a stranger. Bitter experience had taught him that no one at Zion was to be trusted. Everyone was here for the treasure in one way or another. Maybe this Andriot guy was just cagier than the others by pretending not to know anything.

CHAPTER VII
The Observer and the Observed
The Zion Crossroads Plantation Hotel
1980

"What the hell are *they* doing together?" exclaimed Murphy, peering cautiously through the gap in the curtain. Gardner and Andriot had just returned from the Labyrinth Garden where they had visited Joe's grave and were now standing on the south lawn, deep in conversation. "What could they be talking about?"

Sitting behind the desk, Fleming methodically finished his cup of tea without reply. Back in the 1920's when the hotel was thriving, these rooms on the first floor at the back of the main house had been Gwyneth and Fairchild's private suite. Now one was used as Murphy's bedroom and the other a private sitting room and office that he and Fleming both shared.

"And who is this Andriot person, anyway? And why did he say that---about seeing Daddy last New Year's Eve?" Straining to keep them in view, Murphy was forced to duck when the two men in the yard looked suddenly towards the house.

"I don't know but he's lying. Come away from the window before they see you." Fleming wiped his mouth, as if to be rid of a disagreeable taste.

"But why would he lie about something like that?"

"Daddy probably blabbed about the treasure. This guy is just another con man trying to confuse us, is all. And besides---the man he claims was Joe, wore no glasses. Think, brother! He shot a raging elk!"

"Moose. It was a moose."

"Moose, elk, whatever! He shot it straight through the eye! Now you and I both know Daddy was as helpless as a blind man when he didn't have his glasses----and he never hunted a day in his life. Why he didn't even know how to shoot a gun! Am I not correct?"

"True. That's very true." Murphy wisely acted more reassured then he felt.

"No," mused Fleming, absently stroking his bristling beard with long white fingers. "I'm thinking this Andriot character has some other motive."

"Still, it almost seems as if he knows something---but he couldn't--- could he? I mean---." The end to that sentence hung in the air unspoken for it was unspeakable what they had done---burying an empty coffin---and neither one of them had ever mentioned it aloud until this very moment.

Fleming rose up imperiously. "Stop it! Daddy is dead and that man is a liar."

"I-I know. I know. But still---."

"It was suicide! We have the note. That's all that matters."

"Yes, but anyone who thinks about it is bound to wonder why we didn't have his body, Fleming! And what if he isn't dead? I mean, do you really think that he could do such a thing?"

"I said stop it!" And he slapped Murphy hard across the face, sending his glasses flying. "You're acting like a hysterical ninny! Father was mentally ill and wandered off into the forest because he did not want to be found. So of course we had no body to bury!"

Murphy stared at him. "Yes, right."

"Now we will not be having this discussion again."

"Right." Murphy slumped into the wing back chair, hiccuping quietly. But regardless of what Fleming said, he still didn't feel right about the way they had rushed the funeral. They should have waited to see if Joe showed up again because, after all, he had disappeared only to reappear again so many times before. And wouldn't it be rather awkward to explain why they'd already buried him?

But Fleming had insisted on going ahead with the 'funeral'. They certainly didn't want their father's death besmirched by suicide and more scandal, after all he had been through! Besides, what would happen if his body was never found? How could they ever take ownership of Zion Crossroads? They could be trapped in legal limbo for years. Did Murphy really want that?

When it was put like that, no, he didn't and so like the sheep he was, Murphy had followed along with Fleming's scheme. At first everything seemed to be okay. Even when the Coroner had showed up unexpectedly, nothing bad had happened and when a week went by and no government officials had come to arrest them, Murphy dared to think that they were out of the woods.

But then a strange woman had arrived at their front door with seven red suitcases in a state of great anxiety. Her name was Amanda von Hassel and she'd just lost her job and her apartment. Only later would they come to know about her drinking problem.

Within the hour, two men came to join her. The first was a well dressed, silvery haired Professor Valentino, still in full possession of his marbles and coldly detached. The second was Mr. Claude K. Puffenberger, with limp greasy locks creeping over his collar and reeking of used car salesman "Nice digs," he'd announced fingering the big gold chain nestled in the wiry black chest hairs bristling out of his green V-neck polyester leisure suit. "A little fallen down in the arches but a real fine piece of real estate. I think I'm gonna like it here!" Of course, he too had little choice since he was flat broke and hiding out from an investigation into certain financial improprieties at his last place of employment. But that, too, didn't come to light until later.

"Needs a better sign, though," he continued. "Picture this: 'The Zion Crossroads Treasure Hunt Plantation' in big neon lights! Maybe a couple billboards along the highway? That'll really bring in the clientele. So how is the business doin' anyhow?" He popped in a stick of gum. "Care for a piece?"

Murphy had merely stared like the veritable deer in the headlights.

Puffenberger had looked puzzled. "You are Joey's son, right? I mean, you're the spittin' image! Wouldn't you say, Mrs. Hasselberger?"

"Von Hassel," corrected Amanda with tepid dislike, repelled by his utter tackiness.

"Yep---a better sign could do wonders! Now this pamphlet isn't bad but it should be in color and on glossy paper to show more quality," continued Puffenberger waving a copy of the pamphlet Murphy knew all too well as the brainchild of his father's hippy friends and the beginning of all their troubles.

"So where is Joey, anyways?"

As if on cue, Fleming had arrived and with the solemnity of an undertaker, informed them of Joe's recent demise.

Amanda had immediately fainted, (strategically it seemed) into Valentino's arms who along with Puffenberger appeared to be terribly disturbed by the news. Joe had been such a wonderful guy---a special person, they said.

"Well, yes this is true. Now thank you for stopping by," answered Fleming and promptly started shuffling them off to the front door.

But Puffenberger stoutly resisted. "Not so fast, pal. I'm not goin' anywhere!" Whereupon he whipped out his copy of a letter beginning with the fateful words "...I, Joseph Meriwether Bowen..." ; the one giving him the right to live at Zion Crossroads "in perpetuity" because he had "saved" Joe's life. Whereupon, the others produced similar letters.

"And all signed and legally notarized," added Puffenberger, stabbing the document with a thick finger bearing a huge gold ring.

"This is outrageous!" roared Fleming. "I won't stand for this! Get out of my house!"

But rather than being intimidated, Puffenberger only yawned. "Actually," he said, "according to this letter---this is *our* house, too!"

Fleming was all but breathing fire by now. But before he could speak, he was interrupted by a the sound of a piece of old sheet metal flip-flopping like a drunkard across the overgrown yard amidst skittering herds of dry leaves blown from their summer branches. An enormous black thunder cloud had arrived on the back of an ominous wind, bullying its way over the mountain, thrashing the tree tops like dust mops, and anything else that wasn't nailed down.

A sudden fierce pelt of rain slammed the porch swing on its rusty chain right into the library window, sending a mischievous wind frolicking through the house, slamming every door, and knocking the statuette of Robert E. Lee to the floor.

As Fleming and Puffenberger continued to wrangle with each other in the front hall, it was Murphy who'd rushed into the library and discovered a copy of *The Brother's Grimm Fairy Tales,* mysteriously dislodged from the shelf and lying open on the floor, its pages ruffled by invisible windy fingers, revealing a previously unknown envelope. And this was how the Bowens came to discover the existence of Joseph Meriwether Bowen's last Will and Testament.

Meanwhile, back at the registration desk, Fleming was incensed. "You know very well those letters will never stand up in court!"

"Fine then--- that's where we'll see you, in court!" Puffenberger appeared supremely confident, as he was well acquainted with the cold hard hand of the law.

"Fine, then!"

"Fine!"

The two men were standing head to head, bristling and ready to draw blood.when Murphy hurried into the room, wild eyed and dazed. "You can stay!" Then he looked firmly at Fleming. "They can stay."

Fleming turned, aghast. "What did you say?"

Without a word, Murphy handed Fleming the document. As he read it, Fleming's face grew ominously pale. Murphy had never seen such an expression of fury or heard such a vile stream of profanity as that which issued from Fleming's lips.

The Last Will and Testament of Joseph Meriwether Bowen, duly notarized and legal, described in flowery terms, something called the *Confederacy of Zion Crossroads*, a community of like-minded people dedicated to creating a new model of communal ownership, encouraging people to live according to their highest ideals. It also detailed that three utter strangers, people they had never even heard of, were now co-owners and, as such, had the right to live there in perpetuity or 'so long as they so desired'. This was due to the fact that they had `saved his life'. In a sub clause, Joe had added that, 'anyone else who'd saved his life but whom he might not be remembering at the time of drawing up said will was also included.

Fleming, who had been bitter for as long as he could remember was now in flames and, without a word, left the room.

"These people may have a 'legal' right to be here," he later told Murphy, "but one thing's for damned sure---there is no way in hell they are getting the treasure that is rightfully mine---by blood."

"And mine," Murphy had wanted to say but didn't because suddenly he was seeing something in Fleming that made him afraid.

"I said, step away from the window, Brother!"

"They've gone, Fleming," replied Murphy, staring blindly out the window with eyes still riveted on the past.

"Then what are you thinking about?" Fleming always seemed to know when Murphy was thinking something negative about him.

"Oh, nothing," replied Murphy, hastily covering his tracks. "I-I'm thinking I should go take care of some things. There is a problem with the----."

Fleming was back to brooding over his Bible so Murphy thought to quickly make his escape; however, when he opened the door, there stood silver haired Professor Valentino, poised with little black book in hand. Both of them jumped from fright, sending the old man's book and his stub of a pencil rattling to the floor.

"What are you doing here, Professor?" hissed Murphy, hoping that Fleming wouldn't overhear. How long had the old man been standing here and what had the he heard through the door?

"I've seen it! I've seen the Council of Light!" cried Valentino, his blue eyes glowing with a childlike happiness.

"That's very fine, Professor, but you know you're not supposed to be back here in our private space!" Poor old guy! He was just a witless old man, after all. How could Fleming be so hard on him? Murphy bent to retrieve the old man's book and pencil. A tattered, folded copy of the infamous pamphlet had partially slipped from between the pages but without a moment's hesitation, Murphy slid it back in and returned it to the old gentleman.

"Now, please go on back to your room, Professor."

"But I want to tell you something important."

"You can tell me later. Hush now! We don't want to bother Fleming, do we?"

At that precise moment, Fleming voice sounded from behind, and there he was looking biblical and fierce with his long bristling black beard. He informed the Professor that this was a private area.

There was a flat pitiless way about Fleming, perhaps because what he saw was a very flat world of black and white with rules and breakers of rules. He bore no sympathy for those that walk the line between truths, riddled with doubt and wracked with second-guessing. In Fleming's mind, people like that---people like Murphy---were weak. They needed to be led and if they refused to be led, then they needed to be controlled and that was the sum total of his philosophy.

The Professor grasped Fleming's hand with surprising strength. "I have a message from your father, Mr. Bowen---about the fire to come!"

But Fleming was wholly concentrated on extricating himself from Valentino's grip. "Let go of me!"

Undaunted, the old man's rosy countenance blazed with intensity. "You must prepare yourself but do not fear---it will be a good thing! A good thing, in the end."

"I said let---go!"

"Professor! Professor Valentino---you need to go *now*, Professor!" Murphy was pushing but the old man stood like a rock.

"It's a cleansing, you see---a cleansing fire. Just a step---a necessary step."

"Professor Valentino!" In desperation, Murphy shouted into his face to try to break the old man's fixation on Fleming. He was normally so pleasant and quiescent. Only when he was around Fleming did he have these peculiar outbreaks. To his relief, Valentino released Fleming's hand. Looking very pinched and pale, Fleming withdrew behind the door, where he immediately began scrubbing the invisible contamination from his hand with a white handkerchief. He had always had a devout distaste for being touched.

Meanwhile, Valentino stood at the door, frozen by rejection. Murphy wanted to hurry him off, for fear he might do something worse to anger his brother, but the terrible look of sorrow on the old man's face stopped him. It almost cut Murphy's heart in two to see it. He loved the old man and not just because he was kind but because the old man seemed to love him in return.

"Don't take it personally, Professor. You know how Fleming is. He doesn't like to be disturbed."

The silver haired professor turned to Murphy, with quiet dignity. "Oh, I'm not sad for *me*, Malatraya---*not* for me---but for *him*, don't you see---for him." The peaceful light returned to his blue eyes, and he amiably patted Murphy's arm before ambling off, stopping once to closely examine a spider's web on a windowsill then scribble a note in his notebook before moving on.

This was not the first time he had called Murphy by that strange name.

Filled with dread, Murphy returned to the room where Fleming sat behind the desk in ominous silence. "How long was he out there---at the door?"

"He'd just arrived when I opened it," lied Murphy.

Fleming stared down into his Bible as if into a deep, dark well. "He was listening, wasn't he? Spying."

"Fleming, he's just a senile old man!"

"And still you did not get the map, did you! He dropped it right on the floor in front of you and you handed it right back to him! Don't lie, I saw."

"Fleming, I couldn't just take it! Not right in front of him. It would be a betrayal of his trust!"

"His trust? What does that matter? He's just a senile old man. You said so yourself!"

"He still has feelings."

"Keep in mind that the demon working through him is manipulating you and knows precisely what it's doing."

"No, Fleming, no----please don't talk like that!"

"Think, Brother! A `message' from our `dead father'? What else could that be but a demon?"

"It is just nonsense, that's all! Just silly nonsense!"

"*You've* been taken in by him. That's what's happened!" Fleming lowered his eyes and began to read in ominous tones. *"Behold I come as a thief. Blessed is he that watcheth and keepeth his garment lest he walk naked and they see his shame."* He looked up with a penetrating glint in his eye.

The hairs on the back of Murphy's neck stood up. "But what does that mean? I don't understand it." As a rule, Murphy tried to avoid conversations like this but it wasn't always possible.

Fleming read on. *"Babylon the great is fallen and is become the habitation of devils and the hold of every foul spirit.'"* He rose and stood at the window gesturing towards the same flock of buzzards that had for some months been wheeling in lazy circles above Zion Crossroads. "It is evil that attracts them here to the feast."

"What do you mean?" When Fleming talked this way, Murphy got edgy mostly because he didn't feel qualified to understand. "I mean the Demons are upon us, yet you do not apply yourself, Brother. You do not pray. You do not study. Sometimes I wonder if you even believe! Do you have any idea how close you would be to the edge of destruction were it not for me?"

An oily fear gathered in Murphy's stomach, "But I do believe! I do!" Though even as he spoke, he felt the lie like a piece of undigested meat. He knew Fleming was right. It was true. He'd never been religious, never read his Bible like he should, or even ever prayed much.

"They will use your weakness," continued Fleming, reading

the guilt in Murphy's expression with cunning accuracy. "They are subtle as serpents, Brother---subtle as serpents! And I fear they are even now drawing you into their web, trying to set you against me. Are you against me, Brother? *"Come out of Her my people that ye be not partakers of Her sins and that ye receive not of Her plagues,"* intoned Fleming, pausing only because his brother's mind had obviously drifted. "I'm warning you, Brother! If you're not careful you will go right down the drain with your 'harmless' old Professor."

Murphy sat staring at the floor, wheezing sadly. He didn't have to guess which drain Fleming was talking about and he was undoubtedly correct. An Evil Influence did live inside him, a dark ugly thing he kept hidden, a secret hatred for everyone---his moth-er, his father, his brother, and yes, even the guests for the way they always looked through him, never seeing. Even now, he could feel this Creature of Spite thinking inside of him, for it was always there. It slept and ate with him and fed him on bitterness and fear.

 But the worst part was what it had made him do to his father---that terrible wish for his father to simply and finally die and so bring an end to the constant upheaval and pain. Surely, this was a sin that could never be expunged for didn't the Bible say that to think a thing was as bad as doing it? And if this were so, then wasn't he responsible for his father running off into the forest and committing suicide?

Thinking he had Murphy sufficiently chastened and recep-tive, Fleming cleared his throat loudly as he was preparing to read and wanted to be sure Murphy was paying attention. *"And I took the little book out of the angel's hand,"* he read, *"and ate it up, and it was in my mouth sweet as honey and as soon as I had eaten it, my belly was bitter."* He paused dramatically. "You think me severe, don't you Brother. But when the Lord fills you with knowledge, you can't ignore it. You can't pretend that everyone and everything is all sweetness and light. Our father had that particular affliction and look what it did to him. It attracted parasites and thieves." He continued reading in thunderous tones.

"And he said unto me, 'Thou must prophesy again before many peoples and nations and tongues and kings.' He stopped abruptly and continued in a slightly petulant tone, "And I can't do it for you, Brother. No matter how hard I try! Without proper study you are a house built upon sand. The first assault is already upon us. The Demons are at the doors of Zion this very hour. The first

battle is soon to begin and yet you don't seem to care."

Fleming snapped his Bible shut with a steep arch of the bushy brow. But if he was looking for some kind emotional surrender from his wayward brother; he wasn't going to get it. Instead, Murphy's eyes had glazed over and he was wondering if the Old Testament prophets were as difficult to live with as Fleming.

He was also thinking that even though Fleming had heard a Voice that day they were baptized in the river, Fleming was not God. And even though Murphy had only felt stark terror when the preacher had dunked him flailing beneath the brown impenetrable waters, he still had a right to be frightened by the things Fleming had done in God's name, regardless of hellfire. Now that their father was dead there would be nobody to stop Fleming from doing more of 'God's Will'---nobody but himself. And that worried him more than anything.

"So, you see," Fleming was saying, in closing, "the Lord has made it plain. I can ill afford to ignore this situation any longer. A time of cleansing is at hand, indeed."

And a grave terror collected in the pit of Murphy's stomach--for what if this were true?

Someone else had been secretly watching the journalist and the black gardener. Earlier, Jack had observed them talking intently as they headed off to the maze and against Tommy's objections, he'd decided to follow them. Tommy had said it was spying and uncool.

"All's fair in love and war, Tommy."

"Since when is this a war?"

"Trust me. It's a war. What do ya think? They're gonna come and say, "Let's hold hands and skip out into the woods and find the treasure together? Shit. When are you gonna learn people ain't like that? It's dog eat dog from here on out." With that, Jack had departed, stalking in bow legged strides across the mole ridden ground before disappearing into the Labyrinth Garden.

"And curiosity killed the cat," muttered Tommy.

In the meantime, Tom decided to go in search of the circle of stones he had stumbled upon when they'd gotten overtaken by the mist. He had no doubt that this was some kind of ancient power spot. He'd felt it immediately, like a rush of chill bumps going up his spine. They were sometimes called 'standing stones' and, being that they were pure quartz crystal, made them transmitters of the earth's electromagnetic energy. This was far more interesting than finding civil war treasure.

The moment he entered into the forest, that cathedral of trees arching overhead, he experienced the same feeling as before. Deep in his core, a weight was being lifted and an exquisite energy taking its place---a Presence. Yes, it was true---going into the wilderness wasn't really going *out* but more like coming *in*. He'd read that somewhere. This was the real world, outside the man-made crazy box. This was 'in". This was home.

Presently, he came upon two women sitting on a bench at a crossroads in the path---the elfish looking woman, Nealy and her sour faced sister.

The moment she spotted him, Nealy jumped up, waving excitedly. Apparently they'd gotten lost and her sister's back had gone out. As if to demonstrate, Portia shifted her weight, clenching her face in pain.

"We've been going round and round in this horrible forest and still we always end up here!" she growled..

"That's odd. You're really not even that far from the house," said Tommy cheerfully.

"Did you hear that, Portia? He says---."

"I heard what he said!" snapped the older woman. Cringing dramatically, she proceeded to limp down the path, muttering darkly to herself.

The younger sister was clearly embarrassed. "I'm sorry. It's her back." Nealy lowered her voice. "It puts her in a bad mood."

"Well? Are you coming or not?" Portia stood at the bend in the path, glowering at Tom with undisguised hostility.

"Sorry, Portia." Nealy glanced apologetically at Tom. He could see she was used to being the one to smooth things over, sort of like what he did with Jack.

Tom cleared his throat. "Uh, m'am! If you're heading for the house, it's this way."

Portia scowled and reversed course, limping past him with martyred determination. "Oh, so now it's the other way! Why am I not surprised?"

Tom and Nealy looked at each other and burst into silent laughter. The two sisters posed such a contrast. Nealy was pretty not so much in the details of her face but in a soft glow of loveliness, an inner light that danced on her lips and in her eyes. On the other hand, while Portia was not unattractive, the flat look in her eyes and the sourness of her mouth spoiled whatever beauty she did possess.

Portia turned with hands on hips. "What is so funny?"

"Oh, nothing!"

"Yeah, right!" She scowled again and kept on going.

"Somehow I don't think she likes me," he confided in a low voice, once Portia was out of earshot.

Nealy suddenly looked grave. "She doesn't mean to be this way. It's just that she's only recently come through a very hard time. A divorce."

There was a guarded fragility, a slight inner tremor behind her cautious and steady gaze. A wounded bird, he thought. One did not gaze lightly into such sad eyes that looked so deeply. "You know, we've met before," he said abruptly. "Earth People's Park? Back in '73?"

"Yes," she replied calmly showing no trace of surprise. "But you had a beard then. That's why I didn't recognize you at first." She kept her eyes on Portia, as if only half-listening.

"You were visiting my friend, Trip."

"That's right!"

"How did you two know each other?" she asked.

"We were in the streets together during the protests. He's always been like a brother to me so when he told me to check out what was happening up there---I went. A cool place----."

"While it lasted." There was a wistful sadness when she said this.

"Those things never do, it seems."

"Guess not." She said nothing about how he'd helped her to escape minutes before the helicopters had descended, and later how he had comforted her in his arms while she wept. Or how they'd slept that night on the soft plowed earth of a farmer's field, under a sky lit by flaming marijuana fields off in the distance.

"Nealy!" It was Portia.

"Coming!" Though Nealy's voice sounded light and cheery, the look in her eyes was still deeply sad. "I have to go," she said softly and then moved on. There was much that had been left unsaid.

When Tommy got back to the house, he found Jack, sitting on the upstairs balcony smoking a cigarette. It seems he was disappointed. The two men he'd been following had walked into the maze just to look at a grave. "Man, if I had a beautiful wife like that I wouldn't be spending my time tromping through graveyards, that's for damned sure."

"I figured you had the hots for his wife."

"Shut- up, young one." Jack couldn't refrain from a wicked smile. "I just wonder what he's up to."

"Why does everybody have to be up to something?"

"Because they usually are, Tommy. Trust me. I know these things."

"Has it ever occurred to you that you're making most of this shit up?"

"Oh, really?"

"Yeah! Like when you thought Padow murdered his wife and buried her in the backyard and then come to find out she was really just visiting her daughter in California? Remember that one?"

"Hey, the guy owns a butcher shop! He's probably Mafia all the way. If he didn't kill *her*, I'll lay you odds he's killed somebody along the way!"

"See? You're paranoid."

At this point, Mrs. von Hassel's door opened and she came out in her red silk Japanese robe, wearing sunglasses and a turban. A strong presence of perfume and tobacco lingered in the thick warm air long after she had sealed herself into the bathroom.

Jack rolled his eyes. "This place is too weird, Tommy! You done good."

CHAPTER VIII
Panovision: Evening Falls on the Second Day
The Zion Crossroads Plantation Hotel
1980

That evening Amanda von Hassel has retired to her room to pursue her nightly love affair with a bottle of booze. At dinner, the presence of rivals-- the young females--- disturbed some kind of inner balance as if their youth and beauty could somehow make Amanda herself disappear. For reassurance, she absorbs herself in looking at photos of the good old days when she was the 'most beautiful one at the ball.'

Mr. Puffenberger takes up his customary spot on a small wrought iron bench below her window in hopes of stilling his terrible hunger with chocolate covered peanuts. This gnawing in his gut is the curse that has plagued him, the tragic flaw imprisoning him in a never ending lust for food, and robbing him of his heart's desire. He sits, waiting for a glimpse of her in the rosy glow of her pink makeup light. This comforts him somehow, and it will be enough because it has to be. By now he is used to being here on the outside, looking in. Fortunately, long suffering patience comes easily to him, for all his choices were made for him a long time ago. That, if not exactly solace, is at least something he can depend on. It is what he's come to expect from life.

Meanwhile, in his room, Professor Valentino sits in a pool of lamplight, surrounded by stacks of newspapers, poring over an article he has somehow overlooked. He is surprised and uneasy because if he missed that then what else might he have missed? Suddenly the burden of being Keeper of Moments sits heavier on his shoulders. He can't afford to overlook anything. Every detail must be accounted for.
Gardner is nursing a cut on his shin sustained by a careless

swing of the hoe earlier that day. He briefly notes the dust collecting on the draft of his doctoral dissertation, then turns out the light, rolls over and falls instantly into a dead sleep.

Tommy sits on the side of his bed in the dark playing his guitar. He never knows what he is playing until he's playing it. The music shapes itself. It pours out of him like emotion, exquisite, like love. He drifts on clouds of peace.

Up in his attic room, beneath a large Confederate flag, Fleming labors on an old Remington manual typewriter. The essay, entitled, *'The White Race: On the Brink of Annihilation? Why Segregation of the Races is God's Will'* started out as a letter to his state delegate and evolved into a fifty-page dissertation. He's taking great pains with it, fine tuning every nuance, every possible flaw in the argumentation. He is convinced that this will fall on his future readers like a bomb, opening them up to a whole new understanding of life and how it should be lived. He believes that this is in keeping with the mission God has granted him---his role in the Greater Plan---the one he was born to play and which he is only beginning to understand. He still feels awed and flattered that he should have been chosen for such a task.
Once his work is completed, he spends a few moments in ritual reverence in front of the twisted form of Christ on the Cross which hangs on the wall over his bed. Agony is something Fleming can understand. His religious conviction came in adolescence and what he learned was that, in order to survive, one must be allied with Power. He has never felt anything like the joy that others speak of, however. A feeling of failure momentarily darkens his heart and, though he is not a Catholic, he crosses himself solemnly then positions himself on his back, arms lightly folded across his chest, and sleeps without moving until dawn.

Over the past nine months, Murphy has only dared to read the notebooks late at night when he knows he will be undisturbed, for his brother, Fleming, is an early riser and retires to his attic room at sunset. Because there were so many notebooks, it has taken him since August to get to the last one in the stack, a handwritten diary called 'The Boke of Shadows' inscribed with a warning to *'Guard this well on pain of death'*.
It is well known in the family history, that in 1710, the orphaned Meriwether Bowen, at age twelve, sold himself into indentured

servitude, left Ireland, and came to America to work for a wealthy plantation owner in Virginia but nothing has ever been said about why he'd been orphaned in the first place. Now, Murphy sits hunched and sweating in a pool of lamplight until dawn, for this one will prove to be the most shocking story he has ever read.

The Story of Meriwether Morrigan Bowen
County Meath on the Sacred River Boyne
1709

I well remember the day my life changed forever. It was the middle of a harsh winter of starvation and I was but twelve years when my father called me to the barn. I can still see Ma, how she stood watching from the dooryard. At the time, I didn't understand the look on her face but too soon would I discover that there was much they'd been keeping from me. 'Has it all come to this?' I'd heard her say, the night before at the hearth fire, when they thought I was asleep. I didn't think to wonder what she'd meant until the next day when I looked into my father's kind face and saw what I'd not seen there before—stone cold fear.

"There's a book here," says my father to me, half whispering. "This book," and he pulled a worn leather book out of a hidey hole beneath an old trunk, all the time looking back as if someone could be listening. "It tells of secret things, things that you must know."

And fear touched me with her cold finger.

"I was born with the Second Sight," he says. "But my parents taught me to hide my gift lest I be counted for a witch and the whole family burn for it---for as we both know, many have burned and I fear there will be many more to come."

Suddenly, he could not speak as if overcome but grabbed me and held me fast and when he let me go, his eyes were full of tears. "So I learned to keep these things to myself," he said. "Save for this one little book which holds many secrets. Secrets which must never be told."

"So this happened to me when I was but a boy of twelve years just as you are today," he said this in the way he often began his stories though this would be the strangest tale he'd ever tell---and stranger still because it was true. "One summer day I was swimming in the river Boyne and near most drowned!"

"Oh, no!" I cried.

106

"Oh, yes," he said and his eyes gleamed a faraway look. "And as my sight clouded over, I hear the sound of distant bells tellin' me the Fae was near and I hear a voice in my ear saying, 'Come, Wanderer for ye are all wanderers strayed far from home'...so I followed the sound right through the tiniest keyhole straight into the Other World."

"What is it like, Da?" I asked him.

"Oh, it's quite the same as this one, only much lovelier with bells hanging in the trees and flowers blooming everywhere under foot. And as I look, there's a beautiful lady sittin' on a tree stump and she says she's been waitin' for me. Oh, she did look so peaceful, with a rainbow of lights dancing all around her. And wouldn't ya know but it was Lady Boann, Bright Swan of the Sun. Faery born of the Faery blood and Goddess of the River Boyne, speaking with the silken voice of rushing waters. "I've come from the Four Holy Cities to bring up a servant for a special task.' she says. 'Are you such a one, Morrigan Boann?'

And my heart leapt like a winged bird. 'Aye,' says I, not knowing the cost.

Then she showed me a pit under the earth, dark as the grave. 'On the winter solstice, you must go down into that darkness and retrieve four talismans--the Cup of Plenty, the Sword of Victory, the Dreaming Wand, and the Stone of Destiny.'

'But how will I see?' says I.

And she laughed and bells tinkled all around her. "Why 'tis is the Sun Palace of the god, Roth Grian! He will light your way," she said and called me a brave hero as in days of old but while that pleased her it also made her sad for surely a hero never goes unscathed to their glory. "Just be faithful in the dark,' she told me. 'The Light will not fail ye now your oath is given.' And she gave me a ring as a sign of her thanks whereupon I suddenly felt myself being dragged from the river by rough fisherman's hands that poked and slapped me back to life. And as my lungs disgorged the sacred water of the River Boyne, I heard the Faery bells once more, retreating into the distance. Thus I returned to this world of pain, my son, the Faery's Ring still clutched in my hand. This ring I've kept hidden all these many years." And from out of the hole, he took a ring and gave it to me. It was a beautiful ring with strands of silver and gold, woven like tendrils of vine.

'Ten years would pass and I saw no sign. Had I not had the ring she'd given me, I would have thought it all a dream and nothing more. Only later, did I see. I was married and worked as a laborer for Master Charles Campbell and one day we cleared the brush and stones from around a curious mound at the river's bend and there we discovered the entrance to a cave which proved to be an ancient tomb.

"This was in November, and I immediately knew it as the sign I'd been waiting for these many long years. With the others, I had already gone down into the pit and it was just as dark and dank as when I stood there with my Lady Boann. I went sleepless for many nights, awaiting Solstice Eve, when I knew I would have to go down there alone.

"But true to Her word, it was as if some hidden hand guided my steps in the dark, for I easily found the talismans." And he pulled a leather pouch out of the hole as well and inside were a small silver cup, a dagger, a stone of clear quartz, and a smooth wand carved in a language I did not recognize.

"They're so small!" I said.

"Yes, but they hold the heavenly powers, son."

"But how do you know?'

"Because She told me, son!"

"Who told you?"

"Lady Boann, Bright Swan of the Sun. She comes to me in dreams even now and tells me things about the Other World, our true home, where the Tree of Life still grows and where there is no hunger or want and where every wish comes true!"

"But why can't we see it, Da?" says I.

"Because this world we're in casts such a shadow we cannot see and so we are doomed to be wanderers searching for a world as close as breath! But soon the two worlds will once more be as one! Yes, that day is soon upon us, son!"

"What day? What day, Daddy?" and I was crying now because he seemed quite mad and I was afraid.

From the house, I could hear Mama's voice calling, "Morrigan!"

"When the Two Worlds become as One, Meriwether!" And he was impatient that I was so slow to understand. "For the Earth grows weary and longs for the day when the Shadow World disappears and the Holy Cities open their gates once more upon the Earth. Then it will be as if no time has passed, as if no sin has ever cast its shadow on the truth." His face was shining now with joy and his shoulders were no longer hunched and burdened but straight and true. "But first, Mankind must stand at the Gate and choose."

My father paused, his face exceeding sad. "Last night Lady Boann came to my dream. She told me that you, son of my heart, must journey with them to the place where they must go—to the

Fourth Gate."

"Will you be coming with me, Da?" the boy asked.

*But his father sadly shook his head. "Not this time, my son."
And he caught me up in his embrace as if he would never let me go
and we wept together.*

"But where is it and how will I know?"

*"Just follow. She will lead you so long as you never forget your
sacred duty. It's a secret calling given to our family alone! We are the
Protectors of something infinitely precious sent to this dark world."*

*"Morrigan!" It was my mother in a panic at the doorway. "They're
coming!"*

*My father handed me the Book, the leather pouch containing
the talismans and the Ring. 'Guard this well on pain of death, my only
son. Now run, Meriwether! Run!' And that was the last word he spoke
to me.'*

In all the confusion, Meriwether managed to run away and hide
in the woods. All night, he covered his ears to hide the sound of
those terrible screams. The next morning, he'd returned to find both
the cottage and the barn burned to the ground but in the center of the
building, a small section of the floor remained and when he lifted the
board, there lay the chest unscathed.

He took it and trekked deep into the forest, careful to stay off
the main trail until he came to a road and hid in the brush. Presently, a
cart of fodder came by. The man stopped and got out to relieve himself.
He was not anyone Meriwether recognized and because he was old
and hard of hearing, it was easy for Meriwether to scramble into the
back of the cart and burrow down under the loose hay. The next time
he looked up, he saw that he had been taken to the neighboring port
town. Once again, he was able to slip out undetected and disappear
into a crowd of people getting ready to board a ship. But as he had
no money to cross the gangway, he was yanked aside, and put into
a line of rag tag folk preparing to sign themselves into indentured
servitude. And this was how he paid for passage to Virginia while
secretly transporting a book of magick!

The shock of this discovery makes Murphy slam the book shut,
his heart beating like a drum. What he holds in his hands suddenly
feels dangerous. This would be the scandal that would top all Bowen
scandals if it ever got out and couldn't he go to hell simply by having it
in his room? Possibly. Even so, he cautiously re-opens the book and
keeps on reading.

At midnight, Katherine finds herself standing on the balcony, depressed, and a little drunk, she gazes out into a starlit sky, trying to rein in all the crazy mad thoughts churning in her head. It has been a disastrous evening. Somewhere, someone is playing a melancholy tune on a guitar and without warning those damned incomprehensible tears start to flow; the tears she'd struggled so hard to deny.

They were to have made love tonight, and who knows, maybe even conceive a child. They'd drunk a bottle of wine and had just started to get close but she'd gone and said the wrong things. It was that note of blame in her voice that had killed it. Now Stephen is asleep. A few moments ago, she'd stood watching as he slept, knowing he would never agree to a child. What had she been thinking? When had a child ever been in their plans?

Surrendering herself to this strange new anguish, she lifts her face to the heavens, "God," she mutters, "what am I doing?"

Somewhere in the night, the strains of guitar music stops and the silence becomes strangely attentive. In horror she realizes that she is not alone and it isn't God who is listening. It is that jackass that came on to her at the front desk! Of all people to see her like this! She wants to roll herself up into a ball and disappear.

"God, this-this head ache---it's killing me," she moans, pretending she hadn't noticed he was there.

Jack stood up slowly, like a man in a dream. A beautiful woman coming out like this in a white gown, her dark hair, loose, falling over bare shoulders, the curve of her breasts---he hadn't dared to hope for a moment like this with her. But the Old Crow flowing in his veins gives him the nerve to approach her. "This'll cure what ails ya," he says, laughing like a man totally in charge of his world.

Against her better judgment, she accepts the bottle put into her hands and drinks. Nothing is making sense right now. "Thanks," she says, gruffly, then takes another. She is drunk all right and getting drunker.

Fearlessly, he reaches out to touch a straying tear on her cheek. "Bad headache, huh?" A surge of tenderness moves through him. Yeah, he is pretty loaded himself.

She bursts out laughing. The situation is too hilarious and he looks so solemn and childlike.

"Why are you laughing?" He seems hurt, a knot of consternation slowly forming in the middle of his forehead.
Instead of answering, she takes another swallow. This stuff was going down too easy.

"You know, I think you're beautiful," he says. "You know that, don't you?" He doesn't know how he knows to say these things but his heart is open and he is speaking his truth to her; foolish maybe, but fearless nonetheless.

If she were in a normal condition, she would blow this off. She would turn on her heel and walk right out with a smart little comment to show how far she is above all that. She doesn't need his praise or admiration. She is complete unto herself and doesn't need any man. But she isn't in her normal condition, for not only is she very drunk, she is also somewhat insane. An inner mad woman is calling the shots now, and she is just watching it happen like a bad TV show. Out loud, she says, "I have to go," but somehow can't move.

"You think I'm an ass, don't you!" The whiskey makes him reckless and brave. "Hey, I know what you think of me. Don't think I don't." His consonants are a little thick. "And yeah, I don't have the big fancy car. That's a thirteen-year old rattle trap out there. The damned door doesn't open so you have to crawl out the window, okay? And yeah, I work road construction. I work with my hands." He lifts his hands up. They are beautiful, masculine hands, strong, eloquent hands with scars on them, and one thumbnail turned black and blue. His hands mysteriously move her, and the way his voice breaks when he says `I work with my hands', as if he is defending himself against some unspoken judgment. "And I drink too much but I enjoy myself, okay? What's life for if you don't enjoy yourself?"

She looks at him mutely. Her eyes aren't focusing together but she has caught a glimpse of something, some kind of secret shame he carries on the inside. He is wearing a tank top and suddenly she's a little too aware of his well-formed body, his muscular arms and chest, his throat. This is absurd, of course. He's an uneducated jerk. Even the smell of his overly flowery after shave cologne is laughable. Where is her common sense? But she isn't moving.

"You know what I thought when I first saw you?" His voice is husky now and intimate. "I thought—class. Pure class. That's you. You got it, sweetheart. Everything. You got looks, brains. You're going somewhere. It shows."

It is definitely time to leave, but she wanted to hear this. It's embarrassing to need to hear this so much. The world is starting to spin so she takes another slug.

He smiles now in a fatherly sort of approval. Whiskey is good medicine and he can tell she needs it. "Take as much as you want, sweetheart," he says.

"Don't call me sweetheart."

"Sorry." He sways ever so slightly closer.

"And you know what?" she says. "I am going *somewhere*. I am going somewhere because I'm good at what I do. I am damned good at what I do." She is seeing two of him and the whole world is sliding.

"And it shows. It shows." He takes a deep uneven breath. "But you know what else I see? Sweetheart, you ain't happy." He restrains himself from stroking her hair off her forehead.

Oh, god---where does he think he is going with this? But he's right---too, too right. "Okay, you know what? I'm a---*married* woman," There, she used the 'word'. She poked him in the chest with her finger. "And *you* don't have any business telling *me* that *I'm* not happy. Okay? Now I'm *going*, thank you very much." She starts to assemble herself for a retreat.

"Sorry! I'm sorry!" He put his hands on her shoulders then quickly withdraws them. Thunder rumbles in the distance. The air is soft and thick.

She brushes against him as she lurches towards the door. He catches her arm to steady her, his breath on her shoulder. "Easy, now," he says. They are standing very close, face to face, and for a moment, she is paralyzed. "I could kiss you right now," he says, "because I really want to but I'm not because it wouldn't be right. I just want you to know I would never take advantage of you while you're drunk." When he blinks, his eyes close for longer and longer amounts of time.

She could have laughed but she doesn't. "I am not drunk!" she says. "I'm married ---*and* I'm going now." She swerves back into the hall, the floor not quite rising to meet her feet.

Nealy heads outside into the violet hush of twilight, her burden sitting like a stone in her chest. She wants to be completely alone, somewhere without eyes upon her, away from the suffocating energies of the house. It has been too long since she's been back in the country, so close to nature. She needs this time by herself to clear the emotional debris, make an offering, reconnect. She remembers a dream from last night in which she'd been lost among the ancient trees of Earth People's Park, wandering on a path tangled with briars and cloaked in mist. A deep sadness wells up inside, just to think about how free she'd felt back at the Park. She could never have imagined being as trapped as she is now. Yes, she is lost now in more ways than one for if this healing spring is just another delusion, her life will be a long slow descent to the grave.

It had been a stupid argument back in the room, but Portia's words still torment her. It had all started when her sister had dragged out her enormous plastic bag of medications and Nealy had made the mistake of suggesting that perhaps Portia should think twice about putting all those chemicals in her body. "It could cause liver damage," she'd said.

"Liver damage?" scoffed Portia, eyes bulging with contempt. "I seriously doubt my doctor would prescribe something for me if it is going to hurt my liver!"

"Well, actually I've read about cases---."

"Where did you read that? In this book?" She'd picked up Nealy's book on spiritual healing entitled *Heal Thyself* and practically threw it at her. "Is this what convinced you to stop going to the doctors? Nealy, you have a serious heart condition!"

Like a fool, Nealy had answered back. "I just wish you would read this then maybe you'd see the truth in it!" Why did she keep trying to convince Portia? It was useless and only made her angry.

"If it's so true then why aren't you healed?" blurted Portia, "Any liar can write a book! Besides, who knows what kind of demons got hold of you up there at horrible hippy commune you went to!"

"Portia, you know nothing about it!"

"And you are so naïve! You think you're immortal? Like you can't be destroyed? Well, you can. Life is not a happy little fairy tale so you better play by the rules!"

"I am not like you, Portia," Nealy said quietly. "And my life is not like yours."

"I see. So you're bound and determined to learn everything the hard way, are you?"

"I don't see the point of this conversation." Nealy had headed blindly for the door. It would have been so much simpler to have left this vengeful creature behind but the ties that bound them together could not be denied and Portia needed the healing springs just as much as she did.

Portia's face twisted into a mask of contempt. "Oh, so I suppose you're angry now!"

"I'm not angry with you, Portia," she said finally, her tone carefully measured, keeping her eyes averted. If there were the least tinge of blame in her voice, it would only give fresh wind to Portia's attack and they'd be up all night trying to untangle it. It wasn't worth it to argue with her. Better to let Portia feel that all was forgiven. In the mirror, she could see her sister's reflection, haunted looking---Portia, the ghost.

"Well, you're distant now. I can always tell because you're distant." Portia's tone was at once accusing and penitent. "You know I hate it when you're distant."

Nealy had stood with her hand on the doorknob. "No, I'm just tired. I think I need some fresh air."

"You won't be long, will you?" Now Portia had turned to victim, pity me---take care of me---don't leave me.

"Don't worry. It'll be just a little while."

Outside the full moon is rising. Nealy finds a spot on the grass to lie down. She needs to feel earth beneath her. *When you are in trouble, lay on the earth with your head to the north and pray for help.* Tears leak out the sides of her eyes and run into her ears. *You are my Love.* Unbidden, the words form in her mind. Who is saying this? Or is she merely saying it to herself? Somehow it makes no difference. Soft as a bird's wings, her Spirit lifts. The spell of fear loosens its grip. *You are My Love*, says the quiet voice within. *I am Yours, You are Mine. We are One.* It is a signal, a password, and as she has come to expect, a beautiful peace blooms in the core of her being. She is not alone.

Strains of music mingle with the gentle sighs of the breeze rustling through the leaves. Someone is playing a guitar out under the moon. Night deepens around her. Lightening bugs glitter. Silvery clouds float like ships at sail across the moon and her Spirit opens like a flower, as she lies against the comforting bosom of the earth, gazing at the endlessly changing landscape of the sky.

The music drifts into silence. She could have stayed there forever if it hadn't been for Tommy nearly stepping on her. He curses, she screams. "Sorry," they both say in unison, then laugh.

"You probably think I'm strange to lie on the ground like this," she says, sitting up.

"Full moon," he replies. "It would be a waste not to." He sits down beside her and turns his eyes skyward. A vigorous chorus of cicadas swells on all sides. He can feel the delicate beauty of her presence in the silvery darkness beside him.

"Your music is amazing," she murmurs in her soft private voice. "Do you play, I mean professionally?"

"That would be a little tricky since I never play the same thing twice. It's like some people play to remember. I play to forget. It just sort of happens." In the moon glow his face looks as if it were changing forms, like masks; the images of other faces flashing, some old, some young, but through it all, that irrepressible grin sheepishly bobbing up to the surface.

The wind sighs through the trees, caressing their bodies so gently.

"Don't you think it strange that we should both randomly show up here?" he says. "That we should meet again like this? Doesn't it make you think that there must be some kind of---."

"Purpose?"

"Yeah."

She pauses, guardedly. "I don't know."

"Yes, you do!" he whispers fiercely. "You *know*. The whirlwind called you here. When you told that story at dinner, I knew right then! None of this is a coincidence."

She looks at him but says nothing.

The insect orchestral suite intensifies with a grand lightening bug display. Suddenly, she feels completely still inside, and somehow she can feel that stillness inside of him, as well. This strange intimacy seems almost inappropriate, yet, as if under a spell, her body does not want to stir. She wonders if he feels it, too. For no apparent reason she wants to cry.

He touches her arm. "Do you see that?" he whispers in her ear.

"Yes." She catches her breath. "I see them."

Later back in his room, Tommy can't stop thinking about what he'd seen. He tries to explain it to Jack. "It was like these orbs of light moving through the trees."

Jack is sitting by the window, smoking in silence, his mind a million miles away, thinking about his encounter with Katherine on the balcony. "Probably aliens or somethin'."

"Come on, Jack! You don't believe in aliens!"

"Okay, ghosts!"

"You don't believe in ghosts, either!"

"Well then why the hell are you asking me? It was probably just your imagination."

"Then how come Nealy saw them, too?"

"Nealy? So what were you doing with her?" Usually he would have made some kind of snarky insinuation.

"Yeah, we met accidentally in the garden, so shut up about it."

"You want me to shut up? Okay, I'll shut up." And he does which is unusual for Jack. He goes back to his silent brooding, blowing smoke rings out the window.

Katherine throws off her white gown and crept into bed, to lie naked beside Stephen. He is sleeping patiently, the way he always does, never snoring, just silent and peaceful. Though it is suffocating in the room, she needs to feel his body beside hers. He stirs slightly. She kisses his shoulder.

"Katherine," he murmurs.

"I love you, Stephen," she whispers but he is already asleep and dreaming of the Himalayas.

CHAPTER IX
Into the Forest
The Zion Crossroads Plantation Hotel
1980

The next morning while dusting the front desk, Murphy was caught off guard by the sudden appearance of the young Miss Nealy Brown come to report that the day before she and her sister had gone round and round looking for the Healing Springs and gotten hopelessly lost.

"Right," said Murphy, standing rigidly at attention, his eyes shielded behind the glare reflected in his glasses. He tended to be this way around women, especially when they were pretty. It was his armor, his protection, for the truth was that except for that fateful night with Mrs. von Hassel—which didn't really count---he'd never even kissed a girl and to be in close proximity to one ordinarily made him almost uncontrollably nervous.

"So do you think you could help us?" she was asking.

There were a number of reasons for Murphy to hesitate. First, though he'd heard the old legend about an ancient healing spring, he had no idea where it was or if it even really did exist. Second, he was deathly afraid of the forests of Zion Crossroads and had been since the summer he was twelve, the summer of his father's first disappearance. Day after day, the men in search parties combing the woods had straggled back with strange and terrifying tales of paranormal encounters and weird visions. Eventually, the Sheriff had had to call it off entirely because there was no one willing to go back into that mysterious tangle of forest.

The black housekeeper, Leonora, had ordered the twins not to mingle with the men in the search party. She didn't want them to hear something upsetting. Of course, they were already upset being that their father was missing and possibly dead, his body torn apart by wild animals. How could they not be upset?

But one afternoon, a man sitting out under a tree had called to him, begging for water. No one else was around so Murphy had had no choice but to do as he'd been asked. Murphy remembered how hot it was that day yet the man was shaking so badly that the water kept sloshing out of his cup every time he raised it to his lips. Finally Murphy steadied it for him so he could take a drink and that's when he'd begun to talk.

The man told him that while out in the forest, he'd become lost in a thick layer of mist for what seemed like years. "Then something awful happened," whispered the man and the terrible look on his face made Murphy want to get up and run away but the man held him fast with an iron grip. He needed to tell it to somebody, he said, or lose whatever mind he had left. He'd found a place, he said---a circle of stones in a clearing. The moment he stepped into the circle, he heard sounds of weeping and suddenly a naked child appeared, beckoning him over the crest of the hill. There, he saw he saw scores of dead bodies spread across the ground, rotting in the sun.

Later, the man had to be taken to the mental hospital. A 'nervous breakdown' was what the grownups had called it, a term not unfamiliar to Murphy who had heard it in whispered conversations about his own father.

But Murphy did not want to tell Nealy about all that. She might decide he was strange and go away like most people seemed to do. Mostly, he had hardened himself not to care but she was different and he did not want her to go away. Something about her made him want to trust her. Maybe it was that she was pretty but not so pretty that she seemed all that concerned about it; or maybe it was her voice, so careful, with that quiet seriousness shining in her clear blue eyes. It was as if she were really seeing the person before her and he felt oddly exposed for there was so much he didn't want her to see. Yet, despite his shame, she seemed kind and he longed to be seen by her, even if it felt dangerous. Yes, he was like a moth drawn to flame and though never one to think of women directly, (for he could rest assured they would not be thinking of him), he knew that if he were to have a daydream, it would be about someone like her.

Meanwhile, she was pulling out her carefully folded copy of the pamphlet. "No matter which path we took we always seemed to end up back here," she said and pointed to a place on the map where two paths crossed, creating a great figure eight.

Seeing the pamphlet, Murphy's heart froze. Fleming had specifically instructed him to try to get a look at it. "Oh, don't feel bad!

Everybody gets lost," he said, laughing a little too gaily and ending on a ridiculous note. Fleming was right. He did laugh like a ninny but luckily she didn't seem to notice. "Um, may I—um, do you think I could see the um---the uh, map? I mean, the pamphlet?" Without meaning to, he caught sight of himself in the dreaded two-way mirror, inwardly recoiling for he looked like such a great gawking bird with those spectacles and thin as a scarecrow.

Of course." She rewarded him with her warmest smile, making him feel all the more like a vulture as he took the pamphlet she handed over so trustingly. At a glance, it was similar to Puffenberger's which he'd seen once only briefly when it had been left by accident on the porch swing. This, too, showed the Loop and the same familiar network of riding trails but there were added landmarks that he did not recognize with strange titles like The Wall of Adversity and The Ladder of Success. Further along what was supposed to be the Ravine was the so-called Healing Springs.

"You know, I don't want to impose," she said, "but do you think that maybe you could show us where it is?"

He hesitated then before he had a chance to know what he was saying he'd asked her why she looking for the healing springs. By the look on her face, he immediately realized that this was far too personal a question and that it was painful for her. It was a problem with her heart, she said. He was stunned because no one had ever confided themselves to him like this before. On the contrary, he was used to being treated as if he were slightly less important than the wallpaper.

It was too late now to ask if she needed more towels and the subject of soap would never do. No, he had to say something real for they'd stepped over the boundary and something irrevocable happens around boundaries. Whether one chooses to think of it as falling off a cliff or merely stepping over a line, suddenly he was madly in love; which quite possibly explains why he offered to show her where to find the healing spring even though he had no idea where it was or if it even existed.

CHAPTER X
Book of Joe: Part One
The Zion Crossroads Plantation Hotel
1977

Forget the dog! Snowball would have to find his own way back to the house. He had to worry about himself now. Dusk was falling fast and the mist was already snaking its way among the trees. Soon he would not be able to see a thing. A cold panic flowed up his spine in a thin paralyzing stream. This feeling was far too familiar. It was the signal the Gods of Disaster always sent in advance of their arrival.

As a child, he'd feared the Mist coiling out of the ravine at dusk, licking the earth like a serpent's tongue. Stories told of strange things that happened to people foolish enough to get caught in it; encounters with ghosts and Beings not quite of this world, people forever lost and never seen or heard from again.

"Damn you, Snowball! Damn stupid---! Ow!" He was still limping some. The casts had just come off a few days before and in his agitated state, he'd very nearly stumbled into one of the 'Colonel's holes'. "Damn stupid hole! Damn, damn, damn!" He'd thrashed his way through the underbrush like a blind man, a ranting madman. The only consolation was that no one would be here to see him stumble and fall yet one more time.

Just when he thought there was no way out except to die, the Mist drew back like a curtain to reveal a massive live oak tree. He was just having that peculiar feeling that he had been here before when an apple clunked him on top of his head.

"Ow! What the hell?" How odd that an apple had fallen out of an oak tree; and odder still that there was a bite taken out of it!

It was then he noticed a very homemade wooden ladder nailed into the side of the tree. Maybe it was Philip using it for deer hunting. "Who's up there?" Straining to see through the veils of mist, he thought he detected a slight movement in the foliage above. "Philip?" he called out, suddenly savage with fear for something told him this wasn't Philip. Another apple plummeted to earth but this time he deflected it with his arm.

"Drat!" came a disembodied voice from above. The wisps of fog parted, revealing a withered, wiry little man with scraggly white hair and a long beard crouched like a monkey on a sturdy branch high above.

"What do you think you're doing up there?" demanded Joe from the ground.

"I live here, what do you think?" The man in the tree replied, quite impudently.

"You can't live there!"

"Why not?

"Because this is my tree, on my property, and you are trespassing, that's why! I own this forest!" The stinging pain in his arm lent some fire to his anger for he was not normally one to be so confrontational.

"You can't own a forest! That's the silliest thing I've ever heard of! Who do you think you are?"

"Who do you think you are?"

"I asked first!"

"I am Joseph Meriwether Bowen, the owner of Zion Crossroads *and* this forest, *and* that mountain, *and* this tree! That's who I am!"

"Really? Well, you have my sympathies. Now would you mind throwing that apple back up to me? It's the only one I have left!"

"If you want your darned apple then you'll just have to come down and get it yourself!" Joe had never actually been very good at being confrontational.

"Well if you want me to come down, you'll have to help me," said the man, clearly trying to sound pathetic. "I'm scared."

"Scared! If you're so scared how did you get up there in the first place?"

"I can't remember! And now I'm too scared to go back down!" The little man didn't look remotely scared. To the contrary, he clearly seemed amused.

"That's ridiculous! Just take it one step at a time for Pete's sake!"

"But what if I fall? I could break my back? I could break a leg! I could break both legs! Besides, I live here!"

The mists cleared enough to reveal a small poorly constructed tree house. Suddenly, the audacity of this trespasser made Joe want to charge up the ladder and beat the daylights out of him and he was half-way up before he even knew what he was doing. "Don't look down," he told himself.

"What's that you say? Speak up! I'm a little deaf." The old man was leaning way over, hanging like a chimpanzee from one ropey arm.

"How dare you!" Joe was now racing up the ladder so fast his feet barely touched the rungs. It was only when he reached the top that he made the mistake of looking down and his head reeled. They were a good twenty-five feet off the ground.

The little old man, on the other hand, seemed quite relaxed, nesting on some blankets. The platform was fairly spacious but there were gaps between the boards and it was such a long way down. An old plastic tablecloth was stretched across as a roof and he recognized it immediately. "How did you get my tablecloth?" demanded Joe.

"Someone gave it to me." The little man seemed greatly amused by this.

"Who?"

"That fellow there." The man pointed to a small framed photo wedged into the crook of a branch.

Joe stepped onto the platform and crawled over to it for closer examination. It was a picture taken of himself with the twins when they were about three years old. "And you stole this picture, too?" he roared. "Out! Out of my tree!"

"Ironic! Since you are already clearly out of yours," replied the little man with an impertinent wink.

"And what exactly do you mean by that?"

"You've gone off your nut."

"Well, so?" Joe paused. "You're still in my tree!"

"Why care about property rights?" The old man reached into a cloth bag and pulled out a Meerschaum pipe carved in the shape of woman's naked torso. "It's just an invention."

"Oh! And of course, you would say this while smoking my grandfather's pipe!"

The old man laughed like a hyena showing yellow teeth. He was old but his eyes gleamed like fire and he looked utterly mad.

Joe gave a snort of contempt. "Well, go ahead and laugh but the Sheriff isn't going to be too amused when he arrests you for robbery and trespassing."

"Oh, goody! Am I going to get punished?" The old man rubbed his hands together as if it were something to look forward to.

"Yes!"

"But what if I run away?" He giggled devilishly.

"How can you run away if you're too afraid to climb down the ladder?"

"Good point," conceded the little man, then lowered his voice to a confessional tone,   "But you see, it's not that I'm afraid. It's just that the tree wants me to stay. It likes my company. We're bonded."

"A tree can't bond with anyone. A tree has no feelings."

"Who made that rule?"

"It's not a rule. It's a fact."

"Is it really?"

There was now no doubt that the strange little man was insane, possibly even dangerous, and Joe realized that he was indeed in a bind. Not only was he lost in the woods and worse---lost in the mist with night coming on---but he was sitting up in a tree with a mad man. He had no choice. He had to get out of the tree. Joe had to go down the ladder.

The fact that he'd fallen off a three-story roof not nine months before and broken numerous bones was strangely not on his mind. Instead, an inexplicable surge of energy had suddenly made him very positive about going down the ladder. In fact, it felt easy to him. It was an optimism that he was not accustomed to having but it was as if the tides of anger had swept away the clammy pessimism that habitually lurked in the dark crevices of his heart.

"Come on," said Joe. Even his voice was stronger and for the first time in his life he actually felt powerful. It came from deep inside the very core of his being and it felt very good indeed. Suddenly, he knew that it would be easy to go down the ladder and though the darkness and the mist swirled around him, he didn't need to see because his feet knew the way down, as if they had a mind of their own. In fact, his glasses became so intensely uncomfortable that he ripped them off, and this was odd, as he was normally helpless without them.

When he stood again on the earth, he put a hand on the tree and immediately, a bolt of energy, like an electrical charge shot up his arm, spreading into his chest like warm, liquid light and he thought, oh--- that's what this is! He remembered now.

The next thing he knew it was morning and he was dozing in his rocking chair on the front porch of Zion Crossroads with a cold wet nose nuzzling under his forearm. It was the long lost Snowball. "Where have you been, you silly dog?"

"You're out here bright and early, Mr. Joe." It was Leonora, the black housekeeper, in her blue flowered apron, broom in hand.

"Snowball's back! I was so worried."

"Snowball's been back. Lift your feet." She swept away the dirt beneath his chair. "Have you gone and lost your glasses again?" Her voice, like her body, was firm and vital.

"My glasses?" Suddenly he realized he had no idea where his glasses were. How strange. Normally, he couldn't see his way down the stairs without them. Not only was it mortifying that he could re-member nothing about where he had put them, but he couldn't even remember how it was he came to be sitting in this chair.

She lifted the newspaper on the side table. "Not here. Have you checked your pockets?" She was used to his forgetfulness.

Flustered, he patted all of his pockets and still did not find them.

"I'll get your extras."

"I don't understand how I could have--- "

"You just weren't thinkin', is all," she said gently. "People do lots of things and don't even know it. My great-aunt Tilly once put the phone book in the freezer and the pork chops on the telephone stand!"

Leonora's laughter was usually infectious but this time it only made him wonder how long it was before they'd locked that woman away in the crazy house. With his replacement glasses on, the world again came into focus just in time to catch sight of Leonora's expres-sion. Beneath the warmth of her smile, there was a look of concern.

CHAPTER XI
The Two-Way Mirror
The Zion Crossroads Plantation Hotel
1980

After visiting Joe's grave with Gardner the gardener, Stephen Andriot circled around to the front of house only to find Professor Valentino standing in the driveway, dignified and erect, wearing a Panama straw hat and a pale blue seersucker suit. He was gazing off into the distance with a look of consternation on his handsome, rosy face.

"There she goes again!" he sighed. "Well, I suppose she knows the way home, a natural tracker, that one. I was never a hunter, though. Never interested in killing animals for sport."

Stephen Andriot stood beside him, "Lose your dog, Professor?"

"She'll find me. She always does." Valentino continued to scan the tree line anxiously. Suddenly a look of relief played across his face. "There! Sure enough, a rabbit! Good girl, Willie! What did I tell you? She was after a rabbit!"

Andriot could see no sign of a dog or rabbit, but Valentino seemed satisfied. He was going on his daily walk to the mailbox and the journalist, ever sniffing out the story, fell in step alongside. There was something he wanted to ask.

"Mr. Valentino, weren't you once a psychology professor at Berkeley?

The older man looked as if this were something he hadn't quite considered before. "Why yes, I believe I was."

"I thought so! You know, I was a student there back in the mid sixties."

"Really?" Valentino's watery blue eyes were gentle and inward looking.

"So, Professor Valentino, what brought you to Zion Crossroads?"

Valentino paused and surveyed the landscape with dignified solemnity. "Why I'm sure I've lived here for a thousand years."

Andriot was a little taken aback, but he went on without missing a beat. "So how are you enjoying retirement?"

"Retirement?" The old man's gaze drew inward. "No, I've only moved on, you see. Now I am keeping the Record of Moments. I am to keep the record of all of this—this life. That is what I am for, you see." He gave Andriot a keen look. "It is essential to discover why you've come here, otherwise, it's all for naught. Just another wasted trip around the wheel. But now I know!" He stopped and tipped a rock over with his cane. "All that came before was just prelude. Prelude to the dawn, to the beginning. Yes." His eyes were dreamy.

"The beginning of what, Professor?"

Valentino turned with a sudden intensity. "Why we're standing on the threshold of something quite wondrous. Not sure yet, but it will be wondrous. They tell me that much. A new world." He raised a bushy white brow as if Andriot should naturally understand the significance.

Andriot nodded solemnly, thinking how sad that a man once known for his brilliance should have come to this. "So, are you still writing much?"

"Oh, yes. I'm writing, yes---words on a page. Representations. But they don't really contain the information, do they? So where is the information if it isn't on the page?" He looked at Andriot as if expecting him to answer but then went on.

"And have you ever noticed when you are speaking or writing that you don't really know how you're going to end the sentence---until it just happens?"

Again, Andriot felt the old man waiting for him to respond but when he opened his mouth to speak, the old man talked right over him.

"No, you haven't, have you! You're always thinking ahead or thinking back but if you were to record the moments very accurately, you might see that you don't really know how you think. So the more interesting question is not *what* you think but *how* you are thinking at all? Where do our thoughts come from? In other words, *what* is thinking through us? Or rather, *who*? You begin to see that it's a creation flowing from one level of reality to another but the source is really quite mysterious. We take it all for granted, don't we? We think this is all just a static boring reality when we really don't begin to know what is really going on here."

"You know, you are absolutely right about that, Professor," said

Andriot, hoping this might lead to the end of the conversation.

Andriot continued walking with Professor Valentino in polite silence until they came to the dead end road where someone had clumsily propped the mailbox up with a two by four. Andriot opened it with a rusty complaint. Inside was a local newspaper along with two letters addressed to Mr. Fleming Meriwether Bowen, one from the Gray Knights of the New Confederacy and the other from the Internal Revenue Service.

"Interesting," thought Andriot. His mind drifted onto the subject of the article taking shape in his mind and at first he failed to notice the Professor gazing at him intently.

"So do you want to know what's really going on here?" asked the old man abruptly.

"Yeah, sure!" The hotel was in sight. Not much further.

"Well, as the Keeper of Moments, I have been privileged to notice certain inconsistencies in what we call 'Reality' with a capitol 'R'." The old man's eyes widened making him look utterly mad.

Suddenly, Andriot's interest perked up.

"You would think that everything here is strictly objective" continued the professor. "The objects, this forest, our bodies even---everything always the same---moment to moment. But it's not. Moment to moment, it is constantly shifting, changing. It's quite subtle for the most part and we're so distracted by a thousand things we never notice." The professor's eyes gleamed. "So what don't we notice?"

The old man waited, again making Andriot feel like a student called to answer in class. "I don't know. What don't we notice?"

The professor seemed pleased. "Ah! Finally, you admit it! Intellectual pride is our undoing, dear friend. We will never properly understand anything until we surrender it. What we fail to notice is that there is no objective reality. These objects, these trees, this road, even our bodies are like— words, symbols on a page. They merely point to a meaning they do not contain. Like words, they are a medium of expression flowing from a source beyond our understanding. But it is not a static picture, is it? No! It's constantly moving, changing, transforming.

"Your face, for example, my face---you see it most readily in the faces—it's not the same face it was a moment ago. It is an interpretation of a mix of emotions and chemical responses. We live in our interpretation of the moment. Quite limited, actually. So we fail to notice that there is a constant translation of thoughts and desires, not just into words, but into physical objects---or physical reality--- and we are doing it quite as easily and unselfconsciously as we translate words onto a page." The older man beamed.

"But how is this practical, professor?" said Andriot who was suddenly and surprisingly engaged. "I mean, what does it matter? We are stuck here in this reality, like it or not."

Valentino's expression became grave. "Oh, but this is of the utmost practicality, my friend. It's the only useful way to look at this reality. When you truly understand that your experience of reality comes as naturally out of your mind, as words come out of your mouth, then you have found the psychological key to your freedom!"

By now they'd arrived back at the house. Valentino headed cheerfully to one of the rocking chairs and proceeded to read his paper with great interest. Andriot excused himself to go inside to find Katherine. In passing the front desk, he happened to notice the narrow closet door beneath the staircase standing slightly ajar which was how he discovered the two-way mirror overlooking the registration desk. At the sound of footsteps approaching, he impulsively stepped inside and pulled the door shut just as Fleming walked into the room.

Andriot watched unseen as Fleming went behind the registration counter, pulled a tray of medicine bottles out of a drawer, deftly unscrewed the lid to a small vial and filled it with a brown liquid from another vial he had produced from his shirt pocket. He was tightening the lid just as Professor Valentino came inside.

"Time for your medication, Professor."

A shadow of uncertainty flickered across the old man's rosy face. "But where is Murphy?"

"He went to town on errands so I will be giving you your meds today."

"But--."

Fleming arched an eyebrow and the Professor's protest died on his lips. "Very well." He obediently swallowed the blue, the yellow, the pink and white striped pills but when Fleming emptied the vial of brownish liquid into a small cup, Valentino balked. "What's this?"

"It's a new medication sent by the doctor."

Valentino downed it with a grimace. "If anything will kill me, this will be it!" Fleming watched intently as the old man gathered his things and started up the staircase.

"I believe it's time for your medicine, Professor!" called out Murphy cheerily, entering from the back of the house.

Valentino paused. "Oh, but Fleming already gave it to

me."

"He did?" Murphy shot a suspicious glance at Fleming who was by now intently reading his Bible.

Valentino's face brightened. "Oh, yes but Murphy, you must come with me! I have something to show you!" He hastened up the stairs.

Murphy hesitated and Fleming displayed a rare smile. "Yes, Murphy, do go with him to his room and see what he has to show you!"

After they had left, Fleming closed his Bible and was preparing to leave when a spider skittered down the back of Andriot's collar causing him to jerk involuntarily and bump his elbow against the shelf. On opposite sides of the mirror, both Fleming and the man in the closet froze, listening. Sweat trickled down Andriot's temple as Fleming's hawkish eyes tried to pierce the murky shadows behind the surface of the glass that separated them. Fortunately, Gardner suddenly entered from the kitchen.

"I figured you'd want to know that someone's pilfered one of the pies for dinner."

"Three guesses who that someone might be," growled Fleming and they both left.

As soon as he dared, Andriot opened the closet door.

"What in the world are you doing in there?" It was Katherine, coming down the stairs dressed in an apple green tank top and gray athletic shorts, her mahogany colored hair tied up in a ponytail.

"Long story." He felt drained and headed up the stairs.

"Really! Well, I've been looking all over for you!" She put her hands on hips. " Now where are you going?"

"To our room so I can lie down."

She hesitated, mentally calculating. "To do what---exactly?" She seemed to be inferring something but what he couldn't be sure. She hadn't been `available' for sex since he'd gotten back from his trip. The melodramas at the office had taken all her `emotional' energy, so he was pretty sure that couldn't be it. Even so, she could be so difficult to read.

"Sleep." He would stick with the safe answer, but immediately realized this was the wrong one, as her face clouded over with that martyred look she got when he wasn't doing what she wanted him to do.

"I thought we could at least go for a walk since we haven't spent any time together since we've gotten here," she said. "I mean, I thought that's why we came but apparently that wasn't what you had in mind." Beneath her anger lurked the buried hurt. He could see it in her eyes still he couldn't resist a sarcastic jab.

"I thought you wanted to do research on your novel?" he said.

"I can't work on it *all* the time."

Beneath her evasiveness, he sensed she wanted something but as usual rather than just telling him what it was, she needed him to be some kind of a mind reader. Rather than risk an argument, he shoved down his rising irritation and agreed to go for a walk with her.

"Okay, where to?" He asked this in as neutral a tone as he could muster, though to her ears it sounded brusque.

Immediately, she wavered. "You decide."

"Okay, how about the Labyrinth Garden?" At least he could see if there were anymore grave sites.

She let out a huge labored sigh. "Okay."

"So what's wrong now?" Obviously that too was the wrong answer, he thought, having no way of knowing about her weird flashback experience of being pursued and strangled earlier that morning in the labyrinth.

She moved closer and coyly took his hand. "Nothing. I don't care where we go, just so we're together." His eyes narrowed suspiciously. Katherine was usually so independent, even competitive with him. "What's gotten into you, Kat?"

"What? I just thought it would be nice to be together for a change." As usual, her defensive instincts always came across in attack mode.

He shrugged if off. They continued walking in silence but he was far away in his thoughts and after just a short distance he stopped and asked if they were done yet.

"I thought you wanted to see the Labyrinth Garden," she snapped then rephrased in a gentler tone. "I mean, wouldn't it be nice to sit in that stone temple together? You could put your head in my lap and rest."

He shrugged again in that listless way he had when being made to do something he didn't want to do. Her enthusiasm fizzled. Having to drag him on an evening walk was not her idea of romantic.

As they entered the narrow passage of the boxwood maze, the pungent odor once again triggered the same apprehension as it had earlier in the day. The same squadron of gnats was waiting on the attack as well. Of course they only seemed determined to get into Katherine's eyes and weren't remotely interested in Stephen, who became inexplicably jolly. Suddenly, without warning, he slapped her butt hard and dodged into the bushes! "You're it!"

"You bastard! That hurt!" Gone was gentle lady love. Katherine had become the enraged battle axe. "I thought you were so tired!"

Devilish laughter resounded from somewhere behind the bushes followed by an ominous silence, then a flash, and another stinging blow from out of nowhere. Cursing, she lunged and missed but he vanished like smoke. The strap on her right sandal snapped. "My sandal!" she wailed. "And it was my favorite! You are officially dead meat, Andriot!"

Her fury was met with delighted howls from deep in the maze, and then more silence. She waited tensely but nothing happened. Thunder rumbled in the distance as the sun moved behind a gray cloud.

Suddenly, this didn't feel like a game anymore and an irrational terror closed over her throat like a fist. The walls of the maze were closing in on her again and she had to get out. Without knowing which way was to go, she stumbled into one dead end after another.

When a hand reached out and grabbed her, she erupted with a bloodcurdling scream. It was only Andriot but she slapped his face as hard as she could. "Don't you ever do that again!"

"Katherine, what the hell? Calm down!"

He rubbed his cheek, no longer devilish, just perplexed. She'd really hurt him. He was cool after that and walked a little ahead. This was not how she had wanted things to be. She'd acted badly--not very sexy, hitting your lover and calling him a bastard. Now they wandered into the center of the garden like strangers in a museum. She ended up sitting stiffly in the temple while he poked among the plants.

"This really looks like a Greek temple, doesn't it!" she said, hoping he would talk to her but he didn't respond. He wouldn't look at her either.

Stung by his rejection, she pretended to be absorbed in studying the carvings on the columns. She felt foolish sitting there alone but remorse soon gave way to irritation and she decided he was impossibly difficult and why had she bothered in the first place? In fact, two could play the silent game, she told herself.

Then, as if to chastise her foolish pride, a memory appeared unbidden. One early morning, in the cool grey light of dawn, they had reached for each other still blind with sleep, only waking by degrees in the midst of their passion, wholly merged; their minds and bodies melded into one being, in the rapture of tongues, and mouths, skin and scent, the sweet rhythm of moving as one, as if this were all she would ever know or care to know; as natural as being born.

Afterward they had laid coiled around each other in perfect contentment, still safe beneath the waves of daily thoughts, still protected in the half-light of dreams. Words rolling up to the surface like bubbles of air, dissipated without being spoken. `I wish we could stay like this forever,' was what she had wanted to say but didn't. Instead, the phone had rung. It rang and it rang into the empty air. They listened like closed flowers, resisting, as the world hardened around them, all the while knowing that in the end it would have its way. The world owned them more than they owned themselves, and they would pick up the phone, and dutifully put on their watches, and return to the strict procedure of time; life measured out in moments ticked off like items on a `to do' list, their sweet union dissolving like morning mist.

Softened by the memory, she came and stood beside him where he was examining a weedy patch behind the temple. She sighed. "That's a beautiful plant!"

"Wickedly beautiful. Its called Datura, a powerful hallucinogen. There's a story that the American settlers gave it to British soldiers and they hallucinated for eleven days!" He looked at her with a peculiar smile. "In strong enough doses, it'll kill you."

"What are you smiling about?"

"Was I smiling?" he asked, suddenly the innocent.

She laughed. "I'm sorry for— you know."

"You pack a mean punch."

"It wasn't a punch! It was a slap. A playful slap."

'Playful?"

'It's a woman's prerogative."

"That was before women became trained killers.'

"Stop!'"

He pulled her to him and gave her the kiss that she'd longed for. "Is this what you want?"

"Yes," she whispered.

"Then let's go!" He made as if to pull her down to the ground but she balked.

"Here?"

"Why not?"

"No! Somebody might find us!"

"Nobody is going to find us! We can't even find ourselves in this place. It's perfect. Besides who's going to come in here?"

"That gardener, for one. Please, let's just go back to the room. It'll be so much more comfortable."

However, Katherine and Andriot soon discovered that leaving the Labyrinth wasn't so easy. First, they had their usual arguments over which way to turn but every attempt only landed them back in the center. Finally, they had to agree that neither one could remember the way out. Frustration soon grew into genuine concern. Andriot was getting snappish, so Katherine didn't dare say anything about the panic she felt just walking through those dark, claustrophobic passageways. She, herself, was appalled. Never in her life had she felt anything like this. Was this what people called a panic attack? "Breathe through it," she told herself.

They were both on the verge of yelling for help when Katherine spotted an old wooden door set into the hedge and almost totally obscured by branches. "You think this could be a way out?"

"Only one way to find out!" And he immediately began to wrestle it open.

They found themselves in a primeval forest with towering trees exuding a presence that momentarily silenced them into reverence. A sanctuary, thought Katherine. A white feather lay at her feet and she stuck it in her hair.

Andriot looked at her approvingly. "You look good, Kat. You belong here. All the wrinkles have melted away."

"What wrinkles?"

He laughed and took her hand. "Come on. You know you're beautiful."

"Do I?" Katherine wasn't so sure.

He paused solemnly, "You know, I can't give that to you, Kat. Nobody can."

Her eyes misted over with pain. He was right. Nobody could. She would never believe it. He kissed her again, only this time it was simple kindness. If anything, he did understand the real Kat; that beneath her driving need for accomplishment was a big gaping hole of insecurity that she spent most of her energy trying to hide.

They continued on into the dim, green beauty of the forest, possibly getting themselves more lost than ever. But the cacophony of the birds in the branches above calmed her deeply. Life--- this is real life, she thought, sadly. How far she had strayed. Was this what she had been longing for? Could it ever be this simple---not to always be doing but just to be?

"I think I see someone! Hey!" cried Andriot suddenly, waving his arms. It was the gardener trudging slowly towards them up the path, shirtless and bearing a swing blade on his shoulder. He didn't look all that happy to see them for he merely nodded.

"What are you doing all the way out here, man? Digging for treasure?" Andriot was joking but Gardner seemed defensive.

"Working on the trails," he replied tersely. He turned to Katherine with a hint of sarcasm. "So three guesses---you always wanted to be an Indian?"

Her fingers strayed self-consciously to the feather in her hair, once again feeling awkward and strangely revealed in his presence; as if those golden eyes could see right through her.

He smiled coldly. "Yeah, I always wanted to be an Indian, too." He turned to Andriot. "So out for a stroll with the missus?"
As if unaware of the negative undercurrents, Andriot launched enthusiastically into a blow by blow account of getting lost in the maze.

"Yeah, the labyrinth can be real tricky sometimes," said Gardner suddenly aloof. "Real tricky."
"If we hadn't found that wooden door we could be still wandering around in there!"

"Yeah---that good ol' wooden door."
Despite the careful smile on his face, Katherine was all too aware of the suspicious and unfriendly vibe coming from him.

CHAPTER XII
The Art of De-brambling
The Zion Crossroads Plantation Hotel
1980

So what the hell is this son of a bitch up to, thought Gardner, as he walked Katherine and Andriot back to the main house. That's what he'd really wanted to ask. He'd already noticed Short Dude---Jack---sneaking around, spying on him and now he had reason to be suspicious of Andriot, as well. He asked way too many questions.

Gardner didn't like it that they had found the wooden door, either. That was his shortcut to the trail, the final leg leading down into the creek bed that would take him up to Indian Rock. For some unknowable reason, he'd never been able to find this part of the forest any other way but through this old gate set into the hedge. After all that work he sure as hell didn't want these new people to waltz in and find the treasure.

Amanda, Puffy, and the Professor no longer posed any competition. They didn't seem interested in venturing out into the forest anymore; each for reasons they chose to keep to themselves. The irony of this wasn't lost on Gardner. Here, they'd had the treasure map handed to them on a silver platter, like stone tablets from on high. All they had to do was get off their butts and go get it and instead they'd just fallen back into their private traps. Wasn't that the way of it? So many gifts from Life squandered, he thought grimly; he being a prime example.

Gardner had been here now nearly ten months and a very long ten months it had been. In the beginning, he thought getting down to Indian Rock was going to be simple. Gardner remembered his father having pointed it out once, rising like a great monument out of the ravine. "That's what they call Indian Rock, son. See the Indian man's nose and that hole at the top? That's his eye." But knowing where Indian Rock was and getting down to it were two different matters.

Fairchild Meriwether Bowen had turned Zion Crossroads into

a hotel in 1912 and it was known for its riding trails through a pristine, almost primeval forest. But in the 1950's Fairchild handed the business over to his son, Joe, and the long years of neglect began. By the late 70's, the trails had deteriorated. The signposts were rotted and covered over by vines, which made it all too easy to get lost.

The Loop, as it was called, was the easiest trail, and still in good shape but it was aptly named, for the first few months he couldn't seem to find his way out of it. He always ended up back at the intersection where the trail doubled back on itself, creating a giant figure eight---the symbol of eternity. The irony was not lost on Gardner. At the crossover, was a stone bench under a great big old tree, where he spent many days arguing with fate, feeling as if he'd wandered into some kind of twilight zone.

Then came the setback. Oddly enough it happened on the very day that he'd officially quit and given God the whole 'show me' routine. At this point, he was ready to believe that God didn't even exist---or if He did, He was far, far from here. As if on cue, an enormous owl had swooped down from the treetops and led him up a steep path to an opening in the trees, overlooking the ravine. There arising out of the sea of brambles, loomed a massive rock resembling the profile of an Indian Chief. The vestiges of an old sign marked the spot as "Look Out Knob".

But the celebration fizzled as he took stock of the impenetrable tangle of briars that stretched before him as far as he could see. What the hell was he supposed to do now? Cut his way through all those briars? It seemed an impossible task. (In fact, as he would find, no matter how hard he worked, the thorns just seemed to grow back during the night as if the forest itself wanted to prevent him from getting through.)

After this dismal discovery, he failed to notice that a white mist was gathering stealthily in the ravine. All his life, he'd heard the grim stories about what could happen to you in that mist. Panicked, he quickened his pace but was quickly overtaken by a white mist thick as milk.

For the second time that day he was determined to give up when, in a sudden turn of events, the mist opened a narrow passageway leading him safely to the Loop but just as he was congratulating himself, a terrible force slammed him to the earth and everything went black.

Moments later, Gardner awoke alone, pinned beneath the weight of an immense tree limb. Once freed, he limped back to the house, shaken and defeated. The next day, the doctor confirmed his fears---three ribs, broken. There was nothing to do but give him a bottle of codeine pills. He would continue to do the cooking but all outdoor duties were suspended for the time being. Ripping out briars was definitely out of the picture.

His first thought was that he dared not let anybody know about the broken ribs. Fleming Bowen would use this as an excuse to fire him, so he kept it a secret. However, he would soon learn that broken ribs were no joke. His body had suddenly become the enemy. Any sudden reaching, bending, or twisting erupted instantly in knife-like pains. Even sleeping was a torture and the pain pills gave him hallucinations. Not since childhood, had Gardner seen the Colonel's pale image floating in dark mirrors or standing beside his bed, gazing down at him, stirring him from sleep. Gardner threw the pills away and decided to tough it out.

Then Fleming came sniffing around with questions as if Gardner were up to something and made it clear that he'd seen his kind before, always hiding out from the work. He wasn't about to tolerate it, understood? After that it became Fleming's daily goal to think up all manner of hard physical tasks and, though it hurt to breathe, Gardner performed them all, sometimes nearly fainting from the pain.

All of this had transpired late in the fall and had marked the beginning of a very difficult season during which Gardner sank into a brooding depression. If the death of his parents had taught him anything, it was that life ends. Death was no longer just a theory and now there was no one else between him and that final door.

Until recently all that had ever mattered was his career, making the right moves, creating the new 'Garner'. He had, until now, quite successfully cut himself off from his past. It was the progressive thing to do---or so he'd thought. But nothing satisfied his restless mood and that longing for something he could not even name.

When he'd decided to leave teaching and go back to painting, his girlfriend had taunted him, calling it the "most glorious case of self-sabotage" she had ever seen. "Us black folks sure do know how to kick our own ass," she'd said and then officially washed her hands of him.

She was no big loss, really---too cerebral and sarcastic---though she did have a nice body. The sex he would miss. Still, her words had come back to haunt him more than once. Maybe she'd been right. Maybe he was more like his father than he wanted to admit.

Throughout the long winter to come, Gardner had drifted without purpose, his depression sometimes rising into sheer panic. What in the hell was he doing? In the evenings, he tried to paint, but hated everything he produced. Suddenly his angry, fragmented style seemed pretentious and cliche. He brooded enviously over Haden's paintings that hung on the walls in almost every room. He had to admit that he found the warmth of Haden's classical renderings of nature truly powerful and in a strange way, uplifting. He never tired of looking at them.

And the sketches in his diary--- specially the ones of the woman, Abanetha---something about her face, moved him in a mysterious way. He couldn't name it but there was a compelling sadness there, a longing that touched him deeply. Her face began to appear in his sketches. He started to do some realistic sketches---of the house, of the scenes outside his window, something he hadn't done in a very long time.

Though he was lonely, he avoided his relatives who still lived in the county. He'd never really connected with his working class cousins. The 'little prince' is what they'd called him, as a child, when he sat in corners reading books at family gatherings. He still remembered Aunt Harriet, crowing, "Will you just listen to that boy---he sound like a dictionary!" Oh, how his aunts hated to hear Leonora bragging on her darling wonderful Gardner! He could still see those eyes rolling every time she mentioned another of his attainments. They were convinced he looked down on them---which in truth he did.

But deep down, the real reason he wasn't telling them he was back in the county was that he didn't want them to know about his 'up-keep' job. "Following in your daddy's footsteps, huh?" was what they'd say to his face, but behind his back, those eyes would be rolling again with the secret satisfaction that the little prince couldn't make it in Chicago and in the end, was still no better than they were.

Christmas at Zion Crossroads had been a dismal event. A cloud of gloom hung over the household. Everybody wanted to be somewhere else, except for Valentino who was especially rosy. Murphy had bought a turkey, determined that there should be a proper Christmas dinner.

Gardner's first playground had been beneath the kitchen table and he actually did know how to cook when he was in the mood. Leonora had often said that food could heal or kill, depending on the mood of the cook. "So you don't ever want to make the cook mad with you," his father would often say, giving Leonora's broad behind a playful pinch, followed by a happy shriek from Leonora.

Well, there were sour stomachs and a lot of cheerless chewing that Christmas day at Zion, the grim silence broken only by Gardner's unseemly jokes. Afterwards, when Gardner had retired to his room for the night, Puffenberger had come to his door bearing a bottle of whiskey and both had proceeded to get stinking drunk. 'Puffy' as Gardner called him, was the closest thing he had to a friend here at Zion though he wasn't even close to trusting him. There was something oily and avaricious about the man.

There was no doubt in Gardner's mind that the real reason Puffy ever came to bullshit with him in the kitchen, was to filch food when he wasn't looking. Gardner pretended not to notice mainly because he didn't care. As far as he was concerned, all stealing from Fleming was a good thing. But this was the first time Puffenberger had ever actually come into his own private space and something about that made him feel uneasy.

Puffenberger usually did all the talking and that night he was brooding about Frank, the brother-in-law who had double-crossed him. Gardner had heard most of this before, how Puffenberger had worked thirteen years as a regional salesman in Frank's hardware wholesale business and about all the years spent on the road; meanwhile Frank had it cushy in the home office raking in the cash. Frank had promised him a full partnership, only later to deny he'd ever said such a thing then fired him on the lamest of pretexts. By the time Puffenberger got to the part about how skimming 35,000 dollars off the top 'wasn't *really* stealing because Frank had deserved it', Gardner was feeling pretty damned good from the whiskey.

"So how the hell did you end up here at Zion, Puffy?"

Puffenberger sighed. "Well," he said, "it was funny how that all happened." He shifted his big body a couple of times and cleared his throat. "See, the day Frank fired me, I get home and there's a letter from Joe, saying come out to Zion Crossroads. He's hunting for treasure and needs my help. I had nothing to hold me anymore, so I got in my car and I came---only he was already dead when I got here." Puffenberger's eyes blurred with genuine tears that he seemed proud to bear. "Joe was the strangest and greatest man I ever knew."

Yes, he was definitely one of the strangest, thought Gardner--- but the greatest? "So where did you meet Joe, anyway?"

Puffenberger's face softened and for a moment Gardner glimpsed a younger, more open hearted man. "The first time I ever saw Joe," began Puffy, "he was standing in the middle of the highway out in Kansas corn country on one of the hottest damn days of the year. It hit 117 in the shade that day. Flat as an iron griddle out there, nothing but soybeans and corn as far as the eye can see, highways straight as an arrow. You can see for miles in any direction. I remember I had one eye on some storm clouds just rolling up onto the western horizon and the other on this little dot standing in the middle of a lake up ahead. You know how off in the distance, those ripples of heat will make the highway look like it's underwater.

"Anyways, as I got closer, I was thinking--- what the hell is that? A person? You don't often see people just standing in the middle of nowhere…no car, no nothing. I pull up alongside and ask if he needs a ride but he's just staring at the sky. Then I notice it's that yellowish heavy air, so still, and I'm thinking this can't be good. And when I turn around, sure enough there's a monster tornado zigzagging across the plains. I'm yelling, 'Get down in the damned ditch!" It's bearing down on us like a locomotive. I mean, the sound—! It was deafening but he's just standing there, talking. I couldn't make out what he was saying but I swear to God, he was talking to the wind.

"So me, I throw myself in the ditch and cover my head, and I'm waiting, but nothing happens. There's just silence. I'm afraid to look up, but when I do—it's like, what in the hell—?The sun is shining and there's Joe standing there with his arms stretched out. So I says, what the hell happened? And he says, 'It went down the river'.

"Next thing I knew, he was in the car thinking I was going to give him a ride. I figured what could I do? He was probably an escapee from the state mental ward but I'd just dump him off at the next stop. All I had to do was find out what direction he was going and say that I was going the opposite way, see---only he didn't have a particular direction, he was just drifting. We drove for about 30 miles. I tried to get him to talk about himself but he was a blank page. Didn't say where he was going or where he was coming from either.

"Finally we stopped to eat and he follows me into the restaurant and orders a meal. Of course, he doesn't have a dime on him. Somebody stole his wallet, he says. Like I really believe that, I'm thinking. I decide just to bide my time until he goes to the restroom, then make my get away." At this point, Puffenberger was chuckling to himself.

"So what happened next?"

"You're not going to believe this, but after one block, my left rear tire blows out. So I'm going bumpety-bumpety right into the gas station and guess who comes walking up to my window like everything's normal and fine! He helps me with the tire and all the while, I'm thinking, 'Was it him that put the nail in my tire?' Now I really want to get rid of the sucker but it's tough to kick him out when he's being so helpful and polite, so when it's time to leave, he just hops right in same as before.

"I drove straight through 'til dawn, going about 90 the whole way cause I was afraid to stop for fear of what he might do. Finally dawn is breaking and my bladder is about to burst. The light is just barely lifting and just gradually you can start to see that something's wrong with the cornfield in front of us. It looks like it's been smashed by a giant club. Joe tells me to stop so I pull off to the side of the road and he gets out to look around.

"There's a washing machine just sitting there out in the middle of the field and a little further off there's this little doll baby with a pink dress. I'll never forget the way he held that doll---like it was a real baby or something---and the terrible look on his face. I says to come on and let's go but he keeps walking right down into the gash the tornado had left in the corn field until we come to a house. It had been lifted clean off its foundations and smashed on its side about a 100 yards away. You could look right down into the basement and there was a whole family just laying there like they could have been asleep. Joe stood there, shaking all over and bawling like a baby, saying it was all his fault. I try to get him back in the car but he breaks away and runs out into the road. A big semi is coming and Joe lays down right there in the path of this oncoming truck. I say, "What the hell are you doing?"

"He says, 'It's all my fault.'

"'It's not your fault,' I says."

"'No, it is too my fault,' he says over and over. Meanwhile, I'm waving my arms, yelling like a maniac, and the semi is getting closer. I says, 'How can it be your fault that a tornado destroyed their house?'"

"He says, 'If I hadn't sent it down the river, their house would have been spared.'"

"I decided that moment that he was crazy. 'Look, if you hadn't have sent it down the river, who knows how many more houses might it have destroyed?'" I says to him.

"Well, that seemed to make sense to him and he gets up and steps out of the road just before the semi barrels by. Joe was crying and over and over he kept thanking me for saving his life. After all that, how could I not bring him home with me? What I didn't know was that in a way, he was going to save my life, too."

Puffenberger rearranged his bulk, his eyes still fixed on that distant prairie with a wistful expression.

"The night Joe came home with me, my house looked, like some kind of rat had been living there, or a madman with TV dinners, trash, paper cups strewn all over the living room, the couch buried under blankets and dirty laundry.

"You see, not long before that, I'd come home to find a note saying my wife was leaving me for good. I never could blame her. It was my fault. For years I'd acted like home was just a pit stop. Still it was a shock to the system so I'd been pretty much just staring at the TV for the past few months except for when I went to work. I didn't dare turn it off even when I was sleeping. I just couldn't hack the silence. I needed those voices in the background to keep me from thinking. But that first night Joe was in the house I slept like a baby. It was just the fact of having another human being in the house, I guess.

"Yeah, I remember how the bed was still neat and tucked in, the way she'd left it. I hadn't touched anything in that room since the day she'd walked out. It gave me a funny feeling just going in there because I could still feel her, the way everything was still arranged the way she liked it. She was a very neat person. I suppose it was a ter-rific burden to be married to a slob like me.

"So I says, you go on and sleep in the bedroom." I says, "I can't go in there just yet." You know, sometimes I think if Joe hadn't a showed up right about that time, I'd have probably just stayed there in front of the TV set, all covered in mold, a living dead person. Cause I knew I'd blown it and no chance in hell anybody'd ever care about me again." Puffy's lower lip twisted in a terrible way and a solitary tear rolled down his swollen cheek but he seemed too stricken to brush it aside.

Gardner silently poured him another drink, meanwhile secretly hoping the story would soon be finished. Puffy was the kind of guy who naturally assumed others were interested in every last thing he had to say. True to form, he now went on at length, berating himself over the way he'd treated his wife, recounting in punishing detail all the times he'd ignored her pleas for attention and the pitiful scraps of affection he'd tossed her in return. As he talked, Puffy idly flipped the lid of Gardner's box of paints, open and shut, open and shut in a hypnotic rhythm.

Gardner's mind wandered back to the day Puffenberger had showed up at Zion Crossroads for the very first time, along with Aman-da von Hassel, and Professor Valentino. Gardner had been there as upkeep man just about a week at that point, so he was there when they first went out to the forest together to 'find the treasure'.

He was also there, as a silent backdrop, to the muffled consternation and panicked arguments between the Bowen twins. What seemed to really get them all in a lather were the so-called treasure maps. They just couldn't understand how their father could have given them to perfect strangers and not to his own sons.

Gardner, too, was curious on that point but perhaps even more, he wanted to know what had happened to the three 'intruders' that day in the forest. They'd left in such high spirits but each came back alone and shaken, returning to their rooms in silence, never to go out there again. Surely, something drastic must have taken place.

Gardner now noticed that Haden's diary was lying there beneath the paint box, barely concealed. Normally he was so careful to keep it hidden.

"You wanna know what I think?" said Puffenberger with a conspiratorial gleam. Still the lid was flipping open and shut, open and shut.

"What? What do you think?"

As if with a mind of their own, Puffy's fingers shifted the box closer so he could pick through the tubes of paint, leaving the diary totally exposed. "I think there's no f-ing way you're going out there looking for Indian artifacts. I think you're going after that treasure yourself." Puffy gave him a sly wink. "That's what I think!"

Gardner's heart skipped a beat. "Shit, man! I grew up here! Remember? Everybody knows that treasure doesn't exist!"

Puffy mindlessly picked up the diary now, with a devilish smile."That's what Fleming tries to sell me but I don't buy it. Not for one second. That man is ready to kill for it. And you?You're not as stupid as you act. You're educated!" He leaned in confidentially. "So what the hell are you doing here, Gardner? Come on! I'll let you look at my map if you come clean. Hmm?"

"Your map? Why would I need your stupid map to a treasure that doesn't exist when there were tribal people living in those woods for thousands of years! That's the real gold mine, man. There's all kinds of artifacts and shit up there! You know how much museums pay for that kind of stuff?"

"So where are they?"

"What?"

"The artifacts?"

Gardner cleared his throat. What he really wanted right now was to get Puffenberger out of his room before he discovered Haden's diary. "I'm working on it. I'm working on it." He cringed inwardly. That was lame! The alcohol had muddled his lying faculties.

Puffy smirked. "You say this—meantime, you cozy up to Valentino so you can get your paws on his map," crowed Puffenberger, now picking up the diary, flipping idly through the pages. "You think you're being pretty damn slick but Fleming is watching you like a hawk. He's afraid you'll steal the map from Valentino. I'm thinkin' you already have. Am I right?"

"What? Are you crazy, man?" snorted Gardner, as if this were the most ludicrous thing he'd ever heard while trying like hell not to stare at the diary.

"You've probably seen Amanda's map, too!"

"Have *you*?"

Puffy's lip curled. "You know damn well she would never show it to me."

The two men studied each other warily. The fact was Gardner *had* seen Val's map and Amanda's as well. It had been all too easy. The professor was fond of Gardner and had simply shown it to him one day without even being asked. As for Amanda, she was drunk every night and sometimes had to be helped upstairs to her room. To her, Gardner was just the help---an invisible. It had been a small matter to get a look at it with her passed out on the bed.

The thing that puzzled Gardner most was how completely different each map was from the other. There were practically no details in common. Her map seemed to be all about finding the Mirror of Reflection while his had been focused on the Ladder of Success. As far as he could see there was no mention of Indian Rock.

So while he would be interested in Puffenberger's map, he didn't really think he needed it because it was most likely just as irrelevant. In the meantime, Fleming and Murphy were still obsessed with getting their hands on them and it had been Gardner's secret amusement to watch their little games of hide and sneak.

Gardner laughed, hoping that Puffenberger was too drunk to notice the book he was holding in his hands. "You're off in left field, man. I'd never steal from the old man!" Puffenberger belched loudly, self-satisfied. "Everybody steals."

"Everybody does *not* steal, Puffy." Gardner looked him dead in the eye.

This seemed to strike a painful mark and Puffenberger heaved a great sigh. "Yeah, you're right. Everybody does *not* steal. Joe taught me that." He had that far away look in his eye again.

"Great! That's great! Well, I'm pretty tired," exclaimed Gardner, seizing the moment to end this conversation before Puffenberger launched into another long winded story.

But Puffy was not to be deterred. He needed to finish this. "Yeah---actually though, in the beginning I thought Joe was stealing from me."

"Really?" murmured Gardner, his heart sinking.

"One day I got sick," Puff's chair gave an alarming creak as he shifted his weight. "And something sort of snapped inside me. Suddenly here I am bawling like a baby and I couldn't stop. All those months in front of the TV when I could have been crying about my wife and I had to start in front of another guy. It was humiliating. But anyways, Joe comes in, puts his hand on my shoulder, and says, `Is there anything I can do?'

"And all I can think is---raisin toast and tea. You see, my mother had always made raisin toast and tea when I was sick, carried it up to my bed on a tray. She always treated me like a prince when I was sick So next thing I know, he disappears into the kitchen. Only I know there's no tea in there, no bread, and no toaster either because my wife cleaned out all the appliances when she left. So I'm crying, and waiting for him to come back and tell me there's no tea, no bread and no toaster, only he doesn't come back. The kitchen is empty. He's gone.

"So I'm crying even worse now thinking, he got scared and ran out but to my surprise he shows up a couple hours later with some tea and raisin toast. "But," I says, "how'd you make this toast? We don't have a toaster?"

Gardner was about done with the tea and toast story, but Puffy kept right on going. But Joe tells me we do have a toaster! A lady at a yard sale gave it to him, along with a waffle iron. That kind of thing happened all the time with Joe! Once, it literally dropped off the back of a truck, right there in front of the house! At first I didn't believe it! Here he was coming in with gold watches, jewelry, all kinds of shit, and I'm thinking---either he's stealing it or he's taking my money somehow and buying it. So I decided to keep a closer eye on my checkbook 'cause this guy was bound to be a goddamn thief.

"I told myself to get rid of him but at that point I was feeling---well, an empty house is a dangerous thing sometimes. It's so silent and your thoughts keep yapping at you and there's nothing to cover them up, know what I mean? So I was caught between wanting him out and wanting him to stay, all because of that damned silence. I couldn't take it anymore."

Gardner nodded. He did know what that meant.

"But turned out he wasn't stealing anything," continued Puffy. "Though I had to see it with my own eyes before I believed it. I'll never forget that day we were walking down the street and he stoops down and picks up that watch out of a pile of leaves and I says, 'That's a nice watch! What are you going to do with it?'

"'You want it?' he says And just like that he hands it to me. That was a strange experience for me. In my day, I used to steal things now and then. In fact, all my life, I took it for granted that everybody's a thief. Everybody's out to get something for nothing. But I'd never met anybody like Joey before. I never dreamt guys like him even ex- isted! I mean, he wasn't afraid to give." Puffy gazed sadly into the past before resuming.

"Yeah, so— Joey just disappeared one day and I never heard from him again until I get this letter. He's giving me a partnership in this business, see? Because according to him, I had saved his life. I was floored by his offer but then again---not really. It was just like him to do something magnificent like that." The corners of his mouth twitched weirdly and his voice got high and squeaky.

"But you wanna know what the killer of this whole thing is?" he said. "This is the one time in my life I don't have to steal nothin'. He just gave this opportunity to me for nothin'! Nothing! So what do I about it? Nothin'!' Puffy gave a helpless shrug. "I got the map! I know exactly where the treasure is— and still I do nothing but sit here day after day— eating! Food! That's all I can think about— and it's killing me! It's killing me!" He covered his face and burst into tears, his big swollen gut shaking. "They were right. I am a loser! I got nobody to blame but myself! I've fallen into my own trap!"

Gardner reached out hesitantly and patted him on the back, meanwhile trying to keep from snatching the diary from his hands.

"The thing is," continued Puffy, wiping his eyes on his sleeve, "You know, there was always one thing I could never figure out. Why in hell did he give each of us a different version of the map? But now I know---." Puffenberger's face crumpled and his voice got squeaky again. "It was because Joe wanted us to work together! That was just his crazy way to get us to share with each other. That was Joe. Such a crazy loving guy." Puffenberger snuffled back some tears. "He was just so---innocent, ya know? He could never see that the world is just not that way and never will be." Puffy suddenly noticed the diary. "So what's this?"

"It's my diary."

Gardner reached for it but Puffenberger held it aloft, with a suspicious gleam in his eyes. "It's kind of old, isn't it? Way too old to be your diary."

"Okay, it's was my mother's diary. Give it!" He was definitely too drunk now to give a proper lie so he pretended to accidentally knock a jar of his colored pencils to the floor. His ribs delivered a sharp complaint when he bent over to pick them up.

"Your mother, huh?" By his look, Puffenberger wasn't buying it but remembering he had to urinate, he let the matter drop. After two false starts, he heaved himself onto his feet, belched loudly, and left the room.

After that incident, Gardner decided to hide the diary in a better place and that's when he happened to notice a loose floorboard in his closet. Apparently he wasn't the first person to do so, for when he pried it up he found the actual copy of Steal This Book, minus the dust jacket which had been used to disguise Haden's diary. Also, there was an old manila envelope containing several rough drafts of the original Treasure Hunt pamphlet plus more treasure maps---three different versions. There was also a letter that had never been sent, written by someone named Trip.

August 19, 1977
Dear Alexis,
Remember the spaced out dude I was telling you about? Well, he finally remembered who he was and his name is Joe. So check this: now I'm living in an old civil war era plantation house. He owns the place. He was born here and is descended from some old confederate war hero. Ain't life strange, though?

Joe wants to turn this place into a commune, no less and (as the worm turns), Moon's here (surprise, surprise!) He's pushing for some big money making scheme (what else?). It's hard to explain. I doubt if any of us even really understands it. Each of us probably has a completely different idea of how it's going to work.

Anyway it's all centered around this hare brained scheme that Moon cooked up. A treasure hunt with an historical twist, you might say. I get to play a pirate roaming through the woods. Can't wait! (Seriously, no way in hell is Moon getting me into one of those stupid costumes!) Anyway, Joe and Moon are totally swept up in this. I have my doubts though that any of this is going to get off the ground. One of Joe's sons, Fleming, is a really weird, controlling kind of guy---a neofascist if I've ever seen one. In fact, he's stockpiling weapons and ammunition in his out buildings and I'm pretty sure he's organizing a right wing militia. I'm seriously thinking about turning him over to the Feds. Of course they (the Feds) might take that a little weirdly since back in my old Weatherman days I declared war against the government, myself. I guess that makes me a major hypocrite, doesn't it! The real sticky wicket is that I would need to tip them off anonymously. I don't want to get stuck in their cross-hairs at this late date. The war is over!You'd think nobody would care anymore but from what I hear, once they've got a file on you, you don't dare raise your head especially if they think you're a commie. Some of them would just as soon hunt you to the death. (I'm pretty sure Fleming would gladly do the job for them).

When I look at this guy, Fleming, I see a counter image of myself. I mean, truthfully, I almost went so far as to contemplate planting bombs and robbing banks but fortunately I got purged before I could do any damage. I wasn't pure enough for the cause. So the real question is: which is worse? A pinko community organizer power-to-the-people person or a neo-fascist white supremacist? Place your answer in a stamped envelope along with five twenty dollar bills and address it to me. Make it fifty. I'm strapped.

But seriously, the guy doesn't trust me. He's been searching my room every chance he gets which is part of the reason I gotta go. I hear breathing in the hallway (I wish I were kidding). We'll have to talk one on one so I can give you the full low down on the weirdness going on around here.

Peace,
Trip

Trip must have been one of the hippies his father had been writing about in his letters just before he died. It was strange to think that Trip had lived in this very room. What had become of him and why wasn't this letter ever sent? A chill went up Gardner's spine as if Fleming might be looking over his shoulder.

The rest of the winter had been cold and sunless. Not since his mother's death, had Gardner felt despair equal to this. Doubts tormented him and recurring nightmares that ten years had passed and he was still pulling weeds at Zion. Puffy's words had burrowed deep and he was beginning to see that Zion was indeed a trap.

His pride was just about broken but there was one good thing that came about because of the rib injury. He finally understood what it had meant for his father to work until the day he died, climbing ladders with arthritic knees because he couldn't afford to quit. He'd always said he liked to keep busy but the truth was the poor don't have the luxury of being sick or getting old. As Gardner continued his daily duties, in spite of the pain, a burning resentment grew towards the people he served. Sometimes he brooded for days over a stray comment or an ambiguous look from his employers. For the first time in his life, he drew bitter sustenance from small acts of sabotage in the kitchen. It was too easy but it didn't make him happy.

As winter awakened into cold spring and his ribs began to heal, he found himself wanting to hide from the enormity of the task that faced him in the forest--- namely hacking through a wall of briars the size of several city blocks, knowing that it could very well be a complete waste of time. He anguished, he raged. Why did this life have to be so hard? He was an artist, not a manual laborer! Suddenly all he wanted to do was to forget the whole crazy scheme, go back to Chicago, and make art.

But something inside of him refused to budge. No, this was his inheritance. It had been stolen from his family and now the Universe was giving it back. All he had to do was go out and take it. On behalf of the ancestors beaten down by a legacy of failure, he determined that he would never give up. The moment his ribs had healed, he would set to work and that is exactly what he had done. Still, no matter how long and hard he labored, the next day the stubborn tangle of briars were as thick and tenacious as before, as if they'd grown back overnight---as if the forest itself wanted to keep him out.

He had to admit thought, that despite the frustration, cutting out briars had given Gardner a lot of time to think about his life but a different sort of thinking—not the mental gymnastics he'd been trained to in graduate school. Time spent with the earth was slow and empty. Like the kiss of a moth's wings, his thoughts barely touched him. Sometimes he had to laugh. What would his parents say if they were to see him hacking through briars? Gardner? Always so allergic to manual labor?

The vines, he'd come to see as a worthy adversary. He almost admired the cunning way they grew straight up out of the ground, unsupported, like cobras, suspended in thin air, as if knowing somewhere in the nothingness, there would be something to cling to. And wasn't that what he himself was doing-- suspending himself in mid air, living on the blind faith that he was going somewhere?

At first, the thorny barrier had enraged him. He'd tried ripping and tearing at the insidious vines but only succeeded in getting ripped and torn. Finally, over time, he'd come to see the work of cutting through briars as a parable of life itself. Difficulties so often presented as insurmountable are best untangled one strand at a time. Patience requires learning not to dwell on results but taking one step at a time. A book was forming inside of him, "The Zen of De-brambling, a Primer on Living" and it would be a comedy! He would be the dull witted protagonist, hacking his way through generations of ignorance and density, de-brambling an entire history of embedded, enslaved thinking.

In a twisted kind of way, he'd actually come to enjoy this useless labor, losing himself in the sweat, the dirt, the smell of earth, the humming of life all around him. It was a clean emptiness he felt, a witless satisfaction to gaze upon even the smallest square of cleared earth.

As a child, the ravine had always been the forbidden zone. His mother, Leonora, had spared nothing in her efforts to terrorize her young son from ever setting foot into that deep gash in the earth, impenetrable as any jungle. Small children get lost down there and would surely die, she told him. There were ghosts down there, too and a bottomless river and if you fell in, you would fall forever.

It was late June when he'd finally just about finished cutting his way down to the stream bed. From what he could see, it had dried up to little more than a puddle. A decade of drought had done its work and offered yet another chapter to the parable of the briar patch. Legendary fears of the unknown are sometimes vastly overrated. In the end, the hero's battle is ultimately with himself.

CHAPTER XIII
How Val Met Joe
The Zion Crossroads Plantation Hotel
1980

Later, Stephen Andriot went in search of the professor's room. After what he'd witnessed earlier while hidden behind the two way mirror, he was worried about Valentino's wellbeing for something told him that the mysterious brown liquid that Fleming had given the man was not medicinal.

It turned out that Valentino lived in the new wing, on the second floor at the back. At the sound of Andriot's knock, the typewriter stopped and after a delay, the door opened revealing the old man, his shirtsleeves rolled up, his necktie loosened. A few strands of heavy silver hair had fallen over his eyes and he looked preoccupied.

"Hello, Professor. I hope I'm not disturbing you."

Muttering, "Come in. Come in, " the old man hastily pulled Andriot into the room, leading the way between head high stacks of cardboard boxes and bundles of newspapers to a corner occupied by a bed, a chair, and a table with an old fashioned Remington typewriter. He impatiently motioned for Andriot to sit on the bed, and took his place at the table where he continued typing, pausing periodically, as if listening to some kind of dictation inside of himself.

Andriot ventured an explanation for his visit but Valentino stopped him, "I'm falling behind," he said and gravely resumed his typing at tremendous speed. Andriot waited politely. Finally, with a dramatic gesture of finality, Valentino ceased typing and turned his attention to Andriot. "The sheer volume, you understand, is simply overwhelming. If I'm not on my toes, I will fall hopelessly behind." Andriot nodded thoughtfully, as if in sincere agreement.

"This is all highly complex, highly complex," went on Valentino, his beaming composure disclosing an underbelly of sadness. "There's such a lot of pressure in this work, you see. So many details, so much information to correlate." He shook his white mane. "But even so, I have cause to hope that someday---," his faded blue eyes blurred with tears, "—someday everything will come together."

Andriot marveled. Here was a man, once widely renowned for his intellectual brilliance, abandoned in a maze of tangled synapses, and blown neural circuitry, betrayed by the very gray matter that had once made him great.

"Professor, how do you feel?"

"Feel?" The word turned sadly on his tongue. For no apparent reason he became flustered, as if some kind of internal data bank were overloading and threatening to crash. "Simply biochemical responses, you see---feelings---external stimuli eliciting patterned responses triggering a-a- memory or---" Suddenly he was somewhere else, hearing someone else, seeing someone else.

Valentino's mind had been a masterpiece of logic, an intellectual filet knife layering the stuff of life into neat categories. His genius was that of being able to stand outside the emotional realm with absolute objectivity, observing behaviors with a clinical precision that perfectly prepared him for the task of systematizing every form of mental illness into neat categories. He studied his fellow humans very much as one would have studied an alien species, for he was not encumbered by feelings of any kind.

His wife had left him finally after eleven years of having to endure lengthy discourses on the subtler aspects of obsessive-compulsive disorder, the fine lines between bi-polar and simple mania. You'd think it was all the evenings and Saturdays spent alone with their young son while Val remained riveted to his desk, devouring medical journals and pouring out the contents of his mind onto a typewriter with the deadly acumen of a laser. But it was the ballroom dancing that had, in the end, been the straw that broke the camel's back. Of course, Val had never understood why his wife should have suddenly thrown up her hands (literally) and begun shouting, "That's it! That does it! I'm leaving!"

They'd previously enrolled in an Arthur Murray Dance class for Ballroom dancing. "Let's do something fun together for a change," she'd said. It had been her plan for a marriage renewal. It would be something like a second honeymoon, something to remind her of what had possessed her to marry such a man in the first place. What magic spell had taken hold of her mind to convince her that he was 'the one'? Passion? She certainly felt none of that now, not for three or maybe even four years now. Certainly not since the birth when two mutually exclusive worlds had formed: the pristine solitude of his study; and the ceaseless, mind numbing drudgery of taking care of a small child (for God forbid the twain should ever overlap). But she was a patient woman, loyal as a Labrador, and she had been willing to wait---wait until the boy was walking, wait until he was in kindergarten---or until Val finished his Ph.d. She was willing to wait for him to open his study door and put her on his agenda.

The day he invented a system for dancing ballroom, she'd gazed at the paper laid out on the floor, with the complicated sets of symbols and arrows and it had struck her like a hammer's blow. The man simply could not feel---not even the rhythms of a dance. His physical being, as beautiful as it was, might just as well have been made of wood. And in that moment, their marriage cracked open like a nut and she simply packed up the child and left. When he'd asked her why she was leaving, her parting comment was simply, "Why should I bother telling you when you couldn't possibly understand?"

Years later, when he'd won the prestigious Harmon Award for Scientific excellence, he was interviewed for the radio. He did not break down when he mentioned having lost his wife and child. No, it was not until he spoke about the day he'd received a standing ovation for his research that his voice had begun to crack with emotion. His wife had been correct. His work was the only love of his life. Indeed it was his life until the night he met Joe when everything he thought he knew was suddenly called into question.

Stephen Andriot possessed immense reserves of patience which was what made him such a good journalist. He was willing to allow his subjects to open up at their own pace. He was drawing upon that now, as he sat quietly waiting for the Professor to return from his little mind trip. Meanwhile, lightning licked the western sky now bruised by banks of murderous black storm clouds; the kind that had teased them before only to rumble off without leaving a drop to wet the thirsty ground; as if the blessing were purposely withheld. Andriot couldn't know that the lightning had sent the old man off on yet another journey, back to the night he'd first met Joe six years before.

He began to talk.

That night there had been lightning like this, leading to one of the most vicious storms he'd ever seen. Rain poured out of the heavens so fast and furious that within hours the entire landscape had been turned into a raging flood. Creeks had burst from their banks, overflowing roads, and washing out the small bridge at the base of the hill where Valentino lived.

He'd found Joe dangling from a tree. Though not normally given to acts of heroism, Valentino had rescued him that night. With thunder and lightning flashing all around them, he'd taken his small rubber boat, used for fishing trips at the summer lake place, paddled out, and tied it up to the tree. The victim, shivering, and soaked to the skin, had flopped down into the soft rubber boat, causing it to bounce most alarmingly. They were both terrified but managed to maneuver back to his house on the hill where it was safe.

At first Joe had seemed confused. He didn't know his own name, or where he was from, babbling incessantly about *them*, and some kind of mission he had to perform. Valentino's immediate assessment was that perhaps he was having some kind of psychotic break. However, when Joe suddenly started conversing on lofty planes of scientific abstraction, quantum physics, and theoretical mathematics, Val was instantly captivated. Obviously this was not an educated man, but a savant, a rare genius! Excited about the possibilities for research, Val had just secretly turned on his tape recorder when the power went out. In the darkness lit only intermittently by flashes of lightning, he continued to pump Joe with questions drawing him into a discourse on the nature of reality that lasted well into the night.

By the end of the night, Val himself had entered a state of high abstraction---a sympathetic trance state perhaps. Nevertheless, he found himself on a mental plane of such clarity that he could quite literally feel the mathematical identity of any thing that came to mind. It was the most extraordinary thing that had ever happened to him. He suddenly had the power to summon any knowledge he desired and watch it bloom inside his mind like a flower.

He felt that he could have gone on forever, expanding this experience of knowing. In his excitement, he tried to capture something of the extraordinary importance of this experience. *"This completely redefines what knowing is,"* he wrote blindly in the dark, *"and where it comes from. In fact, it redefines what the mind is."* Soon, the overload got to him and he fell deeply asleep. When he awoke, his notes from the previous night were as dry and meaningless as dead leaves. His exalted mental acuity was gone and so was Joe with only a handwritten note to prove he'd ever been there. "Thanks," it said, "for saving my life."

Several years went by and he never forgot that incredible experience. In fact, he craved more of it so when he'd received the letter from Joe inviting him to the treasure hunt, he'd jumped at the chance.

Perhaps this would be his chance to study Joe, perhaps to tap into that exquisite state of knowing once more---that genius state. However, he'd arrived at Zion Crossroads only to find that Joe had died.

For him, the treasure had never been about physical gold. The moment that he saw the treasure map, he knew intuitively, that this was something far greater. The Wall of Survival, the Ladder of Success---all these features clearly pointed to a transformational experience and this was what he hungered for with every particle of his being. Ever since his experience with Joe, his academic research had lost its savor. It felt utterly lifeless to him. He didn't want just a body of information in a book, he wanted to be that body of knowing, the way he'd experienced it that stormy night.

In a sense he got what he wished for but not in the way he would have liked. That first day when he, Amanda von Hassel and Puffenberger went in search of the treasure, they'd found the first landmark, the Wall of Survival---a stony outcropping jutting out of the hills--- but then they'd gotten separated in the mist.

His first reaction was relief. Now he wouldn't have them getting in his way. He had nothing in common with these people. They were on a very low level, as far as he was concerned and he wanted nothing to do with them. As if in answer to his thought, a mist rolled in and separated them. He found himself alone on a path that led him directly to a ladder leading up into a tree house. This had to be the second landmark---the Ladder of Success, it merely confirmed his belief that he was the one destined to find the treasure.

He'd climbed all the way to the top when it hit him---this wonderful state of intellectual exhilaration, the one he'd been longing for---just the way he'd experienced it that night with Joe---only this time instead of seeing the beautiful symmetry of the universe, he was made to see only himself, how his intellect had made him into a machine; how he'd sacrificed his wife and his child for ambition. It was a crushing blow. He'd gone up the ladder a supremely confident man in charge of his world only to come back down, broken, and weeping uncontrollably.

Returning to the hotel in utter defeat, he'd gone to sleep in despair, longing to be changed in some way, to be set free from the prison of his mind, so that he could finally feel. During the night, something happened. Later, the doctor would conclude that it had been a simple stroke. Everyone said what a terrible thing had happened but in an odd way, he'd merely gotten his wish. He'd been set free from his mind. Now he was free to feel.

CHAPTER XIV
Jack and Amanda
The Zion Crossroads Plantation Hotel
1980

"Addiction is a way of getting stuck in little patterned responses like separated rooms of the mind, where pleasure becomes a thought rather than a sensation. It becomes a symbol of pleasure rather than an experience. It becomes a remembered pleasure, that has always taken place in the past not the present. It blocks the perceiver from receiving the nourishment of the present moment, in the form of blessings from the Seen and Unseen. Addiction is a fear of losing that moment of comfort and pleasure, a fear that if we don't pursue it, that moment will never come again, so we manipulate, and we orchestrate that moment over and over and over and the fixation is not pleasurable at all but stressful and blocks the subtle pleasures of the moment."

Excerpt from Joe Bowen's notebooks.

Jack woke late with the usual feelings. Slamming into a wall---that's what returning to life felt like for him every single day. He was thirty years old and couldn't remember ever not feeling this bad in the morning. Surely, there must have been a day when he had risen free and joyous with the sunshine inside of him. He just couldn't remember it.

The muted images of last night's encounter with Katherine on the balcony surfaced like a dream, a shimmer of joy dancing on the razor's edge of disaster. It was all coming back, how close he'd stood to her, the scent of her dark hair and her skin still in his nostrils. But what had he done and what had he said? And more importantly, had he made an ass of himself? Still, hope foolishly fluttered in his veins---

as if he had a chance in hell with a woman like that. Even he knew that after all these years he was still just as clueless as he'd always been.

Emerging from his room just as she had been coming up the stairs---now that had been bad timing. Her dark hair pulled back into a tight little knot had made her look even more severe than the deadly look she'd leveled at him. If he'd just left well enough alone and said something like, 'hello'--- or 'hi'---or 'how's it goin?' it wouldn't have been so bad! But no, he couldn't do that because he was so damned dense! Because his head hurt too much to think straight! "Listen, about last night," he'd said. "Just forget about it, ok?"

"What are you talking about?" He didn't know a voice could be so icy. And the way she'd stared right through him? Two bullets couldn't have left such a hole.

He should have just walked on by but he had to show her how stupid he was and try to answer her. "I just don't want you to think that *I'm* thinkin'----." Yeah, that's what he said and then he saw *him*, the husband, coming up on the landing right behind her. The shock made Jack inhale down the wrong tube and suddenly there he was almost choking to death on his own spit.

She walked away without a word, cool as a cucumber. Meanwhile, the husband was asking him if he was okay and pounding him on the back. The married couple swiftly disappeared into their room, while Jack stumbled blindly on down the stairs and out onto the front porch. He needed a cigarette bad and a few moments to collect his dignity. He should have been used to this by now, he told himself bitterly. Trying to get somewhere with a woman always turned catastrophic and humiliating. Yeah, he had a talent for humiliating himself.

The von Hassel woman was already camped out in the far corner of the porch, wearing dark glasses and a wide brimmed straw hat and sipping down a tall glass. From the careful way she moved her head, he could tell she had a hangover, too. She wasn't wearing any lipstick and beneath the dark glasses, he could see her eyes were bare. She asked him for a light, then held a long thin cigarette to her lips, the ones with the slogan, 'You've come a long way, baby'. These were the cigarettes for all those women's libbers, he thought with secret amusement, as he lit it for her.

"So what you got there," he asked grinning, indicating the glass.

"Lemonade," she said, with a wink, "with a little pick me up."

"Where could I get one of those?" he said.

"Right here," She poured from a pitcher on the small table into an extra glass.

"How did you know I was coming?" he asked, suddenly more jovial. A good drink made for an instant comrade.

"I'm always prepared for company." she replied with a knowing smile. Her voice was comfortable, like smoke and whiskey.

He settled into one of the rocking chairs. At least somebody wanted his company even if she was almost old enough to be his mother. She was more subdued than she'd been the night before at dinner and that suited him fine. Flirtatious, coquettish types always put him off center. For the first time, he felt like he could relax a little around this place. He could tell she was a hell raiser from that scene she'd made on the stairs that first day, so he fielded a comment on the run-down conditions of the hotel. Griping about a mutual adversary usually made for good conversation.

She took the bait immediately. "This place is a joke," she said. "If they ever want to make any money, they're going to have to do a lot better than this. But it wouldn't be like this if Joe was still around."

"So everybody keeps talking about Joe. Who *is* Joe?"

"Joe Bowen. He was Murphy and Fleming's father but how he sired a couple of sons like them is beyond me. Joe was a very special man. He's the reason I came here to Zion Crossroads in the first place."

"Were you, you know, married or---"

She smiled a little wistfully. "Oh, we were never in love---not 'in' love--- but I loved him more than I've loved any man and that's a fact. Joe was different."

"How do you mean, different?"

She thought for a moment. "He was alive. More alive than any person I've ever met. I think he lived more in one minute than most people live in an entire lifetime." She touched the coolness of the glass against her cheek and smiled sadly. "I truly miss him. He always used to say that *I* saved *his* life but I know it was *mine* that he saved. But that's a long story."

"Well, I got a long attention span." Unlike the other stories he'd heard her tell, this one he wanted to hear.

She gave a deep throaty chuckle cut short by a smoky cough. "Well, you asked for it, then." Unlike her performances at the dinner table, she now seemed uncertain as to how to begin. "Well---hell---I met Joe Bowen back in what---71?" She squinted, sucking the last draw from the stub of her cigarette and expertly flicking it over the railing. Just like a guy on the road crew, thought Jack. On the surface she liked to come on all fluff and femininity but deep down, she was earthy and solid. He could trust that in a woman.

She had just been divorced for the sixth time, from Wilhelm. "The only man that ever left me," she told him with a mixture of pride and pain, a brave smile pasted over a tragedy. "Wilhelm wanted a real woman, you know, the kind that cooks and cleans and has babies. Not someone like me. He surely didn't want someone like me. I told him that from the beginning but he wouldn't believe me. I thought I was immune but I fell for him pretty hard and I won't lie. It hurt like hell when he left." She drained her glass and refilled it from the pitcher. "More?" She topped up his glass before he had a chance to say no, which he wouldn't have anyway. "Funny how it hurts even now after all these years. Ridiculous, huh?"

Jack shook his head. He knew what she was talking about. "What hurts hurts," he said.

She flashed him a grateful smile then continued. "So, the first time I ever saw Joe, he was being attacked by a couple of wild dogs in an alley. I'd been drinking alone that night, going from bar to bar. Now don't get me wrong. I'm no man hater. I've been married six times for Christ's sake but after Wilhelm left, I was ready to swear them off for good. I figured I'd be a whole lot better off with my cat and my birds. I figured I hated men for awhile. You know, sometimes hatred is the only thing that keeps a person alive. I don't know if you can understand that but it's true."

Jack said that actually he did understand that, very well--- more than she might think. Their eyes locked in a moment of mutual understanding.

"Well, then you're an honest man because most people--- most 'good' people would never admit such a thing. But I've never pretended to be 'good'. I have too many bad habits." She lit another cigarette and blew out a long stream of smoke before she continued.

"You know, I've often wondered about that night. What was really going on because at that very moment, I had just imagined a scenario in which Wilhelm would be dying in a car accident, and calls me to his side and says, "Baby, I shoulda never have left you." Then of course, I'd be sayin', "Sorry! Too late, loser!" That's how my mind worked in those days. I make no apologies. I was vindictive as hell but that was before Joe. Anyway, there I was stumbling down a dark alley---a woman, alone---stupid and drunk---talking to herself like a madwoman.

"The only one around was this man sitting huddled behind the trash cans and suddenly these dogs rush out of nowhere, and they're coming straight at me. Of course, now I know that my murderous thoughts attracted that kind of energy. I've learned that much since then. Anyway, so there I was thinking I'm already dead but they go right past me and attack him instead. It was the most vicious, horrible thing I'd ever seen. I was sure they were going to rip him to shreds. I was insane with fear, screaming my guts out. I remember I threw my purse at the lead dog and missed of course, because I never could throw worth a damn.

"And the next thing I knew, the main dog was completely calm and this guy is stroking its head, talking just as soft and nice, and all the other dogs sort of slithered away. So I went over and asked him if he was okay and I'll never forget the way he looked at me. It was like he knew me. Of course, I'd never seen the guy before and you know how bums can be, always trying to con you. I just asked him if he was okay and tried to make my getaway but his arm was torn up bad. I knew I couldn't just leave him there, so I offered to help him get to an emergency room somewhere.

"Well, I was so drunk that the only place I could manage to get to was my own apartment which was close by, so he came with me. I think I must have passed out on the couch. Anyways, I don't remember anything until waking up the next day and he's humming away in the kitchen. Right away I got suspicious, thinking maybe he'd taken advantage of me while I was too drunk to resist but then he brings me this nice tray of scrambled eggs and toast, and I felt ashamed for thinking such a thing.   And here I was the one supposed to be taking care of him."

She shook her head, chuckling. "But apparently he'd cleaned up his arm himself and it already looked so much better than it had the night before. Anyway, we're sitting at the table and he starts rambling on about how people sometimes get lost and how he used to be lost but now he wasn't. I thought he was just looney tunes but then he says, 'I think we've known each before.' So I says, 'I've never seen you before in my life.' And he says, 'No, I mean in a past life. I cheated you in that lifetime and I am here to help you now." He said this just so matter of fact, like 'I'm here to fix your water heater, ma'm'. Then he started telling me things about myself and right away I realized that he did know me, in a deep way, a secret way, like nobody had ever known me before.

"'I said, how do you know all this?' And he just said, 'I don't know how I know.' And the way he said it was so sincere, so truthful, and humble that I started to cry. He must have talked for hours---all about my divorces, my ex-husbands, my whole life---everything.

"He kept saying he didn't mean to pry. He just wanted to help, that I was on a dangerous path and he didn't want anything bad to happen to me. So he wound up staying a month. He didn't seem to have anywhere else to go and didn't seem to care. Joe was like that." She was interrupted by a pair of finches, dive bombing a crow out in the yard.

"So you really believe in all that---about past lives?" asked Jack.

"Of course! To me it's only logical that we've lived many lives before. I hope so, anyway---I know I could use another shot."

"My brother is all into that kinda shit. Went and lived in a hippy commune, the whole nine yards---but me, I never went in for that kind of thing."

"Well, it doesn't matter---though I'm getting that you and I have known each other before. Yes---definitely. Hmmm." She looked at him thoughtfully.

"Really?" He felt unexpectedly flattered by this comment and a little awed. "What makes you think that?"

"I guess you could say it's a feeling I get---I sense it. There are things I just know." She sat quietly for a moment. "I wasn't like that before I met Joe. He sort of unlocked me."

"So what was he like?"

She smiled warmly. "Oh, he was---not like any man I'd ever known. He was---he was like a child, sort of innocent but very kind and wise. Nothing bothered him and when I was with him, I felt so different." Her voice softened with wonder. "I felt beautiful."
"But you are beautiful."

The smile faded. "I mean beautiful on the inside. There's a difference. You see, I've never been the sweet and giving little woman in the kitchen type but it was easy to be kind with Joe. I didn't mind cooking for him. I even stopped drinking---for awhile anyway." A lonely tear escaped down the side of her cheek but she didn't bother to brush it away.

"And at one point, I even wondered---was I in love with this guy cua I'd never felt that close to any man without sleeping with him. But it was never about that with him and that's what made it so confusing. Our relationship was just as pure as two kids holding hands in Sunday school. I didn't know how to act. I admit I tried to seduce him one night and he acted like---I don't know---like he didn't quite get it. I was insulted. I'd never been rejected like that before. I remember yelling at him, 'Are you a homo or what?' But he just looked at me and said, 'Is this the kind of box you're in?' That's how he would talk---sort of symbolic. I said, what are you talking about? What box? And he told me, 'If you're living in a box your whole life and you've never been outside of it, then the box is all you know. So how do you even know there is anything but the box?'

"I said I was not in any damn box. I wanted to lash out. He was seeing my weakness---me, the goddess of love and so desperately alone. So I just broke down crying. I cried for three days straight. Three days! It was like a flood of everything bad inside of me just pouring out. I fell apart.

"Joe took care of me the whole time. He brought me soup and tea and toast. He turned on the lights in the evenings and every morning opened the curtains to let in the sun. I was like a leaky faucet. The tears kept coming and coming and when it finally stopped, I was completely numb, like an empty shell with no feelings at all. I asked him, 'What's happening to me?' He said, 'You've stepped out of the box.'

"I just yelled at him. 'What are you talking about? What box? Can't you talk normal so I can understand what the hell you're saying?' I was a mess.

"He said, 'It's an invisible box. That's why you don't know about it. You can't see it because it's everything you think and everything you feel but it's not all that you are. You are something else.'

She stopped short of telling Jack about what had happened one special night, in the glow of the streetlamp streaming in through the window. Could anyone who hadn't been there understand how there could have been another light, soft and blue, settling in around them like an embrace? And, yes, she would have to say that it was love, like an energy, penetrating her deepest self and she'd felt totally merged with him without his having laid a finger on her. He said he'd never come to anyone like this before. Years passed and she still would not understand what that had really meant but she'd guarded this memory like a precious jewel. No, she would not allow anyone to say this was crazy so she skipped over that part and continued with the story.

"Anyway, he just disappeared one morning and I didn't hear from him again until last summer."

"So how did you end up here?" asked Jack. In the shadow of the wisteria vines, the atmosphere on the porch had softened almost imperceptibly. The 'lemonade' was finally kicking in.

She shrugged. "I was invited. He had this crazy treasure hunt thing going on."

Jack's attention perked up. "You gotta map?"

She laughed. "Think you're gonna get rich, huh!" It was like she'd read his mind.

"Nah! Well, maybe---why not? It exists, right? It's out there somewhere."

She laughed even louder, then she grew serious. "You think you know why you're here, but you really don't. That's one thing you learn pretty quick around this place--- nothin' is ever about what you think it is." Her cigarette was finished and she felt around inside the pack for another but it was empty.

Without being asked, he produced one of his stubby filterless cigarettes and lit it for her.

"Oh, my god! You smoke these?" She took a drag and spit out a tiny shred of tobacco. "Oh, well! Beggars can't be choosers. I wish I could stop but that ain't happenin'." She sighed and settled deeper into her chair. "I know I should quit drinkin', too but that ain't happenin' either---at least not any time soon. But at least now I know why I do it."

"Why do you?"

She looked at him sadly. "I drink to keep myself from all my regrets." Then she smiled. "Is that why you drink, Jack? Do you have regrets?"

He smiled sadly. "I guess I gotta a fe Who doesn't?"

She gave him a long wistful look but it wasn't him that she saw. It was that day last September when she had gone out into the forest with Puffenberger and the Professor to find the treasure. Looking back, it seemed so long ago, like another life. She was a different person then. She didn't know herself like she did now. She hadn't looked into the Mirror of Reflection yet.

Valentino and Puffenberger had been at each other, like two roosters, competing in that mindless way men often do. All she'd wanted was to get away from the both of them then without warning, the mist had crawled in, oozing around the roots of the trees, quiet as a snake, filling up the air until they couldn't see each other anymore. She'd called out but there was nothing but silence in every direction.

She'd stumbled upon the Mirror of Reflection quite by accident. It certainly wasn't because she was following the map. The Mist just rolled back and there it was. It wasn't what she would have expected either for it wasn't a mirror at all but just an old stone birdbath filled with dirty rainwater. However, when she looked down into it, a stream of understanding flowed into her mind, permitting her to see herself quite clearly. For the first time in her life, she saw the real motivations that lay behind every thing she'd ever done, the selfishness, the greed, the need to possess, and behind it all the desperate longing to be loved by a man because of the belief that without a man's love, she didn't exist at all.

With a sinking heart, she understood that the treasure was something she would have to find by journeying inside herself—so she could finally learn to love and be loved, not for her body, not for her looks, not even for her personality. Her attachment to all of these she must relinquish and this was devastating because she already knew that this was a price she would be unwilling to pay. Later, it came as no surprise that instead of rising up to meet the challenge, she fell back into her drinking again and with a vengeance.

"I could have been a great singer," she told Jack, in her dusky voice, "but I was a fool. I threw away my chances at a career---all for love. That's why I came here---chasing after that dream. I never gave a damn about the treasure and still don't. But I get here and Joe was dead. Bad timing, huh?"

Why she was revealing all this, she didn't know. It wasn't anything she wanted to talk about because now she would have to think about things she didn't want to think about. She gazed appreciatively at Jack's muscular body, a fine sheen of sweat gleaming on his neck and shoulders, a finely wrought workingman's body. She'd always felt most comfortable with a workingman. Maybe he wasn't really so young and maybe she wasn't too old.

"Ever had your cards read?" she asked abruptly.

"A carnival once."

"They probably told you a beautiful blonde was in your future, right?"

"With lots of money."

The headache had melted away now and she felt more like herself, the self she wanted to be, free and easy and happy. "When's your birthday?" She set the tray with the pitcher and glass onto the railing, and pulled the table between them.

"July 15."

"A Cancer. Hard on the outside, vulnerable on the inside and moody as hell, right? Here. Shuffle the cards and cut them three times." She handed him a deck of oversized ornately decorated cards. He did as he was told.

"Now pick one pile." He did so and she pulled the top card and placed it in the center of the table. "This card represents the issue. Knight of Wands. That's definitely you: a sexual male, aggressive--- impulsive though. You need to prove yourself but you have a tendency to fight your way to where you don't belong. You get scattered, lose focus. You must learn to think before you jump!"

Jack was all ears now. *Use your head for something besides a hat rack!* was all he'd ever heard growing up.

"Still," she continued, "once you're focused, goals are easy to attain." She didn't know where all this was coming from. Ever since Joe had showed up in her life, whenever she did the cards, her mind just showed her things and she'd learned not to question it. She flipped over the next card and laughed.

"What's so funny?" he demanded.

"The Mother Goddess. They're telling you to open yourself to the Her gracious abundance." That's gotta be me, she thought, smiling to herself. Yeah, maybe he wasn't too young for her after all.

"They?"

"He, She, It, Them---a rose by any other name is still Divine, babe. You don't think this is just arbitrary coincidence, do you? Just wait and see how it all turns out and then decide. Personally, I don't believe in coincidence. It all means something. And trust me, sometimes I wish it didn't."

She pulled the next card. "This is above you---in your Conscious Mind---Princess of Cups. A younger woman---an elusive beauty--- someone you can see but not touch, someone you are very emotional about at the present time." She raised her eyebrows seeking verification. He remained tight lipped. No way. This could mean his ex---or maybe even Katherine. Elusive was the key word, he thought ruefully.

"And this---," she said, pulling forth the next card with jeweled fingers. "This represents your Unconscious Mind, the Eight of Pentacles. Interesting. There is a door you must pass through, an initiation. A test."

"A test?"

"Something you need to learn or maybe it's just something you simply need to remember." He shook his head. "No? Doesn't ring true? Wait a few days and maybe then you'll see it."

She flipped over the next card, then nodded. "Ah, the High Priestess! This position represents that which is behind you, moving you forward, perhaps giving you a shove. Again, you have arrived at a gateway. Some kind of important transition. The High Priestess separates the wheat from the chaff. So again, some kind of test. Anyway they want you to look deeper. Lead from the heart." She looked at him hard. "Does it resonate?"

He stared at her blankly.

"Dull thud, huh? Well, give it a moment. At some point, it usually clicks and you get your ah ha moment! So this," she continued, turning the next card, "lies before you---Six of Wands, a card of victory, triumph over adversaries but not without a warning."

"What do you mean warning?" A chill went up his spine.

"There will be victory and glory, but keep in mind that victory sometimes has certain pitfalls—self-delusion, overkill. You might just might want to ask yourself, who is the real adversary here because it may be you."

Jack smirked. This was no news to him. He'd known for a long time that he was his own worst enemy.

Sensing his disappointment, she hastened to add, "Still, it's a strong card in your favor. All obstructions will be overcome." The next card was the Ace of Cups. "A very powerful card, A direct link to Source. Love, pleasure, satisfaction—-spiritual nourishment, maybe. At any rate, no matter what your troubles, it's always easier to bear with a little love coming your way."
There was a momentary lull between them and they both knew they were thinking the same thing.

"So!" She slapped down the next card. "Hmmm. Soon, you'll be facing a choice---opposite directions— absolute destruction or the perfect balance of opposites." Drawing the five of Swords, her eyes glazed over. "All that glitters is not gold," she murmured in a far away voice. "Swallowed pride, humiliation—always afraid somebody's out to play you for a fool. Yes?" After a dramatic pause, she lifted the last card and placed it on the table. "Ahh! King of Pentacles. With the King, there is no compromise. He is Authority manifest. Perfect balance between natural and spiritual law. Better know yourself well when you work with this energy. You don't want to muddy it with stupid shit. Think beyond reactionary patterns but join with Him and you will dance the victory dance."

Jack was stunned. He could have said he didn't understand it but deep down, bells were ringing. Yeah, he needed to prove himself so bad it was burning a hole in him. Here he was, thirty years old and getting nowhere fast for no matter which way he turned he was blocked by somebody pissing on him and making him do something stupid. "How do you know this stuff?" he asked.

"It's all in the cards."

"No, nobody ever told me things like this before. How did you do that?"

"Don't ask me. It's just here." She tapped her forehead. "I just know certain things. Enough to get myself in trouble, okay?" She smiled ruefully and wrapped the stack of cards into a purple scarf and slipped it inside a purple velvet bag.

"What do you mean by that?"

"Just that maybe it's a good thing Joe isn't around. I would have let him down anyway with all my bad habits." She regarded him intently. "You know, Jack---something is happening around here. Some kind of a door is opening. Or maybe it's more like a bridge and either you cross over or you don't. What happens if you do? I don't know, but maybe something wonderful. And if you don't, you get to stay in your trap and life goes on until you die, right?"

"So why are you here?" asked Jack.

She drained out the last of the lemonade. "I don't know," she said, but she was lying. She gazed out at the distant tree-lined river, winding its way through rolling pastures until it disappeared around the bend and her eyes welled with tears.

Joe had been dead three days when she'd first arrived at Zion Crossroads. She'd never fainted before in her life but when they'd told her the news, everything had gone black and suddenly she was out cold. However, it wasn't until later that she would remember what she'd seen while unconscious. It was Joe, standing there smiling, looking impossibly fine. "I'm glad you've come," he'd said. This was the reason why she hadn't left Zion Crossroads. She was waiting for Joe.

What happened later was certainly not something for Jack to write home about. What would they say if they saw him sliding out of bed with a woman almost old enough to be his mother? By the time he was ready to leave, Amanda was already passed out and snoring lightly, mouth ajar, a jeweled hand lying coyly across her pink satin bodice. Nothing had actually happened beyond a few kisses, a few caresses. It had all been rather drunkenly sweet. He felt bad for her really. She'd let down her defenses and it was her vulnerability that made him so uncomfortable. He felt strangely responsible and though she was so out of it that he could have dropped a sledgehammer, he tiptoed out of the room so as not to wake her.

After the tarot reading, they'd spent the rest of the afternoon hanging out on the porch, talking and yeah, he'd opened up to her about his life---not just the kind of things you want people to think about you but the real stuff, the way you feel deep down. After dinner, they'd ended up on the porch again only this time the drinking was of a more serious nature. Amanda was dressed to kill and he had to admit that in the lamp's glow she did look pretty damn good. And sure, the whiskey had something to do with it but illusions can sometimes be useful.

"Often I wonder why it is I didn't marry Joe when I had the chance. I mean, he really did save me," she'd said. "After Wilhelm left, who knows what kind of creep I might have thrown myself at if Joe hadn't come along." Her laughter stopped, strangled in a smoker's cough. Jack tactfully looked aside while she struggled to catch her breath. "Excuse me." She cleared her throat with a loud hack and then hawked it expertly over the railing. "Sorry about that," she said, then continued on without skipping a beat. "Yeah, a woman will do that sometimes when she's hurt just to feel some comfort. Women are weak that way. I guess we need love more than men do."

"I don't think that's necessarily true," he'd said. "Maybe men need love just as much, maybe more."

This seemed to surprise her and they'd looked at one another quite frankly, her beautiful eyes, no longer hidden behind dark lenses, measured his. "You're a workingman. I like a man who works with his hands, out in the elements," she'd said, though she couldn't help but think that the eyelashes were much too long for a man.

Once things got personal, it would have been arguing with gravity to keep it from ending up where it did.

Now he sat alone on the balcony and drank some more, thinking dismal thoughts and getting drunker. It was almost midnight and he was feeling more alone than ever. His life was going nowhere, at least nowhere he wanted to be. Of course the real issue was that he had to stop drinking. Seeing her so drunk and pitiful had disturbed him. He didn't want to end up like that but that's exactly where he was headed if he wasn't already there.

A knot of desperation turned over inside of him. He wanted to get out of his head, away from these thoughts. Where was Tommy, anyway?

Tommy always made him feel better, safer somehow. A flood of emotion swept through him. Tommy was always so patient even when Jack was being a jerk. Tears of love sprang to his eyes. Suddenly he wanted to tell him how much he cared.

The room was dark when he entered. He felt around for the lamp switch, knocking something over with a loud crash. He cursed and flicked on the light.

"What the hell!" It was Tommy shielding his eyes from the glare of the lamp. He'd been asleep and now he was angry.

"Sorry! Sorry!" Suddenly Jack felt ashamed for being so drunk. He couldn't even focus his eyes. "I just want to tell you somethin', okay?"

"Turn off the damned light!"

"But first I gotta say somethin'!"

"You're drunk! Turn off the fuckin' light and go to sleep!"

"I'm just trying to tell you something, dammit!"

"Well, now is not the time, okay? If you weren't so stinkin' drunk, you'd realize that!" Tommy rolled over and stuck his head under the pillow.

Jack would rather Tommy had knocked the shit out of him than talk to him in that tone, like an adult talking to a misbehaving child. He stood there, swaying stupidly, feeling shamed. "You son of a bitch! I'm just trying to tell you that I love you!" He punched his brother hard in the shoulder.

Tommy did not move. "Leave me the hell alone," said the muffled voice from under the pillow.

Jack's anger instantly soured into regret. Why had he done that? He always ended up doing the wrong thing. Still, he stubbornly resisted the urge to apologize. He'd already done enough apologizing. He slammed the door on his way out and went downstairs to smoke cigarettes and brood. He'd made a royal ass out of himself again. What if Tommy had seen him with Amanda? The thought made him sick with dread. He could just see Tommy and that Nealy girl, laughing about it together.

As he was passing through the front hall, the table lamp in the library suddenly blinked on. At first glance nobody was in the room. Maybe a bad plug, he thought so he stepped in to turn it off. There on the table in the greenish lamp glow there lay a long, silver letter opener. He picked it up and a terrible thought slid into his mind. How easy it would be to shove that blade into Tommy's back. That would teach him. A shiver of dark power ran up his arm and into his chest. He felt stronger, taller.

That's when he saw him---a man standing by the bookshelf, dressed in 19th century clothes and wearing long side burns. The phantom locked eyes with Jack and that darkness in the middle of his chest grew so heavy that it hurt to breathe.

"Are you a reader, Mr. Sprack?" interrupted a voice at the door. With a gasp, Jack turned to see Professor Valentino standing there, his rosy cheeks and quiet eyes shining with peace, a halo of white hair. "I couldn't sleep and I came to find a book."

That dark pressure inside of Jack instantly collapsed and suddenly the atmosphere in the room returned to normal. The man by the bookshelf was gone. Jack set the letter opener back on the table with a trembling hand. "Yeah…I guess I couldn't sleep, either."

"Here." Valentino pushed a volume into Jack's hands. It was *The Brother's Grimm*. "A good book can make all the difference." The old man gave him a grandfatherly pat on the head, as if he were a small boy being bundled off to bed. "Sleep *well*, Jack."

Jack remained there sitting in the lamplight, quieted by a subtle reverberation traveling from the top of his head where Valentino had touched him and settling into his chest like a warm nugget. He opened the book and there slipped between the pages was this short handwritten poem.

THE FOREST OF GHOSTS
Before one is free to enter the Inner Garden
One must journey through a forest of ghosts,
Ghosts of the dead past, layered onto the living present.
All the players in your story, hidden behind masks,
Masks you have given them, masks they do not know they
wear,
Ghosts in broad daylight, unwitting actors
in the private Comic-tragedy you call Life.
So when the Enemy appears in the face of your brother,
Or the stranger at your side and the urge comes to strike
out,
Strike back, get revenge, straighten someone out,
 do not be fooled. Obey and you join them
to wander among ghosts, a stranger to your own true Self
Which is pure, Unfailing Love.

Joseph Meriwether Bowen June 1977

Jack sat down and wept. Fighting had always come easy to him. It was in his blood but getting along, saying sorry? That was the killer. No, he was born to be a warrior. His father's people had all been Poles, who'd fought the Nazis from the sewers with such stamina and bravery, that even their enemies had to admire them. Jack was proud to have come from such people. No, all his wooden-headedness was meant for fighting oppression but he was short. Nobody takes a man seriously when he's short. Nobody had ever taken him seriously. They'd called him a stubborn jerk so long he'd come to believe it, when all he really needed was something noble to fight for, a real enemy. Maybe he'd always been fighting the wrong battles.

Burdened by the full weight of his tragic failure as a human being, he slowly mounted the steps back to his room where he stood over his brother, whispering, "I'm sorry. I'm sorry." But Tommy was deep in slumber and did not hear.

CHAPTER XV
Dreaming in Panovision
The Zion Crossroads Plantation Hotel
1980

Despondent, Jack sleeps in the car. He rarely dreams and if he does, never remembers them. But tonight, he is standing in a field that stretches out towards the forests of Zion Crossroads glimmering with fireflies. Wild whinnying cries echo through the dark forest, then with a flash of light, a magnificent white mare bursts from the trees, recklessly galloping through the undergrowth, pounding hooves reverberating into the earth. Heart beating like a drum, he longs to ride her but is afraid. His feet will not move. The horse reels, heading straight for him. Terrified, he falls to the ground as the mare rears up, pawing the air above him. Jack is screaming. "Not me! No, God! Not me!" The horse suddenly wheels and veers off into the woods. Jack awakes with tears on his face and the taste of earth in his mouth.

Tommy is dreaming as well but without image or sound. He is drifting in a sea of blue light. The lightest touch of an invisible hand on his head lingers for a moment even after he awakes.

On the balcony, Nealy lies enraptured beneath a breathtaking moon and so enraptured and not one perceptible thought appears in the emptiness of her mind. When Her Lunar Majesty slips behind the trees, sleep draws her into joyous dreams of running naked through an ancient paradise shrouded in drifts of pink mist, penetrated by shafts of glistening light. She runs without effort of any kind, for her bare feet know every dip and curve of the earth. She comes to a turn and there is Tommy. "Where are we?" she asks.
"At the Crossroads," he answers.
She briefly wakes into a thick belt of stars along the Milky Way, her mind mute with sleep then dissolves into a very different sort of

dream; a dream of struggle, still barefoot but now in the snow. She is climbing with great difficulty, slipping until she falls down an embankment and lands at the feet of a stone Goddess. Again, Nealy asked, "Where am I?" And the statue remains mute and inscrutable then opens its eyes. "Don't you know? You're in Paradise!"

Nealy awakes with the voice of the goddess still vivid in her mind. Transfixed, she holds the moment in her heart, before a third dream swallows her. This time she is standing in a creek, at the foot of a great stone. Water issuing from a cave high above, gushes in a silvery waterfall that glistens with sparkling light. She steps into the sheet of falling water and opens her mouth to drink. A tiny gleam of euphoria began searching through the cells of her body, searching...

Katherine too dreams of a forest stream by moonlight, but it is not a euphoric experience. It is a desperate struggle, gripping terror, and gnawing grief, as she struggles against physical exhaustion, to carry two heavy leather sacks. The muscles in her arms burn, her breath is labored, and the rocks cut her feet. She doesn't allow herself to look down from this perilous ledge high over the water, and then now she is somewhere dark and airless pushing, pushing something into a shadowy hole.

In Gardner's dream, he is out in the woods with his wheelbarrow full of tools, heading for the briars in the ravine. Someone is following him, a gaunt, bleak figure covered in dust and cobwebs. It is the Colonel. Dead leaves hang in uncombed hair, grown past his shoulders; his eyes yellow and vacant, his hand, a grasping claw encrusted with old blood. Even so, he is surprisingly agile, leaping out of a deep trench with ease. Gardner awakes in a pool of sweat.

Puffenberger lays on his bed in the blue glare of a bad late night movie, sweating in his undershorts. He is despondent. Somehow, the current of his thoughts has led him back to the day they first arrived with their treasure pamphlets— the day they learned that Joe was dead. That was also the day the three of them had traipsed out into the forest to look for the treasure and gotten lost in the mist. He's never told anybody about what happened to him there. It is too shameful, too horrible to even think about; and he thought he'd buried it for good but now here it is, staring at him through the haunted eyes of that starving child with bones showing through his skin.

He, Amanda, and the professor had started out together in a

spirit of cooperation but now things have deteriorated. Valentino's huge ego has rubbed Puffenberger's self respect in the wrong way---or is it the other way around? Regardless, it is just like every other rivalry over a woman, in this case, Amanda, the gorgeous slut. Plainly, the situation is quickly going from bad to worse when they'd suddenly get separated by that damned mist. That's when it gets really bad. For a while, Puffenberger seriously believes that he's not going to get out of there alive. In fact, he may have died without knowing it because it feels like years have gone by. That's when this terrible hunger begins, the hunger he would never satisfy. He knows that now. Starving and exhausted, he'd stumbled dispiritedly upon an enormous hollow tree. Ten people could have stood inside. Looking down he sees something metal, half buried, glinting up through the dirt and dead leaves. It is a cauldron. It comes easily out of the ground like a great turnip, with these words engraved on the lip: *Ask What Ye Will.*

Suddenly, the moment he thinks of it, an entire roast chicken materializes in the cauldron. At first he dismisses it as nothing but a hallucination, but it smells so fragrant and savory and when he lifts a drumstick, it tastes so good. He gobbles it down, along with the mashed potatoes, and corn that also appear the moment he thinks of them. Green beans and muffins quickly follow but he is only hungrier than before. Now, not one but two lemon meringue pies came out of the cauldron and so the food keeps coming, exactly according to his will. Hours that feel like years slip by as he thinks up all his favorite dishes until he senses a presence. Someone standing close to the en-trance to the hollow tree—a child, a small child with huge eyes and a swollen belly and an arms and legs, painfully thin. body. Puffenberger had grabs the cauldron and draws back into the shadows, pretending not to see her, sniffing around a chicken bone previously tossed out onto the ground. After waiting to see if there will be more, she'd wan-ders off into the mist.

Puffy awakes on the hard ground inside the hollow tree but there is no cauldron. He searches everywhere but finds nothing.

Amanda dreams she is looking in the mirror and another face clouds her image, a disturbing face, the hard lines of sorrow, the hol-low eyes, the bitter mouth. She turns away. She does not want to see this face nor the other faces she knows will come, like masks, flitting one to another, all images of the self she does not want to be.

Fleming has been lying awake in his bed for some time. A

memory of Leonora, like a thorn in his mind, keeps him awake. Once when he was fourteen, she'd reprimanded him and he'd retaliated by saying, "You would not treat me like this if you knew who I was."

"And just exactly who are you, Mr. Fleming?" she had asked in that mocking tone as if he were just a stupid child.

He'd answered with a cold secretive smile. "I am the Anointed One."

"Then where is the love in your heart, Fleming?" was her stern reply and she'd left him standing alone, his proud smile fading from his lips. This had been the moment he'd decided she would pay for the sin of not recognizing him.

Murphy is also awake, reading further into the Ancestor's mysterious Boke of Shadows. The young Meriwether, as the tale continued, after witnessing his parents burned at the stake for witchcraft, and escaping down to the docks, had been indentured to a wealthy Virginian, owner of a vast tobacco plantation on the wide delta of the James River. Luckily for young Meriwether, his master was a wise and kind man who, when he found that the boy was clever and knew how to read, took a special interest in him.

There were many long passages in which young Meriwether wrote passionately about wanting to better himself, to learn more, to be as good as he could possibly be. Seeing his parents burn had sent the message deep into his heart: Don't cause trouble, don't play with fire. He was suspicious of the Boke of Shadows but took his father's warning very seriously and never showed it or the four talismans to anyone.

By the end of his seven year contract, he was trained in carpentry, masonry, and farming, all the other skills he would need to live on his own. When the time came, his master, gave him his freedom, a sack of gold coins, and a parcel of land in the western region. If Meriwether worked this land and developed it for tobacco and hemp, he could ship it downriver to his master's plantation and he would be paid for his produce.

It so happened, that this land was located deep in the Indian's Sacred Hunting Grounds so anyone settling there was subject to attack but Meriwether was young and bold and smart enough to weigh the risks against the fact that he had no other choice. The year was 1730 when Meriwether made his way upriver to the site, taking with him the small chest of talismans. In the family's official version, the Ancestor had heroically battled savage Indians and every kind of danger to preserve his homestead; however, Meriwether's diary told a different sort of tale. In his diary, he was a candid fellow and rather humble about his faults so he described in painful detail how he had foolishly arrived in the autumn with little time left to build his cabin before winter set in. As it had to be made of green logs, it rewarded him by turning into a leaky sieve just as a miserable and brutal winter set in. By early February he was at starvation's door. He vowed that if he survived, he would head straight to his former master and beg to be taken back. He hated the rustic life and was terrified of the Indians; however, perhaps not terrified enough for one day, in the madness of starvation, he stumbled upon a rabbit caught in a tribal snare. He was in the process of stealing it when an arrow nabbed him above the left kidney. Meriwether went down without a fight and the Indian disappeared with the rabbit leaving Meriwether for dead. Meriwether's sentiments, before passing out cold, were that he was finally going to get to die and end this horrible life.

However, this was not to be for after a time, he felt himself being jostled and pulled across the ground. Gliding in and out of consciousness, he considered that possibly he'd gone to heaven, though he would not have expected heaven to be quite so painful, for he was feeling every sharp rock and branch along the way. Perhaps, he reasoned, he was on his way to hell instead. However, as it turned out, neither was the case.

His assailant turned out to be the local chief's youngest son, who'd been soundly scolded and ordered to bring the wounded man to their camp. Thus Meriwether's life had been saved. Chief Louah turned out to be a powerful medicine man. He'd taken him to a beautiful waterfall beneath a great rock formation which he reverently referred to as the Ancestor. Louah performed strange rituals, applied evil smelling potions to his wounds, and Meriwether slowly began to come back from the edge of death.

It was one night, during his recovery, that he was awakened from his stupor to see a beautiful white swan gliding to the spot where he lay beside the healing water. "Hail, Meriwether Morrigan Bowen, son of your father," she began and turned into a beautiful woman, radiant with spiritual light and who identified herself as Lady Boann. "Welcome to the crossroads between worlds, hidden in the fields of Time and the Dream of Death. Have no fear, for you are yet eternal and eternal you shall remain, just as drops of perfect rain, drawn from the Ocean of All Being, are never lost but forever returning to the One." And she proceeded to teach him about the Four Talismans: the Cup of Plenty; the Healing Wand; the Stone of Destiny, and the Sword of Invincibility. These, she explained, had been taken from this world and not until such time as mankind were ready to receive such powers would they be returned. In the meantime, he was instructed to hide them "in the crystal eye", a small cave at the top of Shamalah, the Ancestor, the great crystal rock beneath which he lay. Struck dumb by her mighty presence, Meriwether lay very still as she touched her wand to his wound and immediately all sign of it vanished.

Later he found himself waking from what he understood to be a strange dream only to find that he was, in truth, completely healed. He went back to his leaky cabin to resume his suffering ways, having completely forgotten the instruction to hide the talismans in the cave of the crystal rock as the Swan Woman had told him. It was only by sheer coincidence, that one day he was thirsty and, having broken the last of his clay mugs, suddenly remembered the old silver chalice in his father's chest. He fetched it and while drinking the water from the spring, his mind wandered into a daydream about wine. He hadn't had wine in such a long time that he quite longed for it and so much so that indeed he could almost taste it on his tongue. The flavor was so vivid that he had to look twice and, to his dismay, saw that the water had in actuality turned to wine.

At this point, Lady Boann's words came back to him with piercing clarity. "This is the Cup of Plenty from which no one goes unfed," she had told him. "Ask what ye will." So he began to experiment with the powers of the chalice, always with the intention of putting it in the crystal cave as he'd been told, but thinking that perhaps he would do it later. In the meantime, he manifested great wealth for himself. From the Stone of Destiny, he learned that if he placed it under his pillow, it sent him traveling in his dreams to far off places, indeed to other worlds. And if he became ill, he would use the wand to make himself better. He had no use for the Sword of Victory as he lived in peace with Chief Louah's tribe.

When he began building his new house, and a much bigger and grander house it would become, he created a secret interior room, hidden behind a moving bookshelf, where he kept the Talismans and his father's Boke of Shadows. By this time he was married with a son of his own and whenever he needed something, he simply went into his secret room and manifested more gold. But he always kept the Talismans and the Boke of Shadows secret, hoping that one day his son would be mature enough to handle the powers, although clearly the boy, having been given so much, had grown spoiled and selfish.

Meanwhile, Meriwether himself grew less and less interested in the earthly plane and spent his nights traveling to the celestial cities in the Otherworld with Chief Louah.

Every evening at prayers, his father would say a word of thanks to Lady Boann. At one point, the son finally thought to ask, who was this Lady Boann?

"She is my benefactress." replied Meriwether.

"Is she the one who gave you all your gold?"

"Yes. She is the one."

"Where is she?"

"Far from here, son."

"How far? In Ireland?"

"Yes. In Ireland."

His son begged his father to speak about where he'd come from but all Meriwether would say was that his parents had died and he had been forced to come to America as an indentured servant and that good fortune had given him to a generous Master. One year, the crops failed on all the neighboring farms and yet their fields and gardens continued to yield abundant harvests and their larder was always full. Seeing that his father continued to have even more gold, enough to build the largest mansion west of the fall line, his son began to ask questions. He was getting old enough to see that one and one did not make two but Meriwether's answer was always, "Good Fortune is on our side."

Now at the time, another tribe of Indians moved in from the south and started attacking white settlers, killing and looting across the region. Yet a secret barrier of peace seemed to protect all of Meriwether's property and they remained untouched by any violence. Meriwether knew that it was his relationship to Chief Louah that kept them safe for though they were a small tribe, the Chief was a great healer who drew respect far and wide. Then one night, his son observed his father coming out of the secret room. "Is that where you keep your gold, father?"Meriwether was startled but calmly told his son that yes, this was where he kept his gold and that when the time came, he would give his son the key to the secret room.

"When will that be?" asked the son.

"When you have grown to be a man," replied Meriwether.

In a year or so, his son, having just turned eighteen, came to Meriwether and told him of his decision to join the British in military actions against the French and their Indian allies. But his father strictly forbade it. "In this house, we serve only the God of Love Eternal," he said.

His son scoffed at this. "Even the Bible says that God is a wrathful god, and will side with us against our enemies."

"What enemies do you speak of, my son?"

"These filthy tribes. We need to rid ourselves of them once and for all. They are nothing but savages, Father, a godless people! And they are a danger to everything we have made here! Besides, they say their sacred mountain is full of gold and if that is true, then I aim to get it for us. This is our property, Father. They don't belong here."

"But they were here long before we ever came and they're our friends," protested the father.

Hearing this, the son grew sullen. "Why can't I ever go into that room, Father?"

"When you are ready and not before." And Meriwether was very firm about this which was unlike him, for until now there was nothing he would ever deny his child because he did not want him to suffer as he had suffered.

But the son only grew petulant. "I'm eighteen and a man fully grown. How could I be more ready?"

To this, his father could only answer with silence. The readiness he spoke of was not anything the son could even understand; and in his heart of hearts, Meriwether feared that day might never come for he knew his son to be utterly selfish and proud. The son bowed and and with a false show of respect, withdrew but that night while his father was deep asleep and traveling to other worlds with the Stone of Destiny, the young man broke into the room. There he found nothing but what appeared to be an old silver cup, a carved stick, and a stone dagger made from the purest crystal; the Stone of Destiny being at that moment under Meriwether's pillow. The Boke of Shadows was also there in the room, but his son ignored it, not ever having been interested in reading.

It was the dagger that drew his attention. He liked the way it felt in his hand and so the next morning it went missing along with his son and a small bundle of his clothes for he had left that night to join the army. Seeing that the secret room had been broken into and the talisman was missing, troubled Meriwether deeply; but he would not understand the full repercussions until that terrible day some months later when his son returned with the militia in force to wipe out Chief Louah's tribe.

Lady Boann's instruction to hide the Talismans in the crystal cave suddenly took on new meaning. He had made a grave error for so long as his son possessed that dagger, he would be invincible. This was something Meriwether knew he must not permit, so the night before his son was to leave again with the militia, ready to travel deep into the Ohio River Valley the next day, Meriwether found the stone dagger in his belongings and took it back. Not knowing it was gone, the son left, never to return for he was later killed in battle.

By the time Meriwether's wife had given birth to a second son, Meriwether had already made sure the talismans were hidden in the cave at the top of Indian Rock as Lady Boann had instructed. Without the Cup of Plenty, Meriwether was left to rely on the usual means of attaining prosperity but he had already created a fortune of such magnitude that it was not difficult to increase it. Still, he had been changed. Gone was his self respect, for he had betrayed his duty to protect the talismans and as a result, betrayed his friend, Chief Louah. That dark cloud of guilt would haunt him the rest of his days.

Then one day in early spring, at a time when Meriwether had reached his old age, he was sitting wrapped in a blanket, warming himself in the cold sunlight. A man appeared in the distance, coming through the trees and to his surprise it was the old Chief Louah, looking just as he had always looked.

"I thought you were long dead!" cried Meriwether, dreading the old chief's anger.

The chief squatted down on the earth at Meriwether's feet, still just as lithe and limber as a green bough, and lit his pipe. "I have been in the Other World," he said, offering the pipe. "Smoke with me, friend, as we have done in days of old."

"I am glad to see you, as well," said Meriwether, relieved that Louah still called him friend, yet shamed by it for he knew he could never be so forgiving in such circumstances. He apologized for his son's actions and said how much he grieved over Louah's great misfortune.

The old shaman nodded solemnly and said that he too felt sorry for what happened but perhaps even more for what was going to happen to white man's people.

"Why is that?" Meriwether had asked.

"Destruction and sorrow, like a bird, always returns to its roost," was the old Indian's reply. And in that moment, Meriwether understood that a chain of negative circumstances had been unleashed that would curse him and his family for generations to come.

CHAPTER XVI
Book of Joe: Part Two
The Marriage and Falling Off the Roof
The Zion Crossroads Plantation Hotel
1948-1976

Joe was born inside out, his intestines literally outside his body, and only due to the pluck of the doctor that delivered him, was he able to survive the emergency of his birth. It turned out to be something of a trend. As if by design, he would always be fragile like a caterpillar torn from its chrysalis too soon.

By the age of three, he was already legally blind and saddled with glasses thick as coke-bottles. Even with his eyesight corrected, his clumsiness only continued into adulthood where it reached rather stupendous proportions. Joe was continuously plagued by accidents, and after a time, the only reasonable conclusion was that it was yet another manifestation of the 'family curse.' No one ever wanted to talk about this, but it was there on everyone's mind every time something bad happened.

By the time he was twelve, he'd fallen down the stairs six times, fallen out of a window (slipped on his mother's silken sheets right off the bed and out the open window), had to be cut loose from a tree that fell on him, burned himself (so many times they'd all lost count), gotten run over by the tractor twice, drank kerosene by accident (he thought it was Seven Up), and got stung by an entire hive of bees---not to mention severe allergic reactions to his mother's perfumes causing asthmatic attacks, not to mention that when he was nervous, he suffered attacks of hiccoughs that could sometimes last for hours---and this was just the beginning of the list.

His wife, Mary Glenn Dodson, a woman tending toward fanciful notions, remained convinced that she should have spent her life on the stage instead of bogged down with housewifely chores in a Civil War era plantation house going straight to the dogs. But it was the birth of twins that nearly killed her and drove a wedge into an already shaky marriage.

She'd never had the temperament for children in the first place and having two just amplified her misery. She became despondent and detached during their infancy. Fortunately for the children's survival and Joe's sanity, Philip, the 'colored' hired man, married a young woman by the name of Leonora, who subsequently took on housekeeping duties and would look after the twins when needed. Later, Leonora claimed that the reason she'd waited so long to have her own child, was because the twins had put her in the 'wrong mood' for children.

Mary Glenn was mostly inert, spending most of her days on the couch painting her fingernails, smoking cigarettes, and reading celebrity magazines. Taking care of the children by her self always put her in a petulant mood. Sometimes, she'd throw dirty diapers at Joe when he'd walk in the door and cry and give heart-wrenching performances about how her life was a disaster. Though Joe was ordinarily a very understanding person, try as he might, he never did understand Mary Glenn. He'd hug her and give her flowers or a new dress and that would calm her for a while, but she was basically too disappointed to be happy for long---disappointed in life, disappointed in her self, disappointed in him. Why she'd ever married him in the first place she didn't know. This was her favorite harangue, and he could only agree for he was not a romantic figure though she said he would have been halfway handsome if it weren't for those god-awful glasses he wore. Also, he was an embarrassment, always bumping into things, knocking things over, forever causing a scene in public.

She was convinced that she was too beautiful for the ordinary life she was forced to lead. She was the kind of girl who could have been discovered by a movie producer in a drug store, if she hadn't been buried out in the middle of nowhere chasing after Joe's thankless brats.   Of course, the worst part was that having babies had just about ruined her figure and that had always been her biggest asset.

It was at a high school cotillion that he'd first met Mary Glenn, a plumber's daughter with a social climbing mother. His mother had pushed him to join, hoping that it would help him get over his cataclysmic shyness. At this point, Joe was tall and gangly, his glasses even thicker, and though he'd lost his stammer, he'd assumed an unattractive slouch, an unconscious attempt to fold up inside himself so as to become entirely invisible. But the cotillion had provided a protected realm where if a guy was methodical, he could learn the dances and depend on getting a partner no matter how dismal he was at conversation.

Seeing the opportunity to marry into an aristocratic family, Mary Glenn's mother had pushed her daughter to strike up a relationship with Joe. At first, the young woman couldn't be bothered. She had her sights set on Carl, the captain of the football team, but he ditched her in favor of her best friend. Determined to prove that she couldn't care less, she now aimed the full force of her charms at the next nearest target, Joe. In the weeks leading up to prom night, she aggressively played up to Joe, throwing her arms around his neck in the hallway at school, walking with him hand in hand, bragging to her friends what a dreamy kisser he was, and how rich he was.

The truth was she was more enamored of Zion Crossroads than she ever was of Joe, himself. She pictured herself walking through the halls in a long gown, the lady of the manse. In a sense, she fell for her own dis-information campaign and began to almost really believe that she *was* infatuated with Joe---almost.

Needless to say, Joe was hopelessly smitten. He had never received such attention from a girl before, and Mary Glenn was one of the prettiest in school with bright laughing eyes and thick curly brown hair that she wore down the middle of her back. But her figure was her best feature, and she took great pains to display it to the best possible advantage. She thought of herself as the next Jane Mansfield or Marilyn Monroe, and she imitated their hard boiled, heavily made-up 'glamorous' look.

The night of the prom, she had convinced him that he was much better looking without his glasses and with those gentle golden eyes of his, he was indeed. Waving aside his concerns at not being able to see, she assured him that all he would have to do was to hold her hand and she would lead him everywhere he needed to go. Anyway, who needed to see in order to dance? During a break, they left the steamy gymnasium and joined a group of her friends out amongst the trees, drinking stolen gin. Later, in the back seat of a car, under the spell of a perfect moon, she gave herself to Joe and in that reckless moment, Joe's fate was sealed.

One month later, it would be too late to turn back. Her daughter now pregnant. Mary Glenn's mother triumphantly set the wedding date, and by August they were man and wife. Joe didn't know which end was up, but he was happy anyway, even if he had now become an official blot on the family name. His hopes for conjugal bliss were short-lived, however, for soon it became clear that the only person Mary Glenn would ever be interested in was herself.

They moved into Zion Crossroads with his parents. Almost immediately, Mary Glenn and his mother, Gwyneth, began butting heads. (It was 'distaste' at first sight. Gwyneth could spot a shallow, self-centered girl a mile off.) Then there came the fateful news: the doctor had detected two heartbeats. Mary Glenn would be delivering twins. Joe was the only one who failed to comprehend the true dimension of the problem this presented and foolish enough to be excited by the prospect. Only later would he come to understand the reason for everyone's glum expressions.

Before the twins were a year old, Joe's parents suddenly decided to retire to Florida, leaving the hotel to Joe. (Gwyneth was through being Mary Glenn's `nanny in residence', never thinking about how she had used her own mother-in-law for just such a purpose.) Suddenly, at age twenty, Joe was a husband, father of two, and proprietor of a deteriorating hotel. It was soon evident that Joe lacked his parents' entrepreneurial flair, and thus Mary Glenn sank into a black depression that would last for twelve long years.

But when Leonora's son, Gardner, was born six years after the twins, that had been the straw that broke the camel's back. He was a beautiful child but suspiciously light-skinned. His father, Philip, was admittedly light skinned as well, but the eyes---like Joe's---were golden, the color of river sand glimmering up through sunlit water. Joe denied it of course, but Mary Glenn wasn't blind. Those were Joe's eyes in that child's head.

Mary Glenn had hurled accusations of infidelity. She'd even demanded Leonora's resignation, but that had only been temporary as it soon became clear there was no one willing to come and take her place raising the twins. Still this had become her first weapon of choice and her justification for throwing Joe's clothes out into the hall and locking him permanently out of their bedroom. (Her rage was only somewhat assuaged when Leonora's husband, Philip, showed her a photograph of his own grandfather who bore the same golden colored eyes.)

She fed the twins on stories that Leonora was a voodoo priestess trying to seize control of Zion Crossroads by poisoning her with those wild plants she supposedly used for 'medicinal purposes.' For a time, she even stopped eating any of Leonora's food (except when it was just too irresistibly delicious).

As the years passed and the business went steadily downhill, Joe's wife retreated into a sullen depression and continued to leave

Leonora to run the household and raise the twins. Then after twelve years of marriage, Mary Glenn decided to leave.

That summer it rained every day for a solid month. The roof leaked like a sieve, and it was feared the whole thing was going to cave in. Every pot, pan, and bucket was being used to catch the leaks, and the air was filled with the *plink, plink, plink* of drips. Meanwhile, beyond the curtain of rain, the backyard had become a rushing torrent. The lawn furniture, toys, stray gardening tools, all had been carried off to the river.

Joe spent his days, roaming the rooms, emptying buckets and pans, followed by Mary Glenn screaming at him that if he'd fixed the roof last fall like he was supposed to, this whole mess wouldn't have happened! The ladder was still propped up against the side of the house from the previous October, for god's sake!

The real reason he hadn't done it, of course, was that he just couldn't make himself go up that ladder. There was something about ladders that filled him with dread. He had bad dreams about ladders. Seven times that day he'd almost walked under the ladder and saved himself only at the last moment. Seven times. The number seven gave him a distinctly uneasy feeling. A feeling of doom had followed him from room to room, right behind his raging wife.

The human mind must have order, and when a person is subject to so many accidents, one begins to weave a personal mythology as a protection against the seeming arbitrariness of fate. Joe was ruled by superstition and quickly learned the old rule: never say never, for as soon as he said it, it was sure to happen---to him.

He'd also learned to be very careful about his thoughts, because they had a way of coming true. For example, on a Tuesday it would occur to him that it sure would be easy for that window to fall and smash somebody's finger then sure enough, by Thursday the window would have fallen and smashed his finger.

Everyone said it was his imagination, but he knew better. He'd read about it once. It was called the 'self-fulfilling prophesy'; however, having a name for it didn't change a thing. In fact, it only made it slightly worse because now he was positive beyond a shadow of a doubt that whatever catastrophe came to mind was sure to happen. This led to desperate preventative measures such as putting his fingers in his ears while whistling and other odd behaviors.

He was equally superstitious about patterns. If something repeated three times, that was ominous; but seven? And Thursdays? Bad things always happened on Thursdays! And *that* day, the day

Mary Glenn packed up and left, was a Thursday. He was so distraught that he walked right under the ladder and didn't even care. Then like a man on death row, he picked up his bucket and climbed the ladder to the top of the roof. It was still raining and not the best time to repair a roof but he was driven by a vengeance towards himself, towards the ladder, towards the roof, towards her, towards fate. So he mounted the ladder anyway, sobbing convulsively, daring himself to fall. The rain mixed with his tears and he could barely see.

It didn't take any time at all. Disaster is like that---one little moment. He took a step out on the roof and lost his footing. His only thought as he was falling to the ground was that at last he could die now and get it over with. Afterward, he didn't remember hitting the ground, but he did remember waking up in excruciating pain with shattered arms and legs as Philip, the hired man, lifted him into the back of the truck and carried him to the hospital.

Leonora had always considered Mary Glenn white trash, a woman more concerned about her hair than her own children and figured Joe was better off without her. But Joe's despair was so deep that she finally wrote a letter pleading with the absent wife to please come back. "If not for Joe, come back for the sake of your boys because now it's like they've lost both parents at once," she wrote. The unwritten half of that sentence no doubt was: and I'll have to look after that little devil, Fleming. A week later, a letter arrived from Mary Glenn's doctor, saying she had a nervous condition and wouldn't be back for a while. She needed a period of complete rest and separation from the family. Everybody knew she'd never return.

After the accident, Leonora tended to Joe, faithfully bringing him food he rarely touched, sitting beside him with idle chat, and when needed, holding his hand. The Bible was her most powerful weapon against any trouble, so she put one on the side table with a sunflower seed on the cover just to see if it was ever opened when she wasn't around. That seed never moved.

Joe spent most of his time propped up on the front porch. Indoors, the walls made his thoughts go round and round in a mad rage. Out of doors, he just felt empty like everything that he had ever been had been crushed into clean dust and carried off on the wind. He was like an abandoned house boarded up and vacant, the voices of his household echoing down the long dark hallways of his mind. His sons soon learned there was nobody home and left him to himself.

"It's all them painkillers," Leonora would say, plumping up the pillows under his broken legs and refilling his water glass. "You won't feel like yourself until you're offa them things." But her optimism failed to make a dent in his gloom. It was so unlike him not to nod or acknowledge her comment in any way. She'd always liked Mr. Joe. He wasn't in the least bit mean, always treated her well. She really did hate to see him like this, looking so lost, and she only hoped and prayed he wasn't thinking about doing something crazy like, well, she didn't even want to say the word.

When Joe disappeared inside the wreckage that had become his life, he started remembering things--- little things, words spoken, opportunities missed, little dark pinpricks of pain, pushing doggedly through like tiny ants and he was far away, just watching them. At times, he heard his grandmother's voice, just as clear as if she were sitting beside him. Sometimes, she'd sing like she used to do when he was young, but mostly she was talking. He couldn't always tell what she was saying because the numbness was like a haze all around him, but he sensed that she was trying to tell him something important. He'd loved her probably more than he'd ever loved anyone. Granny Irene was a plain spoken woman, raised among illiterate Scotch Irish mountain folk, and though she'd never learned to read, she was wise from the ground up.

He brooded. Everyone had said, "poor Joe---more bad luck." Yet, this was no ordinary bad luck governed by chance but almost a deliberate misfortune being imposed upon him. He thought a lot about the Curse in those days after the accident, about Fate. All his life, he'd sort of assumed that this was just the way his life was supposed to be, fraught with peril and doomed to failure. But now he sensed something more terrifying than any catastrophe; that perhaps there were those who lived peacefully, successfully, even happily. That this could be true was almost too much for him to bear. For life to be a misery was one thing when it was shared by all, but to think that some could escape and that he had not, made him feel like a man starving outside a banquet hall. Yes, he'd known plenty of people who did not share his fate. And now a question rose up out of the dull wonder, bludgeoned, and drunk on pain and codeine, into an anger sharp as blood, "Why? Why me?"

Everyone knew that Leonora wielded the only real authority in the house. Joe was just a figurehead. She was the one making all the decisions about the house, the money, about Joe's hospital business, his doctor's appointment and about the care and discipline of the twins.

From the age of twelve when his mother had walked out, Fleming had been butting heads with Leonora. It was clear that he did not respect her or his father. "You're not my mother" was Fleming's standard retort whenever she corrected him. Leonora could have commented on the fact that his mother never bothered to write or call or even invite her sons to come for a visit, but that would have been too cruel. But despite the fact that Fleming was not remotely likable, she felt sorry for him.

And as for Murphy, well he was nothing short of pitiful, just like his father, skinny and uncoordinated with those gosh awful eyeglasses that made his eyes look big as eggs. He was forever falling down and breaking a tooth or a bone, just a calamity waiting to happen.

She'd decided a long time ago, she was doing this job for the Lord because it certainly wasn't for money or for the thanks she got from anybody. That she knew she would never get, but that boy Fleming made the job harder than it needed to be.

For example, she knew beyond a shadow of a doubt that Fleming was hitting little six-year old Gardner when she wasn't looking and doing other bad things and blaming Gardner for it. Gardner was forever running in, crying that Fleming had done this and done that! And there'd be Fleming just as cool as a cucumber, with an airtight alibi, looking innocent as the driven snow. And then there was the time he'd locked Gardner up in the root cellar of the old summer kitchen ---a dark dank hole in the ground, full of spiders and rats. Thank God she'd heard Gardner's sobs or who knows how long Fleming would have kept him down there!

For that she'd given Fleming a whipping he would never forget. She didn't care what anybody said, no little white monster was going to abuse her child. She'd marched right out into the yard and when she'd confronted him, Fleming had just smiled that contemptuous little smile that made her see red. She'd grabbed him by the hair and yanked him right off the swing. He'd whooped and hollered plenty, fighting like a little cat but she was stronger, and held him with one hand and beat his backside as hard as she could with the other.

"Don't you *ever* mess with my child again, or I'll beat you so you won't never set down for a week! You hear me?" He'd twisted out of her hands and run off, yelling, "Get your sorry black hide away from me!" She'd run after him but he was too quick. In a rage, she'd thrown a bucket after him and missed, then collapsed on a bench and wept. She'd never been so angry or so close to losing all self control in all her life. Her hand had hurt for three days after. Things always had a way of getting ugly around that boy, Fleming.

Joe had apologized for his son. He'd called it 'indefensible behavior,' but that didn't change anything. He still couldn't control him. Nobody could. And then Fleming had gone and poisoned that old stray dog that had been hanging around the place. She'd found it in convulsions in the back yard with all three of the children standing around watching.

Fleming, just as cocky as he could be, claimed it was a scientific experiment but when she'd pulled young Murphy aside and made him tell, she'd gotten the real story. Fleming had given the dog poison. And then little Gardner had relayed that there had been other animals as well---mice, rats, even cats. She'd spanked her son just for being a part of the whole thing and sent him off to bed, crying. She'd given Murphy a good talking to as well though she couldn't bring herself to spank him. He'd fallen off the porch and broke his arm just a few days before and still had a big bruise on his forehead. He looked too pitiful to punish, besides it was Fleming who was the real culprit.

That was the day she'd headed up to Fleming's attic bedroom to find that he'd put a lock on his door. She'd pounded on the door, and shouted threats but to no avail. He refused to open it. In a rage, she went to find Joe who was sitting in a lawn chair under the shade tree beside the house.

"You have got to do something, Mister Joe! Fleming just killed a dog! Poisoned him! And he's locked his door! Won't let nobody in! Lord only knows what he's doing up there! Mr. Joe, I won't have that! I won't have a twelve year old boy shutting me out!"

But Joe said nothing as he was transfixed by two dragonflies mating on a leaf floating in an old rain barrel under the eaves. Her words were tearing small holes in the stillness and he just wished she would go away.

Her husband, Philip, had tried to draw her away, saying, "It was just a boyish prank. Boys will do cruel things at this age. It's in their nature!" But it was more to protect Joe from upset for who knew what could happen to him if he went over the edge again.

But Leonora refused to calm down. "This is not natural. I'm telling you he enjoyed watching that dog suffer! Now that ain't right!" From then on, she would argue that he needed to be sent to reform school but talking to Joe was like talking to the wind. She would wage a lonely campaign, pitted against Fleming in an unspoken war that would last the rest of her life. She was not one to give up when she knew she was right, and she knew there was something wrong with him---bad wrong. There was absolutely no remorse in Fleming's character. Consequently, there was no way she could ever make him sorry for what he did and that frightened her right down to her core.

"I hope you're going to do something about this," continued Leonora, careful to leave the 'for once' off the end of that sentence replacing it instead with a heartfelt sigh. She'd had to bite her tongue more times than she could count when Joe delivered his tepid 'disciplinary talks'. Joe muttered something indistinct. He was really too far away to care.

"...and what are you gonna do about your own self? Mr. Joe? Are you listenin' to me?" Her voice broke through the spider webs wrapped around his mind like a shaft of cold hard sunlight.

He blinked stupidly, trying to think. "I don't know."

She put her hands on her hips and contemplated him for a moment. Her practical no-nonsense nature had given her an unerring contact with reality that spared no one. "You gotta pull yourself together, Mr. Joe. How long you gonna sit here in no man's land grievin' over that woman? She ain't worth it! You know it and I know it."

"Really?" Joe spoke like a child whose mind was still thick with sleep.

"Lord, I knew it from the first moment I laid eyes on that Miss Finger Nail Polish Queen! I never seen anybody spend so much time polishing her nails as that woman. Seemed like that was just about the only thing she ever cared about. She certainly never gave that kind of attention to your kids. In my book, that ain't no woman to grieve over. Now that she's gone, I say let's have a party!"

For a moment it looked like Joe was breaking down again, but in fact, he was laughing. It just hurt to laugh.

Leonora joined him, her rich, booming laughter rolling out like a force of nature shaking up the dark. Then she gathered up the used dishes and left him to stare into the empty afternoon. A shapeless form moved in the darkness of his mind, turning it inside out. Something was trying to get out into the light of day but just what it was he couldn't say.

After that conversation with Leonora, Joe started to improve. Daily, he showed signs of returning to his normal self. In the evenings, he watched television with the boys. He started to laugh again. The relief felt throughout the household was palpable. The windows were open again. There was a sun shining after all. It had been two long years.

Joe started making plans--minor plans--but plans just the same, for new improvements to the house, better advertising to bring in customers again. With help from Philip and Leonora, he made lists of things to be fixed, supplies to be bought. The house needed paint, the kitchen and bathrooms needed plumbing work; also the annex needed new mattresses in every room. He drew up the Master Plan, a new improved Zion Crossroads. They would need to hire another person eventually but, in the meantime, he and the boys would get outside and help Philip to get the ornamental gardens back in shape. Zion Crossroads had always been known for its gardens. It wouldn't get done over night but these were the things that had always set Zion Crossroads Plantation Hotel apart from the competition. His mother had been an avid horsewoman and Zion had always been known for its riding trails. He would fill the stables again and refurbish the trails.

The sticking point was as always the money. Hospital bills and now alimony payments had made serious dents in the trust funds (stock interests left over from his mother's inheritance, mainly.) Despite this, Joe was surprisingly optimistic. He had a new lease on life. He was turning his back on the past and stepping into the future. More than anything, Joe needed something to work for, a direction, a goal. The fact that he'd never been much of a businessman had been a serious disappointment to his parents. They'd been such dynamic business people. Maybe now he would finally make something of himself. He took out a second mortgage on Zion Crossroads so he could get the money he needed to forge ahead.

He was still afraid of ladders, however. Everyone could see that though they pretended not to notice when he'd come up with any available excuse not to climb one. To short circuit the problem, Philip would always volunteer first, despite his arthritic knees, and if he wasn't around, Leonora would do it. Nobody wanted to see Joe sweat it out and more than that, no one wanted to see him fall for deep down everybody knew he was accident prone as ever. The only thing that had truly changed was his attitude. He remained stubbornly cheerful regardless of how many times he stumbled or broke this or dropped that. He was making a determined effort now to be positive.

And things were proceeding fairly well until one rainy day in March.

Joe decided to go into town to pick up some supplies at the

hardware store. On the way back, he stopped into the little café for a cup of coffee. He noticed an old man sitting in the back. He was small and spidery with a wispy white beard and a nut-brown complexion, as if cured by the sun and the wind. From where Joe sat in his usual booth, he could see the top of the man's head. The thin wiry gray hair stood up off the scalp in careless drifts, as if the man had just gotten up from a nap and hadn't bothered to comb it.

Something about the old man made Joe anxious, and he had to use every ounce of will power not to get up and leave, but he convinced himself that it was crazy to think like that. However, when he did get up, the old man got up as well and followed him to the register and then the man smiled and gave Joe a sly wink that sent tremors of terror up his spine.

Joe forced himself to nod to the old man in a cordial yet distant manner and pretended not to notice when the old man followed him out onto the sidewalk. He turned down Washington Street, and soon was in a full-blown panic when the man did likewise, keeping just a few paces behind. Joe quickened his pace, just short of a run, and ducked into a shoe store. The old man lingered outside, pretending to look at the shoes in the window, but Joe sensed that he was really waiting for him. Was he a mad man, one of those psychotic killers?

Joe tried on about nine pairs of shoes before the old man finally disappeared. Joe felt obliged to buy a pair though he could ill afford it and headed back out onto the street. It was empty in both directions. Relief, verging on euphoria surged through him. He stepped lightly down the sidewalk and turned onto Maple Street where he'd parked his car and there stood the little man, leaning up against a tree. He smiled and waved.

Like someone imprisoned in a bad dream, Joe wallowed through heavy air the final ten paces to the car. Thank God he'd left it unlocked. He turned the ignition and drove off, tires squealing and panic roaring in his ears like a locomotive. He need not explain this--- not even to himself. He just had to get away, get far away, and never look back.

When the red car swerved into his lane, he did not see his whole life in review. Instead, he saw the little white haired man sitting up in an oak tree, eating an apple. Then everything went black.

The twins were fourteen years old the first time Joe disappeared. It wasn't long after the car accident. After spending six weeks in a coma in the intensive care unit, he woke up one day, and asked for some Hawaiian Punch. Leonora drove him home and put him in his old hospital bed in the living room. It was summer and very hot. The twins came and sat beside his bed and watched TV but nobody had much to say. Two weeks later when he was feeling stronger, he drove back into town and didn't return for six months.

The entire household was thrown into chaos. Leonora had the police looking for him in ditches and local bars even though Joe had never been a drinker (though his life had given him plenty of reason). Finally the Sheriff organized a manhunt. Men and dogs combed the forest, but after several days the sheriff had to call the whole thing off. Local myths about the Colonel's ghost had the men on edge, and there had been unsettling experiences in the Mist that no one wanted to discuss.

In the end, the Sheriff couldn't say whether Joe wasn't still out there, maybe laying at the bottom of that ravine, but there was no possible way to get through all the briars that formed an impenetrable barrier on either side.

"If truth be told, Miz Leonora, I can't find nobody willing to go back into that forest," he told her. A month passed, and they could only assume Joe was dead. Maybe he'd fallen into the river and drowned. Maybe he'd killed himself. Maybe his body was somewhere in the mountains, slowly decomposing where no one would ever find him.

Leonora called Mary Glenn and told her the bad news. Mary Glenn's response was that she couldn't possibly take the boys right now. She was going through some kind of therapy, and her nerves just couldn't handle it. But her sister let slip the real story. Mary Glenn was getting married again and moving to Texas. She'd found a rich oilman.

The boys would never see her again, and as far as Leonora was concerned, this was no big loss. In the two years since their mother had been gone, the woman had only called a couple times, usually saying things like, "I bet the girls are all over you boys by now that you're so big and handsome. I bet I couldn't beat those girls off with a stick! My little men! I'm so proud of you!"

When Murphy would ask was she coming home for their birthday, she'd call him honey and then whine about her bad back being too messed up too travel. Then she'd pour on more 'sugah' and 'sweetie pie'. "Lordy, this bill is going to cost me an arm and a leg. Honey, I gotta go. Happy Birthday, sugah!"

She wouldn't call again until Christmas and that was just to say that the presents would probably be coming a little late. Packages would arrive just after New Year's Eve containing things like turtle necks that squeezed their necks so they couldn't breathe, and pants that were up around their ankles.

Leonora felt sick about the whole situation. Some days she told the boys that their father had probably just gone off to be by himself for a while or to visit his cousin in North Carolina. On other days, she'd say that maybe he'd had some kind of accident and couldn't get in touch. Secretly, she feared he'd finally done away with himself. What made it all even more unsettling was that not one month before his disappearance, he'd given her power of attorney over his estate and guardianship of the boys. Leonora could only assume he'd known all about Mary Glenn's re-marriage and just plain given up.

One month later, Leonora decided they had no choice but to conduct some kind of memorial service. The funeral director said it wasn't totally unprecedented to have a funeral without a body, for instance in wartimes. He didn't want to mention the other reason. She put an obituary in the papers hoping it would bring in some distant relative she didn't know about.

The day of the memorial service arrived, and there was still no word from any distant cousins. Mary Glenn had sent her excuses. She had chronic migraines and couldn't travel. Undaunted, Leonora prepared a feast and along with the twins, Philip, and Gardner, set off to Sunnyside Baptist Church. There a whole congregation sat and listened thoughtfully as she and Philip and the Reverend Gaines testified to what a fine man Joseph Meriwether Bowen had been. The suffering of the Biblical Job was the subject of the preacher's sermon, which everyone agreed seemed fitting for one so ill fated. Fleming and Murphy were the only white faces in the crowd.

Towards the end of the service, a disturbance at the back of the church caused everyone to turn around. At the door stood a man silhouetted against the blazing sun pouring in from behind him. Thinking maybe this was perhaps some long lost cousin, Leonora hurried down the aisle to greet him, only to find that it was none other than Joseph Meriwether Bowen himself.

Whispers of amazement rippled amongst the congregation. "Praise God! Praise God! He's alive! It's a miracle!" How was it that he'd managed to appear just at this particular moment and where had he been? Hands were pulling him towards the front, but he shrank back into the foyer, as if to avoid the glare of all the attention. Amidst a general hum of consternation, Leonora quickly drew him into the dim seclusion of the church office where all the choir robes were hung and shut the door. Joe was pale and trembling.

"Where have you been?" She knew she sounded like a mother accusing a bad child but she couldn't help it. Without a word, he'd just up and left her with the full responsibility of those very difficult children (there was another word which a Christian woman could not use); and all this anxiety and worry not to mention the trouble of setting up this memorial service and fixing all that food! She thought about the food. All that work! She had to sit down!

To give him credit, Joe was apologetic to such an extent that she wound up begging him not to be so hard on himself. In the final analysis though what she really wanted to know was what on earth had happened?

"That's just it! I don't know." His golden eyes magnified through the thick lenses of his glasses looked monstrous and frightened. But though he acted like a nervous wreck he was tanned and had put on weight. Details like that did not escape Leonora's attention..

"What do you mean you don't know?"

He raised his voice forcefully, "I mean I do not know! It's all gone! Everything---erased! All of it!" He sank into a chair and ran trembling fingers through his wiry hair. He was in a cold sweat and breathing fast. "Last thing I remember I was going into town to pick up some nails, and next thing I knew, I was somewhere in Newport News. He tossed a newspaper folded to his obituary down onto the table beside her. "That paper says October. How can it be October? It's supposed to be April!"

"We thought you was dead, Mr. Joe," she said.

He broke down and wept like a child.

Through all the troubles she'd nursed him through, she'd never seen him cry like this, and it frightened her. She stretched out a consoling hand and said how it was all right, but it was an empty gesture. She didn't believe it for a minute. However, one thing was for sure, she said. Joe needed to be examined by a doctor. Maybe there was something medically wrong.

"Yeah, like I flipped my lid."

"No I mean maybe there's some kind of--- I don't know--- medical explanation. Some kind of condition, you know? Maybe some pills he can give you? They got pills for everything these days."

Joe would have laughed if he hadn't been so miserable. "Just don't let them do that electric shock stuff on me. Please! I'd rather you shoot me than go through all that."

Leonora dismissed this with a flurry of pats and 'Oh, come now's', but in truth his words disturbed her deeply. She'd always been a firm believer that no trouble was too big for the Lord, but Joe's desolation alarmed her. He was slipping away, and maybe she wouldn't be able to pull him back this time. Then who would be stuck with the twins? Maybe it was selfish of her, but suddenly she was in no mood to beat around the bush.

"Mr. Joe, you gotta snap out of this and stop all this crazy talk! You've got to straighten up and find your backbone! You're a man, ain't ya? If God gave man dominion over the earth and all its creatures, surely he can give you dominion over your own self. Now it's time to take it!"

"I can't! It's too much! It's too much!" He was writhing in self pity, and she really just wanted to slap him silly, but managed to compose herself and continue in a milder tone. "Now we don't need to think on everything all at once; just figure out what comes next. If we just put it in the Lord's hands, tomorrow will take care of its self." She lifted up her hands as if releasing an invisible burden into the air.

Joe raised a tear stained face filled with gratitude and pain. "I thank God for you, Leonora. Without you, I'd---!"

"Oh now, now---." She pulled a tissue out of her sleeve and handed it to him. "Like I said, we'll just take it one step at a time, and tomorrow see what the doctor says." Joe nodded. The simplicity of this notion was somehow comforting to them both.

Amnesia was the doctor's pronouncement. It had to be. A man doesn't sustain seven concussions without some consequence. Joe and Leonora smiled at each other as if this were good news.

"Well, then I'm not crazy!" Joe said.

"No, you're not crazy!" The doctor smiled, too. And then all the smiles dimmed a bit.

"So now what do I do?" Joe asked.

The doctor shrugged. "We'll just have to take this thing one step at a time, Joe."

Joe and Leonora looked at one another and nodded. They had already figured that much out.

Fleming, unlike Murphy who wept and carried on, showed no outward sign that he was glad when his father returned after his first disappearance (or as they would come to call them, 'his amnesia trips'). Joe had not been a good father. In all fairness, it is hard when one is treading water in a constant flood of calamity. His attention had always been chiefly upon himself and his troubles, and so he didn't really seem to notice Fleming's cold detachment. Besides, there was enough attention from others to make Joe feel welcome. Even a reporter from a local paper came to do the inside story of an amnesiac. (Leonora shooed him away.)

Part of the problem was that during Joe's absence, Fleming had begun to see himself as the man of the house. He was nearly fifteen years old and had decided his father really was the moron his mother had always made him out to be. ('Jack-ass' was what Mary Glen had always called him, as in `what has the jack-ass done now?"). That's how she talked about her children's father and she didn't care who heard it, least of all Joe.  She said, `Hell's Bells' all the time, too. Leonora had washed Fleming's mouth out with soap more than once for saying that one. She said only trashy people talk trashy talk, and it was no secret that she thought Mary Glenn was just a social climbing piece of white trash. Mary Glen despised her in turn, and so the two had learned to avoid each other like commanders of opposing camps, with the kids bouncing back and forth between contradictory orders. "Mama says we can have cookies anytime we want to!"
"Not in my kitchen you don't! Now get your behind out in the yard and don't come back in 'til I call you for lunch!"
Or "Leonora says we got to take a bath and go to bed."
"Well Leonora don't know every damn thing . Come here and give yo' mama her back rub, sugah."

Perhaps it was an indication of the trouble yet to come, that Mary Glenn had changed her hair color three times that last summer at Zion Crossroads; but Fleming had been aware of the turmoil in the household long before that. Up until the age of nine, the emotional storms and icy periods of silence between his parents had never seemed anything other than completely normal to him. But suddenly, when he was nine that had all changed. His mother began to get migraines on a weekly basis, and would go into seclusion in her bedroom, the shades drawn against the light. She'd lie on the big four-poster bed with an ice pack over her eyes. The least little noise could send her into convulsions of pain and muttered threats that were not very motherly.

As a young child, his mother had regarded Fleming as a demanding, uncompromising creature, whose only purpose was in making her life a living hell. Murphy had been the cuddly one. Ejected from his mother's lap early on, Fleming soon grew accustomed to being ignored. He became independent and aloof. Food and the art of being picky was his primary method of getting attention. The mixing or touching of food groups was utterly repellent to him. The carrots and potatoes had to be strictly separated or must be thrown out entirely. Against her better judgment, Leonora found herself catering to his eccentric wishes for fear he would starve himself to death and so his power to control consolidated at an early age.

Murphy was the obedient one and didn't get punished by Leonora nearly as often as Fleming, causing the latter to decide that she hated white boys who dared talk back. But though Murphy was compliant, he was also a whiner and when Mary Glenn had a migraine, his whining absolutely sent her over the `edge of distraction' as she'd always put it. Fleming was smart enough to see that by holding his tongue, he could stay out of her line of fire. It was so much nicer to watch Murphy take the heat for a change. Getting Murphy all worked up and watching him run crying to mama was a pleasure rivaled only by chocolate ice cream for mama was more inclined to smack the bringer of bad tidings than to trouble with details.

Mary Glenn had never been the sort to sit down and converse with her children, and certainly not with Fleming who was about as welcome as a hangnail. However, she did like to complain and that requires a listener. Fleming soon learned that to have an honored place by her side all he had to do was listen; for with regard to the slowness of Joe, the stupidity of Joe, the ineptness of Joe, she had endless volumes of bitterness to unload.

After her venom was spent, she would go on and on about the noble past, romanticizing it beyond all recognition. It was these conversations that instilled in Fleming a longing to reclaim the greatness of the Bowen name for she painted the Colonel as nothing short of a sainted hero and the Bowens as extraordinary people with aristocratic bloodlines running straight back to the Irish Kings. (This was, after all, why Mary Glenn had thrown herself at Joe in the first place. It certainly wasn't because of his charm and good looks.)

But living in this degrading poverty was an insult to the family name, and it was all Joe's fault and the northern hotel guests, as well. She hated northerners with a virulence matched only by her contempt for niggers and Jews. She'd learned all about the conspiracies and plots at her own daddy's knee, a grand dragon in the KKK, and like him she preached contempt night and day with Fleming soaking it all in. As it was, he showed a real flair for the art of contempt and, like so many, would grow to mistake it for intelligence. Sharing this point of view with his mother made him feel wanted and safe, and in the end would be the closest thing to intimacy he would ever feel with another human being.

Another of her favored pastimes was obsessing about the treasure, and what they could do with all that money. On this subject, Mary Glenn had a rich imagination and just about the only time she was ever in a happy mood was when she was taking the boys on imaginary journeys all over the world.

"We can go anywhere in the world we want to---just name a place, sweet pie! Where you wanna go?" It was a game they played, each person adding on the next place. "First we'd go to Paris," she'd say, her head wreathed in clouds of Taryton cigarette smoke. "Paris in the spring. I've heard it's beautiful there in the spring."

"Would we still live here at Zion Crossroads, Mama?"

"Are you kiddin' me? Why I'd shake the dust off my heels so fast---but first, I'd get me a big bull dozer and tear this nasty old place down and build me a real house---a mansion with twenty-nine rooms and ten bathrooms!"

But the subject of treasure could put her in a bad mood, too. Somewhere along the line, she'd become convinced that Joe was hiding the treasure map from her. From the very start, his snob of a mother had poisoned his mind against her. And this wasn't her imagination, either since Gwenyth's first official act was to keep Mary Glenn out of the Will.

To make matters worse, Joe had repeated to Mary Glenn what his mother had privately told him; namely, that no white- trash- gold-digger who had purposely gotten herself pregnant so she could trick Joe into marrying her was ever going to get her hands on Zion Crossroads. This had set in motion an internal war between the two women that would eventually drive his parents out of the hotel business and down to Florida for an early retirement.

After this, Mary Glenn would remain in a permanent state of suspicion about any number of things---for instance, the family jewels. During their engagement, Joe had mentioned an heirloom diamond ring that supposedly would go to his future wife; however, she'd never seen the first glimmer of that ring. She was pretty sure her mother-in-law, Gweneth, was behind the scenes making sure of that. But perhaps Joe's biggest mistake was telling her a certain story about his grandmother.

Irene was his father's mother, a beautiful, but untutored country girl from the West Virginia mountains who'd married into the family, young and prematurely pregnant. Her reckless young husband had soon grown bored and disappeared with a redheaded poker playing dance hall drunk and was never seen or heard from again. His parents had no choice but to accept their pregnant daughter-in-law into their home, where she stayed for the rest of her life. Her mother-in-law made no secret that Irene did not meet her high social standards, for though Irene was extremely beautiful, she had never learned to read or write. Never feeling she truly belonged, she lived apologetically, almost as an indentured servant, working hard to `earn her keep'.

She scrubbed and cooked and eventually took care of the Colonel, who was well into his 90's by the time he died. They'd eventually had to lock him into a third floor bedroom to keep him from wandering because he'd gotten into the annoying habit of going down into Haden's library and pulling all the books off the shelves. Everyone assumed he was just mad as a hatter and still searching for the treasure map he'd misplaced during the Civil War.

 Though Joe was only seven years old at the time, he still remembered the stale odor of the room where the withered old patriarch sat day in, day out in the stifling gloom, shrouded in blankets and still barking orders. His grandmother, with her soft ways, was the only one who knew how to sooth his storms of temper. His rages echoed daily through the halls of Zion, while the rest of the family hid downstairs. "Despicable worms!" he called them. But she was his lamb, his doe eyed lady of compassion, a saint, for she alone had taken the time to rub his painful limbs and pour soup down his withered gullet. In the end, the only person he would even speak to was Irene. Everyone else avoided him like the plague.

After his last foray into Haden's library, a padlock was installed on his door. Even so, that day Irene had come upstairs to find him in a triumphant mood, indeed he could hardly keep from giggling. The old man had really fallen off his nut this time, but this only made him more gleeful. He'd found it, he crowed after so many years of searching! He'd found his brother Haden's diary!

"Don't you see? Now I know where the treasure is." His small shrunken eyes were bright with awe. "Of course, God would only allow this now that I am too old and decrepit to get to it." It was God's punishment for something he'd done long ago, an unspeakable thing, he'd told her, turning the leather bound book over and over in his trembling blue veined hands. "But at least now I know."

Later, he would weep, something she had never seen him do. He asked her forgiveness. She told him there was nothing to forgive.

As ugly as the Colonel was to everyone else, he'd always been kind to her and she felt protective of him. Underdogs tend to stick together.

"Oh, you don't know. You don't know," he'd murmured and sank into a bleak silence. That afternoon, he demanded paper and pen. He refused to eat or to allow anyone into the room until he was finished and then insisted upon seeing Bill Farley, his lawyer friend of many years. The two of them spent nearly an hour up there. Excited murmurs rippled throughout the house. The old Colonel was getting his affairs in order! Farley was uncharacteristically tightlipped on his way out, making a beeline for the door and leaving them to wonder if the Colonel was finally getting ready to die.

When the Colonel started talking again, he was rambling in and out of the past. His mind had 'come loose' was how Irene had put it to her little grandson. Sometimes the Colonel thought he was still a young man, and that she was his wife. That's when he flew into rages and threw things at her. Apparently, he hadn't liked his wife very much. But if Irene could just manage to touch him and get him to look her in the eye, he would always calm down and remember she was his lamb. Then he sank into a brooding silence, unaware of his surroundings at all, while she moved about the room, quiet as a nun, freshening his bed sheets, sponge bathing his evil smelling body with gentle hands.

Suddenly, on the last day he announced, "I'm a bad man, a very bad man. Why do you bother with me?"

"You're not a bad man," she told him.

"Do you like me then?" he asked.

"Yes, I like you."

"I like you, too." He smiled for a moment, basking in some measure of peace before the darkness clouded his eyes and he was lost again.

Later that night, a terrible storm took down an enormous oak tree just outside the house. Its branches smashed a hole in the southern window of Haden's library. The next morning Gardner's father, little Philip Bell, found him. Philip was just seven at the time and his own father, who was the upkeep man, had given him the onerous task of lugging firewood up three flights of stairs to the old man's stench of a room. Years later he would tell the story in vivid detail of what he saw when he opened the door; the Colonel sitting up in his chair, stone dead, eyes staring as if at something far away.

Everyone agreed that he was better off now since he'd gone stark raving mad; however, it turned out he hadn't been nearly as crazy as they'd imagined. At the reading of the Will, it appeared that he had been quite coherent— enough to vilify in minute detail everyone in the family for every last grievance they'd committed against him. As the ultimate slap to the rest of the family, he bestowed ownership of Zion Crossroads to little Joseph who was also just seven at the time. To make matters worse, at the reading the lawyer produced a sealed envelope addressed to Irene for 'her eyes only'. Instantly, the household was abuzz with jealousy and suspicion, causing them to wonder if perhaps they shouldn't have done a better job shining up to the Colonel and indeed to Irene, for out of loyalty to the Colonel, she never did show that letter to another living soul except little Joe. Being illiterate, she was somewhat in a bind and needed someone she could trust to read it to her. The problem was that he couldn't read very well and try as she might to get him to sound out the words for her, he soon became restless and whiney. There were two many big words, he said. So she finally gave up.

She never said another thing about it until a year had passed when she called him into her room in the old servant's quarters behind the kitchen and told him to pull up the floor boards in the closet. It was dark in the closet, and he had to feel around with his hand. He remembered being afraid that a mouse might be hiding in that dusty hole but it turned out to be nothing but the Colonel's letter. She told him to bring it to her.

"Now I just had me a good idea, son," she said. She was pale as the moon and some of her teeth had fallen out but she was still lovely with her long silvery hair flowing over her bosom. "The Colonel made this here letter for you because he knew that someday you was a-gonna go and fetch the treasure." Her gentle blue eyes rested lovingly on his little face. "You're a big boy now I want you to take it and hide it someplace where nobody else will ever find it. Nobody but you. Can you do that for Granny?" She'd always talked to him like that, so positive and kind, as if nothing in the world could he do to disappoint her.

"But it's your letter, Granny!"

"Oh, no---no, no! It's yours. It's always been yours. I been just a-keepin' it for ya--- just for a little while but now I reckon it's time to give it to ya. That's okay with you, ain't it?"

"I guess so."

"Now, I know you'll do a good job a-hidin' it. I reckon you have a lot of good hidin' places, don't ya?"

Joe nodded because he had just the place in mind—inside

the book of fairy stories he'd been given at Christmas, 'The Brother's Grimm'.

Within the next few months she would be dead and his small life would lose the protection of her love. From that day forward, he would drift through life alone and over time forget about the letter and the Brother's Grimm.

Years later, after he'd been married, he dimly recalled his grandmother having once given him an envelope with a treasure map in it, but could never rightly recollect where he'd put it. Determined to awaken his memory Mary Glenn got a book on hypnosis and tried to hypnotize him into remembering where he'd put the letter but he'd just fall asleep instead. At some point she'd give up and declare him an idiot, at which point, he'd make a beeline for the barn where he would work on his perpetually broken down truck until it was safe to come back, that is until the next time the moon was full and the books in the library would mysteriously wind up in a pile on the library floor. Everyone knew it was the Colonel's ghost up to his old tricks but to Mary Glenn it was a sign that the Colonel wanted to help her find the treasure map. Obviously, the map was still in the library somewhere.

If Leonora dared to put the books back on the shelf, she'd rush downstairs, cussing up a storm. No one was ever to touch those books, least of all Leonora as she was probably just itching to get her hands on that map. Why else was she always cozying up to Joe, running to get him any little thing?

Mary Glenn was well aware that in Leonora's eyes she was nothing but 'white trash' and that she didn't approve of Mary Glenn's careless, self-centered ways. And though Mary Glen was completely bored with everything having to do with the hotel business, she resented the fact that it was always Leonora's opinion Joe sought when decisions were to be made. She grew suspicious that her rightful place was being usurped. Her daddy had warned her of that very thing and damned if Leonora's child didn't look like Joe with those golden eyes!

She knew that in town there was talk and that grated on her. Usually on Saturdays, Mary Glenn would take the twins to town to see a movie. She was obsessed with movies and frequently went twice a week. Afterwards, they would go to the soda fountain at the pharmacy to get ice cream sundaes. Usually they would sit on the spinning stools at the long pink counter, where Mary Glenn put herself on display, pretending to read romance novels while secretly monitoring the surreptitious looks she knew she was getting from the men. She prided herself on being compared to Marilyn Monroe and consciously imitated her style.

But the in the days following the birth of Gardner, she'd suddenly taken to hiding in the back booth, protected from scrutiny. Coming from the wrong side of the tracks in a small town, Mary Glenn had the instincts of an alley cat and though no one dared say anything directly, she knew just exactly what they were thinking.

Women in town had never warmed to Mary Glenn anyway. They didn't appreciate the way she flashed her body around when their husbands were looking. However, their friendship had never been what she was after; it was their envy that she craved. She'd sacrificed everything for that Bowen name, just so that somebody would finally want to be her for a change. Who cared if they only hated her all the more?

But Joe had really done her in good this time. She'd suffered a lot of humiliation in her life but this was the ultimate slap to her pride. Sometimes in moments of desperate longing, she thought back to the first time she'd seen Joe at the cotillion ball. Her mother had pushed the two of them together. She said it would be a good match. He was a Bowen, after all, and that meant something or at least she used to think so---though not anymore. She wondered now if she'd ever loved Joe. Maybe, in the beginning there was something, but what had she known then about love? Just a lot of fantasies borrowed from the movies. Now she knew better. 'Love' was about as real as Santa Claus and the Easter Bunny.

The boys would be oblivious to all of this melodrama about Gardner until they were twelve years old and their mother had left and their father had fallen off the roof. It was a Saturday afternoon. Leonora had dropped them off to go to the movies and they'd gone over to the soda fountain for ice cream like they'd always done. They could have sat on the stools if they'd wanted to since their mother wasn't there, but now even they felt the need to hide, so they'd slunk into the last booth in the darkest corner. Neither one was in much of a mood for fun anyway. So much calamity in such a short amount of time has a way of taking away the taste for it.

They were eating their ice cream in silence when the tail of something sounding very much like the name, 'Mary Glenn,' floated over the tall wooden divider between them and next booth. The boys pricked up their ears and held their breath to listen. It was two women and the first one sounded like she knew what she was talking about.

"Well, you know what broke up that marriage, don't you?"

"You mean besides the fact that Mary Glenn was the biggest bitch walking?" They sniggered wickedly.

"All you gotta do is look at their colored woman's child! He's got them Bowen eyes as sure as I'm standing here."

"You're sitting!"

"You know what I mean!"

Their laughter would echo in Fleming's ears for years to come for like all Bowen's he did not let go of injured pride easily. Unlike his brother, for whom injury was more like a slow leak, Fleming molded his pain into something dark and hard with sharp edges---suitable for a weapon.

At first he'd tried hard not to believe it. The very thought that he and Gardner could be related was so utterly horrifying and repellent. Yet every time he looked into those pale golden eyes, what else could he think? Therefore, it must be true. Gardner's eyes were the exact same shape and shade of his own father's eyes--- golden, like river sand and his nose, so straight and thin---not like the other Negroes. Now every dark and suspicious thing his mother had ever said about Leonora bore fruit in his young mind. It was true, then. It was Leonora who had destroyed his parent's marriage and driven his mother away.

He began spying on Leonora to see if she was really after the treasure, like his mother had always maintained. Maybe she'd already tricked his father into giving her the map! Later when Joe disappeared, Fleming went to Leonora and demanded to know who was in charge of Zion Crossroads now that his father was dead. Leonora had tried to explain that Joe had given her power of attorney over all of his legal affairs, but Fleming had shouted her down.

"Nobody but my mother should be in charge! Not you! Mother was right! You're just trying to steal Zion Crossroads from us!"

Leonora was in a bind. She felt she couldn't tell him the truth, which was that Mary Glenn had no interest in coming back. She was not the one to tell them that their mother was getting married again and moving halfway across the country, either. That was something their mother should have told them herself and no matter how much she despised Mary Glenn, she was still the boys' mother. No, to say anything would have been too cruel, so Leonora made up a story that their mother was too sick to travel. That was why she and Mr. Philip would be looking after them, just like they always had, just like their

Daddy had wanted. Everything would be fine.

This comforted Murphy some, but Fleming remained aloof. He sensed Leonora was not telling the truth and inside he wondered: had she and Philip done away with his daddy? It was entirely possible being that they were just gold diggers and who was there to stop them now? Nobody. Nobody but Fleming.

In those days, long distance calls were still very expensive and children did not make them on their own. It just wasn't done. But Fleming found his mother's number and called her up.

"Oh, I can't go back there, Fleming!" she'd said, sounding grieved but determined to be brave. "Leonora would make it a living hell for me! No. Your daddy wants her to have it, so let her have it all. I gave up caring a long time ago! If that's the way your father wants to treat me after all that he's put me through well then there's nothing I can do about it. He obviously doesn't want me to have anything to do with you boys. Leonora poisoned his mind against us. She never liked me or you boys for that matter! Not from day one! We were horning in on her territory. And now the proof is in the pudding! He up and gives her Power of Attorney? Can you imagine? A nigger has legal authority over Zion Crossroads! That is the most degrading part of this whole mess. No, I can't come back there and I won't. Not ever again."

This was very dramatic and convenient for Mary Glenn. She got to bow out permanently, smelling like a martyred rose. Her last words to her son were to warn him that when he came of age, he must fight for control of Zion Crossroads. He and Murphy were still the legal heirs and, above all, he must make sure Leonora never got her hands on that treasure map. "It's your heritage, Fleming ---more than mine. I just married in. You're blood. Just remember what the Colonel sacrificed for you. Now he's counting on you to protect and defend---protect and defend." Mary Glenn had a talent for inspirational monologues aimed to rile up bitter blood. Fleming took this all into the deepest chamber of his being, where it took root and then drew back into the shadows to watch and wait.

At some point, Fleming began to notice Philip's daily treks into the forest. The upkeep man was supposedly hunting but Fleming suspected that wild turkey wasn't the only thing he was after. He decided they should follow him into the woods and see what he was really up to, but Murphy balked. While that manhunt was out looking for Joe, he'd heard enough disturbing stories about the Mist to convince him never to go in there again. Besides, what if they got lost? What if they saw a ghost?

Fleming had pushed him down into the dirt calling him a goddamn coward. Fleming had just started using these powerful words, making Murphy feel weak by comparison. He still thought it was a sin to say such things. Leonora would wash your mouth out with soap if you cussed, but Fleming didn't care. Ashamed, Murphy stumbled behind Fleming out into the forest and that is how they came to have their first encounter in the Mist.

Of course, later Fleming would never admit that they'd gotten hopelessly lost in the thorn bushes but they did. And, as Murphy had feared, just when they could move no further, the Mist had appeared, coiling low around the trees like a wreath of serpents. Already scratched and bleeding from thorns, Murphy collapsed into blubbering defeat. He should never have listened to his brother because now they were sure to die! Fleming promptly delivered him a knuckle sandwich and after that, Murphy kept his complaints to himself.

Later, the details would grow foggy, like wisps of a dream. They'd gotten separated for a time. Murphy had burned his throat raw screaming Fleming's name but Fleming hadn't heard a thing. All Fleming knew was that one minute he'd been wrapped in fog, and the next minute, it'd simply opened like a door revealing a path. He'd followed it into a stand of dead trees choked with vines that caught hold of his feet and slammed him down into a deep hole. He lay there, flat on his back, the wind knocked clean out of his body, and looking up he saw the Colonel staring right back down at him.

Later Fleming would boast that he'd commanded the ghost to leave, but this was a lie. In truth, he was terror struck, helpless against the cold power of those black empty eyes. Down, down, down he felt himself falling, spinning, down, down, down, and then nothing. When he awoke, the Colonel was gone. A cold wind blew dead leaves across the empty hole and he'd pulled himself out. Fleming never told anyone about this. Indeed, he would rearrange the details so as to hide it even from himself.

Murphy had a very different experience. When Fleming had not appeared, he'd sunk to the ground beneath an enormous tree and cried himself to sleep. Later he would confuse the order of events. In truth he'd felt the warm hand on his shoulder before he fell asleep, but somehow later he would recall it as having been just a dream; and in the `dream', a voice had said, "Everything will be all right."

The next thing he knew Fleming was roughly shaking him

awake saying, "Wake up, idiot! I don't know about you, but I sure as hell don't want to sleep in the woods tonight."

By the time Fleming was fourteen, he had grown well past the stage of taking much pleasure in tripping his brother or poking him with a fork under the dinner table. There were other, more cunning, manipulations that satisfied. For instance, he learned that by merely suggesting it, he could cause Murphy to have an accident. This was way more entertaining---even more than drowning mice in a bucket. Still, it did not alleviate his basic lack of happiness. Later as an adult, he would remember very little of his childhood, as if a black curtain had been drawn and for all practical purposes blocked it from his memory.

Sometime during adolescence, he decided that there was nothing out there but chaos and black empty space. Almost daily, he contemplated suicide with a grim reverence. He rehearsed it in his mind. Purely by chance, he found an old volume in the library on poisonous plants. He hid it in his room and studied it when in the grip of his darker moods. By day, he searched for the wild plants, datura and hemlock, poke berries, belladonna, oleander, and transplanted them into what he called his poison garden. He taught himself to make infusions and decoctions from stolen whiskey. He accumulated a whole shelf full of poisons and began experimenting on small animals, killing mice and rats, and an occasional stray dog or cat that wandered in. In his mind, it was serious scientific experimentation, but also something of a hobby. Living out in the country could be so very boring.

It wasn't long after the poisoning of the stray dog incident that Joe disappeared and what with all the turbulence of the search and thinking Joe was dead, Leonora decided to take the boys to a tent revival for some spiritual tenderizing. The boys had rarely seen the inside of a church, as Joe had been an Episcopalian in name only, but now that Leonora was in charge, things were going to change on that account.

The revival took place every night for a week under an enormous tent, culminating in a baptismal service on Sunday morning at the river's edge. The Reverend was a famous out of town preacher with shiny chocolate brown skin and glittering black eyes in a three piece cream colored linen suit. Though Leonora had told them all the way over how he had a `power for preachin', at first, he'd seemed quite ordinary, complimenting the flowers on the altar and the fine dinner the ladies had prepared for him that afternoon. Then he'd made a few false starts, like somebody trying to jump over a fence, breaking off each time with an apology. "I ain't hooked up just yet, brothers and sisters," he'd say and a voice called out, "Take your time, Brother!" Everybody laughed and the preacher just smiled. Suddenly it was like pulling the kinks out of a rope. His body gave a powerful jerk, and---electricity! He was a man possessed with spiritual fire. Soon the people were swaying and reaching for heaven, crying, "Yes, Lord! Sweet Jesus!" With comic genius, he proceeded to put on a one-man show, wearing all the many masks of the Sinner. They howled with delight over the follies of Everyman but before the night was done, the tears would be flowing, those clean, wholesome tears of repentance. That's when he would hammer them with the sufferings of Christ and the certain fate of those who failed to heed his warning. When they were sufficiently broken down and crying out for mercy, his tone would soften and he would lay on the tenderness and the `Coming Great Baptism of Souls', preaching to those who were to be saved that very night from the eternal fires of damnation.

"Total immersion!" he cried. "It ain't gonna work without total immersion cause you can't get to God with just one toe! You can't get to God with just one finger! A little dab will not do ya, my friends! A little dab on the forehead just ain't gonna do ya! No ma'am! No, sir! You gotta put your whole self into it. Your whole self! You gotta jump right in and let yourself be changed! Let your old self die, right there under the water! Let it be washed away! Let it all go right on down stream so when you come back to life, you're a new man, a new woman. Total immersion my friends! If you want to sit close to the throne you gotta give your whole self to the Lord!"

Fleming had been anything but enthusiastic about being made to come here. In defiance of Leonora's poisonous eye, he'd persisted in little snickering comments just to make Murphy laugh. But the preacher was a good salesman, and had the powers of persuasion necessary to call out even the hardest of hearts. His vivid accounts of the roasting bins of hell was what finally got Fleming's attention and convinced him that the preacher could read his innermost thoughts. The Reverend astutely left the crowd on that precipice to ponder a fiery end. And so, even though Fleming had a mortal dread of water, it was a greater fear that forced him down into that river, the fear of fire---the eternal fires of damnation.

Thus, when the preacher called the people down into the river to receive the Holy Spirit, and Leonora had shoved him into the line, Fleming did not resist. He waded right out into the river and gave

himself into the preacher's big work hardened hands, plunging him down beneath the dark, ominous water. In the terrifying confusion of bubbles and the swirling white sleeves of the preacher's robes, a voice spoke plainly in his head. It said, "Do your duty."
He was lifted, gasping and coughing from his watery purification, more terrified than before. Now he knew! God was real after all and if God was real, then hell was real and of that he could have no doubt. For Fleming, religion would never be about Love, for this was a dangerous vindictive god who could destroy him on a whim. But suddenly Fleming had a real reason to worry. Apparently this god wanted him` to do his duty' but he had no clue what that duty could be.

The next day, his fingers accidentally discovered the rosary Mary Glenn's Catholic grandmother had sent her as a plea to come back to the one true Church. It had gotten shoved between the seat cushions where it had been carelessly dropped and forgotten. It was a large white plastic cross with the usual figure of Christ, naked and twisting with pain on a plastic beaded chain.

A jolt of fear shot through his body. This could be nothing less than a Sign from 'The Voice' that had spoken to him under the water. He hung it on a nail above his dresser, over the collection of relics that had once belonged to his mother. They were simple things, but she had touched them once, and they were all that he would ever have of her.

Accustomed as Fleming was to inflicting pain on animals, it was only natural for him to begin wondering what it would feel like to put a nail through his own flesh. Would this satisfy The Voice? Was that what this God required of His followers? Perhaps this would keep his certain punishment at bay. He was anxious about this for there was no doubt in his mind, that if anyone was going to hell, it would be him.

When Leonora saw the marks on his arms and legs, she panicked and the next day took him into town to see the doctor. Doc Ranson, the comfortable old country doctor who'd diagnosed Joe's condition, had just retired. A new doctor had taken his place, a skinny, high-strung fellow, not long out of medical school, with a sallow unhealthy complexion, and purple stains under his eyes. The downy black mustache and goatee gave him the look of a boy dressed up in his father's suit.

His name was Tarlton Mercer, and unlike Doc Ranson, he liked to use a lot of technical jargon to impress the patient with his superior knowledge. However, when it was the patient's turn to talk, he seemed distant as if suddenly more important issues occupied his thoughts. His hands showed that he was not accustomed to physical labor for they were soft like a woman's, small boned and white as a fish belly with black wiry hairs growing in tufts on the fingers. Leonora found his compulsive habit of chewing on his soft downy mustache particularly repellant.

But though Leonora did not think much of him, it was either this or drive sixty miles to the city. So she told him about the cuts; how Fleming's mother had run off, and that his father had disappeared. However, it wasn't until she mentioned Fleming's habit of torturing animals that she felt she had the doctor's undivided attention. Indeed, at the word 'torture', his eyes had flickered with a penetrating interest.

When Doctor Tarlton Mercer took Fleming into his office and closed the door, he asked how things were going for him now that his parents had left and proceeded to get an ear-full about how Miz Leonora was trying to 'completely take over' Zion Crossroads, how she'd manipulated his father into getting the Power of Attorney, drove his mother away, and probably even been sleeping with his father judging from the looks of her child.

Tarlton Mercer sat nodding his head as if he weren't in the least bit surprised. "Son, no wonder your mother can't come back."

Fleming leaned forward and continued in earnest. At last he had an ally. "And now Leonora's trying to make out like I'm the crazy one. What's she bringin' me here for if she ain't just tryin' to get me sent off to some reform school or worse! She just wants to get me out of her way."

The doctor's eyes gleamed with recognition. He was seeing something here that fit an all too familiar theme: sneaky niggers running roughshod over the whites. "Probably because you're the only one with the guts and intelligence to stand up to her," he said in a judicial tone.

"Yes sir, I am. But Mama says I gotta wait 'til I come of age before I can take over. In the mean time, there ain't nothin' I can do about it!"

Doctor Mercer put a consoling hand on Fleming's shoulder. "Young man, sounds like you've got yourself a problem. But there's one thing I want you to know---you are not alone. I am going to help you but this is going to have to be kept in strict secrecy. I'm talking absolute 'State Secrets' here. There are plenty of folks that'd raise a holy war if they knew. You don't dare speak the truth these days and times. The truth tellers of this world are under the thumb of Caesar.

What Caesar says, goes."

Fleming was confused. "Caesar?"

The doctor leaned forward, animated now as this was his passion. "O ye who have ears to hear, sit up and listen! There's plenty of folks like me who have come to see the truth and we must not let them run us over! Too much ancestral blood was shed for that to ever happen. Now we got a lot of cowards and ignoramuses running things up in Washington so it's up to the few. It's always been like that, son. Civilization has always depended upon the few. The masses are just a bunch of sheep. Now you sound like you've got your head on straight. You've got common sense and we need young folks with common sense."

"Fairly normal behavior for a boy, Miz Bell. The hunter instinct," was Dr. Mercer's smug assessment after consulting with the boy.

Leonora's face burned with indignation. "Cutting on your self is not normal behavior, Doctor. Common sense will tell you that!"

Plainly, he did not care for her tone, for his pallid smile was anything but friendly. "Well, I'm sure you think you know what `normal' is. What did you say your position is in the household? The maid?"

"I'm the housekeeper---sir." Again, her face burned. She was careful to keep her eyes glued to the floor for fear of the look she might give this pasty-faced young snot.

He turned away without comment and busied himself with his notes. He had put her in her place and the interview was over. Even so she stubbornly remained in her chair until he finally looked up.
"Are you going to help the boy or do I take him somewhere else?" She added more sweetly, "I mean, he really needs some help---doctor."

He yawned, as if infinitely bored and replied that yes, he would like to see Fleming on a weekly basis. There was a youth group that perhaps he could attend.

"But you know Miz Bell, boys his age who are under a dominating female influence often resort to such behaviors. It's called survival. If a man is going to feel like a man, he can't have a woman dogging his every step." Leonora saw the unmasked hostility lurking beneath the young doctor's exaggerated appearance of boredom.

Leonora left quietly but in her mind she muttered, "Well, thank you Mr. Know it All." Clearly, this guy wouldn't know how to wipe his own behind if he had one.

And this was how Fleming started attending the Confederate Youth Council meetings. Every Tuesday, Fleming would go straight from school over to the basement of the old town hall where a group of about fifteen boys ranging from ages ten through eighteen would gather to hear an old man they called H. R. talk about the glory days of the Confederacy and teach about their heritage, about the heroes of the south. Every meeting began by singing Dixie and the recitation of the CYC's Creed:

"We pledge ourselves to preserve pure ideals, to honor the memory of our beloved Veterans, to study and teach the truths of history (one of the most important of which is, that the war between the States was not a rebellion nor was its underlying cause to sustain slavery); and always to act in a manner that will reflect honor upon our noble and patriotic ancestors."

"The Catechism" subtitled The Children's Guiding Text, was in a question and answer format.

Q: What causes led to the War Between the States from 1861 to 1865?
A: The disregard of those in power for the rights of the Southern states.
Q: Where was the first slave ship built and launched?
A: In Marble Head, Mass., in 1636.
Q: What was the feeling of the slaves towards their masters?
A: They were faithful and devoted and were always ready and willing to serve them.
Q: What is considered by historians as the decisive battle of the war?
A: Gettysburg.
Q: Why?
A: Because it was conclusive evidence to an unbiased mind that the Federal supplies and forces greatly outweighed and outnumbered the Confederate forces.

Dr. Mercer came to pick him up from the meeting and afterwards, took him to The Dixie Diner where'd they talk `politics'. His favorite subject was the conspiracy of the government to take all the power. He took out his little Bible and read to Fleming the passage about the Mark of the Beast which was of course the government's social security numbers.
"Duh! Why can't these people see it? It's staring us right in

the face!" He'd work himself into such a state, that spit would start flying out of his mouth. "Somebody has got to have the courage to tell it like it is before this country goes completely over to the communists! Do you realize the government can take everything you have if you don't pay your taxes. That's not right. That's slavery. If that's what being an American is going to be, then I don't want to be an American anymore."

This was a shocking declaration the first time Fleming heard it, but after awhile, it started to make sense. He found out that there were a lot of people out there who thought this way; people who had never really surrendered the Cause. It sounded noble and exciting and dangerous, too.

"No, I'm not an American," young Dr. Mercer would say, "I'm a citizen of the Confederate States of America which has been under military occupation for over one hundred years."

And he had plenty to say on the subject of the blacks. In Doctor Mercer's opinion, the colored people were getting too big for their britches, horning in where they didn't belong and always causing a commotion. They needed to be put in their place. They were an inferior race, cursed by God ("It's right here in black and white!" he'd say, waving his Bible above his head) and they'd better calm down or there was going to be some serious trouble. Then he'd wink a dangerous and powerful looking wink. He intimated that the Brotherhood was preparing themselves even now for a civil war. "And I'll be right down there, defending the City Hall if I have to. Now you're getting to be the age where you gotta be thinking ahead, Fleming. You're lucky! You know that? You're eyes have been opened young. You've got a chance to really do something for the Cause."

After a time, Doctor Mercer suggested inviting Murphy to the meetings, as well. Fleming didn't want his weenie of a brother tagging along, but he went along with it just because he respected Doc Mercer so much. Well, Murphy made it to one meeting, then promptly went home and squealed everything to Leonora and she hit the ceiling. She had Philip take Fleming's door off the hinges, found his Confederate Flag, all his KKK literature---everything. She immediately forbid his going to any more meetings or ever seeing Doctor Mercer again, but this only made him more defiant. He stole back the flag and hung it up on the porch. She tore it down and burned it in the barrel out back.

He called Mercer secretly that night and told him everything. The good doctor was predictably outraged but said since she was the legal guardian there was nothing he could do, but promised that he would pursue this in court. He never did. In a few months, he moved to Atlanta to a more lucrative practice, and Fleming was left in isolation. His mother was gone, his father presumed dead, and it was just him and Leonora vying for power, tooth and nail. "Do your duty," the Voice had told him at his baptism. Now at least he knew what that duty was. Yes, he was alone but avenging heroes had to be alone. That's what made them heroes.

CHAPTER XVII
Val's Ceremony
The Zion Crossroads Plantation Hotel
1980

The next morning, Jack found himself waking up in the backseat of his car with a royal hangover but though it felt like a sledgehammer pounding into his brain, it was his pride that hurt him more as the events from the night before came roaring back into focus. He'd made a complete ass out of himself not only by getting drunk with Mrs. von Hassel on the front porch but then parading with her, for all the world to see, up to her room. No doubt, Tommy was laughing his butt off right now---wherever he was because he wasn't in the room. Yeah, he was gone and so was the metal detector. That son of a bitch had already cleared out, and was probably out in the woods looking for the treasure without him. Jack scowled. His hand still hurt from punching him.

Tommy awoke early and saw that Jack's bed had not been slept in. It had hurt to see his brother the way he'd been last night, so drunk he couldn't focus his eyes. When he got like that it was like he was another person, someone Tommy didn't recognize. He just hoped Jack hadn't done anything too stupid like falling into a hole somewhere. It filled him with sadness to think that his brother had finally graduated to being a serious alcoholic, like their father had been. His arm still ached from where Jack had punched him.
That's when Tommy had noticed the heavy, leather bound volume of The Brother's Grimm on the bedside table. Jack must have left it there but he had never been a reader so this was puzzling. Tommy opened it and that's how he came to discover an envelope tucked between the pages. It was addressed to 'My dearest Irene from Colonel Carter Meriwether Bowen' in a stiff old fashioned hand. Inside was a rather confusing deathbed confession to a murder that

had apparently taken place over a hundred years ago but along with it were clear directions to the treasure, along with a hand drawn map showing trails in the woods, the ravine, the creek, and a big x on a spot labeled Indian Rock.

Tommy read it then folded the letter and put it back in the envelope. So the prophetic dreams he'd had about this place meant something after all. A quiet exultation swept over him. Jack was going to flip out when he saw this! Maybe when they found the treasure, Jack could finally be happy again! Maybe he'd even stop drinking!

Barely able to contain his excitement, Tommy had hurried downstairs. The metal detector wasn't in the corner where he'd left it so Jack must have already gone without him. Again, another puzzling turn as Jack rarely got up early when he didn't have to.

Downstairs, the only ones around were Gardner, who was sweeping the porch and old Professor Valentino who had just returned from his daily walk to the mailbox.

"How was your walk, Professor?" called out Gardner in the chipper voice he always reserved for Val.

"Quite beautiful. In fact, I'm beginning to see just how beautiful everything really is." His gentle blue eyes rested affectionately on Gardner's quizzical face.

"I guess---if you don't look too hard," said Gardner, his eye straying to the old pizza box that had been used to cover the broken library window. It was now dangling from a single strand of tape.

"Ah, but that's the whole point. Sometimes one must look just a little bit harder. As Keeper of the Moments, I have come to see that now. Yes. And as you do, you begin to notice that this---all of this---is really a sort of conversation."

"A conversation, you say?" Gardner's attention now strayed to a wasp nest being constructed in the corner of the porch ceiling. Another thing to put off until tomorrow.

"A secret conversation," said Val.

"Uh huh." Gardner gave Tommy a surreptitious wink. "And with whom is this conversation taking place, Professor?"

"With *Them*, of course."

"You're losing me, Val." Gardner was finished sweeping and clearly impatient to leave. Val opened his mouth as if to go on, but before he could get a word out, Gardner had hurried back into the house. "Gotta go, Val! Catch you later!"

Valentino stood gazing at his shoes, his lips moving soundlessly.

"So why is it secret?" Tommy asked from the shady end of the porch from where he'd been listening.

Val looked slightly puzzled. "Why I suppose it's only secret because people aren't paying attention. It's secret like a flower blooming. You don't know why or how or when it happens but it blooms all the same."

"So how do they talk to you? Can you hear them with your ears?"

"They talk to me through everything. They want us to know that They're here and They want to work with us, and show us how to live. It's not just me, you see--- but it's you, too. They want all of us to be happy." He pulled a small stone out of his pocket. "If you like I will show you something."

"Sure. Show me something." The others would have smiled but Tommy maintained a respectful solemnity. Val was not the only one who had seen. He'd had experiences since his days at Earth People's Park that he'd never told a living soul about because they would have called him crazy, too.

"We must go to the Labyrinth." Val turned and led him down the curving stone walk, past the old cement pool and into the shadowy recesses of the boxwood. Here the air was humid and thick with gnats humming in the air around their eyes.

"You see? They're cleansing our energy fields before we go in," murmured Valentino. "We must allow them to do their work." He stood like an obedient child getting its face scrubbed. "I've noticed that my vision is improving daily, you see? Soon I will no longer need these at all." He lifted his spectacles up in a gesture of salutation. "Now, let me show you how I've made Them my Helpers."

They wound their way through the maze, past the small sanctuaries in the little cul de sacs. "You know there's always the unexpected nook here in the Labyrinth. I always find something I've never seen before---often something wonderful and just so perfect." He stopped suddenly. There before them, perching in the dark foliage of the boxwood, was a long white feather. He took the feather gently and stuck it into his thick wavy hair.

"A greeting, you see, a way to call my attention, that is all. So we can assume now there is something here to notice." He made his way into a small cave-like indentation where the bushes grew together over a gap large enough for two people. Valentino immediately went in and sat down. "I just love this place, don't you?" Val said, nestling himself in.

"It's wonderful," replied Tommy, following him in. "Have you been here before?"

"No, never. Not before this moment. It may not have even existed before this moment. That is another thing I have learned about moments. Reality is never so real as we should like to think it is." Suddenly, the old man gasped with pleasure. "And of course, what do you think---but a Faery Ring."

He pointed at the circle of moss etched in new grass and leafy clumps of a small purple flower. In the very center was a large flat stone with an indentation almost like a bowl, filled with water. "Oh, thank you, thank you, Love!" he whispered, tears blurring his clear blue eyes. "They have provided a healing altar. Here is where I shall receive my second sight!" He removed his glasses and placed them on one corner of the flat stone. "These are but symbols you see? And how perfectly they fit the stone. Now it's your turn to make an offering, if you wish."

Tommy rummaged around in his pocket and produced a small square stone he'd picked up once long ago. "A symbol of all that I carry with me," he said, placing it on the flat stone beside the glasses.

Valentino removed the feather from his hair and laid it across Tommy's stone. "A token of friendship. May our Spirit Friends help us to see what we need to see in order to be free." He looked at Tommy and Tommy looked back at him. "The others think I'm mad. Do you think I'm mad?"

Tommy thought for a moment. "Do what you feel, man. It's all good."

The professor nodded gratefully. "All right then." He placed a loose flower petal on the surface of the water in the stone bowl. Presently, a dragonfly arrived to perch delicately on the lip of the petal, its long antennae stroking the surface. "It is collecting the essence of my desire,"he whispered, his blue eyes bright with wonder. "Is is showing that my request has been honored and how much they treasure our every prayer." He fell silent for a moment. "Tremendous evil has been done here, you see, which is why the Gate to the Otherworld has been locked for some time now. Certain powers kept there are not safe in this world." The light in his eyes flickered. "And it will not be opened so long as Mankind shall continue to create suffering or until it has made him wise."

Tommy remained spellbound and speechless. Suddenly, the foolish old man appeared wise.

Deep in the silence, Tommy heard the tiniest sound of a bell ringing.

Val's eyes gleamed. "They're calling us to understand!"

"Understand what, Professor?"

"That this world has no power!" He reached into his breast pocket and withdrew a bottle of ink then started to unscrew the lid. "May I show you something?"

"Professor, what are you doing with that?"

The older man drew it to his lips. "Watch!" And he began drinking it down.

"Professor!" cried Tommy, fighting the urge to snatch it away. "This is not a good idea!"

But the old man stubbornly persisted and when he was finished, smiled broadly, displaying blackened teeth.

"Oh, my god! Professor, what have you done?"

The old man's eyes glimmered pure madness now. "But it has no power!"

Tommy's first reaction was to quickly get him to a doctor but then judging by his energy field (which strangely enough, Tommy could actually see) Valentino's cocoon of gold and indigo was vibrant and expansive in all directions.

He'd read about people able to see that kind of thing in books about body work but until this moment, had never actually seen it for himself. Tommy laughed. "Well, I guess you're okay!"

Valentino grinned. "Fear not the mystic union," he said.

CHAPTER XVIII
Searching for the Healing Spring
The Zion Crossroads Plantation Hotel
1980

The next morning Murphy left very quickly after breakfast was over and practically started to run when he saw that Nealy was following him, as he fervently desired to avoid her.

"Mr. Bowen!" she'd called out in that seductively sweet voice that sent delicious chills throughout his body. "I'm sorry but is now an okay time to show me where the Healing Springs are? Or are you busy? Cuz you said—."

"Well, yes I did say that." He stood at an awkward angle, his body turned away from her, as if it still meant to go somewhere else.

"The forest is so huge and it's so easy to get lost," she said, sheepishly. Her smile was like a charm and deep in the dark crevices of his fear-encrusted heart, his resistance began to flounder. Oh, damn his foolish heart. Love was not for him! But excitement and danger quickened his blood and he found himself checking to make sure Fleming wasn't watching. "Well, all right," he said, thinking he would walk very fast and keep his eyes straight ahead as a precaution.

They walked in silence for a good while, as Murphy battered his brain for something to say. "Do you think the world will end by fire?" he said finally, and quite out of the blue. He knew it was an odd thing to start out with but he didn't want her to think that he was a bore with nothing interesting to talk about.

Despite the awkwardness, she seemed to give the question some serious thought before answering. "I don't know," she said, finally. "Sometimes it does seem like a distinct possibility but I like to think that the good in mankind will win out in the end."

He snorted. "What good is there in mankind?"

She fixed her gentle gaze upon him. "You think mankind is evil?"

"I know man is evil because I am evil." He looked away. "It's in my blood---apparently." He was thinking about his ancestors burned for witchcraft.

"But don't you think that's just a little drastic to say. I mean, no one is perfect but you're certainly not evil. At least, I don't think you're evil."

"Well, you don't know me very well," he replied solemnly, his large protruding ears glowing brightly red. "For one thing, I never pray. I never read the Bible and I never go to church."
He hurled these words like accusations but she shocked him by laughing out loud. "That's ridiculous. You can still be good and not do any of those things."

He gawked like an indignant owl. "If I am so good, then why am I continually being punished? Tell me that!" Until now, they'd been going uphill but suddenly the terrain leveled off into a wide plateau. Here the forest seemed to be dying. Huge trees stood like white ghosts, caught in a stranglehold of vines. However, in the midst of this was a large clearing inhabited by a circle of large stones. "What's this?" he exclaimed, for never having been brave enough to go this deep into the forest as a kid, he had never seen this before. On closer examination, the stones proved to be solid quartz crystal, each carved with strange hieroglyphs and standing a good twelve feet high.

"Oh, my god! It's an ancient ritual circle,"murmured Nealy, mostly to herself. These were the standing stones Tommy had told her about. She moved, as if drawn, to the center stone, a low rectangular slab also of crystal. "Amazing!" She pressed her whole body against one of them and closed her eyes. A dark cloud seemed to pass over her face. "Something bad happened here," she said.

Murphy stood awkwardly by. "Actually a tribe of Indians once lived here and when the British came---."

"Many people died," she said softly. "A massacre."

"Yes," He stared at her. "I guess that is what you would call it."

"Women and children." She stared as if at something he could not see.

A somber silence descended upon them. "Destruction is like a bird---it always returns to its roost," he said, suddenly remembering what he'd read in the Boke of Shadows.

As if stirred from a dream, she turned to him. "What did you say?"

"Something the old Indian Chief said to my Ancestor a few years after the massacre." He paused. "When I read that, I couldn't help but think about what it says in the Bible---'the sins of the father shall be visited unto the third and fourth generation'." That was one biblical quote he did know by heart for surely he was a victim of this legacy of sin---the Bowen curse, murder, and witchcraft.

She nodded thoughtfully. "What goes around, comes around."

"You sound like my father's friend, Moon. He was a hippy from Vermont who used to live here--- for awhile anyway." Again, this was another subject he would rather avoid.

"Vermont? You don't mean, Earth People's Park, do you?" The light in her eyes glimmered mysteriously.

"Yes, that's it. You know about that place?"

"I lived there for a time back before it fell apart," she said. "Yeah, I knew Moon very well, actually!" Another coincidence? This was all too weird, she thought.

Murphy looked at her with apprehension. What would Fleming think about this? "So are you a hippy?" he asked. Fleming had a raging dislike of all hippies, especially because of what had happened with their father.

"There are no more hippies, Mr. Bowen. They've all vanished into the hills like the Faeries," she said. Despite her small softness, suddenly she seemed quite tough.

"Fleming thinks that all hippies are evil."

"What do *you* think of them, Murphy?"

Hearing her use his first name gave him a warm feeling. "I think they were the beautiful people who saw beautiful things. It may not have been real what they saw but it was beautiful." He looked away, sadly. "I wonder where Moon has gone. I miss him."

"Moon is a wanderer, Mr. Bowen. He never stays anywhere very long."

Later, when Murphy returned to the front desk, there was Fleming with his suitcase and dressed in a Confederate uniform, all ready to leave for the semi-annual Gray Knights conference. This time it was going to be in Richmond and he was going to spend the night.

"I saw you out there with Miss Brown. What were you doing with her?" By the poisonous tone of Fleming's voice, Murphy instantly knew he did not want to be in this conversation.

"We were walking in the woods."

"Why?"

"She wants to find the healing springs and I---I'm---."

Fleming's smirked contemptuously. "And you're what?"

"I--I'm helping her." He took refuge in watering a spider plant that didn't need it.

Fleming shook his head disparagingly. "Oh, what a tangled web we weave when first we practice to deceive. I've had a bad feeling about that woman, Brother."

"But you always have bad feelings! Why must you always be so suspicious of everyone--hic---Fleming?" Here we go with the hiccoughs, he thought dolefully. He always felt like such a child when he hiccuped in front of Fleming.

"She's a hippy woman, you fool. I'll lay you odds Moon sent her here to finish his dirty work. You don't really believe that story about the whirlwind, do you?"

From the day their father had brought Moon and Fleming to Zion Crossroads, Fleming had them pegged. They were parasites and con-artists bent on stealing Zion Crossroads right out from under their noses. Even Murphy had to admit the idea of a whirlwind coming and wrapping the pamphlet around someone's leg was somewhat far fetched. Still, he couldn't believe she had any ulterior motive. She was too sincere.

"She couldn't lie, Fleming. She's not that kind of---hic---person."

"Women like her are never as innocent as they seem," retorted Fleming with authority. "They always want something. First they get a man talking about himself and then they seize control."

Murphy swallowed ruefully. It was true he had talked way too much. "Well, if you got to know her, you'd see. She's really very sweet."

Fleming's black eyes glittered with superior knowledge. "Eve was oh, so very sweet, Brother---and look what happened. Remember Satan uses sweet things to make us fall." And with that Fleming drove off to the Gray Knights Conference.

Ten minutes later, Murphy slipped and fell down the stairs.

CHAPTER XIX

"Be careful how you tell your story to others---but especially, to yourself."

Joe Bowen

The last time Joe had disappeared for any length of time was in 1978. He was gone for exactly one year, and when he returned, he'd changed dramatically. His hair was down to his shoulder blades, and he smoked 'weed'. He brought two companions, a small slender fellow dressed like a Hindu with a long braid down his back calling himself Moon, and Trip, a wooly, disheveled cynic and one-time war protester who wore dark tinted glasses even at night. They'd recently been ejected from a place called Earth People's Park by a gang of pot dealers with no politics, (just a lower form of dirty capitalist and the most contemptible kind of human being as far as Trip was concerned.)

The 'commune' as such had died long before this after a devastating drug bust had wiped out the core of the governing council. Trip had been the last one to remain, like the captain of a sinking ship, holed up in a deteriorating trailer amidst the wild splendor of six hundred acres on the Canadian border with a ninety -nine year lease. A beautiful dream gone to shit.

Trip now officially classified himself as a grandstand observer a.k.a. 'The Hermit', sitting back to watch Society self-destruct. But this was just a rationalization to make him feel better. At heart he was still an activist burning to change the world, and it was killing him to sit in the backwaters fending off the brain dead cowboys camped out on Park land (an inherent problem with the open-door policy, he'd come to learn).

After 'The Crash,' they were the only ones to come back, like cockroaches; they weren't about to pass up a free ride. Soon they'd turned Earth People's Park back into a marijuana patch only this time rigged with elaborate booby traps, (bear traps, hidden pits, vicious German shepherds, beehives). They'd taken to wearing ten gallon hats and pistols strapped around their beer guts hence the cowboy title. They reminded him of what the real cowboys must have been like in the Old West before pavement and the law, mud caked boots and mayhem; mayhem by night and muddy hangovers by day. They lived in a small enclave of shacks and tipis on the western end of the property, and he pretty much kept himself to the east. Trip tried to have as little contact with them as possible.

Occasionally, he'd see them up at Ted's Market where they congregated at the outdoor pay phones, slouched against a dented old Pontiac with the mismatched fender, smoking homemade cigarettes. Meanwhile their foul mouthed women in patchwork denim skirts haggled with the welfare office over the payphone out front and their brood of dirty brats pestered passers-by for money.

Trip didn't like them, and they didn't like him. He'd made it known he had an itchy finger on the shotgun which he kept hanging over the front door of his trailer, and they knew to leave him alone. Sometimes months would go by, and he wouldn't see or hear them which was fine by him. He was lonely but not that lonely.

The only real company he had anymore was Moon, who was more than anything just a ball and chain around his neck. Moon had never been anything but a hanger-on in the community. One of those self-absorbed vegetarian fanatics always in your face about chemicals and animal rights and organic this and 100% cotton that. He'd never 'got it' the way Trip 'got it.' He had no politics. He was just a Rice Eater. Trip's credo with regard to people like this was basically: Fuck rice! He'd eat a steak if he damn well wanted to! He'd eat a Twinkie and lick his fingers after every bite just to upset people like Moon. "Have a bite," was the way he'd taunt him. "You know you want it!" Shit! You'd think Moon would be sent straight to hell for eating a Twinkie. He was an airhead. They were all airheads, but he was King of the Airheads.

Still, Moon was now the only other person who came back to Earth People's Park. Everyone else---all the `committed' people, the ones who'd really `gotten it' that this was a whole new world they were hatching here, they had scattered like seeds in the wind. Now it was just him that was left and Moon who only seemed to show up when he'd run out of money or gotten kicked out of some ashram or commune he'd been crashing in.

Moon was, in a word, a royal sponge, but at least he was company, annoying company true, but better that than facing the long brutal winters alone. Trip had done that once and it wasn't long before he'd been talking to himself in public, like that day Joe had made his first appearance.

It was late February, during a temporary thaw. Trip had come to town to do his laundry---a semi-annual event, aside from occasionally swishing his underwear around in a bucket. No running water in the trailer made doing laundry a bit of a problem. Whenever Moon showed up, there was usually a big production of boiling all the sheets in a big pot on the wood stove making the whole trailer smell like wet dog. But for some reason, Moon was late in coming that year. Maybe he'd finally joined the Hari Krishnas like he'd been talking about.

Trip would never have admitted it, but he'd been lonely---lonely enough to want to see Moon coming through the door. He'd spent the entire winter alone with the exception of a few encounters with the cowboys that did not exactly count for human interaction.

Also, one of his dogs had died. Maybe that was what had put such a dark cloud over him. He'd had to shoot her to put her out of her misery. Plus, he'd burned his novel three times which was probably a record. Usually he only got that disgusted once a year. It had become sort of a cleansing ritual like expunging the demons of the past, but how did a person expunge a demon that was like a rubber ball? No matter how hard he threw it out of his head, it just kept bouncing right back in.

The day he'd stood on the sidewalk in the middle of town, talking to himself, had marked the beginning of a rude awakening because for the first time in his life he'd had good reason to question his own sanity. Maybe he really was losing it and just didn't know it. While furtively scanning the street to check if a stranger had seen his lapse, he'd caught sight of his reflection in a store window. It had been a deadly experience. What he'd seen was a ragged, wooly headed wild man, the kind one generally expects to find rummaging through trash cans in the alley.

It was the shock of having seen his entire person that did it. I had been a while, since the only mirror in the trailer was so small it could only show a quarter of his face at a time. So when someone tapped him on the shoulder, he'd jumped a foot. However, it was only a tall skinny guy with big fish eyes peering through coke-bottle eye glasses; and for some incomprehensible reason, he was holding Trip's wallet.

"What the f---?" Trip's first reactions were usually attack first, ask questions later, so assuming the worst, he'd ripped the wallet out of the man's hand with such force that it had thrown the guy off balance and sent him sprawling across the icy sidewalk. Instantly, a clear vision of the mouse hole in his coat pocket slid onto Trip's mental screen, informing him that the wallet had no doubt fallen out and the poor guy was simply trying to return it. Swept by waves of self-recrimination, Trip was quick to offer a hand.

"Damn! I'm sorry, man. Sorry. Shit! Didn't mean to freak on you---hey, thanks for returning my wallet! Really, man!"

The guy didn't seem at all upset, but just patiently reassembled his long skinny limbs and then stood there expectantly like a lost puppy waiting for someone to take him home. Judging from the way he was dressed a la Salvation Army--- the layers of flannel shirts two sizes too small, the mismatched plaid polyester pants, the dirty orange knitted cap pulled down low over his forehead---Trip had him pegged for the druggie and / or escaped mental patient variety. That kind of trouble, he'd learned from bitter experience, he did not need. Still there was a mildness about this guy, a vulnerability, and for some reason Trip didn't object when Strange Dude followed him into the warmth of Lula's Laundromat. What the hell, the guy had returned his wallet. He could have run with it.

They were the only ones in there and to discourage any conversation, Trip kept his chin tucked down into his navy blue pea coat, (which he suddenly noticed was full of dog hair and crusty stains) and pretended to sleep. He peeked a few times to make sure Strange Dude wasn't staring at him but the guy remained sitting, perfectly straight, his eyes closed, a tiny smile on his lips, as if he were listening to soft music that nobody else could hear---definitely a mental case.

At one point, there was a jingle of bells at the door, as an older woman came in. Trip recognized her as the owner of the place. She ran a disapproving eye over Trip and Joe who continued to sit there with his eyes closed and that idiotic little smile on his face. She reminded Trip of a tiny bulldog with her protruding lower jaw and heavy jowls, as she strutted over to where Joe sat and gave him a nudge.

"You got laundry?" She shouted like he was on the next block.

He opened his eyes as if he were surprised he was there and not somewhere else.

She didn't like this. Trip could tell by the way her face hardened. "I said, you got laundry?" Joe shook his head. "Then what the hell you doing here? You on drugs?" He shook his head. "If you're on drugs, I don't want you here! Understand? I've had it with you junkies and pill poppers! You go on and trash somebody else's place! Better yet, get a damned job and go trash your own place!"

Trip spoke up. "M'am, don't worry about him. He's with me."

"And what are you doing here?" She turned on Trip with equal venom.

"Just doing my laundry, m'am! And for your information, I don't 'take' drugs or alcohol."

"Then why don't you go get a haircut so you look halfway decent? What's wrong with you people? You tryin' to go back to the caveman days, or what?" With a scowl she left, making a point of adjusting the No Loitering sign on the front door on her way out.

Though Trip had done his share of drugs, his name had come from a bad trip not a good one. Marijuana made him paranoid and acid was a nightmare of self-induced psychoanalysis. He didn't need it. When he had to, just to be sociable, he'd pretend to take a hit or two when the peace pipe came around but for the most part, he liked to keep his head on straight. Besides, he could see what all the dope had done to the movement. He had no doubts that FBI undercover had done their share of dope peddling. A perfect way to tame the wild activist-- give him a joint and he'll spend the rest of the day worshipping a daisy.

When his laundry was done and he was on his way out, something made him pause at the door. Sure, maybe Strange Dude had had a mental breakdown, but he seemed harmless and Trip was lonely as hell so that's how Joe ended up at Earth People's Park.

Joe didn't speak and Trip didn't know his name, so for convenience, 'Strange Dude' evolved into 'Dude'. 'Dude' turned out to be an easy companion. He may have been a bit off, but he hadn't pulled a knife on him (yet) and he had no problem doing dishes (a *big* plus). And (an even *bigger* plus) he seemed to prefer staying outside during the daytime, leaving Trip the luxury of the cramped trailer all to himself. Being that it was early March, there was still snow on the ground, but Joe kept the picnic table cleared off and that's where he sat for hours at a time, just looking at the trees with that blank expression. Meanwhile, inside, Trip hammered away at his old Remington typewriter in another full scale assault on 'The Novel that Would Change the World', (working title: Albatross #5).

True to form, just when Trip had come to the idle conclusion that three would definitely be a crowd, Moon showed up--- and this time with half his head shaved. Apparently, half way through his Hari Krishna initiation he'd changed his mind. A black cloud threatened to descend on Trip's mental equilibrium as he pictured Moon spreading out and taking over with all his beads and leatherwork and tie-dye paraphernalia which was how he made his money.

But the real problem with Moon was that once he started talking, he never shut up. The trick was not to look at or speak directly to him in the first place. That way he would generally remain quiescent in his parallel universe of mantras, rice, and beads; hence the no-talking-before-noon policy. This was just how it had to be in a tiny trailer in northern Vermont in the dead end of winter.

However, Joe threatened to upset that delicate balance because he gave the impression of being such a good listener, and Moon had a lot to talk about---like how the whole situation had gotten *really* hung up with all this like really--- *stuck* energy---like people not communicating about feelings---and he *really* couldn't vibe with that cold, analytical left brained type shit. His psyche needed to be in an open space with a lot of like, *heart* energy.

Of course, this was basically the same story he gave every time he was on the rebound from another ashram experience gone amok. Needless to say, back in the trailer there was absolutely no 'heart energy' since the last thing Trip ever wanted to do was to talk about his feelings but that did not seem to deter Moon from coming back.

Trip was on the verge of one of his semi-annual Giving-Moon-the-Boot explosions when Joe simply got up in the middle of Moon's monologue and walked outside. A good audience was hard to come by up here since Trip never listened to a word he said, so without skipping a beat, Moon followed. This soon became a trend and as the weather warmed (it was an early spring that year), Moon moved his beadwork outside where he and Joe would sit, Moon talking, Joe listening. As time went by, Moon was teaching Joe how to string the beads, how to work the leather, and how to smoke pot.

Moon was a 'pothead'. He smoked morning, noon, and night. He called it 'straightening out his head' but in Trip's opinion it only made him more difficult to communicate with. It was working out well, though. Joe didn't seem to mind listening to Moon's babble and it definitely kept him out of Trip's hair so he could work on his novel. He'd been infected by a resurgence of optimism (sort of like a virus that kept coming back) that maybe (maybe) it was finally going somewhere.

For both Moon and Trip, there was something very comforting in Joe's silence. Whether it was because he was such a good listener or because half the guy's mind was blown, either way it felt safe to reveal themselves to him.

Come April, Trip and Dude set off down the muddy trail for an official tour of Earth People's Park. The first place they came to was

Moon's Pyramid built of plywood and logs. It had a dirt floor and low slotted windows that came about knee level, sort of a wooden teepee. Trip pointed out the open smoke hole at the top which had always been a real problem when it rained, making it totally impractical in every way and impossible to heat, (and which was, of course, why Moon was always hanging out at the trailer). But ironically it was still standing, unlike Trip's first home, which he referred to as the 'The Hovel', now a pile of rubble slowly being reclaimed by the forest.

They passed another lonely log structure, the lopsided door hanging in despair from one hinge. Within, stood a rusty wood stove and an iron bed frame covered in dead leaves and drifts of crusted snow blown in through gaps in the walls, silent witnesses to a life come and gone. The spring thaw had already unsealed the earth smells, the damp rotted wood and moldy leaves, the smells of decay.

Trip stood in the doorframe, gazing into the dim enclosure, an unspeakable heaviness closing over his heart. Before long all of this would be gone forever like it had never existed. "This is where the dream hits the cold hard ground, my friend. A helluva lot of work and colder than shit in the winter." He smirked. "Yay! Build your own house! Be self-sufficient---right!"

They continued on until they came to an imposing log structure nearly two stories high. Outside the door, Trip stooped to pull a rough wooden plank up out of a pile of leaves. Brushing off the dirt revealed the words, `Freedom House`. He smirked again and tossed it back on the ground.

"Welcome to the Council Lodge built in nobler days. What a work party! Wish you could have seen it, Dude. Everybody helping out. It was one big family! Yeah, one thing's for sure, we sure could throw a helluva dance! Raise high the roof beams, man! Best party ever. Watch your step." Inside, the vaulted ceiling was open to the sun where it had collapsed on one end. Shards of sunlight poured through, illuminating the young saplings that had grown up through the rotted floor. A black crow perched on the broken edge of the roof then flapped his wings and disappeared skyward.

"I kind of like the skylight effect we got going here, though I can't say it was in the master plan." Trip picked his way past a pile of rubble to the remains of a bench. "You see, *this* is my novel, Dude. The dream of Eden briefly come to Earth. People sharing and living in harmony and peace and how it all came to shit."

Joe sat on the bench and gazed up at the blue sky with the light pouring in, the image of the broken roof caught in the reflection of his glasses. Trip had heard that it was a bad idea to tell anybody about your idea before it's written but something about Joe made you want to spill your guts because you knew that no matter what you said, he'd remain perfectly normal about it and never say a word. It felt very safe and private---sort of like talking to a priest in a confessional or better yet, like talking to yourself.

Sometimes he thought that maybe he talked too much around Joe, but this stuff was burning a hole in him right now and maybe the damned book never would get written. You just couldn't know things like that. Maybe he just needed to purge his guilt. Maybe that's what the novel was really all about.

He sighed and took a seat beside Joe where he too gazed up at the sky. "It may not look like much of anything now, but for awhile we really had something, Dude. What this was supposed to be---you see---." He paused for a moment, the corners of his mouth pulled down hard in order to control an unexpected wave of emotion. "This is where we took our stand, man---a society based on consensus and free will---an incredible group of people. Yeah, it was pretty incredible."

He brooded in silence, his fingers twisting the ragged ends of his wooly beard, a sad bear of a man. "But when it comes right down to it, most people only really care about themselves. Only a very few are willing to live for their ideals, willing to make the sacrifices, to do what it takes." He shrugged, plunging his hands into the pockets of his jacket.

He rambled on. He'd always had the idea that he was supposed to do something important. He'd been one of those brilliant whiz kids who was supposed to grow up and be something important, like the president or at the very least have a doctorate. Everyone in his family had a doctorate---even his dog was named `Doc`. But he'd been a rebel, an atheistic, communistic drop out (for awhile anyway, that is until he'd figured out that bullshit). In the process he'd thumbed his nose at everything society stood for, the war, greedy materialistic, paternalistic capitalistic bullshit. Oh, yeah. He'd had no patience for sitting around while history was being made, so he'd dropped out and went into the streets to earn his badge of honor, fighting against the Vietnam War. He'd gotten beat up pretty bad, too---even spent time in jail, the whole nine yards.   But by the time the Feds killed those students at Kent State, he already knew that it was all going to shit---the whole sick society was on the verge of a breakdown.

He sighed. "Those were desperate times, man. And then I met David and Erika. They showed me that the Movement couldn't just be about breaking down barriers. It had to be about building something. What a high that was---I mean, they had a vision of community and it felt---holy, like destiny---like we could really make it happen. And then this land just appears, like manna in the desert---six hundred acres way the hell up here in no man's land Vermont---with a ninety-nine year lease. It was like the hand of God just opening the way and all we had to do was walk in.

"But you know how things go. Egos started making trouble. Jealousy crept in and over a woman, no less. Can you believe it? The oldest pitfall known to man and we fell right into it." He smiled sadly. "We both loved her. How could we not? She was an incredible woman. Jealousy is a horrible thing, man. It's like deformity of the soul. It makes you want to hurt the people you love the most." A solitary tear spilled down into his grizzled beard but he made no move to brush it aside. This was the part of the story he hated the most, the part that always hung him up when he tried to write about it, the part he wanted to throw into the fire and forget.

"David and Erika were into weed. To them it was sacred, like religion. I never got that. It just made me feel paranoid and out of control. I always hated that feeling. I like to stay clear, you know? But that was how they generated the cash flow, growing it and selling it in the cities. It was a reasonable economic path to take for the times, I guess. But I fought them on it. I mean anybody with half a brain could see that it was only a matter of time before the Feds caught on to us. But David was, I don't know---magnetic---and I'm not. Anything David said was like, "Yeah, man! Let's do that!' Me? I was like a fly buzzing against the windowpane. I was too into 'fear-based thinking,' they said. I needed to stop being intimidated by 'society's rules' and find my 'power.' That's how they put it, utter bullshit as it was.

"There was a huge bust. My father had just died so I was back home at the funeral when it all went down. I didn't know what was happening 'til I got back. David and a bunch of them had been arrested and were sitting in jail, the marijuana fields were burning, and everybody else had split. Erika was desperate. All she could talk about was how we needed to get David out of jail. She wanted to raise money for a lawyer and I---I argued against it. Oh, you should have heard me! It was too late, I said. It'd be a waste of time, a waste of money. I sounded just like my father---time and money! But the truth was that I was secretly glad that he was in jail, my tribal brother, man. I was glad so I could have Erika to myself. In the end, I turned out to be just like all the other jerks out for themselves. That's how much I cared about the council. I killed it with my jealousy." He stopped for a moment, a terrible look on his face.

"After that things pretty much disintegrated overnight. Everybody was gone, Erika, everybody---everybody but me. I hid out in a cave all through the fall and when winter came, I started living in the trailer someone had left here. I guess I was waiting, just holding on. At first, I told myself this was just a temporary set back. If I hung around, I thought, they would all return and we could pick up the pieces and move on but that just didn't happen. It's been seven years, man and all this time I'm telling myself that I'm doing the right thing, holding down the fort, so to speak. But the real reason I'm staying here is that I'm afraid. I'm afraid to go back out there to the `real' world. I've gone too far out to ever think about going back."

On the way back to the trailer, he and Dude took another route and came upon a flock of buzzards tearing at the headless corpse of a large deer. The cowboys were into collecting heads with antlers that could be stuffed and sold and left the bodies to rot. Trip shook his head. "Assholes."

One morning, Dude smoked weed with Moon, laid down on the picnic table and stared up at the sky, then got up and told them that he was Joe Bowen, that he lived in a place called Zion Crossroads, and he needed to get home because his sons would probably be wondering where he was.

That night the cowboys showed up with their guns, drunker than piss and shouting for Moon to give back the pot he'd stolen from their weed patch. For added emphasis, one of them sent a bullet through one of the trailer windows.

"Damn it, Moon. What the hell did you do that for?" Trip couldn't give a rat's ass about Moon, but nobody messed with the trailer. He grabbed his shotgun from over the door, and being that he was an excellent marksman and not staggeringly drunk, scared them off with a few well-placed shots.

Watching the cowboys beating their hasty retreat, Moon let out a howl of exuberance, cut short by a blistering scowl from Trip. Moon hung his head. "Sorry! Guess I screwed up, huh."

Trip sighed. "Well, I'm sick of this place anyway. Let's get the hell out of here."

"Where'll we go?"

He looked at Joe. "How about Zion Crossroads?"

They ended up hitchhiking when Trip's old van died somewhere on the New Jersey Turnpike. All the way home, Joe had been looking forward to going home with a warm expectancy, but one that quickly cooled when he encountered the limp welcome from his sons. Murphy was distant at best and Fleming down right cold, bluntly informing him that the housekeeper, Leonora, had died nine months before. She'd passed away in her sleep one night of heart failure. She was fifty years old.

The household was a very different place without Leonora, who had ruled with a mirthful, if iron hand. Clearly, without her, conditions had fallen into filth and disarray. But Joe had changed too, and it wasn't just the long hair and beard. The man the twins remembered had been forever ensnared in some secret inner muddle, preoccupied, absent. But now he was looking out at the world with clear, searching eyes as if seeing his sons for the first time.

Leonora's husband, Philip, was the only one who acted like he was glad to see Joe. In fact, the better word would be 'relieved.' They sat up late in the kitchen talking first about Leonora's sudden passing. Maybe she was ready to be done with this ol' world, Phillip had wondered aloud. Tears had filled both men's eyes. Joe could hardly believe it. Leonora dead? She had been the very essence of strength and vitality, a lifeline through many difficult times.

Philip went on to talk about how things had been since Joe had left over a year ago. Though Joe's `amnesia spells` were nothing new, it still threw the household into a tailspin. They couldn't know if he was alive or dead but they'd been determined to keep things afloat, trusting that Joe would return like he always had before.

Then without warning, Fleming had come back home. Philip hesitated as if this were something difficult for him to talk about, "You just really need to understand how Fleming has changed, Joe." *He was bad before but nothing compared to now*, was what he could have said, but didn't.

When Fleming went to college, he'd stayed away. He was through with Zion Crossroads and for twelve years they'd neither seen nor heard from him. He'd left, a sullen rebellious teenager, and returned a hardened zealot; the kind that Philip despised and feared, the kind who used the Bible to justify hatred of Blacks and Jews. Fleming had left magazines around the house preaching about the rise of the New Confederate Nation and neither Philip nor Leonora had had any illusions about what that meant.

There'd been tension, especially between Fleming and Leonora. After being back home only a few short weeks, he'd begun pressuring her to hold a funeral for Joe and officially turn Zion Crossroads over to him. Leonora had stoutly refused. As far as she was concerned, Joe was coming back just like he always had and she was just taking care of things until he did.

Shortly after, Fleming accused her of stealing from his grandmother's trust in order to take Zion over for herself. It was the same old argument they'd been having before he went away to college. Ever since the twins were twelve years old and their mother had packed up and left, Leonora had been in charge of everything--- raising them and keeping up the household---and Fleming had always chafed under her dominion. She had been a powerful woman in her day, physically strong, her deep cocoa colored skin shining with vigor, her mind and tongue sharp as a razor. They'd both always known she could whip his tail any time she wanted to and wouldn't hesitate to do so, but now things had changed. He wasn't just a skinny kid anymore. He was a grown man, and he was white.

Something happened to Leonora over the next several months. For the first time in his life, Philip saw his wife slipping under the shadow of doubt, and though she'd tried valiantly to hold on to Zion, she knew she was losing her grip.

"She held on as long as she could, Joe. She always believed you'd come back, but he got to her this time. He got to her real good. I'm sorry, Joe."

Joe looked puzzled. He didn't understand what Philip was sorry about, but Philip wasn't through yet. "Cause, you see, that's when Fleming started bringing in those Brotherhood people for meetings and all."

"The who?"

"The people who write *this* filth!" Philip produced a magazine from the cabinet. The New Confederates they call themselves! He's one of them, Joe."

Joe could see that Philip had aged. He'd gotten streaks of gray in his hair, and his face had lost its inner light. Of course, Leonora had only been gone now for nine months or so, and he knew how hard it was to lose a wife. Yes, he did know that much. Joe patted Philip's shoulder comfortingly and said everything would be all right.

"You've got to do something about this, Joe, or I'm afraid that it won't be." Tears clouded Phillip's sad brown eyes. "I'm just so glad you're back."

Joe promised he would talk to Fleming, though he felt Philip was probably overreacting. There'd always been that sort in the community, clinging to the past, whistling Dixie, but it was usually just a lot of hot air. As for Fleming, well, he'd always been a difficult person, but he was intelligent, and Joe felt sure he could reason with him.

Returning to Zion Crossroads had never been easy for Joe. He had many painful memories here. The walls held the ghosts of depression that followed him like shadows from room to room. He had hoped this time would be different, but the first night spent in his old room had been restless and difficult. In the end, the only room that felt safe was Haden's library. Perhaps it was the windows that opened to the east and the south, bathing it in light throughout the day that endowed it with the protection of a welcoming Spirit. This had been Haden's sanctuary, where he'd spent many hours absorbed in his art. Top to bottom, the walls were still lined with his books, undisturbed now for a hundred years. His rosewood desk looked out over the lawns and the forests beyond as it always had and still hanging on the walls were his paintings depicting wild magical glades, waterfalls, and secret glens, each a summons to buried longings. This had been the room Joe had seen in his mind when he'd envisioned coming home.

But changes had been made. A Confederate flag now hung stretched across one window like a curtain casting a reddish light into the room, and on the mantel there were small statuettes of southern generals from the Civil War. The morning after his first sleepless night, he went to the library and calmly pulled down the flag.

"What are you doing?" Fleming was standing in the door behind him, his brown wiry hair standing up somewhat in disarray. *The Bowen hair. Never very suitable for the clean cut look*, he thought.

"It dims the light. Here." Joe folded it and handed it to his son, who took it, his face an unreadable mask. There was an uncomfortable silence.

Joe tried to think of something to say. "So, are you now a history buff?" He indicated the statues of the southern generals. "Philip tells me that you worked in a book store for several years."

"If you wish, I will remove them." Fleming behaved as one did towards a stranger, mechanically correct, impersonal. Of course it had been years since they'd seen each other; light years if the changes they had undergone could have been calculated.

"No, no they're fine where they are," answered Joe, mildly. "You know, I was a bit interested in history at one time, but that was a while ago."

Fleming got straight to the point. "I need to know just how long you plan to stay *this* time, Father."

Fleming had begun calling him 'father' instead of `daddy' when he was twelve years old, the year that his mother left, the year Joe fell off the roof, the year (and he realized this now in a sudden rush of clarity) that Fleming had officially declared his independence. With a pang of remorse, Joe realized that he could remember very little about his son's childhoods. So much of his life had been lost.

"I don't *intend* to leave, if that's what you mean." Intend. That was the operative word. Joe could not claim anything more definite than that for when had he ever been in control of anything, much less his life? He couldn't guarantee that tomorrow he wouldn't suddenly forget who he was and wander off.

"And how long are your friends *intending* to stay?"

Joe remembered Fleming as having been something of a bully, full of mischief but when did he erect this wall of cold superiority?   "I suppose my friends will stay as long as they wish." Joe paused. The truth was that he didn't want his friends to leave. In fact, he felt closer to them than he ever had to his sons.

Fleming nodded grimly and turned to go, pausing at the door. "They are paying, aren't they? They're going to pay?" He said it twice as if Joe might not have gotten the message the first time.

"No. They're my guests. Why should they?"

Fleming lifted his chin, and looked down his short pinched nose condescendingly. "You've been gone a long time, father. Perhaps you are not aware of the financial situation."

Joe could have pointed out that Fleming had been gone a long time as well or that Zion had been in a bad financial situation for decades; ever since his father, Fairchild Meriwether Bowen, had left him the business and gone off to Florida. But Joe said nothing.

"Of course, you realize we're in this state of affairs largely due to your frequent absences," continued Fleming in a lecturing tone.

"I thought Leonora always ran things quite well."

"You 'thought' but did you ever bother to check up on her? An ignorant Negro woman with barely a high school education? Not a very smart move, Father."

"Leonora was smart as whip and fully capable of doing whatever was asked of her."

"Then what happened to Grandmother's trust? Hm?" Gwyneth's trust was how they'd been surviving all these years---investments in railroads, oil companies, Coca Cola and such. "I've been looking at the books, Father. Try it sometime. You may find it enlightening."

"Leonora would never have stolen from us!'

"Father, don't be naïve. She had the run of this place and full control and, believe me, she used it. 'Praise God, hallelujah…Mr. Joe is in a coma, I's got my hand in the cookie jar and ain't nobody lookin'.'"

"She was a good woman. The truest Christian I ever knew. My God, Fleming! Leonora was like a mother to you! You owe her some respect! She took care of us through thick and---!" Joe's face crumpled with emotion, "---through thick and---!"

Fleming's face hardened into a knowing sneer. "Sometimes I have to wonder who it was you really cared about, mama or her?"

Joe had slapped Fleming's cheek before he even knew what had happened. Though they had never spoken of it, Joe was well aware of the rumors spread after the birth of Leonora's son with the golden eyes.

Fleming's bitterness was triumphant. "She still owns you hook, line and sinker, doesn't she, even now." He turned and left, leaving Joe in confusion. He had hoped that this time, things would be different, but Zion Crossroads was still a troubled place.

Joe moved into the library full time, and by staying up all night and sleeping by day, he and his friends managed to avoid the twins and Fleming's disapproving eye. Deep into the night, they smoked the magic weed and bullshitted. Experience had taught Joe that he should expect nothing more than loss and sorrow, that joy was scarce and only for the lucky few, but the walls of Joe's world were cracking, and he was learning to see things differently. His new friends were showing him that perhaps there was another way to live. It was as if he'd been asleep his whole life, and now he was finally waking up.

Life was not a tragedy. It was an adventure, 'the Spirit's grand experiment' as Moon called it. There was no right or wrong way to do anything, no external authority to answer to. All authority, all power came from inside one's self. The power of decision came from following the flow, surrendering to the now. Joe grew to admire his friends and the free-form existence they aspired to---living moment to moment, unconcerned about money, immune to guilt and social disapproval.

The old assumptions that formed the basis for what Trip contemptuously called the 'collective ego bullshit' or 'society', were all called into question. Why did you have to wear a suit and tie, or cut your hair, or go to church on Sunday to know God? Why couldn't you go on Tuesday? And why go to church at all? Couldn't you be with God in the woods or at a bus stop? And why must you wear shoes or sleep during the night instead of the day? Who made those rules? After all what was right for one century was absurd in another. Once bleeding patients was the thing to do, and now that was considered barbaric. At one time, a man of importance wouldn't be caught dead without a wig, and now he would be laughed out of the room.

Everything was relative. Truth—Reality---it was merely a subjective experience. Maybe everyone's Truth was different according to his belief, and so everyone was a world unto himself---correction, 'herself' because why can't God be a female?   You make your own truth, therefore it did not behoove anyone to criticize anybody. Each person was his own authority.

This was so completely foreign to Joe who felt obliged to ask permission for the least little thing. Could he open the window or turn on the light; could they go in or go out? In answer, Trip was typically blunt, "I don't know, man---can you?" This made Joe feel like a weak and foolish child, always waiting for approval. But it also started to make him think.

For the first time, Joe asked himself how it was that he had never been able to exert authority over his own life? His parents certainly had. Why hadn't it passed on to him? Why was it that he had felt so unworthy, as if it were always best if *they* made the decisions. And then of course, when he *did* take a risk and decide something, there had always been his wife to criticize because it was invariably the wrong one. He was conditioned to doubt himself, as if making a decision was going out on thin ice ready to crack. Like wearing shoes one size too small, he felt confined by rules and petty standards he would never think to question.

Joe had never before heard such a flagrantly rebellious philosophy as the one Trip and Moon preached, but it was also strangely liberating. He began to consider that, as fantastic and even absurd as some of it sounded, Joe *could* make his own rules--that is if he could only be that brave. Trip's ethic was: whatever floats your boat. His vision of a new social order based on openness and community and self-responsibility with a higher standard of equality and personal freedom, was like a fresh wind blowing through Joe's mind, which was, of course, floating on clouds of marijuana smoke.

Moon talked endlessly about something called enlightenment, a new consciousness. It was all about 'Oneness'---oneness with God, oneness with humanity, oneness with nature. Smoking the sacred weed, as Moon called it, was more like a sacrament between them, gently lifting them into a realm of peace, in which the moment became endless and deep with possibility, in which the simplest thing became profound.

Moon's dictum was to do everything you normally do, only do it stoned and that way She would teach you. "Weed is a Teacher, man. She's sacred. People don't get that. They think it's just to party and get laid or something but to me, that is a total waste. The party scene, man, is like so totally missing it. It's all about obedience, man. She won't teach you if you don't obey. You've got to pay attention and then do."

Joe was at first mystified by Moon's eccentric ways. Moon was often seized by inspirations like deciding that the furniture needed to be rearranged because the energy of the room was all wrong, or to lie face down on the earth under the full moon, to soak up the earth vibes. Joe found himself wading in the moonlit river or walking at midnight into the forest barefoot on the cool ground, learning to feel with his feet when his eyes could not see.

Moon was often inspired to 'do art' while stoned, and the library soon became cluttered with paintings and drawings. Joe also began experimenting with colors and lines. Moon's rule was just do it. Don't judge it. It's not good or bad, it just is. It's Life, man. Moon was big on spontaneous expression, letting it flow. 'Go with the flow' was another rule. Let the drawing draw itself, he said.

Joe's drawings were a revelation to him, for he had shut the door on creative expression early in life after flubbing recitations in front of his mother's friends. But now, under Moon's benevolent tutelage, he gave himself permission to express without censorship. The results were similar to cave drawings with stick figures and abstract shapes and designs. Moon declared it to be `mystical' and that maybe Joe had been a cave dweller in a past life. "Maybe," he said, as if seeking to look behind Joe's eyes into the center of his being, "maybe, you were a shaman." This seemed to carry a great deal of significance for Moon, not realizing that Joe didn't have a clue what a shaman was.

And then one day, Joe had the *experience* of the 'drawing' drawing itself. It felt like another mind thinking through his mind, guiding his hand. The lines simply flowed out from his pen with a confidence and intention that were not his own. Yet he was participating, for he was feeling the impulse and knowing exactly what it meant. It was a drawing of himself, not the outer but the inner self and hovering over him was a sinister tangled configuration with claws dug deeply into his chest. Instantly, he knew that that was the Curse. When the drawing was complete, a line of words flowed out as well, written in an elegant old fashioned script. It was a question. 'How do you know what you don't know?'

Moon regarded this with grave admiration. "That's heavy. You're there, man. You're really getting it, now."

For the first month, Joe barely slept. A furious torrent of creativity had been unleashed, streaming out of Joe's mind night and day, as if to make up for a lifetime of suppression. He was fifty-one years old and obsessed with drawing arrows, arrows in wild profusion, eyes with arrows flying out of them, heads that opened up with arrows spewing in all directions. His drawings looked as though they'd been created by a madman; yet, though he was driven, he felt utterly joyous. At last, he was coming out of the dark tunnel and the world that welcomed him was glorious and new. He plastered the walls of the library with drawings. He filled notebook after notebook with streams of words that flowed from the inner font of his consciousness. Only Moon seemed to understand that this was a good sign. Everyone else, Trip included, could only assume that Joe had finally lost his mind completely.

Fleming began looking into having his father institutionalized. This would provide a convenient pretext for evicting Moon and Trip, whom he considered little more than con-artists bent on getting something for nothing from a mentally unstable man. They had obviously brainwashed his father, pure and simple. What else could explain his bizarre behavior? And though he himself considered kitchen work beneath him, Fleming resented Moon for taking over the kitchen with his strange eastern foods, cooked with foreign and offensive smelling spices that clung to the walls of the house. In fact, he loathed the very smell of Moon's person. The reek of patchouli, in his opinion, was an unmanly scent.

And then there was the suspicious odor emanating from the library late at night, which he only later came to realize was the pungent aroma of marijuana cloaked inside the sweet heavy scent of incense. Moon did, however, keep himself clean, which certainly couldn't be said for Trip whose standards of personal cleanliness had seriously eroded after years of living without indoor plumbing.

Though Murphy wasn't exactly happy with the presence of these 'intruders', he balked at the idea of putting their father away in a mental institution. Maybe Fleming was judging them too harshly, he said. Fleming's only response was, "We shall see, won't we!"

This was not the first time he'd considered doing this. In fact, it had been in his plan from the moment he returned to Zion Crossroads in 1978. He was 33 years old and had lived in Richmond for 15 years during which time his father had gone off on numerous 'amnesia trips', leaving Zion Crossroads totally in the hands of Leonora. At the time of Fleming's return, his father had just disappeared again and Leonora was as usual trying to hold things together. Fleming promptly informed her that he was now in charge and his first official act was to install the two-way mirror in order to 'keep watch' on the small vault under the registration desk. This was a clear signal to Leonora that she was now under scrutiny, that the power struggle was officially over, and that he had won.

Leonora, however, had not rolled over without a fight. Before her death there had been an ugly confrontation. On her side, she held stubbornly to the notion that Joe would return, eventually, just as he always had, and that Zion Crossroads still belonged to him.

Fleming had dismissed this notion with open contempt. "My father surrendered all rights to Zion the day he abandoned us and even if he does return, I'll simply have him committed. Everybody knows he should have been put away a long time ago!"

"Shame on you, Fleming!" Leonora wanted to slap the mockery right off his face but she restrained herself. Suddenly she realized that she'd underestimated this strange, angry young man and for the first time felt afraid.

Fleming sneered. "Don't play high and mighty with me, Miss Leonora. How can we be sure you haven't been siphoning off Daddy's money all this time? It would have been so easy with nobody here to stop you!"

"How can you talk that way to me after all I've done for you and your family! And for precious little pay, let me tell you! Precious little!" Leonora was an imposing figure when riled to indignation, her nostrils flaring, her eyes lit with fury but Fleming merely shrugged, unimpressed.

"You know something?" he said. "I could never figure out why my father was always under your thumb, doing everything the way you wanted it. How was that ever right?"

"What are you talking all that nonsense for?"

"Nonsense? You drove Mama off! That's right! She couldn't stand it anymore, to see you strutting around like you owned the place. But what I want to know is, where is my grandmother's money? Where?"

She lifted her chin and hardened her eyes but her body was shaking. Never had anyone assaulted her dignity in such a hurtful, malignant way! Not even the worst narrow minded racists in town had ever tried to hurt her like this. "How do you think I've kept Zion Crossroads afloat all these years, Fleming? The `business' sure ain't been doin' it."

But he remained coldly unconvinced. "You mean to tell me my Grandmother's fortune, all the stocks, everything, is gone?"

"Think, Fleming! Medical bills! Your father has been in and out that hospital for over twenty years! You know what it costs to stay in a hospital for even one day?" She was on the verge of tears, but she was damned if she would let him have that satisfaction.

"How convenient for you!" he crowed. "Well, it's over. I'm in charge now, and we will no longer be requiring your services!"

Leonora was so angry she spit in Fleming's face. Afterward, she would regret that, not just because it was unbecoming of a Christian woman, but because of the look of conquest on Fleming's face. And though Murphy later successfully pleaded to have Philip and Leonora remain, Fleming had indeed won the battle. He now wielded the power over all financial and household decisions, and Leonora, not knowing her days were numbered, was never again to rest easy at Zion Crossroads.

CHAPTER XX
Kat and Portia

Having watched Fleming, drive off in a civil war uniform, Stephen Andriot was immediately back up in his room, scribbling notes at a fevered pitch and so absorbed that he didn't look up when Katherine came in. She stood there mentally tapping her foot, waiting for some kind of acknowledgement and when it didn't happen, she exploded.

"I don't know why I even bothered to come here!"

"I'm just getting these notes down before I forget them. This place is blowing my mind and the article I'm going to write is going to get me a Pulitzer!"

"A Pulitzer? Really? A little cocky, aren't we?"

"You know what a 'neo-confederate' is?"

"A neo who?"

"They're the people who want to bring back the Old South--- the Confederacy!"

"That's absurd."

"Yeah, well we might think so but apparently they are taking it very seriously. Gardner was telling me---."

"You mean you've been talking to the gardener?"

"Yeah. He says there's this group. They call themselves the Gray Knights. They're stockpiling weapons and ammunition right here at Zion Crossroads! I saw it with my own eyes!"

"So is this what you're going to be doing the whole time? Writing notes and sneaking around spying on these stupid people?"

"May I remind you, oh thou great hypocrite, that you are writing notes all the time, too! Not to mention gossiping on the phone to that idiot assistant of yours!"

"Okay fine, but I'm trying to stop now because---."
"Because?"

"Because I thought this was supposed to be a chance to---well, so we could---you know---be together." She felt her face burning with humiliation for having to spell it out. "But I feel like I've just been chasing you around all weekend and all you do is avoid me!"

Stephen rolled his eyes. "How am I avoiding you? I went for a walk with you, didn't I?"

"Technically, you were walking, yes." She picked up her notebook and started to flip through the pages as if she didn't really care. "Well, I guess I'll be seeing you---sometime." She headed for the door.

"You're never happy, are you?"

She stopped dead in her tracks and turned, rage rising to a boil. "Never happy?"

He knew he'd stumbled into the danger zone but tried to retain the appearance of calm. "If you could just look at yourself right now, Kat."

"Look at *myself*? I'm supposed to look at *myself*? How about you look at *your self* for a change?"

"You know, I really don't have time for this, Katherine. I actually have more interesting things to do than get sucked into your little junior high school melodrama."

Her voice rose to a higher pitch. "Melodrama?"

"Yeah, melodrama! Lately, all I hear from you is complaining!"

"What you call *complaining*, I call explaining. It's called communicating your feelings! Ever heard of it? Of course you're so out of touch with your feelings that half the time you don't even know what they are!"

"So what you're saying is that just because I don't exhibit that seething neurotic whatever-it-is you identify as 'feelings', that somehow makes me psychologically unbalanced?"

"Sometimes feelings are messy and difficult, Stephen! For those of us who weren't born with a silver spoon in our mouths, life isn't just a walk in the park!" She pressed her lips together as if she was finished but it kept bubbling out of her. "In other words I think you're just a little bit shallow, okay? You're perfectly happy just living for yourself! In fact, you know what I think? The only reason you stay with me at all is because I don't ask too much from you!"

"What?"

"I let you go wherever the hell you want, all over the world, whenever the hell you want, for as long as you want, and I never say a word."

Stephen looked genuinely shocked. "If you're so unhappy

about what I do, then why don't you clue me in every once in awhile. I mean, how am I supposed to know if you don't tell me? I'm not a mind reader, you know!"

Angry tears boiled up into her throat. "You would never quit your job for me! How could you? It's your life! And for that reason I know it's completely insane for me to even think of having a baby with you!" There she'd said it, the dark insane thought that had been festering unspoken inside her.

"A baby! Is that what this is all about!" To her dismay, he howled with laugher.

"What's so funny about that!" She was indignant.

"Your sister had a baby so now you have to have one, too!"

"You make it sound like I'm competing with her or something!"

"Well, aren't you?"

"Have you ever heard of a biological time clock? Well, it turns out to be real!"

"Katherine! You really think you'd be happy staying home with a puking, pooping, crying little baby? Come on, get real. You'd be bored inside of a week and have that kid popped into a daycare center so fast---."

"How do you know that?"

"Because I know you, Katherine! You are not the motherly type! You're too independent, too self-self---."

"Too self-centered? Is that what you're trying to say?" She looked calm but he knew better. "And you're perfect, I suppose?"

"I didn't say that." His instinct was telling him to make a run for it. He had gone too far and if he feared anything in life, it was Katherine's vengeance when she felt victimized. "What I meant was just that— you don't let anybody stand in the way of your dreams!" *Talk about putting a band aid on a seething volcano*, he thought.

Her beautiful face hardened into a mask of pure contempt. "You know, I'm not the only one who is self-centered in this relationship!"

"Katherine, let's not go there! Please."

"Go to hell, Stephen!"

That's when he got up to leave. Stephen had always refused to subject himself to her hostility.

"Why can't we ever have a serious conversation without you dancing out on me?"

He paused at the door, "Kat, you're the one with the phone glued to your ear 24-7. Remember?" And he'd left.

She sat stunned on the edge of the bed, staring at the empty space where he had been. Why had she lost her cool, like that? He never responded well to emotional outbursts. She shouldn't have jumped the gun. She should have bided her time, prepared him first before spilling the idea of a baby. She should have said that sometimes a door, that we didn't know was there, opens and we just have to walk through it; that they could talk it through.

She should have said things like that but realistically Stephen wasn't one to sit around talking about feelings. He never had been. His attention span was far too short. He liked to have a good time and keep things moving. She couldn't imagine him in the domestic scene with children, not at all. It would be too tame. Stephen thrived on wilderness, danger, adventure, and he would never change. Waves of desolation washed over her. She tried to meditate but it was no use, and it was too late for breakfast so she decided to go out for a jog.

Portia, too, was headed for the woods, though at a more ponderous pace. Her feet and back were already hurting and she'd woken up exhausted. With grim willpower and cursing every toe-pinching step, she trudged across the uneven ground in her thin-soled shoes, but it wasn't exercise she wanted. Nealy hadn't slept in her bed the night before, and Portia was worried.

When she'd asked Fleming at the registration desk if he had seen her, he'd merely lifted one cold eyebrow, and informed her that Nealy had gone off into the woods with his brother. This did not sound at all good to Portia. In a fury, she'd immediately headed out into the forest to find her errant sister. What was she thinking, wandering off with a strange man? Sure, he seemed harmless enough but the crime shows were full of people like him, shy and fumbling on the outside, repressed perverts on the inside. He could be a rapist or a psychotic killer!

The low hanging sky was a sullen gray as the older sister trudged stalwartly into the forest, her mind in a dark mutter. It was bad enough that she was being forced to associate with these horrible people in this horrible place that didn't even have air conditioning—but now she had to go out into the filthy bug infested woods to rescue her sister who was too stupid to realize she was in danger!

Having encountered one of the Colonel's holes, she was forced to take a detour in her pinching shoes through the thick underbrush. "Nealy? Nealy!" she wailed, catching her hair and clothing on small branches, "Where are you?"

After floundering in this fashion for a good while, Portia discovered that no matter which way she turned, she always ended up under the same big tree. The third time around, she noticed an old wooden bench buried in honeysuckle vines. Despite a deep abhorrence of nature, she forced herself to clear them away so she could sit down to rub her aching feet.

As naturally as a ball rolling downhill, her thoughts turned to the girl in the newspaper—the one who'd been found in the woods stabbed fifteen times. A renewed panic erupted and sat on her chest like a cement block. How could Nealy be so stupid, so trusting? Clearly something terrible had happened. It just wasn't like her not to sleep in her own bed! Portia's mind whirled round and round. Oh, why did she care so much? Sometimes, she couldn't explain it, even to herself! She loved her little sister, of course, even though that quiet spiritual glow and unwavering forgiveness could be so irritating. She just wished the girl would show some common sense now and then because disaster was surely coming. She could feel it in her bones.

Suddenly, she heard a sound. Someone was coming through the trees!

"Nealy!" she cried but it wasn't Nealy. No, it was that horrible woman again, that Katherine, in her cute little jogging outfit! Right from the start, Portia had taken a profound dislike towards this woman who was, at this moment, the absolute last person she wanted to see.

Unaware of Portia's anxious face peering out of the foliage, Katherine stopped at the big tree and bent over, winded from running. Portia hesitated to speak. Maybe if she kept quiet, Katherine might just run on by and leave her in peace. Of course, if she ran on by, Portia would still be lost and alone in this horrible forest— so grudgingly, the older woman cleared her throat.

Katherine shrieked. "Oh, my god, Mrs. Reed!" She laughed a little. "You startled me!"

"Sorry." Regardless of what she said, Portia always looked suspicious and sour. Nevertheless, Katherine decided to be pleasant. "Lucky you found a bench!" she exclaimed before pressing her face down into her knees for a final stretch.

"Yes," answered Portia stiffly, taking note of Katherine's long beautiful legs while tucking her own under the spreading tent of her dress. She hated her legs. They were hopelessly fat and on no account would she ever let anyone see them. "Have you seen my sister by chance?"

"No, sorry. Mind if I sit down? Whew! Humid, isn't it?"

With a blank nod, Portia slid over as far as possible, suddenly feeling very fat and unhappy about her overly fried hair-do. An uncomfortable silence ensued. "She never came in to bed last night," she said.

"Really?" Katherine sat down. *Get a grip, lady. She probably spent the night with that hunky guy, Tommy.*

"I was told she went out into the woods with that man, that Murphy."

"Well then, there you go. Actually, she mentioned to me something about him helping her to find the Healing Spring." Katherine looked up at the tree spreading above them. "Wow! This thing has gotta be at least 200 years old."

"I just can't believe she'd be so naive," grumbled Portia. "Wandering off into the woods with a strange man. "

Katherine gave her a cool smile. "Nealy looks like a big girl to me. I'm sure she can handle herself." *See? I'm being pleasant.*

Portia sneered. "That's what your type likes to think, don't you? That you can handle anything--- running everywhere, dressed in practically nothing! And then you're surprised when someone tries to rape you!"

Katherine stood up rather abruptly. *Come to think of it, maybe Nealy ran off to get away from you!* "Guess I'll get going," she said.

"It's the law of natural consequences," continued Portia as Katherine started to saunter off. "We're not living in the Garden of Eden, you know! Hey! Do you know how to get back to the house?"

"Lost, huh?" Katherine paused to give her a smug look. "Okay, sure. It's that way." Portia's wide thin mouth soured. "I just came from that direction."

"Sorry but I'm *positive* it's that way."

Portia scowled. "And I'm sure you're always correct."

Katherine shrugged dismissively. "Okay, you can follow me if you like." *That was totally rude but I'll ignore it. Just don't complain all the way back.*

Portia stood up, wincing dramatically and clutching her back. "I guess I have no choice, do I?"

Katherine pretended not to have noticed, started at what she thought was a slow place but soon she had left Portia and her complaining behind.

"I'm supposed to have back surgery this summer you know," cried Portia, angrily.

After that Katherine had no choice but to keep pace with the woman, speeding up and circling back to check on her. They continued on for some time, the tortoise and the hare, until Portia abruptly came to a full stop. "I thought you said you knew how to get back!"

"What are you talking about?" snapped Katherine, who's patience was quickly wearing thin.

Now it was Portia's turn to be smug as she indicated the very same old tree with the bench. "Apparently, we're going in circles."

Katherine rolled her eyes. "Okay, so we missed a turn. Big deal!"

"Well, what are we going to do?"

Katherine sighed. "Just sit here. I'll go find the way out then come back for you."

Relieved but suspicious, Portia sat on the bench. "You sure you'll come back for me?"

"Of course I'll come back for you!" *Silly* fool. Katherine started off down the path.

"You always thought you were better than me!"

Katherine stopped short. "What was that?"

"I said, what makes you think you'll find the way? You couldn't before!"

"That's not what you said!"

"Yes, it is!" The expression on Portia's face confirmed that she was telling the truth but Katherine had heard something distinctly different.

Suddenly a flood of memories came reeling through Katherine's mind---a shadowy hallway---a woman holding a crying infant---imploring and angry all at once. We have known each other before.

"Are you calling me a liar?" demanded Portia, glaring indignantly..

"What?" Katherine, who found herself staring at Portia open mouthed.

"I said, are you calling me a liar?"

"Huh? No, no—I'm just—never mind. Sorry."

"You didn't answer my question," persisted Portia, in a snide tone.

"What question?"

"What makes you think you can find your way now when--!"

"Trust me," interrupted Katherine in a harsh tone, "I'll find the way back!" She turned smartly and with an ear splitting scream fell right into one of the Colonel's holes.

Everything went black. Suddenly her ears were ringing and her head felt as deep and wide as the universe. Meanwhile, with no particular sense of urgency, Portia limped over to Katherine, lying at the bottom of the Colonel's hole. "Are you alright?"

Katherine looked up with a strange new clarity at the woman peering down at her and the name Charlotte to mind. This woman's name should be Charlotte.

CHAPTER XXI
The Storm
The Zion Crossroads Plantation Hotel
1980

All day the heat had been oppressive. Inside, the house was an inferno and the murderously hot day had left everyone in a paralyzing funk. At dusk, a deliciously cool breeze licked the treetops, as thunder rumbled irritably in the distance. Those limply gathered on the porches greeted the coming storm with cheers and murmured prayers of encouragement, as flashes of electricity flickered in and out of a giant thundercloud, nosing its way in from the west.

The clouds turned ominous, and when the storm hit, it was with terrifying ferocity. Lightning lashed the sky like jagged whips, the wind thrashing the trees into a furious dance, driving the rain like daggers into the parched earth. Frightened, everyone moved indoors, clustering at the windows to watch the awesome and destructive power of nature. The electricity instantly went out, engulfing them in darkness.

Soon the beam of a flashlight appeared from the dining room. It was Gardner, summoning the guests to the front parlor where Murphy had lit candles. Puffenberger immediately started complaining that his television had gone out right in the middle of his favorite show.

Gardner regarded him scornfully. This was the fifth straight year of drought and not a drop of rain since the night before Joe's burial, exactly nine months before. "It hasn't rained in nine months and you're complaining because you can't watch TV! Way to set your priorities, Puffy!"

"Gardner's right!" added Amanda. "You're being utterly selfish! We need this rain, and I for one am not going to complain. Besides, now I can take a shower that lasts more than three minutes."

"Mrs. von Hassel, it will take more than this rain to get the ground water back to normal," replied Gardner. "Besides, most of it is just running off into the river. The back yard looks like the Mississippi right about now."

Everyone crowded to the other window to get a better view.

"Where's Fleming?" asked Amanda.

"Probably up in the bat tower summoning the lightning," sniffed Puffenberger.

There was a sprinkle of laughter, but Murphy looked uncomfortable. "Fleming isn't here," he said. "He's in Richmond and won't be back until late tomorrow." He purposely left out the fact that he was attending a meeting of the Grey Knights.

"Yeah, didn't you see him, Puffy? All decked out in his Confederate uniform?" muttered Gardner, rolling his eyes.

Puffenberger glowered. "Ah, yes---the South will rise again." There was another round of snickers.

Just outside the circle of yellow candlelight, the darkness was collecting around them thick as black velvet.

"So what do we do now?" Portia's her pale face looked grim in the dim light.

Without a word, Amanda unwrapped her deck of tarot cards from a silken scarf and set them on the coffee table.

"Those are tarot cards, aren't they!" cried Katherine.

A clap of thunder directly overhead drew them a little closer together.

"You know the Tarot?" Amanda turned her attention to Katherine for the first time since her arrival.

"I had a friend in college who used to read the cards for us."

Amanda gave her best smile. "Would you like me to consult them for you now?"

Murphy cleared his throat. "Uhhh---I don't think this is a good idea."

"Why?" asked Katherine.

Amanda rolled her eyes. "He's afraid that Fleming will have a fit."

"But he isn't even here!"

Murphy shook his head firmly. "He says the cards are evil."

"Is that what *you* think, Murphy?" This gentle question came from Nealy, her eyes gazing at him calmly from across the flickering candles.

"I don't know but—." murmured Murphy, his glasses reflecting the candle flames, his face pinched.

"Then, good grief---give it a try!" Amanda was less inclined to be patient with her bumbling landlord.

"Yeah, Murph," chimed in Gardner, "Don't be such a chicken shit."

"Don't push him into something he doesn't want to do!" It was Portia speaking now. "He might be right. Who knows? They could be evil."

"If it is the Devil you're thinking of than *that* is who will answer you. It is entirely up to you who you choose to consult," replied Amanda unperturbed.

"Why don't you ask Jesus to help you?" offered Valentino, his face shining sweetly in the candle glow. "Or possibly Astrea or Vista. They can be very helpful, too." A furtive exchange of amused looks flew around the circle.

"Or what about Cupid or Comet and Blitzen!" boomed Puffenberger, striking a comical pose. Everybody roared with merriment.

"Quiet!" Amanda held out her hand. "For this, I must hold your hand so I can attune to your vibration." Murphy shyly took her bejeweled hand. "Now ask your God to help you think of a question, or a subject of concern. Hold it in your mind and pick a card."
Murphy hesitated, stricken with anxiety. Part of him suddenly wanted to pull a card very badly but he was more afraid of Fleming than of any evil spirit.

"Go ahead, Murph," said Gardner giving him a reassuring nudge. "He'll never know. Promise."

True, Fleming wasn't here, thought Murphy. "Okay but just this once." He took a deep breath and pulled a card.

Amanda nodded approvingly. "Three of Pentacles! This indicates commercial success through effort and training, some kind of a partnership."

"Partnership?" echoed Murphy blankly.

Gardner clapped him on the back. "It means the business, the renovation and everything! Way to go, Murph! It says you're on your way!"

"It does?" A cautious smile spread across his face. "That's what it really means?" There were encouraging smiles all around and a tiny cheer rose up from the group.

"Pick another card," prompted Amanda. "This will inform us of any challenges you face."

Braver now, he pulled the next card.

"Seven of Pentacles." She paused, as if weighing what to say next.

Instantly, his face clouded with apprehension. "Well, what does it mean?" He could see that the picture showed an entrance with boards nailed over it.

"I told you this was a bad idea," muttered Portia darkly.

"This is the blocked door," continued Amanda. "It indicates inertia, alienation, lost opportunities---or of course it could possibly refer to laziness---"

"Oh." Smitten, Murphy nervously adjusted his glasses. He just hoped to God he wouldn't start with the hiccoughs. "Well---thank you---but I think I'm tired now so---" He rose abruptly to leave.

Gardner pulled him roughly back into his seat. "Where ya goin', Murph? She ain't done yet! Right, Mrs. von Hassel?" He gave Amanda a rather severe look.

Amanda sighed deeply then closed her eyes as if seeking deeper within. "This card also indicates that a new vision is required to overcome such deep seated blockages. Abundance is all around you but you fail to see it."

"There now!" cried Gardner cheerfully, "That doesn't sound so bad, does it? Do another card, Amanda."

"Okay, the last card---your Ally."

Murphy pulled a card, a little more fearful now. However, this one was met with a genuine smile from Amanda. "Ah, the King of Wands, the Spiritual Warrior! He will equip you with the ability to overcome all odds."

There were exclamations of encouragement all round during which Valentino leaned over and whispered in Murphy's ear. "He's waiting...he's waiting! You're not to worry, you see?" Val's eyes glittered brightly in the candlelight making him look frighteningly mad.

Murphy smiled weakly but inside he quavered. Even the sound of it---a Spiritual Warrior---made him feel slightly queasy.

"Proud of ya, Murph!" cried Gardner, clapping the wretched fellow on the back.

Amanda turned to Gardner like a cat pouncing on a mouse. "Now it's your turn!"

Everyone laughed, but Gardner tossed it off like it was no big deal.

The Sun Child was his first card. "Sun Child. I like that!" he crowed. "That's gotta mean something good!"

"The Brightest of Blessings are upon you," continued Amanda.

"The gifts of the gods shine like the sun."

Treasure shines like the sun, he mused to himself.

"It also indicates that you need to stand up for yourself by voicing your truth."

The next card he got the Beggars Card. There was an audible groan amongst the group.

"Ah--too bad, Gardner!" crooned Puffenberger with a malignant grin.

"Hard times, poverty, loss, lack of comfort—" Amanda droned on, her eyes rolled up into her head, making her look very weird in the candlelight.. "Survival cannot be found from institutions or organizations at this time, perhaps indifference from friends, family, discouragement—wanting more, needing more, searching, always searching for more, more, more!"

Gardner's smile faded. He felt unmasked. Murphy hung his head in sympathy. He knew that this had hurt Gardner's pride.
"However, things are not as they seem," she continued on a brighter note. "There is always a choice, always something one can do to change the situation. Trust your instincts."

The last card was called The Beloved. "The card shows two ancient trees, their branches entwined in a love knot." Amanda gazed at Gardner as if straining to see something off in the distance. "Two souls, perhaps an ancient love returning."

Gardner's expression was unreadable, subdued now. He wasn't relating at all to this last card. All he could think about was the Beggar's message.

Amanda's eyelids drooped and her voice took on a sharper tone of command. "And one more!"

Gardner looked startled, "You mean you want me to pick one more card?"

Amanda's voice grew deeper and slower, as if she were slightly drugged. "No. Someone else."

"Let her read your fortune, Kat." Andriot seemed amused by the whole scenario.

Amanda turned unseeing eyes upon Katherine. "Yes. This is the one. Give me your hand." Thunder rumbled. Amanda took Katherine's hand. A collective shiver went through the group as everyone realized Amanda was in a trance.

Katherine handed her first card to Amanda who did not even look at it, but only held it with her eyes closed. "They are waiting to give you the guidance you seek, however you must do your part and put yourself in the right place at the right time. The answers lie beneath the surface."

Amanda waited dramatically in silence, eyes closed, head tilted back. After a few moments, Katherine went ahead and tried to pull the second card but two cards came out together. She tried to put one of them back, but Amanda stopped her. "They want both." Katherine handed her both cards. Amanda seemed lost in thought before finally speaking. "The Chariot indicates that you are to move forward in trust. Spirit will be your warrior. And this--the Tower--counsels you to free yourself from false pretense, take the risk of flying rather than falling." She inhaled deeply and let it out in a long slow gush. "An enlighten-ment is at hand, a shift in your thinking—embrace the encroaching change."

Katherine glanced at her boyfriend who was not doing a very good job of concealing his skepticism. "Go ahead, Kat. Pick your next card." He gave her a sly wink.

With the third card, Amanda's eyes flew open with a look of shocked recognition; once again, the image of two ancient trees, their branches entwined in a love knot.. "Ah, the Beloved." She reached to her left for Katherine's hand and to her right for Gardner's and put them together. "Ancient love returns. Love who you are; not who you pretend to be." Amanda's face was shining with joy. Those, whose hands she held, quickly pulled away from her grasp.

Suddenly something heavy crashed to the floor above them. Portia squealed, involuntarily grabbing Murphy's arm. "What was that?"

"That wasn't thunder," declared Jack.

Everyone shushed him, straining to listen.

"Probably just the Colonel," murmured Puffenberger. "Must be the full moon already. That's when he usually shows up."

Amanda, who had fallen back against the seat cushions, nod-ded weakly, as if exhausted.

"They say that after the war, he went mad looking for his lost treasure," continued Puffenberger in a provocatively low voice. "And he's still out there wandering around, digging holes. Some say you'll see him along about dusk, at the edge of the woods, just standing there."

"Dawn and dusk, the veil between worlds grows thin," mur-mured Amanda.

"Professor Valentino sees the ol' Colonel! He has regular con-versations with him, don't you Professor!" prompted Gardner.

For a moment, Valentino seemed mildly confused then his face cleared. "Oh, my yes but when he comes knocking at my door, Eloram won't let him in."

Suddenly, there came the sound of a bell from somewhere deep in the house, gradually growing louder. Anyone living at Zion Crossroads for any length of time knew what that bell meant.

The Bowens had always simply accepted the Colonel's presence in stride as if he were just another resident of Zion Crossroads. He was a relative, after all. This included all the typical ghostly annoyances like creaking floors and slamming doors, objects moved from place to place, lights going on and off. The sound of the Colonel's footsteps up on the third floor in the wee hours of the night sometimes made it hard to sleep. Even so, the worst thing he would ever do was to pull all the books off the library shelves, and pile them on the floor—something he did a couple of times a year.

The next day, Leonora, would be washing the walls down with bleach, muttering threats of an exorcism if he didn't straighten up, but this ghost was tenacious. His portrait in the dining room watched over all her efforts with contempt. his essence was indelibly stamped (like a stubborn stain) on the very identity of Zion Crossroads, and what it meant to be a Bowen.

Gardner's father, Philip Bell, was born the same year as Joe, and they'd grown up together. He was just a young boy when the Colonel died but still vividly remembered a man, ever seething with righteous indignation, going out every afternoon to dig for the treasure he'd buried before the war. It was said that he'd forgotten where he'd buried it.

In his time, the Colonel had had a reputation for being a war hero and a godly man, but according to Gardner's father, the old man had also had a demon temper, always preaching the downfall of society morning, noon, and night. His anger was chiefly aimed at the North and the federal government. In public, his temper had been viewed as righteous, a sign of intelligence and loyalty to the `Cause'. The South may have surrendered at Appomattox, but the Colonel certainly never would. He still waved the Rebel banner proudly, standing at the bulwark of hatred and contempt for everything Northern.

At home, the family, who had to endure his fiery outbursts over whether the eggs were too cold, or too runny, or too crisp, had a different opinion of him. In other words, life at home with the Colonel was hell. He seemed to despise everybody. Highest on his list was of course `the coloreds'. "Don't ever let them outnumber you," was the primary directive aimed at his progeny; and he didn't care if the colored servants heard him say it or not. But above all, he hated Northerners even more.

It was his grandson, Fairchild, coveting that northern dollar, who had transformed Zion Crossroads into a hotel and called them guests. Nonetheless, the Colonel called them invaders, insisting that the house needed fumigation after they'd `stunk up the premises'. In the Colonel's eyes, the mere presence of these strangers in the sacred halls of Zion was a sacrilege, and he made no attempt to conceal how much he despised them.

At any given moment, there was no predicting what offensive thing he might say or do, and that became the reason they'd eventually enthroned him in a room on the third floor. By then he was too feeble to go out digging for treasure. Thus, for the rest of his miserable life, he sat alone in his room, brooding over dark things, incessantly ringing his call bell.

It was a fearsome dark room, windows shut, drapes drawn against the light. The Colonel suffered from phlebitis and fervently believed his ungrateful family was purposely freezing him to death. As a young boy, Gardner's father had had to keep the wood stove in the old man's room constantly burning; all the while, holding his breath against the stench of old flesh in that hot airless room.

In his final days, the Colonel had become completely delusional, talking to people long dead and forgotten. However, his obsession with finding the treasure had never stopped so Fairchild had installed a latch on the outside of the door, to keep the old man from wandering off. The day the old man finally died, there had been a storm the night before with high winds that had taken down an enormous old tree on the eastern side of the house. It had nearly fallen on the house; indeed one of its great branches had broken right through Haden's old library window.

Little Philip had found the Colonel's corpse still sitting up in his chair, staring with a horrible certainty, his mouth ajar, waxen and gray, the veins already breaking down like spider webs below the skin. It was a terrifying experience for a young boy, though it would later become one of his best stories. Philip had always been a great storyteller, so Gardner knew all kinds of things about the Bowens; the back stair kinds of things that white folks would never want the world to know. This covert knowledge was passed down and became the underbelly of the family history, for truthfully, it was a part of the black folks' history, too. These families were entwined by a perverse destiny, their women raising the whites' children, their kids growing up together as playmates, sometimes, knowingly or not, as blood kin.

As a ghost, the old man proved to be as moody as he was in life, at times appearing old and shrouded, emanating misery and complaint. When he was angry, however, he was young and violent, and prone to breaking things

The story was that shortly after the Colonel's death, Joe's grandmother, Irene, had gone in to clean things out, but a heavy vase had been hurled at her head, crashing against the wall. That was the last time anybody had even tried to go in there. And that's when it had all started, the weird greenish light glimmering through the shuttered windows, the creaking of the old floor boards, and the sound of uneven footsteps punctuated by the sharp thump of the cane on the hard wood floors; and always the sound of the bell ringing deep into the night. The Colonel's room was still up there on the third floor, unchanged from the day he'd died, the door sealed by layers of cobwebs and dust.

Years later, after Joe had fallen off the roof, Leonora would sleep at the big house so she could tend him through the night. On those nights, Gardner had lain in the dark beside his mother, frozen with fear, listening to that bell ring and ring and ring. Once, Gardner awoke to find the Colonel standing beside the bed staring down at him. His mother, sound asleep, never heard a thing.

For some reason, Gardner hadn't been able to explain why he was crying so hysterically. He had seen some *thing*, was all he could say. "What? What did you see?" she'd asked but he was tongue-tied and she had little patience for twenty questions in the middle of the night. If Gardner woke 'Mister Joe' with all his whining, she informed him in no uncertain terms, he was sure to get him something to cry about. Needless to say, Gardner got a hold of himself pretty quick.

As an adult, Gardner hadn't thought much about the ghost until one morning, as he was rising up through that gray watery dimension between dreams and reality, the Colonel's face had appeared, twisted with grief. His mouth moved as if he wanted to speak but only a long agonized groan came forth. The Colonel was asking for help. That much seemed clear.

"I've always heard that the air suddenly gets cold like a freezer when a ghost is around," Portia said. Regardless of her pious opinions, she had a morbid interest in subjects that terrified her.

"The best way to tell if the Colonel is lurking about," suggested Puffenberger, "is from the smell---think damp wool---better yet, smelly damp wool socks---socks that haven't been changed in about three months. God, if his feet smelled that bad in real life, the stink alone could have stunned the enemy into submission."

Everyone laughed except Murphy. It was extremely ill-advised to make jokes about the Colonel's ghost. Murphy glanced uneasily at the gilt framed mirror above the mantle, fearing the Colonel would be there, watching from his world. This was the reason Murphy had broken seven mirrors.

As if in answer there came another loud knocking sound, this time from within the walls. "This is not something we should be talking about," blurted Murphy.

"A ghost can't really do anything to you unless you open yourself to them," replied Amanda curtly.

Puffenberger issued a loud contemptuous snort. "That's right! I'm not afraid of the ol' flea bag. Just tell him to take a hike! That's what I do!"

Thunder rumbled, a little more subdued now. The storm was moving off. Katherine was the first to leave, announcing that she was tired and going to bed. After falling into the hole, she still felt strange literally almost beside herself, as if not completely in her body. Besides, she was tired of being scrutinized by the others, after Amanda's unsettling tarot reading.

The others followed soon after, as the storm had calmed down, the thunder becoming just a low grumble off in the distance. Weak flashes of lightning lit the way back to the rooms, where cooling breezes ruffled the curtains, and the soothing drumbeat of a steady rain would lull them off to sleep.

CHAPTER XXII
Panovision: Dream Bodies Over Zion
The Zion Crossroads Plantation Hotel
1980

"The Invisibles do not blame us for forgetting them. They only wish us to know that they have not forgotten us."

Chief Louah

As the inhabitants of Zion sleep, their dream bodies rise like a flock of birds from the house of Zion, roaming far and wide.

Nealy finds herself in a grove of tall trees. White feathers growing out of the ground lead her to a thicket beside a deep pool of gleaming water where she discovers a beautiful swan on her nest.
"Welcome to the Crossroads between Worlds. A transformation is upon you," says the swan and she changes into a beautiful woman, radiant with light, and her babies become twelve dancing maidens. Many things are spoken that will not be remembered.

Puffenberger dreams he is lost in the Mist again, coming once again to the same Hollow Tree he'd encountered that first fateful day. "The Tree of Life, hollowed out," he thinks, and suddenly understands that this is, indeed, a fallen world. Stepping into the shadowy interior of the tree, he spies the edge of something buried in the ground. It is, he knows, the rim of that mysterious cauldron that fed him once before. Desperate now, brushing the dead leaves aside, clawing the loose earth away with his bare hands, he finally works it loose. Engraved on its side are strange symbols, words in an ancient tongue. Even so, he knows exactly what they mean. *Ask what Ye Will*. To his horror the cauldron begins to fill with donuts and cream puffs, cookies and cake. "Stop!" he cries. Stop!" Off in the distance, a bell is ringing. Sobbing, Puffenberger continues to eat.

It's his old Nazi nightmare and Andriot is hiding in a small closet, frozen with fear while fighting a powerful urge to sneeze. Slowly the door creaks open, slowly, slowly. It is Fleming with murder in his eyes and suddenly Andriot is floating free above his body. Somewhere someone is laughing.

Jack dreams that he is in a fight for his life. He and Fleming are clutching at each other's throats, rolling on the floor; his only thought being that Fleming is stronger than he looks. Awaking, he feels strangely exhausted, yet relieved that it was only a dream.

In his dream, Gardner is playing a violin. As if the instrument is part of his own body; the music moves through him on streams of exquisite beauty and grief.

Murphy is trapped in the same dark dream he's had so many times before, and it always starts the same way. He is alone in a dim room, filled with strange rustlings like whispered messages on the wind. An intruder lurks among the shadows, unseen. At some point, there is a sudden glimpse of the shadow man as he disappears behind a door; and the chase begins. In a cold panic, he's running down a narrow stairwell, down, down, endless flights; the shadow man, always just ahead, feet clattering on concrete steps, echoing into the darkness below. At the bottom there is no way out. Trapped now, the shadow man turns, pale-faced, dark eyes, feverish, triumphant. He is lifting a vial and says: "Watch! I can kill the whole world with this!" Then, to his surprise (and he is always surprised), Murphy sees that it is his own face, looking back at him.

This is the shock that usually jolts him awake and this night is no different. Resigned to the fact that he would not be sleeping anytime soon, he switches on the lamp at the very moment he notices that something is missing from his finger. It is the Ancestor's ring with its strange letters engraved on twines of silver and gold. He must have taken it off at some point because it normally fits so snugly---but where is it? Panic and despair well up inside. The thought of losing it is unbearable. This is the ring his father has always worn. This is also the ring his father has bequeathed (not to Fleming) but to himself, Murphy. And doesn't that mean something— that perhaps his father did love him— after all?

Murphy's experience of being a twin so often means that he has no specific identity. When he was a kid, people got him mixed up with Fleming all the time and soon had stopped trying to figure out which one was which. Forever lumped under the general heading of 'the twins', his sense of self has become highly abstract.

This extends even to his father for during his whole life, he couldn't remember ever having had a personal, specific conversation, much less a relationship. Murphy has always been quite literally on the sidelines, standing beside his father's bed in a hospital room or beside his wheelchair on the porch while Joe stared off into space. The boys spent more time watching TV than they ever did talking to their father.

But the day Murphy discovered the ring beside his bed, the conversations between him and his father had begun. True, they were only in dreams but they were conversations all the same; nothing sensational or even memorable, just talking calmly together in a way they had never talked when he was alive. And yes, maybe he's stupid and weak for being sentimental about a crazy man who smoked marijuana and associated with hippies of a questionable reputation. And yes, he feels guilty for not having the moral fiber it takes to truly punish and condemn wickedness, but ever since he'd started having these dream conversations with his dad, all those painful memories have started to yellow and fade like old photographs.

About 1 a.m. Katherine comes back to consciousness with a jolt.

"Katherine!" It's Stephen shaking her awake.

Katherine clings to his warm body, still in the grip of the horror of the nightmare. It's the same one she'd had earlier of being chased through the boxwoods. The breeze coming in through the window is blessedly cool and the room peaceful with the shushing sound of the steady rain.

"You cried out in your sleep." He strokes the hair from her eyes.

"What did I say?"

"Something about a jewel. "Don't take my jewel' you were saying. A ring, or something?"

No," murmurs Katherine, still oddly shaken. "Not a ring. It was a child."

CHAPTER XXIII
A Leak in the Attic
The Zion Crossroads Plantation Hotel
1980

The next morning at breakfast, rain was dripping into Puffenberger's coffee. The storm had continued unabated through the night, and by morning, the backyard was still a gushing torrent. Everyone stared at the drips issuing from the right nipple of Venus in the recessed ceiling mural above the table.

Murphy acted as though this were the most ordinary occurrence in the world, for indeed Zion Crossroads had been springing leaks ever since he could remember. He and Gardner immediately went off to explore upstairs only to discover that the light fixture in the upstairs bathroom was filled with yellowish water.

"Looks like a fishbowl," observed Stephen Andriot, who happened to be standing in the hall.

Gardner wasted no time getting to the point. "Murph! We've got to go up to the third floor before Fleming gets back from the Gray Knights meeting." Gardner knew all about fixing roofs. All through childhood, that was all his father ever did, and the first thing to do was to locate the leak. "Come on, Murph! You know we gotta do it!

The color drained out of Murphy's face. Nobody went into Fleming's private domain but Fleming. Fortunately, as Gardner cheerfully pointed out, Fleming was not here, and what Fleming didn't know wouldn't hurt him.

Andriot tagged along, curious to discover exactly how one got up to the third floor, since the front staircase ended on the second. It turned out that a door beside the second floor bathroom opened to a short hallway leading to the servant's back stairs, connecting to Murphy's bedroom suite on the first floor and the mysterious third floor which consisted of a central hall lined with closed doors on either side.

Here the air was heavy and stale. Murphy explained that when

Grandfather Fairchild had turned the plantation house into a hotel back in the 1920's, he had converted what had once been the servant's quarters on the third floor into the family's private living space. Guests stayed on the second floor and out in the Annex. Later this was where the Colonel was kept when he'd finally gone mad.

In the 1950's, after having given birth to Fleming and Murphy, Joe's wife had insisted the family be moved back down to the first floor rooms. She wasn't about to haul a pair of twins up and down three flights of stairs. From then on the third floor would remain empty, (except for the Colonel's ghost) until the day Fleming took it upon himself to move up there.

It was the year they'd turned twelve, the year their father had fallen off the roof, the year their mother had packed up and left. For Murphy it had been a terrible dark time. Until the day Fleming moved upstairs, the twins had always shared a room, but then without warning, Fleming had declared his independence and moved. He'd put a lock on the door and hung a DO NOT ENTER ON PAIN OF DEATH sign on it. This had been a devastating blow to Murphy who, for the first time in his life, would now spend the long dark nights alone.

In a place like Zion Crossroads, this was no easy thing, for when the moon was full the Colonel's footsteps creaked up and down the hall and no matter how far one burrowed beneath one's pillow, it could not block out the sound of that bell ringing deep into the night.

Ordinary children would have called out in confidence for Mother or Daddy to bring them comfort, but not Murphy. Even if they'd heard his call, he could be pretty sure they wouldn't have come. Instead, pale spirits drew near only to dissolve in thin air. So when it felt like all the oxygen had been sucked out of the room, and the temperature dropped, he'd spend the rest of the night sweating under the covers alone.

Even now in daylight, it took a measure of courage for Murphy to lead the way up that dark staircase into the stale suffocating atmosphere above. He now stood there muttering fervent prayers that the leak would be found quickly as Gardner and Andriot began a systematic exploration, opening first one door and then another.
The rooms were still furnished, though covered in sheets and a thick layer of dust and cobwebs. The closed window shades were cracked and yellowed from years of sun, casting the rooms in a sickly yellowish light. Signs of rodents were everywhere. In some, boxes of stuff had been left in disorder. For Murphy, only bad memories lived here, from a childhood spent in almost perpetual fear and confusion

"So which one is Fleming's room?" asked Andriot.

Murphy pointed to a padlocked door. "But don't worry!" he said, fishing a key out of his pocket. "He doesn't know I have this."

Gardner grinned approvingly. "Murph, you sly dog, you!"

But Murphy's expression remained grim.

Fleming's room was a shrine to Christ and the Confederacy. A huge rebel flag, like the one in the library downstairs, hung across double windows, drenching the room in a ruddy glow. Over the plain single bed hung portraits of Jefferson Davis and Robert E. Lee on either side of Jesus, depicted in his crown of thorns, rivulets of blood running down his face. It was the lonely room of a warrior priest.

Andriot picked up the worn leather-bound Bible that lay on his desk. On the inside cover it bore the name, Colonel Carter Meriwether Bowen, scrawled in faded ink

Murphy looked horrified. "What are you doing? Don't touch that!" He snatched the book from Andriot's hands, and reverently put it back. "The Colonel carried this into battle."

Meanwhile, Gardner was trying to open a window for despite the heat, it was only cracked a few inches.

"Don't! Are you, crazy?" yelled Murphy in a panic. "He'll know we've been here! Everything must be left exactly as it was!"

"Don't freak out, Murphy! Jesus! I couldn't open these windows if I tried! They're like glued shut! How the hell does he stand it up here?"

"Heat has never bothered Fleming," answered Murphy simply.

Gardner could have made a smart comment but thought better of it.

Meanwhile, Andriot was examining another book on Fleming's desk. This was also leather bound, and printed on onion skin paper as if it were holy writ but it was entitled Catechism for the Young Confederate Brotherhood, dated 1957. On the inside cover, was a pledge printed in a biblical looking script which he began to read aloud.

"We pledge ourselves to honor the memory of our Beloved Veterans, to preserve their pure ideals, to study, and to teach the truths of history (one of the most important of which is that the War Between the States was not a rebellion nor was its underlying cause to sustain slavery) and always to act in a manner that will reflect honor upon our noble and patriotic ancestors."

Beneath was this handwritten inscription:

"The only reason you are white today is because your ancestors practiced and believed in segregation yesterday. I want you for the almighty KKK.

Yours for White Victory,
Dr. Edward Bless,
Grand Dragon for Christ, Race, and Nation.

He and Gardner exchanged a look. "Well, if you think that's bad, dig this," said Gardner, indicating a stack of typewritten pages beside a manual typewriter. "A treatise written by Fleming Meriwether Bowen entitled: *'Why Racial Purity is Important'*." Andriot stood and read over his shoulder. It opened with a discussion of how the Negro Bushmen were a primitive race, not as intelligent as whites, and though they looked human, they were really just savages. They had bigger teeth for chewing purposes but smaller brains and required supervision to survive. Black's natural overseers were the whites, descended from the Hittites but even the Hittites were a subject race for the world's true masters were the Semites and their descendants were the modern day Jews. The Jews, it explained, were a predatory race with higher intelligence, and the reason for this superiority was racial purity. Jews bred only with their own kind while encouraging other races to mix. This ensured that Jews own genetic fiber stayed intact while others weakened. That way, Jews stayed in control of our government through Israel. The only way to escape this situation was the complete political dissolution of the United States.

"The only hope I see," wrote Fleming, "is a revival of the Confederacy."

"What a horse shit son of a bitch asshole philosophy!" exclaimed Gardner, his throat tight with anger. However, Andriot had heard this kind of blather before and felt only mild amusement, wondering if anyone here realized that he was Jewish. He idly picked up another notebook and riffled through the pages.

"What are you doing!" commanded Murphy, snatching the notebook out of Andriot's hands. "I told you not to disturb his things! He'll know we've---" he stopped mid-sentence, staring at the page filled with signatures, his father's signature to be exact---*Joseph Meriwether Bowen*, written over and over and over. Why had his father signed his name in Fleming's notebook? His mind momentarily stalled.

Meanwhile, Andriot had drifted over to some curious bundles of dried plants hanging over a work table crowded with numerous large mayonnaise jars filled with brownish greenish liquids and labeled Wild Cherry Bark, Swamp Maple , Panic Grass, Belladonna, Oleander Seeds, Datura.

Andriot lifted the one labeled Datura, unscrewed the lid, and sniffed. "The story is that during the Revolutionary War settlers fed some of this to the Brits and they hallucinated for eleven days before they died."

Murphy's heartbeat fluttered. Fleming's boyhood hobby had been poisoning mice and small animals "Just don't touch it," he commanded. "Don't touch anything!" It was his policy not to know too much. It was how he survived, but Gardner and Andriot ignored him and continued rummaging through Fleming's stuff.

"So what are these?" Andriot casually pointed to a large jar filled with cast iron balls.

"Mini-balls. Designed to put a fair sized hole in a man," said Gardner. "Fleming's collected them from each and every civil war battlefield. I mean, War of Northern Aggression, right Murphy?"

But Murphy was suddenly beyond hearing. He was standing before Fleming's dresser. Here, a curious collection of relics were arranged beneath a wooden crucifix bearing the tormented figure of Christ—also, a half empty bottle of nail polish, a woman's hair clip, a squashed cigarette butt imprinted with red lipstick, and a small box with what appeared to be a tiny plastic Confederate soldier bravely standing guard on the top.

All of these objects were ritualistically arranged around a black and white photo of a busty bleached blonde woman draped seductively across the porch step, hair swept to one side, lips parted in breathless imitation of Marilyn Monroe. Beside her was a child, no more than a toddler with curly white-gold hair, his face a blur, his body twisting away---a flash of energy captured by the camera for a moment in time. The words *'Happier Days, Mama & Fleming'* were penned in blue ink across the bottom. Murphy stared at the photo then reverently picked up the box with the tiny soldier.

"Mother gave us these for our ninth birthday. Of course, mine broke the first day. Fleming always took better care of his things." Murphy lifted the lid and the song `Dixie' tinkled out into the suffocating stillness. There, nestled on the cheap red velveteen was the Ancestor's ring, the one his father had left by his bedside; the one Daddy had left for him and Fleming had stolen it from him! Stolen! Murphy pressed his lips together to contain his fury.

"What's that?" asked Andriot, picking up on the stunned look in

Murphy's eyes.

"It's something that belongs to *me*," he replied, as if Gardner might argue about it. Murphy put the ring on his own finger, slamming the lid shut and the tinkling music stopped. He'd made his choice now. Fleming had forced him to it and only had himself to blame.

With that he moved towards the stairs as if to go back down.

"Wait! What about that room on the end?" Andriot pointed to a door bolted with numerous padlocks and covered in a thick mat of cobwebs.

Gardner and Murphy looked at each other.

"That was the Colonel's room," said Murphy, turning a shade pale, "and it has never been opened in my memory."

"But it's over the second floor bathroom and the dining room is below that---right?"

"Leaks don't go in a straight line, you know. It could very well be coming in on the other side of the house! Besides---I'm afraid I---don't have the key."

Gardner pulled a hammer out of his tool belt. "We don't need a key." Gardner knew the import of this moment but forged ahead as if it were no big deal. Murphy trailed behind, stricken with dread.

With the shriek of splintering wood, Gardner wrenched the rusted padlocks loose, shouldered the door open, and stepped into the suffocating stench of dead mildewed air. The light filtering through the cracked and yellowed shades, cast the room in a watery haze. The room looked like it had been ransacked, chairs overturned, drawers opened, clothing strewn about. The broken vase still lay in pieces on the floor right where it had been left fifty years before.

"Listen!" Gardner raised one hand calling for silence. "That sound!" And there it was---the steady plink, plink, plink of the rainwater. They'd found the leak. "There!" He pointed to a spot on the floor where rain was dripping in a steady stream. Directly above was a trap door, cleverly disguised by a decorative molding. "There's where your problem is." He pushed a chair up underneath and with a couple of pushes, the flat piece moved. He stuck his head up into the darkness above. "Hand me the flashlight." Andriot quickly handed it to him. They waited breathlessly below while Gardner flashed the light around. "Yep, I see it. It's coming in right near the peak of the roof." And he was seeing something else--a trunk. His heartbeat quickened. Could this be the treasure?

"Anything else up there?" called Andriot from below.

"Uh---." Gardner was thinking fast. If it was the treasure, no way was he telling them about it. He would check it out first. "Hand me the crowbar, will ya?"

"Here ya go."

With a few whacks the lock came loose.

"What's goin' on up there?"

"Uh---wait a sec!" He cracked the lid open. "Shit!"

"Find somethin'?"

"Naw, just this trunk with a---." He handed down the first item.

Andriot took it from his hands. "A violin case?"

"And---." Murphy handed the last item, a rolled up piece of canvas.

"It's a painting!" Murphy was looking at it as Gardner swung down out of the ceiling and landed on his feet as nimbly as a cat.

"A painting?" He looked over Murphy's shoulder.

"Hey, it's the guy in the painting downstairs---the Colonel," exclaimed Andriot.

A shiver darted up Gardner's spine. This was not the Colonel, though at first glance it certainly appeared to be, for this person had the same high forehead, the same angular jaw, and curly reddish brown hair. Nonetheless, this wasn't the same man. The truth was in the eyes. That look of cold impudence was gone. These eyes were soft, dreamy, fixed on something high and far away; and the color, golden like river sand shining up through sunlit water. This was Haden, the Colonel's twin brother.

"That's funny---!" Andriot turned to Gardner. "This guy has eyes exactly the same color as---!" The moment he said it, he realized that he'd put his foot into something for he caught the fearful darting look Murphy sent in Gardner's direction. Suddenly it all fell into place. The color of Gardner's eyes and those of the man in the portrait was the same. What was it Gardner had said he'd been doing? Family research? A silence descended on the room but they were all thinking the same thing. Two men, one black, one white, most likely related. The plot thickens, mused Andriot. Good material for the article.

"Wow!" Meanwhile, Gardner had removed the violin from its case. "I've always wanted to play one of these things." He set the violin reverently under his chin and drew the bow across the strings the way he'd seen it done. A mournful sound vibrated on the dead air.

"Then take it." Murphy exhaled purposefully.

Gardner just looked at him as if he hadn't heard right. 'What did you say?"

"I said, you may have the violin, Gardner."

"What about Fleming?"

"Fleming is not the only one in charge around here." There was a bitter steeliness in Murphy's voice that Gardner had never heard before.

"Well, thanks, man!"

It's the least that I owe you, thought Murphy. "And this, take this!" He placed the portrait in Gardner's hands but he would not look him in the eye, those eyes, his father's eyes, golden, like river sand; the reason his mother had left so long ago, for wasn't Gardner his own father's secret love child? After they'd closed the door and were heading back downstairs, something heavy fell inside the Colonel's room.

Murphy returned to his room, inflamed by Fleming's treachery but this wasn't just about the ring. Seeing those jars of vile brownish green in Fleming's room, had awakened troubling thoughts about things he'd purposely chosen not to think about---like Leonora's sudden and untimely death. It had never made sense that someone so vigorously healthy should just die like that without warning but he'd buried his head in the sand all because he didn't have the guts to stand up to Fleming.

Because of their mother's limited capacity for affection, the twins' childhood had been a reptilian sort of 'survival of the fittest' and Fleming had always come first. Murphy had never questioned that. His loyalty to his brother had run deep, deep as blood, but now emotions he'd buried for a lifetime, were surfacing with a vengeance. There was no getting around it. He knew all too well what was in those jars and could no longer afford to pretend that he didn't. However, until he could figure out what to do, he would have to be vigilant and bide his time.

When Gardner got back to his room, the first thing he did was to take Haden's violin out of its case. Ever since childhood, he'd wanted to learn to play this instrument but never had had the opportunity or the time. When he lifted it out of the case it felt strangely familiar in his hands and it sang like a voice long kept silent. The very walls seem to rejoice as the sound filled the rooms. Later that night, he dreamed of a barefoot woman with coffee colored skin and a yellow headscarf beckoning him down into the ravine. 'Come,' she was saying. 'Come with me'.

That morning, Katherine had awakened, still feeling strangely hollow after the fall on the previous day. It was as if she had been knocked into another dimension. The colors were so extraordinarily bright she couldn't think of closing her eyes and going to sleep. She wondered if this was what a concussion felt like. Suddenly, a new scene in the slave woman's story starting playing in her mind so clearly that it was like a movie. She quickly got out her notebook. She wasn't about to lose any of this. Here was the scene she'd been searching for in her imagination, and for some inexplicable reason, it was also the one she'd unconsciously been dreading. Yes, the slave woman would have to die in the end. The child would be born and left without her mother. A deep sadness welled up within her.

CHAPTER XXIV
Book of Joe: Part Three
Coming Home to Zion
Spring 1979

Why have you come here?
To correct something?
To forgive someone?
To help someone?
To find someone?
To discover what has been missing?

from the notebooks of Joe Bowen, 1978

The day Fleming set a trap for Moon and Trip (the 'intruders'), he'd left a significant amount of cash on the counter and hid inside the broom closet to watch through the two-way mirror. As expected, Moon soon arrived, but to Fleming's disappointment, took one look at the money and called out, "Hey! I think somebody left some money here!"

Unaware of the ruse, Murphy immediately appeared and collected the money all the while straining to discern any shadowy movements behind the mirror for even he could never be sure that he wasn't being secretly observed. Fleming trusted no one, not even his brother. Thus Murphy was not surprised that, when Moon left, Fleming emerged from the closet.

"What are you trying to accomplish by this, Fleming?"

"One best catches the rat with a piece of cheese, Brother."

"Well, as you can see, he didn't take it."

"Who's to say he didn't know he was being watched?"

"You mean you think he knows about the mirror?"

"I wouldn't be surprised."

"Fleming, you think everyone has evil intentions."

"And you really are so naïve, Murphy, if you think they do not."

Still, Murphy remained unconvinced. Trip, the ragged hippy, though he seemed remote behind his dark glasses, was always willing to help the upkeep man. Poor old Philip, broken hearted since Leonora's death and suffering with arthritis, was unable to do things like he'd used to, but Trip was never above doing the dirtiest jobs. He even helped Philip dig out the septic tank when it had gotten stopped up. Fleming certainly hadn't been of any help. He'd made sure he was nowhere to be seen when that job had to be done.

As for Moon, Murphy had to admit that he somewhat liked him, despite his oddities. For one thing, Moon loved to be in the kitchen, cooking, eating, talking; and for the first time since Leonora had died, it was clean and stocked with good things to eat. Moon was friendly and he really looked at you when you talked. Nobody had ever listened to Murphy before. After talking to Moon, Murphy almost dared to think that maybe he did have something worthwhile to say after all.

Moon had such a positive point of view about things--- not like Fleming, who always focused on what was wrong. To the contrary, Moon acted like everything was beautiful. He even used that word a lot. "That's beautiful, man," he'd say when Murphy ventured an observation.

Murphy found himself pondering things Moon had said. Once Moon had asked if he believed in reincarnation. "You know---like have you ever lived before this lifetime?" Murphy had immediately disavowed ever thinking such a thing, fearful that to even saying the word might somehow be sacrilegious. But not Moon. Moon was free and easy about everything. He believed that he had been an Indian woman in a previous life because of the way he felt about tribal ways, about trees, and nature, and how he loved to do beadwork. This rather horrified Murphy at the time, but even so it was interesting, too--- how Moon wasn't at all embarrassed to say such a thing. He accepted it as a matter of course that he had been all races, male and female, and that he had lived thousands of lifetimes. He even believed he'd been a bird at one time.

He talked a lot about his experiences in places called ashrams with yogis and gurus---all strange words Murphy had never heard before. He asked what a 'yogi' was. The only yogi he knew of was a cartoon character, Yogi Bear. In answer, Moon pulled out a framed photograph of a man with long dark wavy hair, and liquid brown eyes melting with kindness and light. Murphy had always imagined that Jesus might have looked like such a man.

"This is a very famous yogi. Look at that face, man---a fully actualized human being. Beautiful, isn't he?" Moon nodded approvingly. "You just want to keep looking, don't you? You know you can receive grace just by gazing at his photograph or from saying his name or thinking of him. In fact, I think that's what it must have been like to be around Jesus when he was in the physical body. Love is a force, man---a power."

"But Jesus was the only Son of God," blurted Murphy, fearing the yogi's picture could exert some kind of demonic control over him. Of perhaps an even greater concern was that Fleming might be looking over his shoulder. Fleming was fervently opposed to all eastern religions. He preached that all gurus were false prophets of the Anti-Christ, and that people like Moon were unwitting pawns for Satan. Maybe Fleming was right. Maybe Moon was possessed, but even so, something made Murphy want to stay and listen. Something about the picture of the man on the book cover made him want to stay and look.

Moon seemed quietly amused. "Yeah, well, you know there's truth there, but I got some problems with that little word 'only.' Jesus himself said we were *all* children of God. Look it up. Now where I come from, that makes Jesus our brother, right?"

"Yes, but he was God *and* Man." Murphy wondered if this would be what Fleming would have said.

"Jesus also said, 'Have I not told you? Ye are all Gods.' So what was that all about, huh? I know my Bible. Didn't know that about me, did ya! Yeah, I was raised Baptist. I had all that stuff crammed down my throat: breakfast, lunch, and dinner 'til I nearly choked. By the time I left home, I was almost an atheist. Too much church can do that to a person. I had to go out *there*---into the woods---where the Spirit dwells undisturbed by Man, to find my God.

"Now this dude," he pointed to the Yogi, "he says God abides in each of us as Divine Self. There is Only One Divine Self, and it is God, and He is so big that when he wanted to live in the world as a body, it took all of us to express it. Now that makes more sense to me than sending just one representative to some remote corner for 33 years. What about all the poor slobs that were born before he was? Like Moses! How was Moses supposed to go to heaven because he sure as hell didn't know a thing about Jesus. No, I think it's like we're all pieces of God---like refracted light. God is Light. That's in the Bible, too. Look it up."

"Jesus is the Way and the Truth and the Light. No one shall come to the Father except by Me," said Murphy, his blood roaring like a locomotive through his veins. After being steamrolled by Fleming all his life, debates of this sort always put him in a cold sweat. Better to stay safely in the corner, keeping silent, than to be subjected to confrontation and humiliation.

Moon was silent for a moment. "Yeah, that has always been the Church's ace in the hole, hasn't it? That's what's kept people herded into the Churches for centuries like frightened sheep. If I don't sign on, I could burn in hell. Personally, I don't think God works that way, and I don't think Jesus works that way, either. He always said 'fear not' and I say that the other kind of Church teaching is nothing but fear mongering, and I decided a long time ago I will not be bullied into heaven.

"So, I'm not afraid to go out into the world and find out about dudes like these Yogis and Masters. That doesn't change the fact that I still love Jesus, and I always will but—if you don't think Jesus and Buddha and Mohammed and Confucius aren't best friends on the other side, then you're crazy and you don't know shit about Jesus."

Murphy's forehead ached from the things Moon was saying, yet he couldn't say that it didn't make sense, for indeed, though it disturbed him deeply to admit it, some of it made perfect sense.

Moon was, at the time, making a leather pouch with a beaded belt, the kind of thing he sold at something he called 'head shops'. He was preparing his 'stash' of merchandise, and talked about how he would tour around from town to town probably at the end of August. Of course, he would need a vehicle and had thought that maybe Murphy might like to come along to be the driver since he had a car and all. Murphy hedged, saying he really couldn't, but the truth was that Fleming would never stand for it.

Moon wasn't naïve. He guessed the power that Fleming wielded over his brother. Even so, he pushed a little. "Come on, man. Live a little for once in your sweet life. When was the last time you took a road trip? Probably never. Am I right?"

Murphy looked away, ashamed. The smallness of his life was a secret source of pain to him, and yet now that he had a real opportunity to go beyond it, he was afraid. "I've got to stay. I have responsibilities."

"You mean to tell me Fleming can't manage without you for a few weeks, man? Come on, get real." Moon didn't say any more about it. Better to wait a while and see how the situation developed. Just plant the seed and let time do its thing. He knew that Murphy wanted to go but it was an inner battle he would have to fight for himself.

A few days later, Fleming announced that he had decided to clear-cut the forest. He claimed it was necessary in order to pay the taxes. However, Murphy knew that his brother had signed up to be a Tax Protester at a Gray Knights meeting and had no intention of paying taxes. More than likely it would go towards building up his secret stockpile of weapons. Everyone who lived there knew about it, but not a word was said to disturb the conspiracy of silence surrounding all of Fleming's nefarious activities for fear of his wrath.

In Fleming's mind, Zion Crossroads was going to become a rebel compound where he and his compatriots would take their final stand against the Feds. Fleming had been preaching lately to Murphy about the manifesto he had been writing. In it, he was declaring independence from the United States of America. In Fleming's fantasy, the Gray Knights would sound the clarion call and like some kind of John Wayne movie, the South would rise up and take back their country. When Fleming talked this way Murphy envisioned it like some kind of Judgment Day with coffin lids popping open all over the south and the dead rising up to sing Hallelujah!

When Murphy told the others about Fleming's plans to clearcut the forest, Moon 'freaked out' (as he always put it), pacing, and shouting, and waving his arms. First of all, no guests would want to stay at Zion Crossroads Hotel without the ancient and beautiful trees! But this wasn't just a bad business move! It was a crime, a sin! The forest was sacred, couldn't he see that?" Suddenly Moon got a crazy light in his eye. "Tell Fleming that if he wants to make money, we have a better plan."

"What plan is that?" asked Joe, blinking like a near-sighted bird through his coke bottle glasses.

"I don't know yet---," intoned Moon, imperiously, "but it's a plan that is about to be born!"

Trip shook his head, bracing himself for another one of Moon's half-baked schemes.

Meanwhile, Joe was in the midst of drawing an outlandish picture of a body with an enormous bald head being sucked into an ominous black hole. In the middle of his chest, a mournful face peered through a windowpane.

"Who's that?" asked Trip. Though he wasn't attracted to Joe's drawings from an artistic point of view, he never failed to be fascinated by them.

"I guess it's me," answered Joe, simply.

An hour later, only Moon was still awake. Trip was snoring on the couch, his head at an odd angle, a rumpled, furry mound, his round belly exposed beneath the shrunken t-shirt he'd been wearing for yet another week. Joe had passed out on the floor.

As fate would have it, the Colonel chose this moment to make an appearance, melting through the wall like mist. He appeared to be looking for something on the lower bookshelf. Though Moon was prone to get hysterical about things like accidentally getting inorganic instead of organic aduki beans, he was not in the least way upset by the sight of a ghost.

"You were hallucinating!" growled Trip, when Moon jerked him out of sweet slumber to tell him what he'd just seen.

"Honest to Goddess, he was right over there, looking through the bookshelves. He was definitely looking for something. Trip answered him with a snore, so Moon had to wake him up again because he was just remembering a very important dream about a vacation his family had once taken at a place called Pirates Cove.

"Huh?" muttered Trip, smacking his lips through the fog of sleep.

"So I'm on this pirate ship again and it's just like it was when I was twelve years old, man! It had these big white sails and the flag with the skull and crossbones, man! And they're firing these cannons, and we're all dressed up like pirates!"

"Holy Jesus, Joseph, and Mary! Would you let me sleep?" Trip rolled over to face the other direction but Moon just kept right on going.

"And the staff people are, like, sword fighting all around us like Errol Flynn!" continued Moon.

Wide awake now, Trip trudged over to the bookshelf, growling for something to read, anything to block out Moon's incessant yammering.

"What are you doing?" cried Moon indignantly. "I'm trying to tell you something."

"When are you not telling me something? Besides, you know I hate hearing your dreams."

"But this is important!"

"It's always important!" Sometimes having to communicate with this birdbrain was almost physically painful.

"So, the ship lands on a savage island—!"

"Ship? What ship?"

"In the dream, we're on a ship, and they divide us into groups and give us treasure maps. And we go out, and I'm looking for the treasure."

"And did you find it?" By now Joe was the only one listening, as Trip continued to look for a book.

"Well, then I woke up."

"Perfect!" exclaimed Trip, who was listening after all.

"But that's not important! Don't you get it? The idea is the treasure! A gift from the Muse!" Moon had always talked a lot about the Muse. He even left little offerings to Her---the last few bites of his favorite food or a bit of marijuana scattered on the wind. He always said this was probably because he had had a past life in Ancient Greece.

"So we're supposed to go to Pirate's Cove?" Joe had his crazy, confused look with his wiry hair sticking every which way and squinting with all his might because he couldn't locate his glasses.

"No," sighed Moon, reminding himself that Joe's lack of imagination was not something he did on purpose. "But we are supposed to make Zion Crossroads into a Treasure Hunt, except instead of pirate treasure, people will be digging up the Colonel's Civil War Treasure! This is the divine guidance we've been waiting for, man!"

Trip groaned. It was those annoying words '*supposed to*' that peppered Moon's language that made it sound like he had a direct line to Divine Will. That and '*meant to be*'---were favorite phrases in Moon's lexicon but what they really meant was that everybody was supposed to do what Moon wanted to do.

"I even thought of the name. We could call it the Zion Crossroads Plantation Treasure Hunt!"

Trip promptly declared this a lousy idea.

Moon accused him of being hostile, then went on to describe The Vision: people in period costumes meandering around, interacting with the guests, mock skirmishes between Union and Confederate soldiers, and a black slave playing a banjo, singing songs, and telling the `legend' of the Colonel's treasure.

Trip said it was a "shameless capitalistic Disney-fication of a tragic moment in our history", pointing out that it was also racist to have the black slave playing a banjo. "Besides, we don't know where the treasure is or even if there is a treasure!"

"The people don't need to look for the real treasure! It can all be fake! We'll make up the clues and bury some kind of cheap junky toys, or candy, or jewelry. That's all we ever got in Pirate's Cove, and we still loved it, man!"

"But isn't that false advertising?" asked Joe, anxiously.

"Joe, you're getting hung up on the details."

Trip rolled his eyes, "Right! Like details don't matter!"

A shouting match ensued. Nothing set off Moon's dark side quicker than someone disrespecting his Divine Guidance. When Moon got riled like this, he reminded Trip of his mother's feisty little dog Romero. As ridiculous as he might seem, you didn't mess around with Romero. After mounting a respectable resistance, Trip grudgingly agreed to dress up like the Colonel, but only on the condition that he would be made to look very, very scary, possibly with flesh hanging in strips off his face, and/or missing an eyeball. (Moon said it would be easier just to make him headless, but Joe pointed out that that would not be true to historical facts).

Silence fell upon the room, as Moon started writing down ideas for the Treasure Hunt and Trip went back to the bookshelves. Even with Moon's blessed silence, he still needed something to distract him from his unfinished novel which had been hanging over him like a dark cloud---Albatross VI, he was calling it now--- or was it VII? He was beginning to lose count and that was not a good sign. He had the dismal feeling now that he'd never be free of it. To think he could have been an accountant, a simple, predictable life with a clear set of rules that even he couldn't have argued with---but no! He had to go out and try to change the world.

Haden's library proved to be a treasure trove in itself but for a 19th century man of letters, a renaissance man's library. Opening the covers, they gave off the stale musty aroma of a book that hadn't been opened in over a hundred years, yet there was the occasional food stain and folded corner that showed that these books had indeed once been well loved.

From the lowest shelf where the ghost had been searching, there were folders with yellowed sheaves of paper filled with musical notations; pages and pages, handwritten, ink blotches and all. Whoever had made them was no slouch, a philosopher, artist, *and* musician no less. Trip pulled out a sketchbook filled with pencil drawings, watercolors of gardens, landscapes, and female figures.

On closer inspection, however, it appeared to be just one woman and definitely not a white one. Hello! Now this really got his attention. Her sweetly rounded features were more like those of an African. "What the hell? He's drawing pictures of his slave girl, or what?" In the early pictures, she was shown cleaning, dusting, scrubbing floors; hands at rest in her lap, face tilted, eyes gazing toward something distant, something lost. The various sketches showed a woman all at once, strong, proud, enigmatic, and sad. She was a beauty but she had known pain. This Haden guy had been an incredible artist, capturing an inner radiance that made the renderings exquisitely life-like.

Meanwhile, Joe had stretched out on the couch and though he appeared to be asleep, his mind was roaming the wreckage of the past. Talk about the treasure had stirred unpleasant memories about his ex-wife, Mary Glenn, and her vicious accusations then suddenly, he remembered that summer morning in 1934 with his grandmother, Irene.

He was eight years old, but it came back to him like it was yesterday, sitting with her in the library window seat overlooking the rose garden. Everything smelled like roses. Even she smelled of roses. He could still see the dust motes dancing on a beam of sunlight and the letter she held in her hand. She'd asked him to read it, but the handwriting was old fashioned and hard to make out and there were too many big words. He'd quickly gotten restless, but she was more insistent than usual and told him to try harder because this was important.

"The Colonel left this for you, sweetness, so you'd know where to get the treasure. You want to find the treasure, don't you?" However, when he'd started to cry she'd given in and said they'd try again later. He was young and like a gangly long legged colt, too big a boy to be sitting on her lap, but she'd pulled him into her arms all the same and held him close. He didn't mind. Somehow, he knew that she needed this more than he did.

Shortly before she died, she'd given him the letter and told him to keep it safe but he'd never been able to remember where he'd put it. Years after, he'd made the mistake of telling his wife about the letter with the treasure map, and she'd never let him forget what a stupid oaf he was for forgetting where it was.

Later when she had reasons to suspect Joe of having an affair with Leonora, she came up with more sinister explanations for why Joe 'couldn't remember' where he'd hidden it. She'd concocted the myth that maybe he and his black mistress were plotting to keep her out of the loop entirely so that, once they'd shoved her out of the way, they'd be free to enjoy the treasure for themselves.

For all the commotion that it had caused in his life, it was pure irony that Joe had never really been too interested in the treasure lost or found; another thing his wife had found absolutely infuriating.

Thinking now about his grandmother, it seemed odd that the Colonel would have entrusted a letter, revealing the location of the treasure to someone who didn't even know how to read it. She'd grown up in the 'wild hillbilly mountains,' as she'd called them, and so had never learned how. It was her beauty that had drawn the only son of the Zion household to brashly fall in love with her. They'd married on impulse, but he'd proven to be a drunkard and luckless gambler, who would soon abandon her, leaving her pregnant and totally dependent on his family. And though loved by her son, Fairchild, and his son, Joe, she would never be accepted as an equal by the other women of the family and was thus treated little better than a servant.

Joe could still picture her with her mop and bucket, cleaning the floors, cooking in the kitchen, doing the laundry. She was always quick to say that nobody made her do these things. She liked to help. Besides, it was the only thing she knew how to do.

The other women of the household certainly never bothered to touch a broom or a frying pan and weren't even too involved in caring for their own children. They always called upon servants to do those sorts of unpleasant tasks. But when little Joe had been born, her only grandson, Irene had welcomed him into her life with unabashed joy and had devoted herself to him every waking minute. She and she alone had raised him and as a result, he had loved her best.

He couldn't remember much about his mother, Gwyneth, except that she was beautiful and fashionable, spending an inordinate amount of time in front of the mirror and never much liking his hugs for fear that he'd get dirt on her dress or muss her hair. Maternity wasn't her thing and later when Joe's twin sons were born that had been her cue to take off for Florida. She and his father had never looked back.

Suddenly another memory; one so ancient it could have happened to another person in another life, opened like a flower in his mind. He was still the same small boy, perhaps even younger, walking in the verdant hush of the towering forest, endlessly dark, endlessly mysterious. Irene was up ahead, coaxing, coaxing, taking his little hand and pulling him down a narrow path that led to a waterfall streaming into a deep pool. She laid him on the mossy ground and covered him in dry leaves. He still remembered the heady fragrance of living water and earth and the enormous rock towering above.

"The water will take away your bad dreams," she'd said, and she'd anointed his feverish forehead. She'd made him drink it, too, because he was sick with the kind of fever that brings bad dreams. "Lie still now so's to let the fairy lights to heal you, Joseph." Her voice slid over him like a spell, and then she'd closed her eyes and started to sing, and all the sorrow and weariness melted from her face, making her beautiful again.

He remembered the blue light and how it clothed them in a kind of secret joy and he was falling, endlessly falling into a tiny rabbit hole inside himself, becoming very, very small. Yet, even as he shrank, there he was, growing bigger—bigger than his body, floating. And a *closeness* came upon him, as if he and Irene, the tree, and the blue light were all held together in one embrace. Someone else was there, too---someone he could not see.

And as her song faded into stillness, she wept and asked for the Lord's hand upon little Joseph. Then other Lights joined them and he felt many Unseen Hands upon him. As young as he was, he could feel her sadness and reached out to hold her gentle earthly hand. Her cheeks were wet with tears. "You do love your ol' Granny, don't ya son?" she'd murmured, patting his little hand.

Now, basking in the memory of his grandmother's presence, Joe wept. How long he had buried the pain of losing her, living so many years in this numbed state, an exile from his grief. But though it was painful, it was also comforting to think about her again, and he wished he knew more about her people's ways back in the mountains where she'd come from, about the healing powers of nature, the phases of the moon, and what she'd called the Fairy Lights. Her spirituality had been earthy and superstitious, but she'd had a warm, personal relationship with Jesus and talked to Him about everything, right out loud, as if He were another person in the room. He still remembered the prayers she'd taught him, the Lord's Prayer, and another prayer to his Guardian Angels, calling them, 'one to his head', it went, 'one to his feet, one to his left side and to his right, two more abide.'

As a child, Joseph had recited these prayers every night without fail, for he'd wanted to be as good as he could possibly be and believed everything she had told him. But when he was eight years old, his grandmother had died and life started to unfold in an unfriendly way. As he grew older he'd gradually lost touch with that feeling of awe and trust in an All-powerful Unseen Being. Now in light of all the pain he'd suffered, it seemed more like childish wishful thinking and worry took its place as commander of his daily thoughts. Not that there hadn't been moments, like after he'd fallen off the roof, and after the first amnesia episode, when in desperation he'd prayed for help. But in the light of day, he was never sure he even believed that God was real because if He were real, how could He be so cruel?

Trip watched over Joe's shoulder, as the latter put the finishing touches on another picture, this one of a woman holding a child, the moon filling the page behind them, stars scattered across her forehead and on her breast. It was the first truly beautiful piece of art that he had seen Joe make.

"Now that is art, man," he said, admiringly.

"It's not mine," murmured Joe.

Trip gave him a puzzled look.

"It drew itself," explained Joe, quite simply. "I don't know how to draw."

Trip looked at him coolly. "Well, for someone who doesn't know how to draw, you do it pretty damn good."

The next day Moon's bag of marijuana had mysteriously gone missing. Moon spent the entire morning in the throes of moral outrage, desperately searching, only to find the empty baggie in the kitchen trashcan. Who could have done such a reprehensible act?

At this moment, Fleming and Murphy arrived on the scene.

Moon's typically laid-back style was immediately displaced by the wrath of Romero, the enraged chihuahua. "What the hell happened here?" He waved the empty bag accusingly under Fleming's nose.

Fleming raised an eyebrow. "I threw it out the window."

"You what?" Moon's face was like thunder.

Then with deadly calm, Fleming coldly informed his father that he and his parasitic friends would have to leave or he was going to call the police.

"Joe owns this place!" cried Moon. "Not you! It's not up to you!"

Fleming's lip curled into a menacing smile. "I will do whatever is necessary to protect Zion Crossroads from con-artists and evil-doers."

"Who's calling who evil, you psycho son of a bitch?" Moon was up into Fleming's face, chest to chest but Trip quietly pulled him off.

"Cool it, macho man."

Moon violently shrugged off Trip's restraining hand. "Yeah, well you may think you're getting away with something, Fleming but you're not getting your claws on this place. Understand? As long as Joe is alive, things are going down the way he says! Not you! Tell him, Joe. Tell him about the plan."

Everyone looked at Joe. It couldn't have been a worse moment for selling Fleming on any idea, much less this one. Nevertheless, Joe stumbled into a disjointed ramble about transforming Zion Crossroads into a community based on equal partnership, a democracy in its purest form.

"A *community*?" Fleming almost choked on the word. His eyes sharpened into daggers. "Equal partnership? Does that mean equal *ownership*, too? Just where exactly do my brother and I fit into this scheme?"

Joe blinked owlishly behind his thick glasses and the others held their breath. This was not going to be pretty.

"Well, you'll be a part of it, of course. You are my sons," continued Joe. "Now I know what you're thinking, Fleming---the taxes---how will we get money for the taxes. But we've thought all that through, and Moon here has come up with a brilliant plan to create a business!"

"To attract tourists!" added Moon.

"Yes, and we'll call it the, 'Zion Crossroads Plantation Treasure Hunt!'"

"Treasure hunt?" exclaimed Fleming and Murphy in unison. Everything stopped as if Time itself had frozen.

"Yes! It'll be a way to bring tourists back to Zion Crossroads. Isn't that—-?" Joe faltered due to his son's horrified faces. "Moon, show him one of the uh, advertising pamphlets. It has all the details. Show him the pamphlet, Moon!"

"I don't want to see the pamphlet! I want the map!" roared Fleming. Everyone in the room jumped.

"But Fleming, it isn't--it's not---!"

Fleming's thin lips twisted into a bitter smile. "Mother always said you had the map, that you were hiding it from us!"

"But---no, I never---."

"What a cunning liar you've been, Father. But now you've gone too far! I used to think you were just weak and maybe even a little simple minded, but now I'm afraid you are completely possessed by demons!"

"Fleming!" Joe's face crumpled.

"But if you think I am going to stand by while you take my inheritance and pass it around to any Tom, Dick, or Harry who walks through the door— well! You have another thing coming! How dare you!" He grabbed Joe by the shoulders and shook him until his teeth clacked. "How dare you!"

"Fleming!" It was Murphy shouting, fearful that his brother might go too far, but Fleming pressed on. "Are you so brainwashed, Father? Can't you see what these con artists are doing? If you don't wake up they're going to take Zion Crossroads right out from under us! Now, I want that map and I want it now!"

Joe remained mild even with his shoulders up beneath his ears. "Well, of course, you can have the map, Fleming but it's not real! It's just a made up sort of thing, for the—the treasure hunt."

"I'm not sure I can even believe you, Father! Not after the way you've deceived Mother and me. No, I think you do have it. I think you purposely hid it from us all these years!"

"But that's not true, Fleming! That was never true. I never lied to your mother!"

Fleming disdainfully cast his father aside like an old rag. "Sometimes I have to wonder if you haven't lost your mind completely. In fact, I wonder if you don't need to be put away in a mental institution."

"Fleming---don't!" murmured Murphy from the background.

Joe grew befuddled and diminished beneath Fleming's imperious glare. "But you wouldn't do that to me, would you Fleming?" he said. "Put me away? I mean---what have I done that makes you think of doing that?"

"What have you not done to make me think that, Father?"

"I---I only want to try to make things better. That's all."

"When have you ever taken any interest at all in Zion Crossroads? All these years you've done nothing! Absolutely nothing! You weren't even here half the time! And now Zion is falling apart, Father! The roof is leaking, the whole place needs to be painted, we need a new septic system and the taxes have gone up! So how in the world are we going to pay for all that when grandmother's stocks are depleted by your black mistress who squandered---."

"She was not my mistress, Fleming! She was Leonora, your second mother and I will not have you talk about her like that!"

"Get off your high horse, Father! You have no right to even speak when all you do is to sit around half the night smoking illegal drugs with these horrible people you call friends. And now, you waltz in here and try to take over? What gives you the right? I've been the one keeping this place together---not you!"

Murphy glanced furtively at Fleming waiting for his brother to bestow at least half the credit on him, but Fleming was not one to share, nor was he one to admit that it was Leonora who had run Zion, and that it was when she died, that it had started to fall apart.

"Well, I'm sorry for that," mumbled Joe, his voice fraying. The light had gone out of his face, and suddenly he looked old.

"Why did you even bother to come back? Can't you see that you're not wanted here?"

Joe cringed beneath his son's fury.

"Now, I want that map---the real map! Immediately!" Fleming wheeled out of the room in a burst of righteous indignation with Murphy stumbling close behind.

Moon dismissed the twins with an obscenity and resumed his search for the marijuana. Stricken, Joe stared at the floor, guilt gathering like a dark cloud inside his chest. How could he have been so blind? His sons resented him and quite possibly even hated him. And hadn't they ever right?

Trip was watching Joe closely, inscrutable behind his dark glasses and grizzled beard. "Don't listen to him, man."

"But it's true." Suddenly Joe was having trouble catching his breath. The room was spinning. "I haven't done one thing for them or for Zion---not for a long time."

"He's just trying to manipulate you, Joe! Don't let him do that! You're the one in charge! Put him in his damned place!"

But Joe only shook his unkempt head. He knew he had to make it up to them somehow. He had to put the welfare of Zion Crossroads and his sons above everything else! No more sitting around in a marijuana haze, drawing pictures! For once, he would do things right!

The morning after Fleming had verbally eviscerated him, Joe was determined to start a new chapter to prove that he could do better. He met with Philip to discuss the long list of problems they faced. They both agreed that the septic system would have to wait. The painting was do-able but before all that could be done, the roof needed to be repaired. No sense in painting the walls if the roof was just going to leak.

They both looked at each other for a moment, weighing the situation in silence. With his arthritis it was out of the question that Philip should be asked to go up on the roof, and there wasn't the money to hire a professional. Joe took a breath, "*I'll* have to fix the roof," he said and headed to the shed to get the ladder.

Philip dogged his steps the whole way. "Are you sure you should be doing this?"

"I'll be fine." Joe was hoping to appear more confident than he felt. "Besides, who is going to do it if I don't? You're in no condition to do it."

"But what about the twins? Why can't *they* do it?"

"No, Philip. I've been relying on them too much as it is! Now I said I was serious about helping out and I've got to prove that I'm serious. I need to win the boys' trust!"

"But can't you win it some other way besides going up on the roof, for Pete's sake?" Philip didn't want to have to spell it out. He didn't have to. They both knew what could happen.

"I'll be fine," said Joe again with forced self-assurance.

Fortunately, he'd only made it to the second step before it broke under his weight and sent him sprawling. But though he only sustained a few scrapes and bruises, he was shaken to his very core. Philip quietly returned the ladder to its place in the shed and they both tried to forget the whole incident; however, the next day, inside the space of an hour, Joe had lost his ring, his keys, and his glasses.

This kind of bad luck had not happened to him for a very long time, not since losing his mind and going off to Earth People's Park, anyway. But right away, that old familiar feeling of doom rose up inside him.

The ring had been handed down, generation to generation, all the way back from the Ancestor. Joe's father had given it to him on the day he married Mary Glenn, but it had symbolized much more than a marriage. It had represented Joe's new position as head of Zion, head of the home place. And as for losing the keys, well, it had hurt his pride that was already about as sore as a kicked shin, however he could accept this with the same stoic resignation that had sustained him his entire adult life. Life was for losing. Life was painful. That much he had learned.

But without his glasses, he was blind. He wouldn't survive ten minutes without his glasses. After flailing around, cursing like a mad man, knocking over a lamp and banging his knee, he'd forced himself to sit down and think, panic rising up like flood waters.

He'd found himself back in his old chair on the porch, staring blindly into an all too familiar fog, paralyzed with dread. It was happening again. The Curse had returned. He struggled to think. Why did any of this have the power to disturb him at all? Hadn't he gotten past that? Yet, obviously it was still there, some deeply buried pain, as if hidden behind dirty windowpanes.

Maybe it was something he had not wanted to look at or see or know, something he couldn't begin to name, a dull, mute animal pain. Now that he was looking at it, however, it had unfurled itself with virulent ferocity. It wasn't dried up, or desiccated at all. It was still vibrant with life, seething with insinuation.

A wave of loss and unworthiness swept over him, casting him adrift on an inner sea of self loathing so potent, so unbearable that he wanted to twist out of his skin and run away but from what---himself? Still, he knew very well what it was. It was Defeat trying to squeeze the life out of him.

He realized that all his life he had felt this way, impotent, helpless, useless. Memories surfaced of being pushed and prodded into competitions and sports activities that had always ended in humiliation, despair; memories of himself always the one to be hanging back, insecure, and whiny, a disappointment to his father, an outcast among his peers.

Now, after getting to know Moon and Trip, after daring to think that he'd actually escaped his dark fate, here he was slammed back into the same old black hole of desperation! The exhilarating rush of creativity and inspiration that had given him new life, stopped dead in its tracks. Maybe, he thought, if he threw himself off the roof again, this time he would die. But beneath the surface of his defeat, a boiling rage refused to let him---not just yet.

Later, the solution to the problem was quite mundane in the end. He lifted a folded newspaper and there found his eyeglasses. A few minutes later discovered his ring on the windowsill over the sink just as Philip came in to hand over the keys that he had borrowed earlier without asking.

Suddenly it all seemed nothing more than a trick staged by the universe to set off the time bomb ticking inside him. But there would be no pretending this anger away. No! For once it did not bow down and take its place in the corner. That's when he knew that he couldn't stay in this house any longer. There were too many ghosts here. When he heard Moon and Trip coming, he slipped out the back door, past Philip who was working on the car out by the garage, and headed out into the woods. He couldn't bear to see anyone---not right now.

Generally, houses fall apart slowly, invisibly. Destruction, like a slow moving glacier, invades inch by inch, until one afternoon without warning a rotten board gives way underfoot, a window refuses to open, the paint blisters up on the south wall. It is the same way for people. The deep internal structures start to give up and give way, and one morning a person wakes up only to find that there is nothing left inside--- to keep him from falling.

CHAPTER XXV
Book of Joe: Part Four
The Zion Crossroads Plantation Hotel
August 1979

How far can you see into the dark?
As far as you can cast your light.

from the notebooks of Joe Bowen

Rage had given Joe the energy to walk far into the woods, where he slept on the ground that first night. Awakened before dawn by a ravenous hunger, he'd slipped back to the house and stolen enough food to last him, then returned to his camp. He absolutely did not want to be seen by anyone. He wanted to be alone. He had to be alone, and his only thought was that he wasn't going to be pushed around by his guilt or by other people any longer. He was going to do what he wanted to do even if he had no idea what that was because for once in his life he was determined to find out.

All his life, he had lived on the edge of everything, fearing judgment, consumed by failure and despair. Suddenly, he realized that he had to take the center spot in his own life. He had to be the star of his own show, and if he didn't he would die, but he didn't know what he even wanted, much less how to get it. All he could think to do was to sit on the ground under a tree and wait. He wasn't worried that his mind was blank because Moon had shown him how to summon an idea. Just put the question in the mental stew pot and let it simmer on the back burner, Moon would always say. Then do something else for a while. When you're not looking, there it will be---the idea, the answer to your question.

And it turned out to be true, for soon Joe had started to think about tree houses. He was remembering how he'd always wanted to live in a tree house just like the Swiss Family Robinson. Then he realized he was sitting under the perfect tree for a tree house, a magnificent live oak with its majestic limbs outstretched as if welcoming him up into Her branches. The decision made itself. He was going to build a tree house and live there by himself. He was never going back to that nightmare house of Zion ever again.

Over a period of days, he began pilfering lumber from a stack behind the garage; then tools from the shed and other supplies for his new home always careful not to be seen. There were moments when he almost got caught, but to his amazement he always managed to escape unnoticed as if protected by some magic spell of invisibility. It occurred to him now and then that maybe he really was insane like Fleming had said, but even that didn't matter to him anymore. All he knew was that he wanted to be as far away from the world as he could get.

The twins assumed their father had gone off on another one of his amnesia breaks from reality, like he'd done so many times before, so they didn't bother making much of a search. Moon, however, was not one to give up so easily and three days after Joe's disappearance, Moon came upon him sitting forlornly on the ground in the middle of the woods, surrounded by odd pieces of lumber representing failed attempts at building a treehouse. All the initial enthusiasm and confidence had been completely quashed by the unforgiving nature of a two by four.

Fortunately, Moon found nothing unusual about a fifty year old man's decision to run away from home and build a treehouse. Joe was obeying the Flow and that was all that mattered. So instead of asking questions, he picked up a hammer. "You're in luck, Joe! I know everything there is to know about building tree houses! I used to live in one back at Earth People's Park."

By the end of the day, they had built a sturdy ladder that reached up to the first branch. Moon was the first to try it and scrambled up as nimbly as a squirrel. However, Joe held back. Moon could see that his friend was thinking very, very hard about this, so he simply pointed out that if Joe were going to live in a tree, he'd have to climb the ladder.

When Joe did take a breath and climb, it was not because he was brave, but because he could not find it in his heart to disappoint the only person willing to believe in him. However, once he was up there, gazing out into the sea of leaves and sky, all his trepidation vanished. He was in heaven! What a rush! He'd done it!

It wasn't long before Joe was climbing up and down the ladder with total abandon. The building went up quickly and in seven days time they had a structure worthy of Swiss Family Robinson. But on the morning of the seventh day, Joe awoke realizing that it was the eleventh of June, the twins' birthday. A sudden wave of panic convinced him that he needed to go back to the house. Was this, he wondered, the Flow telling him he had to go? In his hurry, he missed a step and skidded down the ladder, scraping his arm.

"You sure you want to do this?" asked Moon. Everything had been going so well the past seven days.

"I'm sure," replied Joe, and promptly tripped over a stump.

"You could send a note," suggested Moon.

"No, I have to go. I've missed too many birthdays as it is." Joe doggedly picked himself up and after ten steps, fell into one of the Colonel's holes.

Standing at the edge of the hole, Moon peered down at Joe sprawled in the weeds. "What is it about that house, man? Your body doesn't seem to want to go there."

Joe lay there, absolutely stunned. "It's the Curse!" Joe was dismal.

Later, Moon and Trip were sitting with Joe in the tree house discussing the situation.

"You know what I think?" Moon was saying, "I think Joe needs to get really clear about this Curse thing before he goes back to the house."

Trip dismissed this as hogwash. "There are no such things as curses! It's all in his head! That house has no power over him unless he thinks it does!"

"Maybe it's a family thing handed down from generation to generation, just like in the Bible, the sins of the father handed down to the third and fourth generation. I mean, let's get real here. Joe's ancestors were slave owners. That's a lot of bad karma! You reap what you sow, man. That's Cosmic Law," argued Moon.

"You're making a superstition out of the whole thing!" Trip was yelling now as if Moon was hard of hearing. "It's Joe making Joe fall into the hole! The curse is all up here!" He jabbed his finger into Moon's temple---tap tap tap---like he was stupid, too. "If you ask me, he's just got to stand up to his fear and tell it to take a hike!"

The raging chihuahua was getting ready to bite. "What are you doin', man? Stop tapping me!"

"I'm trying to pound some sense into you. All this talk about curses is medieval!"

"Why can't you listen to my ideas without getting all mad about it, man?"

"Well, then what are you suggesting? A damned exorcism?"

"Maybe."

"Stop!" shouted Joe, suddenly. "Stop arguing! Just go away and leave me alone!"

Dismayed, Trip and Moon slunk off into the forest.

Moon returned a few hours later, and was unceremoniously dismissed by a flying shoe. Joe did not want to talk to anyone. The next morning, Moon arrived announcing from a safe distance that he had a sack of supplies and that he didn't feel like getting hit with a shoe. Joe peered down from the tree house, his eyes hollow and haunted looking. Remaining silent, he dropped down a string with a note that read. "How do I get clear?"

Moon scratched his head. "Sorry but that's for you to figure out, Joe---not me."

The shock of falling into the Colonel's hole had done something to Joe's nervous system. He felt different, removed, literally beside himself, as if he'd been knocked into the next room. High pitched sounds were moving in and out, sometimes on the left and sometimes on the right, his own voice echoing inside his head. There were rims of light like halos of color around the trees, around plants, animals. Everything had changed.

It was not entirely unpleasant but rather like being suspended in a hollow sort of peace. His ordinary thoughts, felt very far away and unimportant. Like slow persistent ants moving doggedly across the surface of his mind, they had lost all power to disturb him. He was neither asleep nor entirely awake, for the boundaries between worlds had blurred and he was dreaming with his eyes wide open.

Consequently, he wasn't all that surprised when his grandmother suddenly appeared in the tree house, looking just as he remembered, her soft wrinkled face radiant with kindness and wisdom. She talked quietly, as if no time had passed, asking about his problems, but as he wept, her face grew steadily brighter, and younger, and more beautiful until she was blazing with a light so bright that he had to shield his eyes.

"Ask God for help, Josie. Knock and it shall be opened. Ask and it shall be given. If your heart is good and true, He'll smooth out the road for you and lead you step by step but you've got to remember to ask. His hands are tied if you don't ask." And then she was gone.

Why Joe believed in God, he could not tell you, but long ago, he had adopted a fuzzy notion that somehow he had offended Him; that he was trapped in this prison of the Curse as punishment. The question he now struggled with was how was he going to connect to this God because if he couldn't do that, it really didn't matter if he believed in Him or not.

So he looked up and asked the air, "How do I get clear of this curse?" He said it out loud and then he added, "I need help."

After that he must have fallen asleep, for suddenly he is dreaming. He finds himself wading through dead leaves like water. He is on his way back home to Zion. All the colors have drained away, leaving the forest naked and blank. His breath empties out into the stillness that presses against his ears, broken only by the rustling of his feet through the dry leaves.

Suddenly, he comes to a fork in the road. Somehow he knows he has been here many times before and is not at all surprised to find a cardboard box right in the middle, blocking the path. He is just about to push it aside, when he hears a voice coming from inside, chanting: "The World is Small. The World is Dark, so very, very dark. I am Small, I am Dark, so very, very dark."

When Joe taps on the box, the chanting stops. He calls out a soft hello.

Immediately there is a loud scream. "Go away, Demon!"

Joe is taken aback. "I'm not a demon. I'm a friend."

The voice inside only laughs bitterly. "Yeah, right! That's what all demons say." And the recitation begins again, "The World is Small, The World is Dark, so very, very dark---."

At first Joe feels sympathetic and politely explains that if the man would only get out of the box, he would see that there was all kinds of light. But the man inside the box doesn't want to hear it and tells Joe to leave him the hell alone.

Now Joe is angry, and he and the man get into a shouting match. The man maintains that since Joe is a demon, he doesn't need to listen to him. In a fit of anger, Joe kicks the box, shouting to the man to get out. Inside, the man screams as if he were being murdered.

At this point, Joe punches his fist right through the cardboard and begins ripping the box apart with his bare hands. He reaches through the hole, grabs the man, and with superhuman strength, pulls him out. It is like a birth. The man comes out head first, his face still and white, his eyes closed. He isn't breathing. Joe strikes him hard in the heart and the man's eyes jerk open. He is alive. With a jolt, Joe realizes that he is looking at himself.

Suddenly, he is awake, lying on the floor of the tree house, the shock of the dream coursing through his veins. Is this an answer to his prayer? And what does it mean? He thinks about his sons. They would never understand. He doesn't understand it himself, but one thing is sure. He is not in charge anymore. Something is happening. It just is.
With a surge of joy, he realizes that maybe this is the `flow.' Words come quietly into his mind: You are my love. So gentle, yet persistent. You are my Love. I am Yours, You are Mine, We are One. Is he making this up or is this some kind of message from beyond?

CHAPTER XXVI
After the Storm
The Zion Crossroads Plantation Hotel
1980

Fleming returned from the Grey Knights conference filled with a renewed determination to, once and for all, clear out the 'vagrants' which was his new word for the intruders. After years of wandering in the wilderness, the Voice had clearly spoken when the Gray Knights of the New Confederacy unanimously chose Zion Crossroads as their future center of operations. Now there was no doubt in his mind that he, Fleming Meriwether Bowen, was the instrument of God's Plan.

But the moment he'd walked in the front door and heard that melancholy voice of the violin roaming like a restless spirit through the halls of Zion Crossroads, he knew something had changed. Even the gallery of taciturn ancestral faces peering from the walls seemed different, softened into resignation.

Vague discomfort promptly turned to shock as he ascended to the third floor only to find that the Colonel's door, locked and barricaded for decades, had been wrenched open, the thick mat of spider webs hanging in shreds from where they'd been torn aside. He approached his own door with a sense of foreboding. Sure enough, the strand of hair pasted across the crack of the door had been dislodged. Someone had indeed been in his room though after a careful inspection he did not notice any other signs of disturbance.

On a wave of Biblical wrath, Fleming immediately charged into Murphy's bedroom. "*Who* has been in my room? And why has the Colonel's door been opened?"

Though startled, Murphy remained uncharacteristically calm; carefully closing the book he'd been reading and setting it aside before responding. "There was a leak in the roof. It was dripping into the dining room, and we had to find out where it was coming from."

"You? And who else?" Fleming's short pinched nose flared, a warning that he was not to be crossed. Still Murphy kept his composure, though his eyes did slide away at the last moment when he lied and said, "No one."

Fleming's sallow face gleamed with malice. "So you found it then?"

Murphy turned pale, suddenly aware that Daddy's ring was on his finger for all the world to see. "What? Found what?"

"The leak."

"Oh, yes. We---I mean--I found it."

Fleming's eyes narrowed. "So Gardner was up there, as well?"

"Alright, yes---of course Gardner was there." He didn't mention Andriot.

Fleming examined his brother closely, like a wolf sniffing out an enemy. "So who is that playing the violin?"

Murphy hesitated. "Gardner," he said.

"And where tell did *he* get a violin?"

Murphy could have said he didn't know but he was only able to think of that much later when it was too late. Instead, as usual the truth just spilled out. When he was cornered, it always spilled out.

"And you simply *gave* it to him," roared Fleming as if this were the most unbelievably stupid thing Murphy had ever done.

Murphy nodded, swept by a wave of panic akin to what he felt when Fleming used to give him Indian burns on his arm or bend his little finger all the way back as punishment for offense.

"You never fail to astonish me, Brother! Don't you see that being 'nice' to the help is exactly the wrong approach? They get sloppy and lazy then walk all over you!"

Think about what Fleming stole from you! Murphy reminded himself. *Just keep thinking about that!*   And sure enough the necessary stream of anger coursed through Murphy like a dose of courage, and he answered boldly. "Yes, but he's so talented, Fleming! Why should that beautiful instrument lie around in the dark when someone can bring it to life?" Murphy waited for the blow but to his surprise Fleming merely waved his outburst aside for there were more important matters to discuss.

"Read this." He handed Murphy a typed letter addressed to Puffenberger, Valentino, and von Hassel, stating in the bluntest terms possible that they must vacate the premises within seven days or risk being arrested for trespassing.

Murphy pushed his heavy spectacles up his short nose, looking very much like a distressed owl. "You can't do this, Fleming! What about Daddy's Will?"

By now Fleming's cold eye had come to rest upon the Ancestor's ring. Murphy froze, again waiting for the ax to fall, but Fleming said nothing about it. Instead he snatched back the letter. "I conferred with a lawyer this weekend, Brother. He says that since Daddy was mentally unfit, the Will won't stand up in court." He turned on his heel and disappeared down the hall, leaving Murphy with something new to worry about—for if the others were forced to leave Zion Crossroads, he'd be left behind with Fleming—alone!

Dinner was unusually tense. Puffenberger refused to sit next to Fleming and made a big show of switching seats with Valentino, who took his portly friend's usual place at the other end of the table. This in turn caused Amanda to switch with Nealy since she refused to sit in direct view of Puffenberger's horrific table manners.

"What is this? Musical chairs?" asked Gardner. There were scowls all around.

Having Nealy sitting so close beside him, threw Murphy into such disarray that he had trouble aiming the fork to his mouth properly and the food kept sliding into his lap. Meanwhile, Jack acted like his brother Tommy wasn't even there, since he was still angry with him for taking the metal detector and midway through the meal, he threw down his fork and stalked out to the porch for a cigarette.

Amanda von Hassel was next to leave, saying she was going to her room. Likewise, Katherine who'd been sitting, darkly silent, in her place between Andriot and Gardner, excused herself early, saying that she was tired and her head still hurt from falling in the hole. Portia had remained in her customary seat beside Fleming and ate everything on her plate without once looking up.

Meanwhile, Fleming chewed methodically unperturbed, retaining a self-satisfied disposition even when Puffenberger rose up with a dire warning. "Don't think for a moment," he declared, "that you are going to get away with this, Bowen! There will be a lawsuit for breach of contract!" Fleming cast a hard look in his direction but said nothing. Everyone else appeared slightly stunned, all except for Andriot who seemed privately amused as usual.

After a long, uncomfortable silence Professor Valentino began to discourse upon a very rare species of butterfly. The room started to clear out pretty fast after that.

Tommy found Jack sullenly chain-smoking on the porch swing.

"What are you doing out here?"

"I'm smokin'! What's it to ya?".

They hadn't spoken to each other since Jack had punched him in the middle of the night and he refused to look at Tommy even now.

"So where you been all day?" said Tommy.

"Where've *I* been? Where've *you* been?" Jack's eyes bulged.

"I've been looking for *you*!"

"Bull shit!"

"So you're still angry?" Tommy's eyes bulged even wider.

"Yeah, I'm angry. Why shouldn't I be? You take the metal detector and go out there without me? How'm I supposed to feel?"

"What the hell are you talking about? You took the metal detector and went out without *me*!"

"Are you calling me a liar?"

"Well, that's what you're calling me!"

"Fuck you, man!"

"You know, I was gonna show you something but now----? Fuck it!" This time it was Tommy who stormed back into the house which was very uncharacteristic since he was usually the one who patiently hung in there to 'communicate' through difficulties.

Jack held his breath, tears stinging his eyes. "Shit!" He threw his cigarette onto the ground and headed out to the gardens.

Meanwhile, Stephen Andriot had followed Puffenberger back to his room in the annex. "Hey! Can I ask you something?"

"Look, my show's coming on! You mind?" Clearly, Puffenberger was still seething.

"I just wanted to know what the hell is going on?"

"It's none of your business." Puffenberger turned away.

"I'm a journalist. Everything is my business."

Puffenberger paused. "All right but shut the door. There's eyes and ears all over the goddamn place."

Inside, his room was a suffocating clutter, every surface strewn with snacks and empty wrappers, trashcans overflowing; the only chair piled high with clothes. Puffenberger swept the pile to the floor. "Have a seat," he said brusquely, and plopped heavily onto the bed. His body was hugely misshapen and for a moment Andriot realized that Puffenberger's growling bear act was only to conceal the fact that he did not want to be looked at. For once, Andriot spared him the usual scrutiny, and politely looked away.

Puffenberger lit a cigarette. "I'm warning ya. It's a long goddamn story."

"I got nowhere to go and nothing to do."

Later, back in his own room, Andriot sat in the corner writing down as much as he could remember from his conversation with Puffenberger while Katherine slept. He would sit up late into the night, writing with a feverish inspiration for this was going to be the most important piece he'd ever done.

After dinner, as daylight faded into purple shadows, Valentino was in his room gazing through a magnifying glass at a curious stone he'd found on his walk. It almost seemed to have letters etched into it. Perhaps a message in an ancient language? Suddenly he was interrupted by a sharp tapping at the window. He looked up and was startled to see a most unusual bird, indigo with splashes of yellow and red. She seemed intent on getting into his window, for she persisted again and again. He turned out his lamp and opened the window. The bird immediately flew into the room, circled around his head three times then flew out again to perch on a low branch of the tree just outside his window.

Within a few moments, he was outside looking up at the bird. Once again, it circled his head three times and flew off, this time to a more distant tree. The song she trilled, bloomed inside of him like a flower. He smiled. It was not a dead world after all. No, it was very much alive with meaning! He could see this now more than ever. He followed her as she led him deeper into the forest where he disappeared into the gathering Mist, the distant sound of bells beckoning him on.

"Where are they?" It was the next morning at breakfast and both Valentino and Puffenberger were missing. Amanda, hung over in a pink sparkly turban and oversized sunglasses, acted worried and snappish.

Gardner smirked and motioned impatiently for Murphy to pass the preserves---not the grape, but the orange please. "They're probably just sleeping late. Puffy does it all the time." He hit his toast with a generous dab and began the delicate art of spreading it evenly to the four corners.

"But not Val. He never misses a meal. Don't you think that's odd?"

Gardner licked his fingers, anticipating the sweet satisfaction.

"Everything about him is odd."

"Well, he's senile, for god's sake! What do you expect?"

Gardner shrugged, heedlessly crunching on his toast.

Amanda's temper began to simmer. "He could have really lost it this time and wandered off! He could have fallen into one of those damn holes!"

Gardner stopped midway to that second delicious bite and sighed. Amanda was being tiresomely persistent this morning. "Okay. Just to make you feel better, I'll go see if Val is in his room." He put his precious toast down, then on second thought decided to take it with him.

"You're going to check on Puffenberger, too---aren't you?"

He rolled his eyes. "I didn't think you cared but yeah, I'll check on Puffy."

"I'm sure they're fine," murmured Murphy but he sounded anything but confident. Though the others kept their eyes cast down they were all thinking about the dramatic showdown the night before when Puffenberger had flung the threat of a lawsuit in Fleming's teeth.

"Well what if they're not?" muttered Amanda.

Calmly indifferent, Fleming finished the egg section of his plate then started on the grits.

When Gardner finally did return, he looked grim. Valentino's room was empty and Puffenberger was dead.

"Dead?" Amanda had shrieked that awful word in just the same way when they'd learned of Joe's death the previous September.

"I found him in his bed, stone cold."

"I knew it! I knew something was wrong!" she wailed.

Gardner shut his eyes against the mental picture of Puffy in his boxer shorts and undershirt, swollen up like a helium balloon, his face a ghastly gray, a lacework of blood vessels popping out all over his body, eyes staring.

"*You* did this, you son of a bitch!" Amanda rose and hurled herself at Fleming like a vengeful bird, her red silk caftan flapping like wings. Gardner did his best to pull her away but it finally took two of them to restrain her.

Fleming, though momentarily shaken, quickly reassembled his air of disdain and left the room.

Tom and Nealy decided they would go out into the woods to look for the professor.

When the coroner finally came, he determined that, given his enormous weight, Puffenberger had no doubt died of heart failure. Amanda was quite shrill in demanding an autopsy, but the little man did not appreciate having his judgment called into question and replied that he hardly thought it was necessary.

"Still, isn't it standard procedure?" asked Andriot, in a reasonable tone.

"Not unless there is reason to think there's been foul play." The coroner paused for a moment and glanced round the faces in the room. Nobody said anything. They didn't dare with Fleming standing right there. But there was grumbling after that—questions whispered in private and watchful eyes lest they be overheard.

After dinner, Tom and Nealy had still not returned. Murphy began pacing up and down the porch in tortured silence while Gardner and Jack sat glumly on the steps. Amanda von Hassel, creaked back and forth on the swing, fanning herself listlessly with a magazine. The humid air was still and oppressive, the heat barely lifting as the light faded into dusk. Brooding about Puffenberger's unsightly end had left them all drained and discouraged, even as the chorus of night sounds erupted optimistically from the darkening world around them.

"We got drunk together that first night we came here," began Amanda without preamble, her voice low and dusky, pausing only to take long drags from her cigarette. "Joe being dead and all, well--- things got emotional and the boundaries got a little fuzzy." Nobody was listening but still she had to say it. She had to make her confession.

She pressed the cool glass to the side of her cheek. "I mean, we both felt it but I shut it down ASAP. He wasn't nearly as heavy back then but still I could never love a man who was that tacky. He reeked of garlic and used car salesman and dressed in those hideous polyester leisure suits with those god-awful gold neck chains and—."

"We get the picture!" exclaimed Gardner.

She carefully dabbed at her eyes trying to keep the mascara from streaking. "Yeah, well I never liked those big gaudy rings, he wore. Still somehow we were the same, him and me---cut from the same cloth. We both saw it. Right away, we both knew. Oh, yes!" Her eyes welled up anyway.. "Still, I pretended not to see it and when he'd sit out there on the bench beneath my window, night after night, waiting for me---I ignored him. I got mean just to drive him away." She paused, her chin trembling. "Why did I have to be so petty and cruel when we could have loved each other?"

The question hung in the air unanswered.

"I'll tell you one thing, that was no heart attack," muttered Jack in a low voice. He and Gardner had been the only ones who'd actually seen the dead man's body and now they were methodically drowning the terrible mental image in whiskey---slug after slug. "I saw my Pops when he died. He didn't turn that color. He didn't swell up like that."

"You think it could have been poison?" asked Gardner softly, keeping a wary eye on Murphy who was staring at them from the far end of the porch. "I mean---food poisoning?"

"You're the cook, you should know." Jack lit a cigarette. "Except everybody ate the same thing last night, right?"

"It's those cream filled donuts. Remember? There was a half eaten box of them beside his bed when I first found the body----but by the time the coroner came that box was nowhere in sight. So where did it go?"

Both Jack and Gardner glanced apprehensively in Murphy's direction. He looked away, pretending not to have heard, but this information had set his mind reeling. For months there'd been constant war over the issue of cream filled donuts. Puffy had always maintained that Fleming banned them simply because they were the big man's favorite. Admittedly, for them to have suddenly appeared in the house gave reason enough to be suspicious---for wouldn't it be the perfect bait to catch such a prey?

"I'm going back to my room," said Gardner, wearily rising to his feet.

"Be careful, man," murmured Jack in an undertone .

After Gardner had gone, it wasn't long before Fleming's pale face appeared behind the screen door, then withdrew, silent as a shadow. Murphy recognized the summons and went inside where Fleming waited for him behind the registration desk. In the distance Haden's violin wove tendrils of melancholy into the humid air.

"What are they saying out there?" asked Fleming quietly.

"Nothing." But Murphy's eyes darted to the side again and Fleming caught the lie.

"Not nothing---what?" He squeezed Murphy's arm painfully.

"They're worried about Valentino and they're asking questions, that's all."

"Questions?" Fleming increased the pressure on his brother's arm.

Murphy jerked his arm away, his face a war of emotions. "They think something's not right about Puffenberger's death, that's what!"

He raises his voice, angrily. "Fleming, you didn't---!"

"Stop babbling!" hissed Fleming.

"But—!"

"I said stop!" He slapped Murphy hard on the side of the head.

Murphy bowed his head in seeming submission, ears ringing. Even so, he knew what he'd seen up in Fleming's room. The vials full of poison. He had no doubt of that. No, he could no longer pretend that away. He looked up with a strange look in his eyes.

"You've gone too far, this time, Fleming," he said. And then he did something he had never done before. He turned his back on his twin and walked outside, the screen door slamming shut behind him. The violin ceased. In the silence, Fleming stood transfixed, mentally calculating. It was then that he heard it—-a subtle creak, the sound he knew all too well. Someone was standing on the stairs above, just out of sight.

Fleming slipped into the closet quietly easing the door shut and waited behind the two-way mirror. Minutes passed and nothing happened; then slowly, cautious footsteps resumed their descent. It was that cocky journalist, Stephen Andriot, looking like he was up to no good. Sure enough he lifted the telephone receiver and began to dial the phone.

"It's me, Stephen," he said in an urgent undertone, glancing furtively over his shoulder. "I can't talk long but something big is going down here. Ever heard of the Gray Knights? Yeah, the—!" He paused, thinking he'd heard something. "I gotta go." He hung up. Suddenly remembering the reason he had come downstairs in the first place, Andriot headed for the kitchen.

The kitchen was a bleak room, made bleaker still in the unforgiving light of a naked overhead bulb. The appliances looked to be straight out of the 1930's, the linoleum faded and cracked; all in all, a dismal place. He opened the the old fashioned freezer and pulled out an ice tray.

"So you feel that you can just go into our freezer without permission?" It was Fleming, standing in the dim entryway to the back hall.

Andriot turned with that bold, wide-eyed gaze that Fleming found so vexing. "Oh, I beg your pardon. May I have some ice?" Fleming fixed him with a cold stare as if to wipe that insinuating smirk from Andriot's lips. "Take what you will, then---Semite," he purred softly.

Andriot pulled up sharply. "What did you say?" Though barely above a hiss, the word had found its mark better than any blow.

Ignoring the question, Fleming turned and disappeared into the shadowy hall. Andriot took a few moments to quiet the adrenalin racing through his body. Though he didn't like to admit it, even to himself, beneath the angry lump in his throat was fear.

CHAPTER XXVII
Suspicion
The Zion Crossroads Plantation Hotel
1980

Andriot headed back out to the front porch to find Murphy, slumped dispiritedly against a pillar. "Can I talk to you for a minute?"

Murphy blinked up at him like a frightened owl. "Leave me alone!" He jerked to his feet and headed across the lawn with Andriot dogging his steps.

"Wait! I heard what you said to Fleming, back there."

"I said leave me alone!" He dodged under a willow tree some distance from the house, its low hanging branches curtaining him from view.

"I was upstairs on the landing---," pressed Andriot, following him in.

Murphy turned on him in a fury. "Are you insane? Do you want him to hear you? He's probably watching us this very minute!"

"You think he poisoned Puffenberger, don't you!" said Andriot. "And maybe Valentino, too!"

A shudder passed through Murphy's body like a sob but he brought it under control. "Fleming is---." He drew a long tortured sigh. "Everyone is the enemy to Fleming—all of you. That's why you must get away from here! Now! Tonight! I'm afraid that Fleming's gone completely mad. There's no telling what he will do."

"Are *you* in danger, too?"

Murphy shook his head. "Fleming would never hurt me. He couldn't. We're brothers. I'm his blood!" But even as he said this the pit of his stomach turned cold.

"Something needs to be done."

"You don't understand! Fleming is not the sort who loses well. No, he will find a way to win. He always has. Nothing can stop him now and this is only the beginning. That's why you must go. Leave!

I mean it!" He plunged out from beneath the willow tree, stumbled briefly, then stalked with determination across the lawn and disappeared around the corner of the house.

"So what's up with Big Bird? I saw you two talking under the willow tree," asked Jack, as Android came back up onto the porch. Mrs. von Hassel had gone upstairs leaving them alone. Jack held out the bottle of Jack Daniels. "Want some?"

Until now Jack had been stand-offish towards him, just shy of belligerent, but at the moment Andriot needed an ally. "You wanna take a walk?"

Jack looked surprised. "Sure."

As they made their way down the driveway, Andriot told Jack everything---about hiding behind the two- way mirror and seeing Fleming meddling with Val's meds; about the vials they'd found in Fleming's room when they were looking for the leak; about the Gray Knights and the weapons cache in the summer kitchen.

"And then I just overheard them talking in the house. Murphy pretty much accused Fleming.'

"Of what?"

"Killing Puffenberger, I guess."

"I knew that son of a bitch was a psycho!" growled Jack.

"Yeah, and I've gotta get Katherine out of here ASAP." Andriot left and headed upstairs to their room.

Murphy went straight back to his room, his mind racing but not with thoughts about Puffenberger. He was remembering Moon coming to his door at dawn in hysteria the morning he'd found Trip, lying dead on the floor of his room. When they'd gone to see the body, Murphy had had to force himself to actually go in. Even then, one quick glance was all he could muster before shutting the door. Still, he would never blot the memory of Trip's face, contorted with what must have been unspeakable agony, vomit everywhere. It was too awful to describe. And then there was Moon's face, gray with terror and rage, shouting that Fleming was behind it all. "I've known Trip a long time," he said. "He may have been a junk food junkie but he was never sick a day in his life! And you know as well as I do that Fleming has wanted us out of here, so you do the math! I mean, come on! He's been ransacking our rooms, following us in the woods---!"
True to form, Murphy had insisted that his brother would never do such a thing though some instinct caused him to glance over his shoulder.

Murphy could still see the look of withering disgust that Moon had given him. "You are such a slave, man. Worse than any 'nigger'. I feel sorry for you, man."

Within an hour, Moon had cleared out without another word, save a note shoved under Murphy's door, reminding him to send food out to the woods for Joe or he'd starve to death. And that was the last Murphy ever heard from the only real friend he'd ever had.

Later when they were digging Trip's grave and Murphy had wondered aloud if they shouldn't try to contact his family first, Fleming's response had been sharp. "No one is going to miss him, Brother," he'd said. "He's just another outcast drug addict." At the time, Murphy had wanted to say that Trip didn't like marijuana because it made him paranoid but he'd kept silent, even as they had rolled the body into an unmarked grave. Suddenly, it was all too clear that Moon was right. He was worse than a slave and he'd kept his real feelings walled off to protect himself from a truth he did not want to face.

Now he no longer had that luxury. This dark thing was coming into the light and he had to see it, and worse---he had to do something about it. As he was passing Haden's library, he heard a loud thump which drew him into the room. His eye immediately fell upon a large book lying open on the floor, Fairy Tales of the Brothers Grimm. As he picked it up, an envelope slipped out of its pages. Yellowed with age, it was addressed to his great grandmother, Irene Bowen, dated 1934, and signed 'Colonel Carter Meriwether Bowen'.

CHAPTER XIX
Confession
The Zion Crossroads Plantation Hotel
1937

February 16, 1937
Dearest Irene,

I leave this miserable world without a friend but for you, the kindest person who ever walked. You've cared for this old carcass when the others would sooner have shot me like an old dog. I know they laugh behind my back. They call me a madman and maybe I am, but you treat me with respect. That is why I am going to tell you what I will never tell them.

The reason that I never knew where the treasure was hidden is not because I'd lost the map. It was because I never buried it in the first place. You see, it wasn't mine to bury. Never mine. It belonged to my brother, Haden. It was his half of the Ancestor's gold, our inheritance, so I knew it existed but I just didn't know where—not until three days ago when God finally saw fit to reveal Haden's diary to me.

After all these years of searching for it, there it was, right there on the bottom shelf in his library. Oh, this has got to be the biggest joke God has ever played on me because now I know exactly where the gold is hidden, now when I'm too old to go and get it. But God's ways are not our ways and we can never truly understand why things happen the way they do. Even so, it is only fair. I do not deserve that gold and never have.

If I am to have any chance of peace in the next world, it's time to make my confession, and you are the only one on this Earth who will ever hear it, Irene. I am only glad that I won't have to see your face when I tell it, for it is a terrible secret. Yes, though I have played the upright man, the God fearing and righteous man, my soul is black with sin for I killed my own brother. I poisoned him and left him to die a cruel death. At the time, I told myself I had to do it. When he dared to call that pregnant slave woman his wife, I told myself that it was my duty to defend the family honor. But the real reason was jealousy. I'd always been jealous of him, Haden with the golden eyes.

The best of everything always came to him. Friends, women, property---even Father favored him over me. And Haden just assumed that this was the natural order of things. He thought he was invincible! What a fool he was to throw it all away for a slave. But, I could not stand by and watch him destroy our good name! It was the only honor I had left! I tried to reason with him. Why could he never listen to me? No one ever listened to me, so I was forced to take matters into my own hands! I had no other choice! You must agree that I had no other choice! Still, it is a vile thing to kill a brother, and I have been as much a prisoner as any man behind bars.

On the night he died, a messenger from Haden summoned me to come quickly, but I came only after it was finished. I could not bring myself to look upon his suffering. Later, when I was drunk enough not to feel, I accidentally knocked over a lamp and set my own house on fire. My wife and the boy were away, and I was the only one there. I spent the night in a ditch watching the flames, listening to the voices of the slaves raising the alarm. They hoped I was still inside the house, no doubt, for not one of them risked his life to save me. After that, I hid in a tavern and stayed drunk for three days. Everyone said it was hard luck, the house burnt to the ground and my brother dead all on the same

At the funeral, there was nothing but praise for Haden and that only made me hate him all the more. Later that very day, Charlotte and I took possession of Zion Crossroads. It was her idea. She knew nothing of the poison. She would never have gone that far, though she envied my brother quite as much as I. That night, our infant son became very ill, struggling to breathe. My wife was frantic. She'd been told that Abanetha had witchy powers so she sent for her. When Abanetha came, she laid her hands on his little body and the baby commenced to breathe normally. I remember the way he looked at her, straight in the eye, as if he knew what she'd done.

For the next few days, Charlotte and I searched the house for Haden's half of the Ancestor's gold but found nothing. Charlotte was convinced we'd be fools not to think Haden hadn't already given it to Abanetha, otherwise, why had she disappeared? But obviously the other slaves were hiding her, so I made threats then hid in the Labyrinth and waited by his grave until nightfall.

Sure enough, late in the night she appeared and lay upon his grave, weeping. If she had only answered me about the gold but she was so proud, so stubborn---so I beat her. Three days later, the slaves showed me her body. They said she'd gone into labor and they couldn't stop the blood. The child too had died, they said, though I never saw its body, and for all these years since, that child has haunted my dreams.

The war started soon after, and the battlefield proved to be my salvation for it was the only place I could hide from the terrible thing I had done. As a soldier, I was finally a respected man. I rose through the ranks and came into Jackson's inner circle. I gave up drinking and even began reading the Bible, as I was expected to do. But the night I knelt in Jackson's tent and wept, it was not from remorse for the evils I'd committed but bitterness for everything I had lost—for Clarendon, burned to the ground, for always playing second fiddle to my brother and getting second best---for always being judged and condemned by my own actions.

The day I buried him, I cast his clothes into the fire. I would have burnt his portrait and the violin; but I couldn't bring myself to do it, so I hid them where I would never have to see them again. You see, I wanted to forget Haden Meriwether Bowen but that was impossible when it was his face I saw in the mirror every time I looked there. And so the dead live on to punish the living. This is the way he has won.

By morning I shall be dead by the same poison that killed him. Perhaps that will be justice enough to keep me from the fiery furnace. The only good purpose left for me, is to help you, as you have helped me. That's why I'm telling you and no one else where to find the treasure. Follow the creek at the bottom of the ravine to Indian Rock. There you'll find Haden's inheritance in a small cave near the top, in 'the Indian's eye'. It may take some doing but you'll find it. Now I know it is not in your nature to lie or keep secrets but do not reveal this letter to anyone. No one but you deserves it, Irene! Take it with an easy heart and perhaps, you will pray a little for my soul.

Yours truly,
Colonel Carter Meriwether Bowen

On a second page there was a hand drawn map showing the riding trails named for the old Confederate Generals--- Jackson's Loop, Lee's Look Out, Mosby's Ride and running through it was the great ravine, and the creek and a big X on a spot labeled Indian Rock.

What Murphy held in his hands represented lifetimes wasted in mutual suspicion, anger, and pain; a family destroying itself in vain. And he wept as the mournful sound of the violin did a slow dance on the evening air.

CHAPTER XXIX
The Unexpected
The Zion Crossroads Plantation Hotel
1980

On the upstairs balcony, Katherine paused dreamily over the open pages of her notebook, as the distant sound of the violin stirred an inexplicable yet exquisite pain. Suddenly, the image of her character, the slave woman, stepped onto her mental screen---a welcome surprise for it had been months since she had made such a visitation. Aba was pregnant, very pregnant, and holding a book---no, hiding it, behind her back. What could this mean? Katherine waited and then realized that someone else was there, as well.

Katherine strained to get a clear image of this person but all she could see was that unpleasant woman from the woods, Portia; except in her vision she was dressed in 19th century clothes and her name wasn't Portia, it was Charlotte---*small-minded, suspicious, Charlotte---all prickles and snares and tending towards fat.*

"What are you doing in here?" Suddenly Charlotte was speaking. Katherine could hear her voice. Quickly, she picked up a pen to record the scene that had abruptly started playing in her mind.

"I said what are you doing in here?" cries Charlotte, her small piggish eyes almost cross-eyed with indignation. The slave woman looks down, wary of a slap, but is slapped anyway. "And what's that behind your back?"

Aba now boldly stands, eye to eye, with the dangerous white woman. "It does not belong to you!" Charlotte makes a pathetic grab for it but Aba easily knocks her hands aside. "You kill him!"

"Hush your mouth, you vile, thieving bitch!" Charlotte raises her hand to deliver another blow but the naked violence in Aba's dark eyes gives the white woman pause and she calls to her house slave for protection.

The moment he arrives, Charlotte turns on Aba with a triumphant sneer, snatching the book then grabbing hold of Aba's hand. "And what is this? Haden's ring? Why you took this off his dead body, you little thief! How dare you!" Charlotte twists it off her finger. "Your days of queening it around Zion Crossroads are over! The moment that bastard is born, it's gonna be sold and taken far, far away where you will never see it again! You understand me? It will never know who its real daddy was. Never!"

"You will suffer for this!" hisses Aba in a low voice, her black eyes glittering with hatred. "You and all your seed!"

"What was that?"shrieks Charlotte, giving Aba another stinging slap.

Aba grows sullen and holds her tongue but the curse has been laid and that gives her some small satisfaction.

"Take her out of my sight!" Charlotte is trembling with fury as her manservant leads Aba out. "Whip her 'til she bleeds!"

"The Missy angry a-'cause they ain't find Master Hyatt's gold," he whispers once they are safely out of hearing.

Inwardly Aba smiles, knowing that this is the one thing Charlotte will never find.

Katherine paused. The heady rush of images and voices had subsided, leaving her mind still and empty but for a silent prayer of gratitude. At last the novel was speaking to her again! Now more than ever, she knew that this character was not just imagination but in some way very real and demanding this story be written. The distant violin mourned in the heavy heat, triggering an upsurge of love and grief so profound that Katherine could not help but weep, yet why she did not know. All she knew was that suddenly she needed to find the one who was playing that violin.

The ice was starting to drip inside the kitchen towel as Andriot headed back to the balcony, only to discover that Katherine was gone. She wasn't in their room either but the contents of his suitcase had been dumped on the floor. "What the hell---?"

The door closed softly behind him and he turned to see Fleming step out from where he'd hidden himself. He was holding Andriot's notes for the article he was writing about the Grey Knights.

Seized by a reckless anger, Andriot snatched the papers and demanded that Fleming get out. But the bizarre smile on Fleming's face made it clear he had no intention of doing so. Andriot was in excellent physical condition and did not step back. "You don't want to mess with me, you fucking nazi son of a bitch!" He would feel the sting of Fleming's knife before he saw it---before he understood.

And the sound of the violin caressed the failing light.

"So *you're* the one?" Katherine cringed as soon as the words had come so bluntly out of her mouth. Of course, in all fairness it had been something of a shock to find out that it was the gardener sitting on the porch outside his room, playing classical violin.

His demeanor hardened. "Hard to believe, ain't it, Mrs. Tai Chi? But yeah, it's me---Gardner, the gardener, playing the violin."   And he kept right on playing as if she weren't there, the night sounds humming in counterpoint to the violin's melancholy. Suddenly, the world cut loose and started to spin, causing Katherine to sit down abruptly on the edge of the porch, her head ringing; something that had been plaguing her ever since she'd fallen into that hole. Meanwhile, he continued to ignore her but, humiliating as this was, she felt compelled to stay.

"So how long have you been playing, like that?" she asked, closing her eyes and waiting for her vision to settle down. When she opened them again, he was looking at her with thinly disguised dislike. Once again, his beautiful golden eyes made her involuntarily blush.

"Fact is, I never played this thing before in my life." He said this dismissively, as if it were a stupid and intrusive question. "Now if you'll excuse me, it's been kind of a rough day so if you don't mind." Suddenly, the corners of his mouth pulled down hard as if fighting back some unbidden emotion. A cooling breeze lifted the treetops with a sigh.

Suddenly, she could see behind his wall of sarcasm. *He's sad about Puffenberger.* The light faded another notch. "So I guess you and Mr. Puffenberger were close?" He merely stared at her as if that were the lamest of questions.

"Right. Of course, you were," she continued, stumbling now. "Look, you don't have to say anything." She cleared her throat. "You know, I think I'll just go." But she stood up too quickly and her vision went black. Easing back down to the steps, she held her head on either side to keep it from flying apart. "Sorry! I'm just a little dizzy."

But he had begun playing again as if she had already left. The awkwardness of the moment tightened and then she surprised herself and blurted, "It just flows, doesn't it?"

He broke off abruptly, blatantly irritated now. "It what?"

"The music. It just flows. As if it's just---."

"As if it's just— *what*?" he snapped.

"Possessing you." She looked at him stupidly and said it again. "As if it's possessing you."

He stared bullets. "Yeah---that's it."

It was only a grudging answer but it emboldened her. "Like you've been playing it all your life."

He shrugged, softening just a hair. "Art and music come second nature to me." He looked away. "Me and the Muse, we're tight like that."

"I believe that, too--in the Muse," she said quietly, excitement rising. "See, I'm---I write and---," The realization was all coming together and spilling out in a rush. "You know, I kinda just wish I could tell you about this character in my novel? Because well---."

The look he gave her was less than enthusiastic. "Yeah, well like I said, it's been a really rough day."

"----because she sort of just appeared in my imagination one day." Katherine was talking even faster now because plainly the window of opportunity was closing fast. "She was this-----this black slave woman, see---actually in a place a lot like this. Of course, what do I know about being a black person, let alone a slave, but yet Aba has been so persistent—as if it's a story she has to tell."

He raised his hand. "Hold on a second! You say her name is Aba?" His golden eyes were now riveted on her. Suddenly, she had his full attention.

"Yes! That's---that's her name." Katherine pushed the loose strands of hair from her face. "Anyway, I thought it was sort of like your music, the story just telling itself. I mean, it makes me wonder because I even dream about it. You know?."

"What's it about again?" The question came impatiently cutting in.

"It's about a slave woman, actually— who falls in love with her master. Well, *he* falls in love with *her* first. I know it sounds cliché and Hollywood but he's this really enlightened guy, and he plays the violin---actually." She dared not look at him now. "He's an amazing artist, too---a painter---and a poet."

Now they were both barely breathing.

"And---what's his name?" he asked almost in a whisper.

She paused. "Hyatt."

He pulled up short, confused. "Hyatt?"

"Well, that's what I've *been* calling him but since I fell into the hole---," she hesitated. This was getting way too weird. Maybe she should just leave and pretend this whole conversation had never tried to happen.

But he was pressing her now. "You fell into the hole and--?"

"Yeah, well I must have knocked my head pretty good because ever since then---." Her enthusiasm got a second wind, sweeping away all hesitation. "I know it might be kind of hard to believe, but I just seem to know about these people and their lives. I mean, somehow I don't think I'm making this stuff up." She paused dramatically. "In some unfathomable way this character is real---I mean, like she may have really lived----maybe even here!"

He was staring at her again only now with a penetrating interest.

"And when I heard the violin," she continued, "it just came to me that he played the violin and---." She looked down at her hands, suddenly shy. "I don't know---am I crazy? Maybe I'm crazy. I fell in a hole and---yeah, it's probably just a concussion or something. Maybe I should go. I'm sorry for bothering you." She made it as if to leave.

"Wait," he interrupted harshly. He took a deep breath. "Her name wasn't Aba. It was Abanetha."

"Abanetha?" Katherine looked confused.

"And his name wasn't Hyatt. It was Haden." Gardner seemed suddenly half way friendly. "Come inside and I'll show you something that you might find interesting." When she hesitated, he gave a slight chuckle. "It's a book," he said, "but I can't talk about it out here. Someone may be watching us." With a furtive backward glance, Gardner ushered Katherine into his room and closed the door.

The stifling heat hit him like a wall as Murphy reached the top of the steep, winding staircase leading to the third floor. It took tremendous courage even to knock at Fleming's door so he was relieved when there was no answer. Murphy slipped his secret key into the lock and with a creaking complaint, the door swung open.

Fleming's room was serenely silent and thankfully there was no sign of him except that the shelf, where all the vials should have been, had been wiped clean. It took Murphy a moment to realize that a mound on the floor was indeed a pillowcase filled with the brown glass vials. Clearly, Fleming was intending to hide the evidence! Murphy grabbed the sack. If he could just get away before Fleming got back, he thought but suddenly there was a sound at the door.

"What are you doing here, Brother?" It was Fleming.

"This has gone too far, don't you think?" said Murphy.

"I hardly think it has gone far enough," Fleming replied coldly.

"I don't want to hurt you, Brother but it's only fair to warn you that you defy me at your own risk."

"How so, Fleming?"

"You should know by now that I am the Chosen One."

Murphy stared, transfixed by the madness glittering in his brother's eyes, the blood smeared across the front of his shirt. "What have you done, Fleming?"

Fleming looked down at the stain as if he were surprised to see it, then looked up, utterly calm."I have done what needs to be done. Now give me the sack."

"No, Fleming, I cannot. I can't let you keep doing this!"

"As if *you* could ever stop *me*?" Fleming laughed as he punched Murphy hard in the gut then bolted down the stairs with the sack tucked under his arm. Gasping with pain, Murphy lurched through the door, out into the hall, and down the steep winding staircase. He was running now just like his old dream, chasing the shadow man—the man with his own face---down, down the endless stairwell. It was becoming reality.

"I can kill the whole world with this..."

Back in Gardner's room, Katherine sat and waited as he locked the door, shut the curtain; then went to his closet where he pried up a loose floorboard producing a worn leather bound volume.

"I grew up here." He spoke in a low voice as if afraid to be overheard. "And I left, swearing never to come back but when my father passed, I happened to find this in a box of junk down in the root cellar under the old summer kitchen. I don't think it was a coincidence." He handed it to her.

She took the book into her hands. "What is it?"

"This is Haden's diary; Haden Meriwether Bowen, the original owner of Zion Crossroads. It tells the story of how he fell in love with one of his slaves and her name was Abanetha."

She sat with her mouth slightly open, stunned.

He grinned, "Oh, yeah---but it gets crazier because this--- this was the part that changed everything for me." He searched for a certain page and handed it back to her. "Apparently, she wrote this right before she died. It's a letter to her daughter, Jewel, telling her where she'd hidden Haden's gold."

"The baby? She did have a baby, then?" A solitary tear spilled down Katherine's cheek as she read Abanetha's crudely written letter to the child to whom she'd just given birth, the child she would never have the chance to know.

Gardner handed her a tissue. "That child, 'Jul', that she was writing to? That was my great-great-great grandmother. Jewel Bell was her name and it's right there in the family Bible. We just never knew that her father was Haden Meriwether Bowen. According to family history, she was an orphan raised on another plantation, by somebody they called Aunt Zita who claimed her as her own after the real mother died in childbirth. I imagine Jewel grew up never hearing the true story of her father and her mother because she had to remain the hidden child, the secret child. It would be death to her if anyone ever learned the truth. That's why none of us ever knew."

"That she was---?"

"That we, the Bell's---the slaves and servants-- were the true heirs to Zion Crossroads." He watched intently for her reaction.

Katherine's eyes widened. "Oh."

"Yeah---oh!" Gardner nodded with a wry smile. "When I realized that---when I found this diary and read that letter, the whole purpose and direction of my life took a hundred and eighty-degree turn."

"So, this place rightfully belongs to you?" Katherine's mind was suddenly racing to find a way to incorporate this into her novel.

"Precisely. Still, I know that Zion Crossroads will never be in my possession. They would never allow it---not the Bowen's. Nah. The only thing I can hope to claim is the gold---so long as they don't know about it, that is."

"And so you stayed here working as the gardener?"

He grinned. "Overtly, yes---but *covertly* I've been sneaking around the woods and searching for a path to the treasure." Then his smile faded. "It's just taken a lot longer than I'd hoped."

"Why?"

"I'm not sure. I mean, I know where it is. Indian Rock. And you'd think it would be simple, right? But nothin' about this has been simple. Sometimes I almost think that something is---I don't know. It sounds crazy."

"Tell me," she said with quiet intensity.

"It's like something has been keeping me here."

She thought for a moment. "Maybe you've just had to wait for something else to fall into place. Cosmic timing."

"Could be."

"Tell me. What happened to Haden and Abanetha?"

"Yeah, well, it's the story of a great love---crazy, insane, tragic love---the kind that makes a guy like Haden, who's got it all, defy the culture of his day and claim a slave woman as his wife!"

"He did that?" Suddenly she wanted to cry.

"Yes, he did---a very dangerous and stupid thing to do."

"It's what killed him in the end, wasn't it?" she said softly. How she suddenly knew this, she couldn't say. It was just there.

He paused. "Of course, we'll never really know. His diary just ends. But something bad must have happened for Abanetha to have given up her child."

Katherine nodded, recalling the nightmare of being chased through the Labyrinth. "Yes, it must have been something terrible," she murmured as the truth flooded into her mind.

The look she now gave him, he found strangely unsettling. He cleared his throat and changed the subject. "Well, anyway, the good news is that I've finally cut a path down into the creek bed. Once I'm there, I can just----." He stopped abruptly. "You're shaking! What's wrong?"

Her eyes filled with tears. "Nothing---nothing."

Suddenly, outside there was a loud commotion. Through a crack in the curtains, they could see two men scuffling in the yard. It was Fleming and Murphy.

Fleeing out the back door, Fleming had stumbled, giving Murphy the opportunity to grab onto his shirt and together they'd crashed to the porch floor. From there they'd rolled off onto the ground, Murphy clinging like a piece of Saran wrap, and Fleming whacking him like one would beat a carpet that was on fire. The sack of vials had gone flying.

It was an ugly procedure, the two brothers grunting, and rolling over the uneven ground; all the while inexpertly scratching and clawing at each other. When Murphy succeeded in grabbing his brother's beard, Fleming erupted with an indignant howl. In the end it was only by getting Murphy into a chokehold that Fleming managed to extricate himself; and while Murphy lay semiconscious on the ground, Fleming quickly gathered the vials back into the sack and took off into the gathering gloom.

CHAPTER XXX
Book of Joe: Part Six
The Language of Trees

When did the world fall?
Was it really just a momet,
hidden in the mists of time,
like a fairy tale that never really happened?

Or do we just keep falling
over and over
every time we lose ourselves
to dark memories?

Is this how the Garden Gate got so rusty?
Is this how the Happy Land drifted so far away?
Like a fairy tale that never really happened?

Joe Bowen, Summer 1979

After falling into the hole, Joe was deeply disoriented, even slightly disembodied, and sometime in the middle of the night, he became acutely aware of the presence of the trees under which he sat. He felt very sure that they were watching over him in a kindly protective way, and their perfect acceptance flowed like balm over the wounds of his heart.

A question struggled momentarily to distinguish itself then subsided like a sigh into the vast unbroken waters of his mind. There was nothing to understand. He need only accept this gift and rest in the wonder of it. At first, he felt more than heard their communication, the images breaking open in his mind like eggs.

"Now I am officially insane," he said aloud. Again, he felt rather than heard the laughter of the trees. Someone was coming.

The Guardian's first appearance was but a flickering movement, a blaze of light out of the corner of his eye. Joe somehow understood that this was a test and by not being startled, he had passed. Only then did this Being take form in full view, ablaze with light, about nine feet tall, a beautiful perfect body, cocooned in blue light. A current of intensity akin to a physical force compelled Joe to bow before him, holding his heart to keep it from bursting with an emotion he had never felt before; Devotion, a word he had never properly understood, for he had never felt anything like it, not like this.

"Welcome to the Crossroads between Worlds!" The Great Being seemed to speak directly into his mind.

Exquisite feelings erupted like a rush of wings as an invisible hand came to rest on Joe's heart. "Thank you, thank you!" He was crying, tears of gratitude streaming down his face, as an inner light searched his body for every hidden grief. Voices like tiny silken bells floated around him. He opened his eyes to see a cluster of small brown and gold luminous Beings peering at him from the surrounding foliage.

"Leave your ancient pain and come with me," said the Great Being.

Suddenly Joe's entire lifetime reeled before him, every person who'd ever hurt him and every person whom he had hurt. Watching it all play out through every possible point of view he finally understood the perfection of his disastrous life.

"All those kicks and blows were necessary," said the Being with good humor, "to shake you loose from the family tree so you could plant yourself in the earth and grow into your greatness."

At about 4 a.m., Joe floated into a dark dreamless slumber. The next thing he knew, there was a hand on his shoulder. This time when he opened his eyes, he saw Moon's shadowy face peering into his own. It was early. The dawn had barely leaked over the horizon. At first, Joe couldn't be absolutely sure that he wasn't still dreaming but the look of anxiety on Moon's face soon persuaded him that he was not.

"You've got to do something about Fleming, man. He's taking over!"

"What do you mean?" The words no longer echoed in Joe's head, but disconcerting halos of light still flickered around Moon's body, spiking out in streaks of angry red and orange when he spoke.

"They're getting ready to clear cut the trees!" The peculiar intensity of Joe's gaze made Moon wonder if Fleming wasn't right after all. Maybe Joe really had lost it this time.

When Joe finally answered, the words seemed to come from very far away. "Fleming won't listen---not to me."

"Don't let him intimidate you! You are still the legal owner of Zion Crossroads! He can't do anything without your signature on the papers!"

"No," he said, "I can't go back there to that house. You know that."

Maybe it was just that without his glasses he looked so different, but Joe seemed unnaturally calm, as if he were under some kind of spell. Moon wanted to shake him. "You gotta come back. You're the only one who can stop this!" A fiery red spear of light jumped off Moon and bounced into Joe's chest. Joe recoiled as if he'd been struck.

Suddenly, Fleming and Murphy were standing below the tree house. Moon cursed under his breath. They'd followed him and by the looks on their faces, they were not happy. Murphy was the first to speak, sniveling on in his perpetually injured tone about how they'd worried Joe was dead and why in the world was he sitting up there in a tree house?

Joe's response was that this was his home now. Murphy seemed to find this alarming. What was wrong and why wasn't he coming back home? Joe could only stare in fascination as a sickly greenish-colored hook emerged out of his son's solar plexus, latching onto his father's midsection with the tenacity of a leech.

At this point, Fleming shouldered Murphy aside. "So, are you saying that Zion Crossroads is not your home, Father?" The cunning softness of his voice barely concealed a malicious satisfaction.

Moon moaned under his breath. His worst fears were now coming to pass. "Don't let him manipulate you, Joe! You're the boss," he whispered. "*You* are in charge! Not him!"

"Stop this idiocy," commanded Fleming, "and come down out of that tree immediately! There are important papers to sign! I'm warning you that I'm not playing games anymore, Father. Do you hear me?" Joe watched helplessly as a slithering gray tentacle grew out of Fleming's body and grasped Joe's head in a paralyzing grip.

"Joe is not signing any papers, asshole!" yelled Moon in an explosion of angry red.

"And you'll stay out of our business if you know what's good for you!" snapped Fleming. Fireworks darted back and forth between them. "Now I'm coming up, Father, and you're going to cooperate for once!"

"Joe, tell them to go to hell!"

The pressure in Joe's head was almost unbearable. He could barely think. He leaned back against the trunk of the tree and closed his eyes, drained. "Don't argue! Just---please don't argue! Moon, make room for them!"

Moon scowled. "Okay, man but whatever you do---do not sign those papers!" He proceeded to roll up the sleeping mat and dump out the piss pot, the stream of urine coming perilously close to the two who had meanwhile begun scaling the ladder. Murphy gave a little shriek but Fleming could only glare as the papers were gripped tightly in his teeth. Once they had mounted the platform, they looked cramped and ill at ease, their faces twin masks, one tight and disagreeable, the other flabby with self-doubt.

"Sign here and here and---," Fleming was busily making little X's on the various pages of the document.

"Wait just a damn minute! He's not signing anything without reading it first!" shouted Moon.

"He's in no condition to read anything! I'll simply explain it all. There's nothing complicated about it," replied Fleming in a deadly voice.

"No! He's reading it for himself, right Joe?" Moon snatched the papers away.

"Would you please leave? In fact, why are you even here?"

"To protect Joe from you, asshole!"

"Please don't argue!" moaned Joe, taking the papers out of Moon's hands. He reached for his glasses and that's when he discovered that they only made everything blurrier. He laid them aside staring in awe at the paper before him.

"Daddy, what are you doing?" cried Murphy. "Now you don't want to make us angry, do you? Please, put on your glasses!"

"But I don't believe I need them." Joe looked up, his face radiant with joy. "An angel has healed my eyes!"

"An angel?" bleated Murphy, meeting Fleming's smirk with a sidelong glance.

"He was just as real as you are and he told me things!" Joe touched Murphy's shoulder. "There's so much I need to share with you!"

Murphy shrank away from his father's hand as if he were contagious with a deadly disease.

"That's wonderful, Daddy," said Fleming in a patronizing tone. "Now sign the papers!"

Joe shook his head and handed them back to Fleming. "I can't sign this, Fleming. You're going to destroy the forest and that I cannot allow."

"I don't think you understand! Since you let all these people mooch off us for free, we have no money to pay the taxes! If we don't pay the taxes, the government is going to take Zion Crossroads away from us. So either we cut down the trees or sell our ancestral home! Which one is it?"

"These trees are our friends! They're intelligent! They have feelings and they're---they're so full of love! No! We couldn't cut them down!" Joe's voice rose to full strength. "And there is a wonderful Angel who lives here. He talked to me!"

"Are you sure it wasn't a demon, sent by Satan to trick you, Father?"

"He healed me! How could he be a demon?"

"First of all, why would an angel talk to you? No, you must realize that demons will do anything to pull you under their influence. I'm warning you! Lean not to thine own understanding, Father! Trust in the Lord."

"So are you saying that rather than trust my own understanding, I should trust yours instead?"

Above his bristling beard, Fleming's eyes flickered with righteous wrath, "I'm warning you! Turn away from this demon and call upon the Lord to save you from delusion, Father!"

"How can you say you speak for the Lord when your heart is so dark. I see no love in you, Fleming."

Fleming's face contorted with utter hatred. "Get back down to earth and sign these papers! Do it or I will have your friends arrested and you committed to a mental institution!"

On this ominous note, he climbed back down the ladder and departed with Murphy scurrying to keep up.

Later, Joe dreamed again. In the dream he opened his eyes and decided that he must be awake because it was summer, and he was heading back through the woods, back to Zion. Just as before, he came to the same fork in the trail where bright sunlight filtered through the pale silvery trunks of a grove of beech trees, their roots clutching the earth like fists. Only now he noticed that to the right, the earth mounted into high rocky cliffs and to the left it fell away in a broad sweep to the creek bed below. For a moment, he thought that something inside of him must have gotten turned around, for he was unable to remember exactly which way to go home. Then in a glimmering, he understood that he was still dreaming---a dream within a dream within a dream.

He sat on a low flat boulder, absorbing the stillness of the forest, marveling at how real and tactile this dream world felt. Presently, there was a disturbance of wings in the treetops. It was a glorious white swan, heralding the appearance of a man just now emerging out of the trees on the far side of the creek.

With one leap, the man crossed the narrow stream and as he moved closer, Joe realized that he knew him very well. Simultaneously, his memories of being Joe also veered into focus, literally slamming into him, yet without disturbing the curious detachment he felt. After all, he was safely inside a dream. Nothing could hurt him here.

"It's about time you arrived," declared the man, sitting down on the boulder as well. His silvery white hair was pulled back in a long braid, his skin, bronzed and luminous, his face and body, ageless.

It was the same jolt Joe always felt the first moment he saw him, this man who had a way of lurking in the hidden folds of memory, like a forgotten dream. This man he called Luna.

"Sometimes I wonder if there is some kind of conspiracy against me," said Joe, as if they were continuing a conversation from before. "It's as if there's some kind of plot to make everything go wrong." He was thinking of the day when he'd lost his glasses, his keys, and his ring all inside of an hour.

"Nothing is ever as simple as it seems." Luna leaned in closer, his bright inquisitive face beaming with secret amusement. "They were hidden from you as a way to stimulate you---to scare up the Shadow."

A chill of fear coiled up Joe's spine. Indeed, the events of that day had triggered the worst fit of depression he had felt for a long time. "They were purposely hidden from me? What exactly do you mean by that?'

"I mean, you were not finding them because they were temporarily hidden in another field of perception, another world. In fact, there are worlds upon worlds in this very spot, and once you find the Crossroads between Worlds, you can find and have whatever you wish. Thirsty?" He held out his hand and a cup materialized out of the air. "Drink."

Without feeling any particular surprise, Joe took the cup and drank. An invigorating warmth spread throughout his body, touching every cell. Abruptly, he began to shake like a volcano getting ready to blow, and suddenly he was up on his feet, running in place.

"That's right! Run! It'll keep you from flying off into a thousand pieces!" Luna roared with laughter as he seemed highly entertained.

However, Joe was not thinking about any of this. He wasn't thinking at all. He was running just to keep the searing white light that was flooding his abdomen, from blowing him apart. Strangely, his body seemed to know exactly what to do and his breathing automatically shifted into a measured pattern. That's when he discovered that he could move the energy, shape, and calm it.

Suddenly, he saw that his mind was like a house with many rooms, each locked and sealed off from each other; and that Luna was someone he had known for many lifetimes and not a dangerous lunatic but absolutely sane.

"Luna, the crazy one---crazy as the moon," said the man, as if he'd been listening to Joe's thoughts. His eyes beamed with a penetrating light. "That is your name for me, not mine." Suddenly, Joe's mind flooded with memories from the year 1730 when he lived as the first Meriwether Bowen, the ancestor who'd settled this land and was later healed in the sacred spring by old Chief Louah.

"If I had told you these things, you would never have believed them," continued Luna, quite conversationally. "Your mind would have lost that information down the crevice, just like it tries to lose everything else down there."

"Crevice? What crevice?"

"Your mind is split and has forgotten itself. One side is trapped in littleness, in brokenness, in failure, and flaw but the other side side has never forgotten who you really are." Luna tapped his temple with a sly grin. "No, it was better for me to wait until you were ready to remember on your own. Now let's go." In one fluid move, Luna was on his feet and with the graceful ease of a panther, clamoring over the jumble of rocks.

"Where are we going?" asked Joe.

"Up there!" Luna pointed to the top of an enormous stony outcropping shaped like the face of a man.

A shallow ledge carved into the rock provided the path leading to the entrance of a small cave near the top. It was barely large enough to hold two people, and somehow Joe knew this place very well—just where to sit in the curve of the rock, where it cradled the spine just so.   Luna grunted his approval. "See? Your body is no fool. It knows that this is a good place to meet the Shadow."

Joe's jaws were clenched tight. The shaking had started up again, making it difficult to speak but this talk of shadows didn't sound good. The very word caused a lump of fear to form like a fist in his solar plexus.

Luna nodded approvingly. "Yes, this is a good place for you to take back the power it has stolen. But first, you must sing your thanks so the cave will get used to you. She will keep you grounded and help you hold the truth about yourself---all of it---even that which terrifies you most."

"Sing?" cried Joe. Knowing the truth about himself sounded bad enough but the prospect of singing even worse. Waves of un-pleasant childhood memories filled his head with humiliating perfor-mances in front of his mother's friends. "I can't do that! I cannot sing!"

"Of course you can't," retorted Luna, sarcastically. "How can you sing a song of gratitude when you don't have a thankful bone in your body?"

"But there's nothing to be thankful about!"

Luna looked disgusted. "Better yet, don't even talk. Just breathe. The Cave will like that better than fake gratitude." Suddenly Joe felt like a schoolboy who'd been sent to the corner. Meanwhile, it was all he could do to control the shaking that was only just now had begun to subside.

After a prolonged silence in which it seemed Luna had given up on his protégé, Luna finally spoke again. This time he had dropped the sarcasm and seemed entirely sincere. "Of course, all real music comes first from listening---here---on the inside."

The old shaman touched Joe's chest, then fell silent as though waiting for something. Presently, he produced a high, nasal sound that modulated into a soft guttural chant. Musically, it sounded quite ugly but soothing all the same, and then words started to form within the sound.

"Tha--ank you, thank you
bless-ed Life.
Take me
as I am."

There was a long silence then with a mischievous peek, nod-ded that it was his turn.

Joe swallowed hard. He should have known better than to think Luna would let him off the hook. He opened his mouth and the first sound was a harsh congested honk. Embarrassed, he cleared his throat and started again with a half -hearted "Tha-a-a-nk you...Tha-aank you." Then he snapped his mouth shut. "I can't do this."

Luna shrugged, shaking his head. "Well, all right---but make no mistake. The Shadow will come for you whether you like it or not."

"When?" Joe's anxiety was rising.

"That's just it! You never know because it has a nasty habit of sneaking up on you when you're least prepared---a real inconvenience. *Here* it's *you* setting the appointment. That gives you the upper hand! You're prepared and you *could* have your allies all lined up for protection."

"Allies?"

"This Cave, for instance, would be willing to be your ally, but I suppose you're just too important to sing to a cave." He heaved a great dramatic sigh. "Still, I suppose if you want to go on killing yourself, that's your choice and there's nothing I can do about it."

"Killing myself?"

"What do you think the Shadow has in mind---a tea party?" His eyes narrowed into a hard glint of light. "No, my friend. The Shadow does not mess around."

By now Joe was a tangle of rebellious emotions. The childish resistance he felt about singing this song was enormous, like a wall splitting him right down the middle. "No! I won't sing! I can't and I won't!"

Luna dismissed this outburst with a shrug and fell so completely silent that Joe began to feel edgy, worrying that he had offended him. Finally, he exploded, accusing Luna of mocking him.

"There, you see?" answered Luna sternly. "The Shadow already presents itself. Now is the time. Take the first step before it swallows you whole. But then of course, we all know---," suddenly, Luna erupted into a ludicrous operatic arpeggio. "That you can-not, can-not, can-not...si-i-i-i-ng!"

Against his will, Joe laughed.

"I don't ca-a-a-re if it's u-u-u-ugly!" bleated Luna on one long plaintiff note, looking comically forlorn.

Joe swallowed. "But I can't....I ca-a-a-n't!" It was little more than speaking but it felt like a fist in his throat, leaving him gasping.

"That's not true! You *can* but you *will* not!" sang Luna, ending with a ridiculous sounding trill. "But why? But can you tell me why?"

"Because I hate myself so much---that's why!" exploded Joe, then retreated, shamefaced.

Luna seemed not at all impressed by this, or shocked, or sympathetic but acted as if this were all perfectly normal. "Of course you hate yourself," he sang, "and that is exa-ctly what-the Shadow wants— your *love*, your *joy*, your *life*! But-you-do-not-have-to-give-it-to-him!"

For a long moment Joe sat, eyes closed, tears streaming down his face, then without warning, he started to sing. It was hardly more than speaking, just one long sustained note. "And I want to be... free....of that." Joe's voice broke off.

Luna grunted with satisfaction. "Now that. my friend, was an honest prayer, and the Cave Mother accepts it with humility and re-spect."

A silence ensued that could have lasted only minutes but the next time Joe opened his eyes, the moon had risen, casting the world in a silvery glow. Meanwhile, Luna was waiting placidly beside him.

"I have a question," said Joe. Now he was feeling his thoughts rather than thinking them, and they were amazingly clear, like crystal patterns in his mind.

Luna raised his eyebrows. "Good. I was beginning to think you were a lousy conversationalist."

"I'm wondering if there is such a thing as a curse because in my family we have this problem. Nobody ever wants to talk about it but it's always there, just waiting to make bad things happen."

"Like what sort of things?"

"Like losing things or breaking things or falling down stairs or, well—off the roof. While I was growing up, I started to think that if I was very, very quiet, it might forget about me but the moment I wasn't paying attention, the moment I made the mistake of thinking, 'Oh, it would be so easy to fall down the stairs'...the next day... boom... I'd fall down the stairs! So what would you call that?"

Luna yawned, "I guess I would call that a problem."

Joe smiled ruefully, "I call it a curse. Sometimes, I think that it's Zion that's cursed. Something in that house wants to kill me because so many bad things happen to there. It makes me think that I am being punished. Or am I just insane?"

"It doesn't matter what you *think* as much as what you *feel* about what you think. What you think is changing moment to moment. What you *feel* is embedded in your flesh. Your feelings are your pow-er."

"What do you mean?"

"Have you ever had a thought more powerful than rage? Or love? Thoughts are nothing without feeling to bring them into your body, into this world. The Shadow has imprisoned your power inside feelings of fear and dread.”

Again, at the mere mention of the Shadow, the fear ramped up in Joe’s belly. “Are you saying that there is some kind of demon haunting me?”

“What do *you* think it is? Only you can know.”

Joe stared off morosely. “Sometimes, I think it’s definitely got to be a punishment. My ancestors owned slaves here. One massacred a tribe of Indians on this very spot.”

“I know. I was there.”

The two men gazed at one another as the reality of time swept through them.

“I’m so sorry, so sorry.” Joe cast his eyes down and wept. “Surely, there is a punishment for that? *‘Down unto to the seventh generation’.* Isn’t that what the Bible says? The sins of the father? Is this why I feel like I am destined to suffer?”

“A feeling like that can trap you in a thought and drive it right into the substance of your being. That’s why I brought you here. The Spirit of this Cave will keep you grounded, while you go and cut the cords that bind you!”

And suddenly Joe was outside of his body looking down on two men sitting in the cave. With a little shock, he realized one of them was himself. In the instant, he realized that he could fly.

He swooped out of the cave, veering down towards the ground so fast he wondered if he would be able to control it. The speed was unnerving and controlling the levitation was a little scary, as well until he realized that he’d done this all before and soon was confidently soaring above the treetops, gliding over the shadowy forest, under the full moon.

Moon was in the tree house, meditating by candlelight. Joe hovered nearby, marveling. The man that he saw was a montage of subtle images layered, one on top of the other, as if all the faces he had worn through countless lifetimes, were still there, molten and alive, merging and re-emerging. He could feel that his friend was worried. Joe touched his shoulder. “Don’t worry, my friend. All is well.” Perhaps sensing Joe’s presence, Moon sighed deeply.

The next moment, Joe was gliding through the cold moonlit halls of Zion, the very walls exuding that familiar feeling of danger but this did not trouble him. He was free. Nothing could hurt him now. He flowed through the walls into the room where Murphy slept, tucked into a ball like a fetus, sucking on his thumb. On the table beside the bed, the thick lenses of his glasses magnified the face of the illuminated clock. It read 3 a.m.

Luna had been right. He could see them, chords of energy searching for him like blind tentacles. It was as painful to look upon this most vulnerable progeny, the one most like him, the one he should have helped in some way but never could. For a moment, he hovered, powerless in the grip of a paralyzing sadness; but he had come to cut these ties.

"I do love you, son. Forgive me." Murphy stirred a little. "Please don't think that you're alone, Murph. Reach out. Help is all around you."

A look of peace appeared on Murphy's face and Joe left him to his happy dream.

He now found himself outside a small door at the end of the hall, the door which led to Fleming's attic room. Here he met with a mysterious resistance and found that he had to will his way through a cloud of stifling darkness that pushed against him as he moved towards the sleeping form on the bed. It was Fleming, lying on his back, hands folded across his chest, his face so still that he could have been dead. A heavy feeling tugged at Joe's insides. It was guilt for this one he had never been able to love.

For a moment, he felt the urge to touch him, but something in Fleming turned him away. In that instant, Joe saw the lifetime he'd spent as the Ancestor, Meriwether Bowen. It was Fleming who'd played the part of his son, the one who'd called in British troops to slaughter Chief Louah's tribe. Joe had never been able to forgive Fleming in that lifetime, just as he'd never been able to love him in this one. This was but another chance to do so. Was he going to pass it by yet one more time or was he going to let this darkness hold him here? The answer that came was surprising and swift. Behind Fleming's cruelty, he saw that it was really only fear, the fear of failure, and a self hatred deep as his own! A sudden tenderness welled up , like what he'd felt the first moment he'd held Fleming as a newborn baby, so vulnerable, so alien, so raw. Fleming opened his eyes now, blank from sleep but saw only darkness and turned over. At that moment, Joe knew they were both set free to go their own ways.

He traveled back through the halls, floating down the stairs, past the registration desk, and into the library where someone else awaited him. Joe stood now in the center of the room, turning in all directions, instinctively drawing himself into a circle of light. It wasn't long before the double doors into the parlor slowly slid apart. There, hovered the shadow of a cold, oily darkness. It was the Colonel, of course, lurking ever in shadow, imprisoned these many long years in the place of his murderous deed. Growing up, Joe had always been so powerless against that Darkness and even now, could feel it sucking out his will, just as it had always done, feeding off his fear to keep itself alive.

As a child, this ghost had followed him about on dreary days, hovering beside his bed at night where Joe lay like a corpse, shrouded head to toe beneath the sheet, too terrified to breathe. If he spoke of it to his father, sometimes he would get a sympathetic pat but not from his fashion-plated mother, whose only response was a terse command to stop imagining things.

Grandmother Irene was the only one to ever offer any real comfort, along with the gentle reminder that a ghost can't hurt you if you don't pay it any mind. It was her quiet voice speaking to him now from the back of his mind, saying, "You must feel sorry for him, Joseph. He's a lost soul and don't know where to go. Send him to the heavenly Light and then forget him." Now once again, Joe saw that it was not so much the murderous deed but self-hatred that had tormented the Colonel and every generation to follow; the self-loathing buried beneath a hardened heart. Yes, the sins of the father, thought Joe, as pity quietly took the place of fear.

With a victorious shout, Joe burst forth like a comet across the starry sky. Go to the Light! He was not afraid anymore. From there, he sped across fields and rivers until he found Trip in a train station. His rumpled hippy friend looked different, refreshed somehow. Gone was the tired cynicism. He seemed enlivened, bright eyed, like a child looking forward to a journey. The moment he saw Joe, he headed toward him, arms outstretched. They hugged. "Thank you, Joe. Thanks for everything! You have given me so much!" They waved farewell and then Joe was off once more, flying over the treetops under the moon. From below, the voices of the trees whispered, God speed. The deep sadness that had dogged him his whole life was gone and in it's place, the peaceful feeling of freedom.

The next thing he knew, he was back in the cave, sitting, solemn and silent, beside Luna in the creeping light of dawn.

"Tell me what you found," said the old shaman.

Joe smiled to himself. "When I looked at the ones I feared the most, I saw myself there and felt compassion."

Luna nodded as though satisfied. "You call yourself a failure but your work has been on the inner plane, Joe. There, you have made huge accomplishments, more than enough for one lifetime. In the Other World, you are a celebrated success!"

Joe screwed up his brow. "The Other World?"

"You really think there is only one? Indeed, we are of two worlds, you and I. The difference being that yours is but a Shadow of mine."

"If our world is a shadow then what is yours?"

"The Real World." Luna seemed to find this very amusing.

As usual when he was with the old shaman, Joe felt that edginess coming on like something inside him was about to break through another shell, like a chick forever being reborn.

"They called it amnesia, what happened to you," continued Luna, "but that wasn't it at all! And you weren't crazy, either. You just blew your circuits. You allowed yourself to see both worlds at the same time. Like that summer after you fell off the roof? Your dog went missing and you were so worried, you even went into the haunted forest to find her."

Like a forgotten dream, Joe recalled the whole scene, wandering into the forest and coming upon that strange little man, eating an apple in a treehouse. "Wait a minute!" The realization hit with a jolt. "That treehouse hadn't even been built yet! But how could that be?" He searched his mind wildly but could made no sense of it.

"You slipped out of Time, old friend. It's quite a common occurrence in my world."

Suddenly, they were wrenched out of the moment and hurtling at great speed through colors and vibrations, until they came to a great circle of stone columns encircling a temple set in the center of a beautiful garden. Tree-lined marble streets radiated out into a gleaming city, scented by flowers and blossoming trees. A woman floated out of the temple and hovered nearby to water her plants.

Joe looked at Luna in wonder. "Where are we?"

"Don't you remember? You've been here so many times here before."

The woman approached with a broad smile. "So glad to see you again," she said and Joe recognized his Teacher from long ago. She offered her hand and with a surge of devotion, he kissed it. She smiled indulgently, as if this were an unnecessary gesture, then motioned for him to sit with her beside a fountain bubbling stone fountain and when he asked where they were, she replied, "The Crossroad between Worlds."

"So, is this a dream?" he asked.

She lifted a brow. "Everything is a dream. The question is, which dream do you choose to live in?"

CHAPTER XXXI
The Search for Val
The Forest of Zion Crossroads
June 1979

Nealy and Tom had been searching in the forest for several hours without a sign of Professor Valentino when suddenly they noticed something white fluttering in the middle of the path up ahead. It was the Professor's little black notebook, the one he'd always kept in his vest pocket. A playful breeze lifted the heavy heat and riffled through the pages.

"I hope he's all right," said Nealy, picking it up.

"Professor?" shouted Tommy. "Can you hear me? Professor! Where are you?"

"There!" cried Nealy, pointing off through the trees. " I just saw him up through there. He looked straight at me but then just kept going!" Now there was no sight of him anywhere. They both called out repeatedly and for a moment thought they might have heard his voice answering back but it was only the call of a strange indigo bird with red and yellow markings, looking down at them from the tree above. It fluttered off then returned, circling around their heads three times before flying off once more.

"Interesting," she said.

They looked at each other and without a word, began to follow. It wasn't long before they found the professor's straw hat hanging precariously from a low branch where it must have been torn from his head.

"Poor thing must be so confused!" murmured Nealy.

The bird led them deeper into the forest to a treehouse lodged in a spacious live oak tree.

"Interesting," said Tom.

Without a word, they clambered up to survey the grand vista of tree tops stretching far as the eye could see. The structure itself was a falling apart hodgepodge of mismatched lumber. On one end, the remnants of an old plastic tablecloth flapping in the breeze was all that remained of what must have been a roof. A wooden box, an old pot, and a couple of dirty blankets were the only other signs that someone had once inhabited it. From inside the box, Tom produced a pair of thick glasses, a meerschaum pipe shaped like a woman's torso, and a photograph.

"I wonder who this is," mused Nealy, examining the tall lanky man who stared bleakly out of the photo and sitting stiffly beside a pair of tow headed twin boys. They looked to be about the age of two and the man seemed utterly disconnected from them.

"Interesting, but check this out." Tommy's attention had moved on to a spiral notebook with a torn green cover. Scrawled on the inside cover was the name Joseph Meriwether Bowen, 1979. Beneath it, was a weird drawing of a big head with question marks sprouting like sprigs of hair. Exclamation points marched in long rows out of its eyes and musical notes seemed to dance from its mouth. The body, dwarfed by comparison, was not big enough to hold his heart which had a big window in it and a small bug eyed face peering out. On the next page, written in a sloping hand, was the first entry of what was intended to be a diary, dated September 17, 1979:

"Today I found the Other World."

He regarded Neely with an arched brow. "Are we in some deep shit here, or what?"

"Oh, my god!" she cried, clasping her hands to her mouth. "Isn't that what the professor is always talking about? The Other World?"

The mist was, at that moment, silently creeping in and quickly obliterated the ground below. The bird had vanished. Tommy cursed. "I was hoping we'd get out of here before this happened. We might have to stay put for a while until this dissipates."

Nealy shrugged. "My sister will worry but she'll survive. What about your brother?"

"Him? Worry about me? Nah, he's probably hoping I get lost and never come back."

She didn't ask why but the look she gave him was sympathetic.

"It'll pass," he said. "Jack is like a thunderstorm. When he gets mad it's like boom! And then it's gone."

She gave a rueful laugh. "Portia's more like Chinese water

torture— perpetually angry but in a quietly frozen way."

"I don't see how anybody could be angry at someone like you!" he blurted. Ordinarily, he would have kept out of it, but he'd seen Portia in action and it bothered him. Nealy was too gentle to have to put up with crap like that.

Nealy sighed. "She doesn't like my life choices, shall we say."

"Like living the pagan hippy dream?"

"Definitely that—and also for making her come here."

"Right—for the healing springs."

"Yes. It's my heart," she said. "I was born with this bad valve. Lately, its gotten much worse. She wants me to have this horrible huge surgery but I know there's got to be another way." She looked away as if embarrassed. "I know it sounds----."

Suddenly she looked so small, so sad, and earnest that he wanted to gather her in his arms. Instead, he reached for her hand, smiling. "But the whirlwind called you here," he said, referring to the way the pamphlet had been blown into her garden. "Just like the wind brought me."

"That's right!" Suddenly, it was as if the light had come back on inside her. "The pamphlet got blown onto your windshield. Right?"

He gave a solemn nod. "So, is it coincidence that brought us both here— or something else?" Tommy stretched his long body out on the platform and put his hands behind his head. "I thought I came here to find some buried treasure. Now, I'm thinking it's something else, something I really couldn't have imagined."

"Yes," she said, softly.

They were both quiet after that, reflecting how mysterious and wonderful it was. Hours passed. The day slipped into night and still the mist had not abated. They fell asleep as if under its spell and as night fell, it grew cold. At one point, she awoke and found herself sheltered in the curve of his body, breathing in synch, the moon in her eyes. She could feel that he was out of his body, perhaps dreaming in other worlds and a quiet happiness welled up inside her. She lay there with an empty mind. At dawn, she briefly awoke to see someone else sitting on the platform, watching them. In the watery gray light she could see that it was a man, long and lanky, then sleep pulled her hard back into the deep.

CHAPTER XXXII
Murphy's Confession
Zion Crossroads
Midsummer 1980

The next thing Murphy knew, someone was jiggling his shoulder. "Murphy! My god, what the hell happened?" It was Gardner trying to rouse him. From the window of his room, he and Katherine had witnessed Fleming choke Murphy into unconsciousness on the back lawn. When Gardner had opened the door and yelled, Fleming had grabbed the sack of vials and run off.

"Fleming's gone crazy!" sobbed Murphy but not because his eye was bleeding profusely or because his lip was split open but for rage because Fleming had beaten him---again.

"Come on!" Gardner tried to pull Murphy to his feet.

"Wait!" Murphy started groping like a mad man for something on the ground.

"He needs his glasses," cried Katherine and joined the search. "Here they are! I found them!"

But no, it was something else and he wasn't satisfied until he'd found it--- something cool and hard lying in the grass. Only then did he allow Gardner to lead him back to his room.

"This is my fault," he wailed as Gardner gently helped him onto the bed. "He's gone completely insane and he'll kill us all if I don't stop him!" Murphy laid back on the pillow, wincing. "He's killed Puffenberger! And I'm sorry. Gardner, but I'm pretty sure now that he did the same to your mother. He poisoned her just like he poisoned Puffenberger!"

Gardner stared at him. "Poison? You're saying my mother was poisoned?"

"When Leonora died I couldn't be sure, but I should have known. I should have seen it coming! And now Puffenberger is dead, and it's all my fault!" Tears flooded his cheeks. "You must get out of here while you still can!"

"What do you mean you should have seen it coming?" Gardner asked with a deadly calm.

"I've got to find Stephen!" interrupted Katherine and in an instant she was gone. Gardner continued to stare intently at Murphy, waiting for an answer.

Murphy swallowed nervously. "Fleming was always in a war with your mother. He was convinced that she was taking money out of the accounts and he resented the fact that my father had given her the power of attorney. After he moved back from Richmond, Fleming did everything he could to get her out. That's when he put in the two-way mirror so he could spy on her. He wanted to catch her stealing but that never happened. Still, he refused to believe she wasn't cheating us. And then there was the whole issue of the nature of her relationship with my father." Murphy looked down, ashamed.

"Murph, that never happened!"

Murphy laid his hand gently on Gardner's arm. "Gardner, either way, I don't mind. None of that matters anymore. And the truth is, I loved your mother and when she died---." Tears sprang to his eyes. "It never made sense. She was so healthy!" He struggled to compose himself. "But I always had my doubts. I'd seen Fleming bringing in those plants!"

"Plants?"

"The datura. I knew exactly what it was from when we were boys, when he used to make his special concoctions? You remember! How he used to poison those poor animals?" He paused, as if staring down the long years. "Well, I asked him what he was doing with it. He said he was making rat poison. Well, not long after that, your mother died. So even then I knew! I just didn't want to see it." His eyes clouded with misery. "I've been such a coward. I should have stood up to him a long time ago, and now it's too late for poor Mr. Puffenberger! But at least I have this!" He held out the object he'd found in the grass. It was one of the vials of poison that had fallen out of the sack. "It was digging into my shoulder blade where Fleming threw me to the ground." He managed a painful smile in spite of a split lip. "Evidence."

Twilight deepened into violet and stillness, only to be broken by a furious knock at the door. It was Katherine. She was hysterical. Stephen Andriot was dead! Stabbed in the chest! She'd gone to their room, and found him lying on the bed. He was facing away from her, but something in the silence felt terribly wrong. She'd whispered his name, but there was no answer. Something dark on the sheets confused her.

At first, in the dim light, she couldn't discern what it was until she'd come close enough to touch him. That's when she'd seen the knife wound and the widening pool of blood. He was already dead; his wide set eyes open, staring, his face frozen in an anguished snarl.

Flashing on the image of Fleming's bloodstained shirt, Murphy struggled to sit up. "Get your car and leave immediately, both of you!"

"But what about Amanda and the other woman?"

"I'll get them." Murphy stood up, his head reeling.

"Are you insane! You can't go into that house!" cried Katherine. "Fleming is still in there!"

"Don't worry about me. I'll be all right. Just go! Quickly!" He reached out to balance himself, knocking the lamp over.

"No offense, Murph! But you're no match for Fleming right now!"

"I am not afraid of Fleming anymore!" retorted Murphy fiercely.

Gardner stared. This was a Murphy he had never seen before. "Okay. Just be careful!"

The moment he had gone, Gardner began pushing aside a bookshelf, revealing a door.

"What are you doing?" Katherine was pale but outwardly holding herself together. Inside, she was numb, her emotions frozen and dark.

"This room was originally the servants quarters connected to the kitchen but I blocked it off because there was no lock. Be right back." He disappeared into the darkened kitchen but was back in a moment, looking grim. "The phone line is dead."

"What do we do now?"

He could see the panic rising in her eyes and tried to appear confident. "We get to the car, drive to the nearest neighbor. Call from there."

"Yes, okay, okay." All they had to do was get to the car.

Dusk was slowly deepening as they set out for the garage. They were halfway across the yard when a man suddenly emerged from the summer kitchen. It was Fleming. Gardner immediately shoved Katherine down behind a row of boxwoods, where they remained concealed. As Fleming came near, he paused as if sensing his prey. He was carrying a gun. They waited in terror and did not breathe again until he had gone on past.

Adjusting the silencer on his pistol, Fleming expected to find his twin lying on the ground but Murphy was nowhere in sight. A complication but nothing we can't handle, said the Voice inside his head.

From the outside, the back of the house was quiet, the dark windows lined up like silent witnesses. But what had they seen? He stole towards Gardner's door and quietly tried the knob. It was locked and the curtains drawn. He flattened himself against the wall, holding his breath, listening— anxiety and a strange sort of joy twisting up into his throat. Was this not the invincibility of the Lord come upon him now?

Suddenly a light flicked downstairs in Murphy's study just as Mrs. von Hassel's pale face appeared in the window above. She lit a candle then withdrew out of sight.

Treading softly, Fleming headed toward the main house. *First the faithless one, then the Whore of Babylon.* "Yea, the Lord is with me, guiding my steps," he exulted silently and was halfway across the yard when a low growl erupted from the boxwoods. Suddenly, a great white dog charged out and knocked him flat. Pinned down in such a manner with the vicious jaws of this snarling beast inches from his face, Fleming had no choice but to lie completely still. He'd never had a way with dogs so he couldn't charm his way out of this one. His only hope was the pistol tucked into his belt, but one false move could trigger the dog to attack.

Suddenly, there came a long low whistle, "Willomina! Willy! Come!" And the mysterious dog bounded off to where his master stood watching from the edge of the trees before vanishing from sight. Fleming lay there, gasping for breath, his heart pounding like fury. He was almost positive that it had been Professor Valentino.

Fleming stood up and went into the house. First, he must take care of his brother so he wouldn't get in the way, but he wasn't in his room. As Fleming was leaving, he caught a stray movement out of the corner of his eye. Startled, he whirled, only to see that it was but his own reflection in the mirror. That's when he noticed the front of his white shirt, smeared with Andriot's angry blood. *They'd think you were a madman,* joked the Voice. *But they shall be made to see. The whole world will know when the Truth is finally revealed.* In the meantime, he must entertain no doubts. Nothing should be allowed to interfere with his mission! And wasn't everything falling into place, just as it should?

Yet, there was that one troubling detail, namely why Professor Valentino had continued to keep on living? He should have been dead ten times over with all the poison that he'd been given, yet still he survived as if it had no power over him at all? And if he survived that, could his father have also? And if Joe was still alive, could he still be hanging around, somewhere in hiding, waiting to return?

This made no sense, he reasoned. His father had to be dead. He simply had to be. And Fleming must barricade himself against that creeping fear. He must banish that almost magical belief in his father's invulnerability to death. One's loyalty to the cause must remain unshakeable or the Lord might choose a more suitable servant!

But where is the love in your heart, Fleming? Suddenly, it was his father's voice speaking in his mind, asking the question that had plagued him so long. This was the question his father had asked him that day in the treehouse; the same question Leonora had once asked him and that had festered long after they were both dead and gone and out of his way. Where is the love in your heart?

Bitter, savage tears clouded his image in the mirror. How dare they blame him? No one could know how that cursed question had haunted him, night after sleepless night! How he tried to understand, why? Why could he not feel this 'Christ love' that everyone raved about? Had he not agonized over it? Begged the Voice not to abandon him? The Voice that spoke to him at his Baptism under the water, the one that had given him a reason to exist, the Voice that had told him, 'Do your duty'?

Thank God, after years of silent suffering, he'd finally seen this question they'd asked for what it really was----a curse, a witch's curse that Leonora had put on him when he was too young to defend himself. She'd done it to weaken his spirit because he was the only one strong enough to stand up to her.

He thought he'd stopped her when she was finally dead but even from the grave he could feel her working against him. During the long nights, he could feel that darkness---like a cold stone wedged between his ribs, trying to press the very breath out of him. In those moments, he could only force his bony knees to the hardwood floor and beg to hear the Voice that wouldn't come.

Beneath the twisted figure on the cross above his head, the pain in his knees became a strange sort of consolation, connecting him to the suffering of Christ. Surely he was being tested. This was why the Lord had withheld his signs. This was why he'd been forced to wander in the desert without love. He was being tested, to see if he would remain true to his calling; to be a warrior, the Lord's Protector; for who would do it if Fleming did not?

But one night---thank the Lord--- after pleading for a sign, the unseen god had stirred the curtain at the window, knocking over one of the tincture bottles on his worktable. And in that same moment, the moon had slipped behind the panes, casting the shadow of a cross upon the room. That was the moment when everything had changed; the moment when the Voice had finally started speaking to him again, showing him the way.

He quickly removed the shirt, went into the small bathroom to scrub the blood off his hands, then began searching in Murphy's wardrobe for another shirt. Unlike himself, who only wore plain white long-sleeved shirts, his brother preferred short-sleeved multicolored plaids, and the only one left was bright yellow and orange. Fleming had always thought it was horribly garish but now he had no choice but to put it on.

In this shirt, minus the beard, whispered the cunning Voice, as he stood once again before the mirror, *you could be your brother.* Obediently, he went back into the bathroom and proceeded to shave his face clean.

Returning to the room, his eye caught something that he'd previously missed---an open letter on Murphy's bedside table. It was the Colonel's confession to murdering his brother, Haden, and his detailed instructions about where to find the treasure. Tears of gratitude flooded Fleming's eyes. "Lord, thank you for delivering this unto my hand," he said. Truly a miracle has taken place, he told himself, but he had no illusions about the responsibilities this incurred. No, Fleming would not shirk the duty for which he'd been chosen. "Brother, you are officially a dead man for keeping this from me," he muttered, as he slipped a pair of Murphy's eyeglasses into his breast pocket and left the room.

CHAPTER XXXIII
Evidence
The Zion Crossroads Plantation Hotel
1980

Earlier, as dusk had settled in, Murphy was on his way to the mailbox when the sounds of the dog attack arose from behind the house. Immediately he'd broken into a limping run, down the long tree lined drive into the darkening gloom. He was carrying an envelope addressed to the Coroner, and stuck inside was the vial of Fleming's poison.

When the animal snarls behind the house suddenly stopped, the vigorous chirping of the night creatures resumed. An ocean of life surrounded him, and though the road behind was empty, he could only feel heart pounding terror for fear that Fleming was following him.

Murphy ran until he was out of breath and then fell while walking. It was at least half a mile to the end of Zion's long dusty driveway, giving him plenty of time to think about how much of a fool he'd been to let Fleming talk him into holding that funeral with an empty coffin. Every instinct had told him that their daddy could never have committed suicide. He was too much of a coward for that. No, Fleming had forged that suicide note himself and the evidence was in the notebook where Fleming had practiced their daddy's signature over and over. Yes, he'd written it over and over before poisoning him to get him out of the way.

Suddenly, he thought about the Kool-aid. That was probably how Fleming had poisoned their father. Yes, it must have been the Kool-aid. After poor Trip had died so horribly and Moon had gone, Murphy had started taking big thermoses of Kool-aid and sacks of peanut butter sandwiches out to the tree house just as Moon had instructed, which provided Fleming the perfect opportunity.

Why else would that have been the first thing Fleming asked about that morning of their daddy's disappearance? "Was the thermos of Kool-aid empty?" he'd asked. At the time, Murphy had thought that was such a strange thing to wonder about when their father had just vanished. "Well—yes, it was empty! Why?"

"Nothing! I hoped that he'd taken the thermos with him because that would mean he was just out on a hike."

"Without his glasses or his shoes? No, Fleming, he is hardly out on a hike!"

And though Fleming had acted like he was worried, the moment Murphy mentioned calling the Sheriff, he'd abruptly overruled the idea. It would be too humiliating for Daddy if they found him running naked through the woods. A scandal like that would destroy the Bowen reputation and the business along with it, he'd said.

As usual Murphy didn't dare to disagree but couldn't help but think that was odd as well. When had Fleming ever expressed concern for the welfare of the business? And then Fleming had turned around and lied to the coroner and everyone else! Plain and simple lied and to his eternal shame, Murphy had buried his head in the sand. He'd known that what Fleming was doing was wrong, but he just wanted the whole ugly chapter to be over so he could get back to normal life.

Now the pieces of the puzzle that had tormented him for so long, had finally fallen into place. In a day or two, the coroner would be holding all the evidence he'd need, to put Fleming away. Of course, for the others, sleeping innocently in their beds, it would be too late.

After laying the letter in the mailbox, he lingered, agonized with indecision. He should go back, he told himself; all the while gazing longingly down the road ahead, stretching empty and pale in the light of the full moon. It would be so easy just to keep going, on past the ragged fields to the old bridge and the highway beyond. Seven miles and he'd be in town. Maybe a car would pick him up and take him further than that, maybe even to a far city. From there he would move on from place to place, just as his father had done all those times when he'd forgotten who he was. Yes, Murphy could do that, too, just disappear, forget who he was, walk out of his life.

It was a reassuring thought for all of a moment, but Fleming had to be stopped once and for all, and who would do it if he did not? So against every instinct for his own survival, Murphy turned his steps back towards the house. He had to warn the others. He had to protect them and for once he felt no fear. He was ready to die now. He was okay with that. His life had reached a dead end, and nothing mattered more than doing the right thing. He knew that now as he turned back towards the house.

Suddenly, a furious flutter of wings narrowly missed his head! "Hey!" The bird perched on a low branch of a nearby tree and looked at him. Shaken for a moment, Murphy continued walking, keeping a wary eye for once again it swooped low over his head but this time delivering a sharp peck on the top of his head.

"Ow! What the hell!" Now he was indignant and even a little afraid. "Why are you doing this?" Squawking cheerfully, the bird flew to a branch further off. Suddenly, Murphy saw the professor standing with a large white dog at the edge of the forest. The old man raised his hand in greeting.

"Professor? What are you---?" Murphy's question hung in the air unfinished for he saw now that there was another man standing there---long and lanky. The man motioned Murphy to follow as he and the professor disappeared into the trees.

Murphy blinked. "No, it can't be," he muttered as he entered the moonlit forest.

CHAPTER XXXIV
Murder
The Zion Crossroads Plantation Hotel
1980

Freshly shaved, Fleming stood outside Amanda von Hassel's door in his brother's yellow and orange plaid shirt. Though she might be awake, he reasoned, most likely she would be supremely drunk at this hour. Just as he began to draw the pistol from under his shirt, however, the bathroom door opened behind him and Portia Reed came shuffling out in fluffy slippers, her hair in curlers.

At the sight of him she gave a loud shriek, then with a scowl, pulled her bathrobe tight under her chin. "Mr. Bowen! You startled me!"

"Sorry," he said.

With a grudging nod she headed to her door, then hesitated. The face she turned to him was a mask of exhaustion and worry. "You haven't heard anything from them, have you? My sister and that guy? They went out into the forest to look for the old man and they still haven't come back."

For a moment she glimpsed something impenetrably dark in the way Fleming stared at her but then he answered in a calm sort of way. "No, nothing but I'm sure they're all right," he said.

"My sister's so reckless sometimes and I worry myself to death over her!" She stepped closer, lowering her voice confidentially. "Do you have anything that could help a person sleep?"

His eyes slid involuntarily to Andriot's door. "The peace of the Lord," he said softly.

Her eyes misted with sudden tears. "Yes, you're right! I should pray, I suppose!" She paused, scrutinizing his face. "You're not like your brother, are you! You're nice and he's so---."

She thinks you're Murphy, murmured the Voice with a burst of malice. "He's so---what?"

Her lip curled with distaste. "Nasty."

The sting this produced surprised him. He thought he was long past caring about the opinions of others; however, she had found an unexpected chink in his armor.

Suddenly Amanda von Hassel's door opened and there she stood, shamelessly revealed in a low cut, red satin sleeping gown, the nipples of her large breasts clearly visible. "Who screamed?" The repellent stench of her perfume, layered over the stink of cigarettes and liquor, instantly saturated the humid air.

"I did," said Portia. "He startled me, is all."

As always it unnerved Fleming to be in such close proximity to Mrs. von Hassel. It was her flagrant sexuality, along with the smug contempt in her eyes, as if she could read him inside and out. Of course, he would never admit, even to himself, that he feared or desired her, for he hid those emotions under a tight lid of cold disapproval.

Behind her, he could see that her room was lit with many candles. "Mrs. von Hassel, you know the use of candles and tobacco is strictly prohibited on the premises." She looked puzzled as if sensing something amiss. Murphy certainly had never used this imperious tone. Remembering, he added in a humbler manner, "I—I just worry about fire hazard, you know."

"I've never seen you before without your glasses," she said, as usual ignoring any reminders of the rules.

"Yes, well---sometimes I like to take them off." He quickly slipped them out of his pocket and put them on. The world became a blur.

"Huh! Well, too bad. You're better looking without them," she said.

Though sorely tempted to go ahead and make an end of her, he was at a disadvantage now that he had the glasses on. He'd have to remove them, and what if he fumbled getting the pistol out from under his shirt? With Portia standing so far down the hall to his left, and Amanda so far to his right, one or both could easily get away. Besides, he wasn't that good of a shot and might miss. After the difficulty he'd had with Stephen Andriot, he wasn't in the mood for another struggle so he remained cool, biding his time.

Turning back into her room, Amanda paused. "By the way, I saw you fighting with Fleming in the backyard." Her face hardened into pure hatred. "Next time, do me a favor and beat his ass." She all but slammed the door behind her.

"Crude woman," muttered Portia and shuffled off in her fuzzy slippers.

"Good night, m'am." He dipped his head and mumbled the way Murphy would do while the gun, hidden beneath his shirt, renewed it's silent promise to return---but later when they were sure to be asleep.

CHAPTER XXXV
The Shadow's Reflection
The Zion Crossroads Plantation Hotel
1980

The house was silent and dim as Jack eased past the Confederate flag hanging in the library window and slid quietly over the sill. The door to the front hall was slightly ajar, and the glow of a small lamp on the registration desk made it the perfect place to watch and wait for Fleming to reveal himself . But the minutes ticked by and nothing happened, not at first.

After Andriot told him about Fleming's ammunition stash in the summer kitchen, Jack had decided to go check it out for himself and happened to be snooping behind the building, when Fleming had unexpectedly showed up. Through a small dirt encrusted window, Jack had watched Fleming search, first one crate, then another until he'd found his weapon of choice---a small pistol with a silencer to go with it. The moment he left and was out of sight, Jack had broken into the shed and procured himself a pistol as well. An unexpected bonus was finding the metal detector that he'd accused Tommy of hiding from him, adding yet one more reason for him to go after Fleming. The sick bastard had stolen it from their room!

Now Jack was inside the house waiting for the next shoe to drop. Holy shit, he thought, grinning at himself as he peered through the crack in the door. Any sensible person would be terrified right about now, but he only felt an odd exhilaration. It was the daredevil, rising on the adrenalin rush he always got before a fight. Oh yeah, he was more than ready to get this fucker. The house brooded on in silence.

Thinking this was the break he needed to go to Amanda, he headed out into the front hall, his senses on hyper alert. Suddenly every hair on his body stood on end. It wasn't a sound but something else that warned him. He slipped behind the nearest door and found himself in a closet---the one Andriot had told him about---the one with the two way mirror. Maybe some of Tommy's luck had rubbed off on him after all!

He waited but nothing happened. Still, something told him to stay put---and sure enough there it was---the slightest creak on the staircase above and then another. Someone was coming down the stairs, someone who did not want to be heard.

Jack held his breath, as a man in a yellow and orange plaid shirt came into view. Relief flooded through him. It was only Murphy! Jack had his hand on the door handle and was just about to step out when 'Murphy' reached inside his shirt and pulled out a gun.

Jack watched from inside the closet, as the man in the orange and yellow plaid shirt removed his glasses and turned to the mirror and with a triumphant leer, slowly leveled the pistol at his reflection. No way was this Murphy, thought Jack. Heart pounding, he, too, slowly took aim and the two held their positions on opposing sides of the mirror. Did this guy in the orange plaid shirt sense that he was being observed from inside the closet? Jack's hand tightened on the pistol but then the imposter lowered his weapon with a wicked smile. No, he's admiring himself, thought Jack. Sick bastard.

Suddenly there was a loud crack and a jolt, as if a semi-truck had rammed into the side of the house. The lamp on the lobby desk crashed to the floor, plunging the room into darkness. Fleming wheeled and left the room.

CHAPTER XXXVI
Running
The Zion Crossroads Plantation Hotel
1980

Gardner and Katherine were running along the moonlit road on their way to the neighbor's house when the earth began to shake. It came like a crack of thunder, the sound unraveling for miles into the distance.

"Earthquake," muttered Gardner. "As if this night couldn't get any weirder."

After narrowly escaping Fleming in the yard, they had run to the garage where Gardner's car was parked, but the key in the ignition had only produced an empty click. The stink in the air told them that someone had siphoned all the gas. Nobody would be escaping anytime soon, not by car anyway so they'd taken off on foot.

When they'd arrived at a neatly kept frame house, an elderly black lady was already standing on her front porch in her nightgown.

"Miz Lewis?" Gardner called out, as he started confidently up the short driveway.

Mrs. Lewis promptly went inside and returned with a shotgun. "You stop right there! Don't you come one step closer!

"Miz Lewis? It's me, Gardner Bell."

"Who?"

"Gardner! Leonora's boy!"

"Gardner? What in the world---? We just had a earthquake, honey!"

"Yes, m'am! You think we could use your phone?"

"What?"

"The phone! The telephone!"

"Telephone? You need to use my telephone? In the middle of the night?" The poor woman seemed utterly confused and only after a bit more persuasion did she relax her guard enough to lower the shot gun and let them into her small living room.

"I swear this earthquake business is like to scare me half to death! It keeps happenin'. You'd think it's the end of the world or something! And for goodness sake, what are you doin' here? I ain't seen you since you was a boy!"

"Now that's not true, Miz Lewis. We saw each other at Daddy's funeral."

"Oh, that's right. Your poor Daddy. He suffered so with that arther-itus and believe you me, I know all about that. My hip is just about to---!"

"Miz Lewis, I'm sorry but ---!"

"It's that damp humidity, you know. Gets into the bones."

"Miz Lewis, the phone? We've got a kind of situation here---."

"Well, of course! You go ahead, honey! It's in the kitchen."

Gardner immediately went into the next room whereupon the elderly woman turned to Katherine, puzzled but gracious. "Honey, you look like you need some coffee!" She set her shotgun in the corner. "Now don't you worry about this old thing. It ain't even loaded. I used up all my shells to scare off the squirrels getting into my chicken feed. Goodness---Gardner Bell! You just never know who is gonna pop up at yo' door these days!"

CHAPTER XXXVII
Tremors
The Zion Crossroads Plantation Hotel
1980

Jack waited, as another tremor rattled the house. It took him a moment to comprehend what was happening. This was another earthquake! He stealthily slipped out of the closet and crept up the moonlit stairs. By the time he got to Amanda's door, she was standing there, in a panic.

"Did you feel that?" she said. "I was just---!"

"Shh!" He pushed her back into the room. It was lit all around with candles. Softly, he closed the door and locked it.

"What the---?"

"Shh!" He clapped his hand over her mouth.

Suddenly there was a loud creak on the staircase. They moved behind the door and watched in horror as someone on the other side, quietly tried the knob and when it didn't budge, slipped a key into the lock. There was a click and the door swung open.

The man in the orange and yellow plaid shirt stepped into the room, a gun aimed at the jumble of blankets and pillows on the bed. He fired silently, once, twice then walked closer to the bed, his back to the door, and fired a third time.

Jack stepped out and fired two shots in quick succession. Amanda screamed and threw herself on the floor. Fleming turned, roaring in pain and confusion, clutching at his side, shooting wildly. With a warrior's yell, Jack lowered his head and rammed into Fleming full force. The two men fell, grunting, onto the bed, grappling for possession of Fleming's gun.

Fleming was like a demon, all long arms and legs, and though Jack was stronger, he quickly lost control and ended up on the bottom. Screaming like a wild animal, Amanda threw herself onto Fleming's back, grabbing his ears and twisting with all her might. With a roar of pain, Fleming heaved her crashing to the floor.

She fell, knocking the bedside candles into the curtains which immediately burst into flame. However, Jack and Fleming were in no position to worry about that, even as flames shot up the wall. When a gun went off again, Amanda grabbed a high heeled shoe and hammered the back of Fleming's head with all her might. He went limp and Jack threw him off to the side.

"Murphy?" cried Amanda in disbelief when she saw the attacker's face. "And I thought Fleming was the crazy one!"

"Come on, we gotta get out of here!" yelled Jack, pulling her away.

Portia had been standing in the hall, wondering what all the screaming was about, when Jack and Amanda erupted out of the room in a cloud of smoke.

"Get the hell out! This place is on fire!"

CHAPTER XXXVIII
Hidden
The Zion Crossroads Plantation Hotel
1980

Katherine and Gardner were back out on the road to wait for the police when Katherine noticed something in the distance. "What's that?" she said, pointing to a huge orange glow above the trees.

"That's Zion Crossroads!"

As exhausted as they were, they broke into a run. By the time they'd made their way up the long drive, they could see flames leaping up the walls of the great house, consuming it with a mighty roar of vengeance. She made a move to draw closer, but he grabbed her arm.

"Where are you going?"

"To see if someone's survived! They might need help!"

"Yeah, and what if that someone is Fleming? No, I say we stay out of sight for now. Wait until the police come."

Suddenly part of the roof collapsed in a spray of fiery sparks. She stared in horror, thinking of the others trapped inside— Stephen's body, melting in the fire. "You think anyone has made it out?"

"We can only hope," he murmured. He was thinking about Murphy and how brave he'd been in the end— but life was cruel.

They found a hiding place in a grove of trees. From here, they could watch the fire continue to destroy Zion Crossroads. "So much work to build a place like that and so little to destroy it," he murmured.

It's the same for a human being, she thought. All that goes into raising a child and in a moment, life could be taken away.
"The police should be here soon," he said, but they waited and continued to wait as the flames burned steadily on, old timbers collapsing, wires sizzling, until the roar diminished into the crackling hum of a cleansing fire. They drifted in and out of sleep, under the full moon's lonely vigil, as it arced to the horizon.

Hours passed and it wasn't until the eastern sky was rimmed

with light and the great house was a smoking ruin that the police car finally rolled in, passing them by.

Katherine rose to flag them down.

"What are you doing?" Gardner yanked her back down.

She shrugged out of his grasp impatiently. "We need to go and tell the police what happened! What's your problem?"

"I got stuff to do, okay?" he muttered irritably. "And I don't have time to get sucked into their little investigation right now."

"Stuff to do! What stuff?"

"Don't worry about it."

"But you're a key witness! You know more than anybody what's been going on here! What if Fleming *did* survive? He's just going to tell them lies!"

"Like they'd take my word against his? No, more than likely I'll just wind up chief suspect number one!

"Why would *you* be a suspect?"

"Look, maybe where you come from the butler always did it--- but down here it's the black guy!"

"But surely they can't just blame you because you're black."

"Are you kidding? They do it all the time and I ain't taking that chance. Besides, once they make this a crime scene, nobody will be able to get in or out. No, if I'm ever gonna get this treasure, I need to do it now." He started walking in the direction of the house but parallel to the driveway, careful to remain concealed by the bushes.

She stood back. "So why are you going that way? I thought---."

"I need to get my tools from the gardening shed."

"Oh." She followed along.

He stopped. "Now where are *you* going?"

"With you."

"Oh, no---no, no! You go on and talk to the police."

"But I can help you!"

He looked at her sharply. "And why would you want to do that?"

"Because you might need my help." She stopped short of telling him that in some inexplicable way, she'd been there, where he was going.

He stared, caught in a battle between good sense and this sudden desire to let her stay, for there was no denying it. Part of him wanted her with him. Something about her seemed so familiar, something he could not name. He'd felt it from the moment he'd first laid eyes on her. "Research for your novel, right?"

She did not blink. "Yeah—research."

"Okay, have it your way. Just don't screw this up for me. We stay out of sight! Got it?"

"Got it!"

They set off, cutting a wide circuit behind the garage, the old stable, and then back of the summer kitchen. From here they had a clear view of the cement pool where Amanda and Portia now huddled on the stone bench, shivering under Portia's fluffy robe. Fortunately, they were fixated on the deputy and Jack who was at the moment reenacting the fight he'd had with Fleming up in Amanda's bedroom.

Gardner stopped to study the situation. It would be a matter of darting from bush to bush in order to get to the garden shed located at the bottom of the old rose garden, about ten yards from the entrance to the Labyrinth Garden. Crouching behind the summer kitchen, she stole quick glances, hunting for signs of Murphy over by the cement pool but didn't see him. Had he gotten out in time? Where was he? Suddenly, without warning, Gardner sprinted to the shed and slipped inside unnoticed. Katherine remained behind, wondering what the hell she was supposed to do because he hadn't bothered to tell her.

"You're saying that Murphy Bowen came into her room and shot at her?" While the deputy looked down to take some notes, Katherine crept to a bush in closer range so she could eavesdrop on what they were saying.

The cop looked up. "And this happened while both of you were behind the door?"

"We heard him in the hall."

"He thought he was shooting at Amanda,"said Jack, "but she was behind the door with me."

"He shot at the bed!" corrected Amanda. "I keep a lot of pillows on the bed. He must have thought I was still in it. I just can't imagine Murphy doing something like this!"

"True, he seemed nice," agreed Portia. "But who knows about these confederate types? Maybe he was in on it the whole time!"

Jack nodded. "These people have got enough guns stored in that building over there to start a small war." They turned to look.

Good thing she'd moved away from the summer kitchen, thought Katherine. She just hoped Gardner wouldn't take this moment to come out of the gardening shed.

"Really! A small war, you say?" continued the deputy.

Jack's voice rose. "Ever heard of the Grey Knights?"

"The Grey Knights." The officer's tone changed. "Oh sure. They been around a long time---long, long time. And we've heard rumors about weapons before but never thought they'd ever really go that far."

"Come on, you can see it for yourself."

"Okay, but first let me get this straight. Now you say there were how many people left in the fire or unaccounted for?"

"A woman named Katherine and her husband---."

"Stephen Andriot, was his name."

"But that wasn't *her* last name. She had a different name. Can't remember what it was."

"And Gardner, the maintenance guy."

"Anybody else?"

"And of course, if that was Fleming with the gun, then there was Murphy. Murphy Bowen," added Amanda, sadly. "He didn't make it out."

The shock of this hit Katherine in the chest. Poor Murphy.

"And the attacker. You say he didn't make it out, either?"

Suddenly there was a loud clunk from inside the garden shed but Portia seemed to be the only one who'd noticed because the others kept right on talking.

"Wait!" interrupted Portia sharply. "I think I heard something!"

They all stopped, looking warily around but only birdsongs could be heard.

"I didn't hear anything," said Jack.

Suddenly a burning timber collapsed into the fire with a resounding crash.

"Don't worry, honey. No way Fleming made it out of that fire." Amanda patted the other woman's knee. "Jack shot him for heaven's sake!"

Katherine could see that Gardner was watching through the small dusty window in the shed and while everyone's attention was turned towards Jack, she motioned for him to come out.

"Jack shot him?" The officer looked up from his notepad but not before Gardner had gotten safely across to Katherine, behind the bush.

"Twice," replied Jack. "I had to have gotten him at least once. Right, Amanda?"

Gardner motioned and pointed at the entrance to the Labyrinth Garden. Katherine nodded.

"I can tell you that when he fell, it was dead weight," Amanda was saying. "He was unconscious. There was no way Fleming could have gotten out of there alive."

Suddenly, the group's attention was drawn to an interior wall as it teetered and crashed to the ground. Seeing their opportunity, Katherine and Gardner darted into the boxwood maze unnoticed. They were headed for the wooden door, Gardner's short cut to the trail.

Between the hedges, looming high above them, the air was dark and oppressive; the pungent aroma of the boxwood, stinging their nostrils. Katherine's body balked like a stubborn animal, as if something terrible were waiting there. "Stop it!" she told herself and shoving back the rising panic, forced herself to follow Gardner in, as he led the way deeper into the maze; left, then right, then right again and on and on until they came into the center garden. In the gray light of dawn, the columns and statues were eerily silent. Her eyes naturally came to rest on the small temple. Was it her imagination or was there someone lying on the stone slab? With a wave of relief she realized who it was.

"What are you doing?" called Gardner as she headed across the garden.

"It's Murphy! He's okay!" Roused by the sound of her voice, 'Murphy' was sitting up, seemingly a little dazed. "Murphy! We were so worried about you!"

As she approached, she could see that his shirt was splotched with blood. "Oh, my god! You're bleeding!"

Gardner followed, hesitantly. Something about this did not feel right to him and it took him a moment to realize why. It was the glasses. Murphy wasn't wearing his glasses and yet his eyes were completely focused and watchful.

As she drew close, the man grabbed Katherine's wrist with his left hand, smiling victoriously.

"Murphy!" she cried out in disbelief. "Ow! What are you doing?"

Cold fear shot through Gardner's body. This wasn't Murphy! "You should smile more often, Fleming. It actually makes you look human," he said.

Fleming beamed maliciously. "And I have good cause to smile for the Lord has delivered me the prize." With his right hand, he slowly aimed the pistol at Gardner, his smile now an ugly sneer. "O misbegotten seed of unholy union!"

Katherine shrieked and twisted out of his grasp. "Are you insane?"

Fleming winced at his wound but the pistol did not waver.

Gardner remained calm. "As usual, Fleming has been fooled by a lie!" He said this to Katherine, as if Fleming weren't even there.

"A lie?" roared Fleming. "Says who? Your mother? The

conniving whore who stopped at nothing to get what she wanted?"

"Another lie!" shouted Gardner, hotly.

"A woman who drove my mother away so she could have my father to herself?"

"That is not true!"

"But she didn't love him. How could anyone love that rattletrap? No, it was all just a ploy so she could steal Zion Crossroads right out from under us—!"

"Oh, for god's sake, Fleming!"

"Steal—steal! Our fortune right out from under us!"

"Who filled your head with this garbage?"

"My mother! *My* mother! She told me! Everything! *She* knew what was really going on between her and my father!"

"*Your* mother? You mean the selfish, social climbing bitch—? "

"Not true!"

"—who never cared about anyone but herself—"

"Absolutely not true!" screamed Fleming, as if to drown out Gardner's voice. "How dare you even speak of her! She *loved* me!"

"If she loved you so much then why didn't she ever come back for you? Huh, Fleming? Why?"

Fleming froze, bug eyed with fury, the taunting question left hanging in the air. "I'll tell you why! Because she couldn't! That's why!" Suddenly, he sounded like a petulant twelve year old boy. "It was her bad back---her nervous condition---!"

"Come on, Fleming! It was because she couldn't be bothered—because she didn't care! The truth was that *my* mother----!" Gardner's voice broke. "—was the only real mother you ever had, Fleming! And you poisoned her! That's the real truth! You killed my mother *and* Puffy *and* Stephen Andriot---and who else, you arrogant son of a bitch? Who else?"

Hunching over his wound, Fleming's face broke into a snarl. "I had to---," he whined, suddenly more creature than man. Gardner had touched something raw.

"What possible reason would that be?"

Gardner stared pure venom as Fleming's face hardened.

"I had to protect—," he said then stopped abruptly.

"What could you possibly need to protect from them?"

Fleming's face fell. "But the Lord---." The gun hand drooped. Suddenly it seemed as if he didn't know anymore. He dropped down on the stone bench, staring dully at the ground as if the others were no longer there. His gaze, always so unflinching, so unsparing, faltered and drew inward, and in that moment, Gardner pulled Katherine away.

As Fleming numbly watched them escape into the hedges, the birds exploded into a loud cacophony; wild and joyous, reminding him of how high the forest loomed above. Indeed, it was all around him; a vast sea of life, making him feel at once very small, and at the same time expansive beyond the confines of his body. In that moment, he saw that he was really only very insignificant as the awful truth welled up inside him, for he had unwittingly played the Devil's hand.

No one heard the silent gunshot that split the air and even Fleming did not feel his body hit the ground.

CHAPTER XXXIX
The Wooden Door
The Zion Crossroads Plantation Hotel
1980

Gardner and Katherine ran on and on through the shadowy passageways as dawn continued to brighten the horizon. Turning left, then right, then right again, Gardner led the way through the labyrinth, then stopped abruptly. Bending down, he picked up a piece of quartz, looked at the hedge, examined the stone, then inspected the hedge once more.

"It should be here!" he cried, pacing back and forth."Each turn is marked with a stone but where is it? It should be here, dammit!

"What's wrong? Did you miss a turn or---?" Checking anxiously behind, she fully expected Fleming to burst in upon them, any moment but Gardner was too busy having his fit of temper.

"The door! Where's the goddamn wooden door?" He scratched his head vigorously as if to dislodge some kind of confusion.

"What's the matter? Are we lost?"

"No, just—sometimes They move things around in here."

"*They*? Who are '*they*'?

He paused to collect himself. "Or—or maybe I'm wanting this too much! "

"Wanting *what* too much? What are you *talking* about?" Suddenly, she wanted to scream at him but reined herself in. "Gardner, *please*—-just hurry!"

Gardner tried to collect himself. "Look, I know I probably sound like a freakin' madman right now but I'm talking about the Spirits running this joint, okay? Sometimes—sometimes you have to negotiate." He paused, weighing the pro's and con's of further explanation. "It's just that when the wooden door opens for you, it leads into a—-I'm not sure how to say it— but it's like a protected part of the forest. It's as if no one can enter without permission and when the door disappears, nobody goes through. I've been working in this forest now for the better part of a year and that much I have learned. So you decide, okay? Humor me. Pick a direction, any direction."

She stared at him as if he were indeed crazy then shrugged. "Okay, fine. I'm usually wrong about these things but I think it's that way, so we should go *this* way." And there it was.

He raised his hand to give her a high five which she looked at with a puzzled expression.

"It's the black folk way of saying, 'congratulations'," he said.

She shrugged then tried to slap his palm but missed. He shook his head in mock disgust. "White people!"

A ragged grin from her was all it took to melt the tension between them. Without a backward glance, they crossed the threshold into a landscape of exquisite beauty. Here, ancient trees towered above, their branches crowded with songbirds, leaves shimmering in a green haze pierced by golden shafts of early morning light. The land soon fell away to one side, where a large creek lay at the base of a deep and wandering ravine.

It wasn't long before Katherine caught glimpses of a shadowy figure hiding among the trees. Someone was following them. "Fleming *is* dead, right?" she said, finally.

Gardner stopped abruptly. "Why?"

"I just saw someone---over there."

Both peered anxiously into the dense foliage. "I don't see anybody."

"Maybe it was my imagination." she said.

They continued steadily making their way through the forest until suddenly, with a loud boom and a jolt, the earth rolled like water beneath their feet. Frozen to the spot, they waited until the tremor had traveled off into the distance. Everything became still once more. "That was a long one but no big deal." Even so, Gardner looked shaken.

"Can these trees fall on us?" she asked.

"Best not think about that right now," he replied and set his jaw. He would not be giving up now; not after all of this.

They continued along the ridge for some time before he stopped again. "This is the path down to the creek."

"What path?"

She peered skeptically into what looked like a solid bank of briars but he had already plunged ahead into a narrow cut through. She followed down the steep incline, slipping on loose rocks; her skin catching on briars. Below, what had previously been little more than a dry creek bed was now, after the storm, a rushing torrent. Definitely more of a challenge but the banks covered in brambles made it the only clear path to Indian Rock. They could see it jutting above the trees further upstream.

Jagged rocks and huge tree roots growing out of the banks made it slow going against the stiff current but they finally made it to the base of the massive stone looming above.

"The Indian's eye," murmured Gardner, pointing at what appeared to be a small cave higher up. "That's where she hid it. But how the hell did she get up there?"

"Who?"

"Abanetha!" He took Katherine's hand to steady her over a slippery boulder. "Careful, this is a tricky spot."

It happened the moment he touched her. Déjà vu and she knew. She'd been here before. She'd been here before with *him*. "There's a ledge---," she said,

CHAPTER XL
The Cave

Hugging the rock face, Katherine and Gardner inched their way along the narrow ledge leading straight to the mouth of a small cave—the Indian's Eye. From the ground, it seemed nothing more than a small dent, its entrance half hidden behind a narrow waterfall, but in actuality it sloped deep into the rock. Inside, it offered a space wide enough for two people to comfortably sit within its walls of pure crystal that emitted a soft blue ethereal light that made their skins look blue. Back in the darkest corner, lay two leather sacks and a small wooden, iron bound box.

Gardner's eyes immediately lit up at the sight. "That's it! That's the gold! It's gotta be!" But the box was a disappointment— just an old silver cup, a small stone dagger, a smooth quartz stone, and a short carved stick, all of which he quickly decided to leave behind. The leather sacks were another matter.

"Is it the gold?" asked Katherine from the entrance where she sat, outlined against the pink glow of dawn.

He threw back his head and laughed. "It is!" he shouted, after closer examination. "It very much is!" But his eagerness quickly faded.

"What's wrong?" Wisps of her dark hair had escaped the pony tail which seemed less pert and more bedraggled after a very long night.

Gardner's lips twisted into his predictably cynical grin, though his eyes were shielded. "I don't deserve this," he announced, in a solemn and official sort of way, as if this were of great importance. "Not like my mother did, or my father, my grandparents, all of them— straight back to the slave ships." And he thought about that endless night, chained in that terrible dark hull, crossing the sea.

Katherine moved in closer. "Gardner, don't—," she said softly.

He shook his head. "No, no—it's their stories! I feel them inside me, their lives—their suffering!" His voice grew harsh now. "And then I look at me and I have to ask, what have I done? What have I ever done for my people except go off to art school so I could learn to finger paint!"

She frowned. "There is nothing wrong with being an artist! Come on! You're the epitome of an actualized black man. Not many white men have done what you've done— built a professional career doing what you most want to do!"

"You mean, when I'm not chopping weeds and burning bacon?" He laughed scornfully. "Look, I appreciate what you're trying to say, but you ain't *hearin'* what I'm *tellin'* you! I'm *sayin'* I don't *deserve* this gold. But the world doesn't give a damn about whether you deserve it or whether you follow the Lord's teaching or if you're good to your kin, good to your friends, good to your—." His voice caught. "— to your son who never did a real thing for you."

His mouth pulled down hard into a bitter frown. "But did I even thank them for bringing' my bony ass up into this world? I doubt it! But don't worry, Mama! Don't worry, Daddy! Your reward is over Jordan! Right? At least that's what we black folks keep tellin' ourselves— and why not? It sure as hell ain't comin' from this side of the river."

She gazed thoughtfully into his face. "It sounds to me like you're punishing yourself for being successful."

"Yeah, but when you're black, you can't just be a man, living his life after you find a pot of gold. You gotta do somethin' significant. It can't be just about me anymore."

"It's your inheritance. You don't need to carry responsibility for the past! That price has been paid. This gold is only what is owed!"

"My inheritance—huh! Yeah." He nodded. "I like that. It's my inheritance. That's right." He looked at her directly with growing excitement. "And do you understand what this means?"

"What does it mean?"

"It means, I am Bowen by blood. It means, this is my land, my *family* land. It means my great-great-great whatever grandmother, even though she was a slave and my great-great-great whatever grandfather, even though he was a white man, fell in love as man and wife! And the child they made together, grew up, and married the man who became my great-great whatever grandfather! And that *means* something—something you can't disown or pretend away because it *happened*, damn it!" He gave her a look of naked pain. "It may have ended in tragedy but it *happened*!"

"And that's the beauty of the story," she added, softly. "Out of tragic love comes something wonderful—like you!"

Gardner smiled whole-heartedly for once. "Yeah, I guess you could say that." And for a moment, a radiance lit his face like a translucent veil, revealing another face—a strangely familiar face. An unexpected surge of love swept through Katherine, a love she did not understand, and she began to weep but he was too absorbed in examining one of the coins to notice.

"Huh! I bet you this is Lady Bo'ann!" he cried, handing the coin to Katherine.

Quietly, wiping away a tear, she took it. "Who is she?" Imprinted on one side was the image of a swan woman and on the other, a chalice. Touching it left a pleasant glow on her finger tips and it almost twinkled when she held it to the light.

"A Magical Being or what you'd call a Nature Spirit. The Ancestor, Meriwether Bowen wrote about her in his diary." Gardner dug his hand deep into the sack. Instantly, he was stung by a soft electric energy, joyous, and exquisite, darting into his heart like the wings of a dragonfly.

Immediately, he became brisk and magnanimous, stating that he would—"take the gold treasure, thank you very much. In honor of my Ancestors and may it do good for all—somehow!" He seemed suddenly quite proud of himself. "I think that's a prayer, actually—which is funny because I never pray."

"Then call it an intention—that its power be spent always for the good."

"I like that!" He nodded, a slow grin spreading across his face. "Then it's not a prayer. It's an act of power! Honoring my Ancestors is an act of power and every time I do it, I take back a little more." He lifted the coin to the Unseen Ancestor. "Here's to the power they took from you—to the power they took from *us*!"

By now they were sitting hunched, side by side, in the blue crystal light and Katherine started to notice that her mind was flooding with images. Strangely, they were all scenes from her book that somehow felt like memories but as real as if they had happened to her—making love on a summer's day, Haden's agonizing death, the beating, the birth—all of it. What was it about this cave? Pain rose up into her throat like a fist and she began to weep again but now she knew that these were Abanetha's tears, not her own. She was remembering.

A guilty shadow passed over Gardner's face. "Here I am, going on and on about myself when you just—." Thinking she wept for Andriot, he gently touched her arm, but she looked at him with a look so wild and desperate, that he pulled away confused.

"Don't worry! I ain't touchin' you!" he said.

"No, no—it's this cave," she mumbled. "It's doing something to me."

He nodded ruefully. "Yeah, I think it's doing something to both of us." He vigorously rubbed his head, as if to rid it of an unwanted thought, for he too was seeing things he didn't understand.

"What is it?" she asked.

"It's nothing. It's nothing."

"No, it's something or you wouldn't be thinking it! What is it? Tell me!" She was looking at him so strangely now that it made him uneasy.

"I can't! You'll take it the wrong way!" he said.

She turned on him accusingly. "Well, you might as well say it because it's getting in the way!" The air was crackling with the pressure of the Thing Unspoken.

Taken aback, he grudgingly cleared his throat. "Okay—so you know how it is. You see a stranger. You get this feeling and—." His voice faded off. He wanted to look away but couldn't.

"And?"

"And you remember. You *think* you remember—."

"You know me," she whispered fiercely. "As I know you— Haden!"

His body ran cold "I don't know what's happening here," he muttered.

"Oh, but I think you do."

They locked eyes and suddenly, there came a gleam of recognition, and it was as if a hidden door had opened to a forgotten room.

"Abanetha!" he whispered.

"Two souls are we, ever yearning to be One," she recited in a far away voice, a solitary tear rolling down her cheek. "Remember?" She lowered her head and began to tremble. Whatever was happening had gone beyond mere confusion.

Seizing her hand, he pressed it to his lips, searching her face, a white woman's face. "That was the first poem I ever wrote for you!"

"I know."

Gazing in wonder, they examined each other in this new flesh.

"Apparently, I've become a black man in order to find you," he said. "And as for you—?

"I know. I know. When will we get it right, I wonder?" She giggled. "So how does it feel to be black, my dear?" Suddenly, the mood had lightened.

He paused to consider. "Well, I don't know. It depends. What do you think of me— as Gardner, I mean?"

Her brown eyes warmed. "I might say you are not very good at it. You're entirely too arrogant."

He graciously bowed his head. "Abanetha, my love—it is a joy to find you again!"

"Yes, and how nice to be in a body again. Kiss me," she said.

He cocked an eyebrow. "Of course, it *is* 1978 and still such an ugly world. What will become of Katherine's reputation?"

"Katherine who?" She smiled.

"We've searched lifetimes for each other, so I suppose it's worth it—just so long as we don't forget ourselves. You won't start to believe in Katherine again, will you?"

"That prickly pear? Never! But what of Gardner? He's no prize!"

"I'll work on him."

"They both need work though I see possibilities but we're here now—.'

"—no matter how hard it is."

"If only the world were blue," she said, leaning her head softly against his and both fell mysteriously and instantly fast asleep.

All that could be heard was the rushing curtain of the waterfall outside and just when it seemed that nothing was going to happen, Lady Bo'ann appeared and with her, was Joe Bowen.

He lingered at the entrance, only curious at first, looking about. Somehow the cave had grown larger with plenty of room now to walk around. "I've been here before," said Joe. "But why did you bring me here, my lady?"

"Because I want you to see that the treasure is going to Gardner," replied the gentle lady and as she spoke, her radiance softly reached the furthest crannies, setting the crystal walls ablaze with Light.

"As only it should," murmured Joe.

And with that Lady Bo'ann and Joe Bowen receded into invisibility just as Katherine and Gardner woke up.

"I think I was sleeping," he said, fully Gardner now, and little startled to discover Katherine's head on his shoulder.

She yawned. "I dreamed someone was here, watching us."

Suddenly, the earth rumbled, and loose stones rained down the face of Indian Rock.

Katherine bolted upright. "Is this what I think it is?"

"Damn! We gotta get out of here!"

Moments later, they were edging their way down the narrow ledge, backs against the face of Indian Rock. They dared not look below, for a jumble of rocks spelled certain death if they should slip. Fortunately, the tremors held off until they had made it safely to the bottom. They had just begun wading down the creek, however, when a thick white mist appeared in the distance, rolling silently across the water.

Gardner let out a low curse. "Just what we don't need!" He took her hand.

CHAPTER XLI
Crossing the Divide
The Zion Crossroads Plantation Hotel
1980

To what do you call from your puddle of fear,
of 'I can't and never will'
but more fear... more failure,
more defeat...?
Or do you raise your flag,
Wave it and say,
I'm here and I'm looking for you,
O Magic Spirit of Love!
Teach me how to notice you,
How to appreciate your trickery.
How to claim
your offer

Joseph Meriwether Bowen

In the treehouse, Nealy and Tom sleep on, buried in mist, and in their sleep both travel in dreams.

Standing knee deep in a pool of water, Nealy finds herself under a great stone, jutting out from the side of the mountain. It looks very much like a human face with a deep cavernous eye and the proud beak of a nose and the cleft below formed the opening for a mouth. Above the face streams a peaceful waterfall and the air glistens with a diamond mist. Fairy lights flit across the surface of the pool, as distant thunder rumbles, heralding the arrival of a breeze. It tousles the tops of the trees, stirring the water like an entity as it travels upstream, transforming into a beautiful swan, gliding to her nest on the shore.

"Welcome to the Gateway to the Other World," she announces with the voice of rushing water. "This is the message the Earth Mother bids me bring you! Those who have long travailed in this fallen world, heed my words! You are now called to the task for which you have been prepared." Thunder rumbles and a streak of lightning lights the sky.

"I can't because I have a hole in my heart, and I can't seem to fix it," replied Nealy, though even as she speaks, her heart begins to glow with an inner well being.

Instantly, the swan transforms into a beautiful woman, ablaze with celestial light. "The hole in your heart is nothing to fix but only release. It is the stain of an ancient wound borne by Our Earth Mother since the world of pain began," she says. "And it does weigh so heavily upon Her; therefore, We honor you, dear One, for helping Her to carry it to the Clearing Light." The Great Being smiles and beauty seems to blossom all around her, as seven pillars of light appear high on a hill.

"Go there," says the swan woman. "You will know what to do, for you cannot fail."

Even after she awakes, those words linger long in Nealy's mind.

Tommy dreams of sitting in the comfortable embrace of a small cave alongside a wiry, dark skinned stranger, a man with blazing black eyes and hair white as moonlight. Tommy begins to feel a unity with him, as if they were enclosed inside a single, invisible shell. Indeed, he feels a unity with everything around him.

"This great stone is a Magical Being and she honors us by her presence," begins the old man. "She calls herself, Shamala, She is of the First Generation and remembers long before all Words, at the Beginning of Time, when the Ancestors took many forms to manifest this world. They became Rock and Fire, Steam and Rain, Flesh and Earth, and every kind of plant and creature. This was when the Gate was still open."

"The Gate to what?" asks Tommy politely.

"To the Garden of Paradise, of course." And for a moment, the old man's eyes become deep as eternity. "Luckily, She has given us this cave where we can sit inside her knowledge which is wide and deep."

Waking in the chill of dawn, Nealy and Tom found themselves in the treehouse, lying peacefully side by side. By now, the mist had cleared. Looking down from on high, they took a moment to gaze at the forest of ancient trees, then slowly made their way down the rickety ladder. After building a small fire to warm themselves, they sat silently eating the last of the food while trying to reclaim wisps of their fading dreams.

"I dreamed a goddess came to me," murmured Nealy, looking very small and pale. "She took me to a rock of pure crystal, rising like a great face, streaming waterfalls into a deep pool—"

"---and the eye was a small cave," he said, finishing her description. Nealy gave him a look and he shrugged, sweeping the hair out of his eyes. "I think I was there, too. Someone was telling me a story of some sort. Something important—but whatever it was, it's gone now."

Nealy frowned to herself. "So, what do you think we're supposed to do now?"

"You talk like there is some kind of plan."

"Well, isn't there? Just because we don't know what it is, doesn't mean there isn't one."

As if in answer, the strangely colored bird fluttered to a nearby branch then glided to the ground at their feet, pacing boldly back and forth, twitching her tail feathers and squawking loudly as if to say 'hurry it up'. Tommy laughed. Suddenly, there was no question but that they were being led.

They quickly collected their things while the bird repeatedly darted ahead then circled back, urging them forward. The last time the bird vanished, it didn't return.

"Now where did it go?" Tommy squinted into the tangle of forest. "I guess we go that way."

"Wait!" Nealy stopped abruptly, her face ashen. "I think we've been going in circles! Remember that bench? We just passed it a while back. Ohh!" She suddenly doubled over, swept by a wave of darkness. "Not this again!"

"What's wrong?" Tommy ran to her side.

"I think I might faint," came her muffled reply.

"Sit here," he commanded, guiding her to the bench. "I'll find the path to the hotel then come back for you. Just stay put." He set off briskly down the hill but had not gotten far when he spied the Mist, swiftly advancing. Before he could turn back, an impenetrable fog had swallowed the world whole. Suddenly, Tommy lost all sense of direction. He called out to her but the only answer he got was the sound of tinkling bells.

Left alone on the bench, Nealy had wanted to say she would be fine but she wasn't going to be. She knew that now and her mind started to whirl with dark thoughts. The shadow of death had drawn too near. Her sister was right. It was crazy to think Spirit had power to heal. What a fool she'd been, to squander her last chance to live. Life wasn't a fairy tale. It was a journey to disappointment, failure, and death.

"Nealy!" Suddenly, it was Tommy's voice breaking through like hard sunlight.

Freed from the voice of doom, she stood up. "I'm coming!" she cried then walked straight into a dense cloud of mist.

Tommy could hear her voice calling in desperation through the fog. He tried to sound calm. "Nealy! Stay where you are! I'm coming!" She didn't sound that far away. If he stuck to the trail, he'd get back to her just fine. Thankfully, the mist had started to thin and he could see again but only to become doubly confused, for suddenly he found himself in a small clearing. In the center grew an enormous tree, so big that fifty people could have stood in a ring around its trunk and not touched hands.

A breeze whispered playfully through its green branches saying, *all is well, all is well*. Suddenly, an electrical surge of joy shot through his body with the power of a thousand volts as his legs buckled and he fell to the earth, overcome with bliss. Dimly, he heard a voice calling, "Where are you?" It was Nealy.

I'm here, he thought before he completely lost consciousness.

Tommy's voice had sounded close enough to touch, but when the curtain of mist drew back, Nealy discovered that she too was standing alone before an enormous tree, ancient as it was grand, but now entirely dead; hollowed out by the lightning bolt that had killed it.

She stepped within where it was dim and holy and sat on the earth, burned clean by lightning. *A sanctuary of sorrow,* she thought. Suddenly, she heard the crowded voices of suffering and felt the history of the world pour out of the earth through her body like a river of grief. It was the anguish of mothers, the misery of the old and dying, the agony of murder, failure, and loss. Yet, all the while, something inside remained utterly serene. This was not hers to keep, she knew. She was but the vessel, the Witness.

Tommy lay unconscious for a long time, face down in the presence of the great tree; until presently, amid the soft rustle of its green leaves, there came the tinkling of bells, and the sense of someone standing over him. Was it Nealy? he wondered as he came once more into awareness.

Through the mist, he heard muffled voices. She was talking to someone and for a moment, he was certain it was the professor's voice answering but when he looked up, it was only a stranger, gazing down on him.

At first glance her face was difficult to make out, as if subtly veiled in gauze. "Where are you going?" she asked in a low musical voice.

A mysterious joy filled him at the mere sound of her voice. "To find a lost friend," he answered.

This was met with a soft chuckle. "But do you know where you are, my dear one?" Her eyes grew bright with a shimmering inner light. Until this moment, he hadn't noticed how beautiful she was and so much younger than she'd first appeared.

His heart opened like a flower. "Where am I?" he whispered.

"In the Other World, Dear Love," she said, offering him the silver cup that had suddenly appeared in her hand. "Drink deep and shine like the Sun!"

Tommy took the cup and as he drank, a tingling warmth sped through his body as a subtle expansive clarity lit every cell. Then the mist closed around her, and she vanished from his sight. Suddenly, a passage opened through the Mist, leading him straight back to Nealy, where she stood with the Professor beside a great tree. From all appearances, it was the very same tree---yet this one was dead and hollow. Only then did he understand what Lady Bo'ann had told him. He had crossed the Divide to the Other World, a twin world except in it was still perfect as it was created.

The Professor's gaze was clear and blue. "Come with me! We have work to do!" he said.

Tom and Nealy looked at one another and laughed for suddenly, it was the professor who had found them and not the other way around; however, as they proceeded, there would be no more laughing for the burden of grief pressing on Nealy's heart had become unbearably heavy. She was weeping openly now and could scarcely stand. Meanwhile, the mysterious energy was now surging up Tommy's spine with such force that he could barely keep himself from charging ahead.

To their left, a rustle of leaves and a snort signaled the presence of a buck and three does staring wide eyed through the trees. As the human procession continued further up the mountain, many other animals came out of hiding to watch---squirrel, rabbit, possum, raccoon, fox, turtle, mountain lion, wolf, bear, deer all came to witness as insects whirled and every manner of bird cluttered the branches overhead, dipping, and diving in joyous celebration.

"They are part of this," murmured Valentino quietly, his eyes shining.

Presently they entered a haunted wasteland of dying trees, strangled by clinging vines. Despite the eerie atmosphere, Tommy was cheered to see the scrap of yellow t-shirt, waving like a welcome flag from the branch where he had tied it that very first day. Up ahead at the top of the hill, he could see the great circle of standing stones. *All will be well.* The words appeared in his mind, *but* as the path steepened, Nealy staggered with an anguished cry.

"What is it?" Tommy caught hold of her before she fell.

"Can't breathe!" she panted. "It's pressing on me—!"

"What's pressing on you?"

"Souls, so many— trapped souls!" Her breath came faster, as the voices in her head rose to a crescendo of screams and shouts. "Here! It happened here—the massacre!" With a groan, her vision went black as she fell unconscious to the ground.

"Nealy! Nealy!" Tommy shook her vigorously, but she did not respond. "Oh, my god, Professor! You think her heart has—?" But there was no answer, for the professor had mysteriously disappeared from sight. "Where are you? Professor?" Tommy's voice echoed down into the ravine but again, no answer came.

Not knowing what else to do, he carried her limp body to the center of the stone circle. There he gently laid her on a low slab of crystal then knelt and picked up her hand. It had already grown cold. A wave of tenderness swept over him. "Please God or Powers of Light or whatever you call yourself," he murmured softly, "You gotta do something 'cause if there's a human being worth saving, she's it."

"This a good place," spoke a voice on his shoulder.

Startled, Tommy looked up to find the professor standing behind him, clutching a small iron bound wooden box, covered in cracked brown leather.

Tommy exploded in anger. "Where the hell have you been? God, man! I mean, geez! You shouldn't disappear like that!"

"I've been to the Other World," replied the old man calmly, then drew a dented silver cup from the box.

To his surprise, Tommy recognized it immediately as the cup from his dream; and was it his imagination or did Professor Valentino suddenly look younger? Meanwhile, from the box, the professor removed a small stone dagger, a carved branch, and a stone polished to a mirror shine. The old man began arranging the objects in the four directions around Nealy's body, then sat on the ground, as if to wait. "Stay with her," he instructed Tom, indicating Nealy's unconscious form. "You'll know what to do."

Suddenly, a small whirlwind appeared, circling the periphery, whirring expectantly, as if observing them. Some instinct told Tommy to cover her body with his own. Immediately, the whirlwind hovered closer until it was over top of them, pulling at him, insistent, commanding, drawing all the darkness out of her, through him, into itself. In the next instant, a bolt of lightning struck the earth, and the mysterious whirlwind had gone, taking the dark energy with it.

Kneeling beside her, Tommy anxiously searched for signs of life but she remained very still. He was just about to panic when the breath suddenly rushed back into her body and her eyes fluttered open. "Oh," she said and sat up, yawning. "What are we doing here?"

As if in answer, the light changed and with the tinkling of bells, a great white swan glided in through the treetops. The moment she touched the earth, she took the form of a beautiful woman.

"Lady Bo'ann!" cried the professor and they all bowed low, shielding their eyes from the blazing light that surrounded her. Tommy recognized her as the Celestial Being who'd come to him in the Mist.

"Well done!" she cried. "The darkness has fled and the curse has been lifted! " spoke the lady with a voice silken as rushing water. "I bring you thanks from the Earth Mother for carrying the grief of this holy place across the Divide. Not since the days we walked the Earth, has this gate been opened to the Other World."

CHAPTER XLII
The Encounter
The Zion Crossroads Plantation Hotel
1980

"Hold on to the back of my shirt and don't let go, no matter what!" With the flooded creek waters swirling against them, even Gardner struggled to stand upright, but no sooner had they found their balance, then the mist swept in and swallowed the world whole. Now they had no choice but to feel the way with their feet, stepping over the slippery stones, through the rising creek waters until they could scramble onto the path up the muddy bank. Picking their way past protruding briars, they came to the top where they huddled in the roots of a large tree.

"No sense in going any further with this mist. We'll have to wait it out here," he said, shifting the heavy pack off his shoulders. "But fair warning. I've been caught here many times before, so I know. It can do weird things to your head so don't be surprised if you see something."

"Something?"

"Something strange."

She sat hugging her knees to her chest, resting her head against the tree, just wanting to close her eyes. The conversations in the cave had faded to something like a dream and she was too exhausted to think beyond this wonderful peace she was feeling, simply sitting beside him, at the base of a tree. In fact, she was so relaxed that she nearly dozed off, but in the next instant, found herself wide awake.

"What was that?" She sharpened her ears and listened hard, but there was only silence.

"What did you hear?" said Gardner, apprehensive now.

"Someone was calling!"

He listened intently. An owl hooted in the distance, and then he heard it, too---a thin voice calling for help.

"Oh my god!" murmured Katherine. "Is that Fleming — or — ?"

"Shhh!"

Again, the voice called, sounding more plaintive than before. "Help! Help me, please!"

Gardner shook his head. "Nah! Even if he's still alive, Fleming couldn't have made it this far. Not in his condition." Gardner cupped his mouth. "Professor?" he called. "Is that you?"

"I'm over here!" replied the voice from out of the fog.

"It's gotta be the professor," muttered Gardner then raised his voice. "We're coming for you, Professor!" The mist opened a narrow channel into a small open glade ringed by tall trees, but the voice had fallen silent. "Professor? It's me, Gardner! Yell so I can find you!" A shadow flitted behind the trees. "Professor?"

Someone was watching them, but it wasn't Professor Valentino. With dawning horror, Katherine and Gardner could only stare at the shadowy figure now emerging from behind a tree. It was the Colonel, in the fullness of youth, gliding towards them, silent as a vapor. The air suddenly turned frigid and dank and they stood transfixed by the gaze of those deep hollow eyes.

"You've found it," rasped the uneasy spirit, hovering near then receding, his face a changing mask of cruelty, longing, and despair. He smiled his terrible smile. "All those many years I searched, and now you have come to claim it. Haden, the golden child!" He sidled closer now.

Gardner felt his own energy drop, as if it were being subtly drawn from his body.

"I knew you the moment you were born," continued the old Colonel. "Before you knew yourself, I saw that my brother of old had returned! Though your skin was black, I recognized your soul — Haden, the Golden Child! The Chosen One, the one I feared and despised my entire life! And now you have returned, but why? Why this horrible place? That I could never understand, not until the day she arrived, the magazine woman — Abanetha, returned but in white! Only then did I understand why — because your love was strong — strong enough to make you return!!"

His hollow laughter erupted like a sob and echoed among the trees. " And it was that kind of love I could never have." The ghostly old Colonel lifted his voice in an anguished wail like a chill wind, moaning through the trees. "Dear Brother, digging holes in the forest was never about finding the gold. It was only something to keep me from killing myself, because from the moment I took your life, I never had a moment's peace."

The ghost's horrible visage turned white and pale as dead bones. "And while death set you free, I was left to relive that terrible moment over and over. But the worst thing about it was when I finally had to see how wrong I was, when I was so sure I was right! Oh, I tried to believe that I was protecting the 'family honor,' but deep down, I always knew that what I really hated was your goodness, Haden. Yes, it was your goodness that I hated because when I compared myself to you, I could only see a man I hated even more!"

Gardner's voice rang out sharply. "Carter, it's over! Let it be over!"

But the Colonel would not be silenced. "But it's not over! It's not over until I tell you the most important part! Because you see—because it was just that I could not love you, Haden with the Golden Eyes. Strange! It was never *you* who needed to forgive *me*—but *I* who needed to forgive *you*— for being what I could not be! And that's all it ever was!" His voice rang out with laughter.

"Don't you see? Now, at last, I can forgive myself for not being you! Now at last, the Spirit of Love has come to bless my emptiness. Now at last, when I see the two of you, reunited—I find I'm glad!" Suddenly, it was young Carter standing before them, radiant and joyful. "Yes, Brother! With my whole heart, I'm actually glad! Glad you found each other and I wish you joy in it! Thus, with my whole heart I bid you fare thee well!" His visage began to alter and fade, then gently dissolved into nothingness, leaving but a wisp of laughter in the air.

Overcome, Gardner lowered his face and wept.

Katherine rested her hand gently on his shoulder and without a word, he took her in his arms and they held each other tight, his face buried in her hair. "Don't take this the wrong way," he murmured.

She pulled back and looked him in the eye. "I won't." And she kissed him.

In the next instant, the mist receded into the ravine, like an animal returning to its lair; and Gardner and Katherine saw that they were standing on a high hill, overlooking the ravine.

"I think we're done here." He shifted the leather sacks onto his shoulders. From here on out the land leveled out and the walking would be easier.

CHAPTER XLIII
The Other World

Sometimes, you're living a new life; and it happens as easily as passing from one dream to another. It comes first on tiptoe, and before you know it, you've gone from one world to another."

from the notebooks of Joe Bowen, 1978

Before the Mist swallowed up all signs of him, Murphy had been so sure that the man he was following into the forest was his father. Of course, now that he was utterly and completely lost, he realized how foolish it was to have done such a thing. His father was dead! If something bad happened to those people, he would never forgive himself. Of course, when had he ever been able to stop Fleming from doing anything?

This sank him into a deeper state of worry, but his brooding came to an abrupt halt when an earth tremor slammed him into a tangle of briars. Breathless, with eyeglasses torn from his face, he lay there defeated, blind, and bleeding;. *The tears of the father unto the third and fourth generation*—no, that wasn't it. His befuddled mind mumbled into action. *The fears of the father unto the third or fourth generation.* Wait---now how did that go? As usual Murphy's biblical knowledge was a bit rusty.

"Don't you think," interrupted a voice out of the mist, "that it's time we Bowen's begin to see where we are going?" Suddenly there was a hand offering assistance and Murphy looked up into the face of his own dead father. "No more blind stumbling in the dark, Murphy."

The first thing out of Murphy's mouth, however, was not a welcoming, "Oh, Daddy, I'm so glad to see you," but a resentful, "Where have you been?"

His father beamed. "I've been to the Other World," he replied.

Murphy did not stop to ponder what that meant, (or even how he himself was able to see without his glasses) but brushed his father's obscure comment aside. "But Fleming poisoned you! You wandered off into the woods, half crazed with no shoes and no glasses! Your body was never found again! Daddy! What happened to you?"

"Well, son," began Joe in his slow drawl. "It's sort of complicated. Shall we sit?"

Murphy was startled at this point to see two rocking chairs set beneath his father's old treehouse, which sure enough was nested in the tree above. "Hold on a minute!" He looked all around. "How did we get here?"

"The Mist brought us here!" said Joe, his golden eyes gleaming now with an inner fire that made him look quite mad.

"Oh, let's not talk about the Mist, Daddy. Fleming says its evil."

His father's lips twitched with secret amusement. "That's just ignorance talking. We fear it because it shows us what we most want to hide from ourselves. We fear it like we fear change. No, The Mist is a powerful Being, and if we allow it, it will take us on a journey of transformation."

"Oh, Daddy!" Murphy shook his head sadly. How many times had he heard his father talk so crazy, especially those nights holed up in the old library with his strange hippy friends. But no matter how Murphy had tried to reason with him, old man seemed bent on his own destruction.

"Well, all I can say is that no matter what Fleming says, I still love you, even if you are crazy so I don't blame you," was what Murphy had always used to say, but this time he added something about the Dark Thorn. "Now that I know about it, Daddy— I can see how you sorta couldn't help it—I mean, being crazy and all."

"Then you've read my notebooks?" Joe smiled with pleasant surprise.

"Yes," said Murphy with a slightly weary sigh. "Every single one, cover to cover, and almost none of it makes any sense except— but for one thing. The Dark Thorn. That I understand. I've always called it the family curse but, call it what you may, I do understand what you're talking about, Daddy. I just want you to know that."

Joe nodded slowly, listening. "So, what do you think?"

Murphy fell silent, contemplating. "I think you've had so much suffering, it just made you crazy. Now I know about that kind of suffering so I can forgive you. That's something Fleming could never do—

because— Fleming cannot love anyone." Suddenly, Murphy's eyes filled with tears. "Poor thing. He wants to feel it. I can tell sometimes that he does—but for some reason, he just can't. Why, I do not know. I have worshipped him all my life, and he only hates me for it. Even so, he is my blood, and I love him still."

Joe gazed upon his son's face, shining with love. "I see a bright future for you, Murphy. Different from the past. A whole new story is about to be told because you've changed in a wonderful way. Loving poor Fleming the way that you do, it speaks well of you, son. It's beautiful."

Murphy shook his head in despair. "You sound like Moon. He'd always say that everything is beautiful in its own way. I wish I could believe that, but now I just think that we're all doomed to unhappiness in the end."

"Even if life turns into a disaster, it's all part of the treasure hunt, Murphy. Such long, dark journeys always are."

Murphy rolled his eyes. "Oh, please! Not that treasure hunt business again!"

"But that's just what it is, don't you see?" The strange bird swooped down and landed on Joe's shoulder. The old man beamed contentedly. "What you're searching for is not in the outer world at all— but inside, an inner treasure, Murphy. When you understand that, you begin to see your life so differently. That's why I call it a treasure hunt, son. That's what it's all about. Behind all the kicks and blows, there's a purpose, and it's all quite beautiful in the end. Sometimes, the worst things bring the deepest joy— but we've talked about this before. Remember?" Without the googly glasses, his father's appearance had changed. Gone was the hang dog, slack jawed expression, and in its place there was an air of placid self-possession.

"Talk? When did we ever----?" Suddenly, Murphy remembered the dream conversations he'd been having with his father. They'd started up the day after his father's fake funeral. "Oh, I get it! This is just a dream we're having, isn't it!"

"But what is a dream, Murphy?" Joe gazed at him with an inscrutable intensity and the world grew mysteriously brighter. "Another room in reality? Another dimension? Another story?" Out of nowhere, a bit of bread appeared in his fingers, and the bird gently snatched it with his yellow beak. The look of confusion on Murphy's face caused Joe to burst into laughter, and it was so contagious that Murphy couldn't help but join in.

Suddenly, it seemed not to matter that he didn't understand,

for as he rocked, a warm buttery glow was melting the clench of anxiety in his gut. It seemed entirely normal that he and his father should
be sitting on rocking chairs in the middle of the forest—and was it his
imagination or were the trees smiling down on them?

CHAPTER XLIV
Panovision: In Revision
The Zion Crossroads Plantation Hotel
1980

Once the whirlwind has left and all is returned to calm, Tom and Nealy rise from the crystal stone at the center of the circle. Something in the air has changed, if ever so slightly. The curse has been lifted, and all sense of burden has melted away. The breath comes easy and the light has softened to a rosy glow. Like a comforting embrace, the peaceful presence of the trees enfolds them. It isn't long before they find themselves once again, wandering in the Mist. It feels as if they have been here forever, looking for the way home. Instead, they find themselves standing before an old gate set in an ancient stone wall, stretching impossibly high and as far and wide as the eye can imagine.

The gate has been left slightly ajar as if in hopes that someone might think to enter in. Its rusty hinges make it exceedingly difficult to move, but they manage to squeeze through anyway. On the other side, they find themselves in a timeless garden. Ancient trees tower above, shading exotic flowers from the full force of the sun, flowers unlike any they'd ever seen. The air is cool and blissfully fragrant. A quiet peace, filled with birdsong, suffuses the rosy light of an eternal dawn. Someone is singing up ahead. They quicken their pace, eager to meet with what awaits them.

Meanwhile, in a lower dimension of time, three survivors have chosen to sit on the stone bench by the cracked cement pool, watching what was once Zion Crossroads, as it is consumed by flames in a mighty roar of vengeance. Amanda and Portia cling to Jack who shelters them both, his arms spread wide. He tried to go back into the burning house to find the others, but the old structure went up like a matchstick and the smoke and fire quickly drove him out.

Coming this close to death, has had a chastening affect and a deep reverence holds them all, as if suspended in Time. For just this moment there is no past and no future. They think about Fleming's body, being consumed by the fire. He's been turned to ash and bone. He cannot hurt them now. They sit there until the fire burns itself out. No one from the outside world even knows this is taking place. There is no working phone on which to call for help; nor any vehicle with gasoline in which to drive to town. They have no choice but to walk. However, the women are barefoot and dressed in nightgowns.

"I'll go," says Jack, stifling a yawn that travels simultaneously from one to the other. "But first, I'll need to rest." He pulls a blanket out of his car and spreads it on the ground. The three of them huddle together and sleep, almost as if they had never existed.

Jack immediately finds himself in a dream, talking to someone named Tommy. He is struck by the fact that they seem to know each other, like long lost friends—or maybe even like brothers. A surge of love for this person swells up inside him but when he awakes he realizes it was just a dream. There is no Tommy, no brother. He is alone, as he has always been.

Portia dreams the phone is ringing—ringing, ringing and she's running, running to catch it in time. It's her ex-husband. He's trying to tell her something, but she can't make it out. Through the window, she witnesses a beautiful swan transform into a young woman, pale and slight and strangely familiar. The swan woman calls to Portia by name, then beckons her to follow into the glade, where the sun pierces with long sharp blades of light. The swan woman disappears into the light as the sound of the dial tone tells Portia that her ex-husband has hung up.

Amanda dreams of fire, and fury, and Fleming's terrible face the way it looked, so deformed by hatred.

Puffenberger is standing beside her. "You can let it go now," he says. "I have."

"You're dead," she says. "It's easy for you to let go but I have to keep on living in this terrible world."

"I'm just here to tell you, Mandy. There is another way. You see that so clearly when you get over here. I see a lot of things that could have been so different."

"But how? How do I make it different?"

"Just be kind. And give to everyone. Don't worry about what's yours. It'll all come out right. Trust me." He smiles at her with so much love that she starts to cry.

Amanda awakes, puzzled, and relieved that he is still even willing to speak to her, even if he is dead.

Later, when he is rested, Jack starts to walk into town. He considers hitchhiking but there's not a car in sight. At least it's still cool, he tells himself. His mind is strangely hollow and he still feels pretty banged up after the fight with Fleming but none of that matters. He has proven himself and now, he's doing this for the two women who are depending on him. That feels good. It makes him stronger somehow.
Suddenly, there's the sound of hoofbeats, and beyond the sunburnt fields, a white horse appears at the edge of the forest. She breaks into a gallop, and heads straight for him. Jack stands transfixed. Something tells him to hold his hand out, palm up. Sure enough the mare gradually slows to a gentle pace until she is close enough to sniff his hand. After what he's just been through, the only thing that surprises him, is that this does not surprise him. After all, this *was* the reason he'd come to Zion Crossroads in the first place—to ride a horse.
Jack strokes her sleek neck and she whinnies softly. When she bows low before him, he laughs. "No way! No freakin' way!" He slides onto her back. "I'm riding a horse!" They break into a cantor and head for town. Maybe after a lifetime of losing, good luck is on his side for a change.

Maneuvering their way out of the forest, Gardner thinks he has cleverly avoided the 'crime scene', when the mist tricks him once again. To his dismay, he finds himself practically stepping into the arms of the deputy sheriff, who is sleepily examining the smoking ruins of Zion Crossroads. Instinctively, the young black man takes two steps away from Katherine and assumes his role of just 'Gardner the gardener'. Only at the last minute, is he reminded of the leather packs full of gold coins perched on his back. A sense of doom closes in on him.
"Jesus!" The cop stares.
For a moment nobody speaks. There's something familiar about this policeman's face but Gardner can't quite recall.
"You're Gardner Bell, right?" says the cop.
"Yes!" An oily dread gathers in Gardner's stomach. *Here we go.*
"I'm Paul Snead!" The deputy runs his hand self-consciously over a balding pate. "Remember me? From high school? I had a lot more hair back then, and I've put on a few pounds but----hey, you look the same!"

Of course they *would* recognize him, thinks Gardner to himself! To this town, he will always be Leonora and Joe Bowen's 'love child' with the golden eyes.

"I hear you went to art school out west somewhere. That you became a professor, or something?"

"University of Chicago! Yes!" Relief flows in. How ironic that he should finally get this affirmation of who he really is from a southern white policeman.

"University of Chicago, huh! Wow! I thought so! You were always one of the smart ones. Sorry to be so late getting here. All hell busted loose with that earthquake. The power was out all over---three, four fires, houses collapsing. We been dragging people out all night."

Gardner suddenly realizes the heaviness he'd first perceived in the white man's face was simply exhaustion. No doubt he'd been up all night, too.

"What happened here?" continues the deputy. "Somebody called in about a stabbing?"

"Yes," says Katherine. "It was my boyfriend that was killed."

"I'm so sorry m'am." Paul Snead averts his eyes respectfully. "So who made the call?"

Gardener clears his throat. "I did."

Snead politely guides him out of her range of hearing. "So can you fill me in on the details?"

Gardner glances back at Katherine and she gives him a reassuring nod. He marvels. Almost without his having noticed it, something has changed in the world. It feels different being here, different being inside of himself, inside his own body. 'Gardner the gardener' is gone forever and when she looks at him, he knows she is seeing him as he truly is.

"Certainly," he says. "I'd be glad to."

Murphy awakes, finding himself in a rocking chair on the front porch beneath the cool canopy of the trees on a bright sunlit summer day. He must have fallen asleep, for he'd dreamt about his father again. It felt so real this time, almost as if it had really happened. He still feels traces of the warm feeling, the closeness, and yes, the sadness. How long has his father been dead now? He's losing track of time already yet it seems like yesterday that he passed away.

In the dream there had been all these strange people staying at Zion Crossroads and there'd been some kind of struggle. Not a pleasant dream at all but one of those you have to fight your way through, and when you wake up, you're more exhausted than before you fell asleep. He must tell his wife, Portia, before he forgets it completely. The memory is already fading like morning fog, leaving only wisps of memory. Some parts were funny and some just plain weird. She'll enjoy it. She always likes to hear about his dreams.

The temperatures have cooled to a pleasant degree. Sounds of music drift out of the house along with the smell of cooking. Thank goodness his wife is orderly and keeps everything on schedule for the gurgle in his stomach says it's time for dinner. He starts into the house, pausing long enough to gaze upon Zion Crossroads with admiration. All the work on the renovation has paid off. The business is blooming and he's filled with gratitude. This is the life that he loves and he can't imagine it any other way.

In another world, Joe walks out into the rose garden outside of Haden's library window. It is the garden Haden designed over a century ago. If there is one place Joe truly feels joy it is here. He has an abiding passion for roses and has always been an ardent and faithful caretaker. Grandmother Irene taught him the art and it's the only thing that he's been truly good at.

At this moment, it has reached a state of perfection, and today there is one rose blooming that has never appeared here before. It's exquisitely beautiful, almost purplish red with a touch of peachy blush. He gazes at it in wonder, how it glistens with beads of dew, and asks himself, hasn't he seen this rose somewhere before? He searches his memory. A dream, perhaps?

The next moment, he notices her, his grandmother Irene, standing at the edge of the labyrinth, wearing a feathered cap and a long blue dress. She raises her hand in greeting. Suddenly, Joe remembers that thing he'd forgotten and realizes he's known it all along—that there is always another door to open, where once there only seemed a wall.

Instantly, the most delicious effervescence tumbles like a waterfall, from the top of his head to the tips of his toes. He asks himself, what is this? He has felt this before, this feeling of being very small and as wide and deep as the universe. It takes him a moment, and then the answer comes to him. This is Home. It feels like home.

"Come!" she says and with that Joe simply follows.

THE END

"Like twisting vines seeking blindly, this journey begins, fearless and foolish, going somewhere and nowhere, only to end, as all life stories do, in ambiguity. Yet the Gate to the Other World remains open to All who choose to enter in."

Lady Boann

www.ingramcontent.com/pod-product-compliance
Lightning Source LLC
Chambersburg PA
CBHW031159310726
48969CB00001B/149